BY JILLY GAGNON

#famous

All Dressed Up

All Dressed Up

ALL DRESSED UP

A NOVEL

JILLY GAGNON

BANTAM BOOKS
NEW YORK

All Dressed Up is a work of fiction. Names, characters, places, and incidents are the products of the author's imagination or are used fictitiously. Any resemblance to actual events, locales, or persons, living or dead, is entirely coincidental.

A Bantam Books Trade Paperback Original

Published in the United States by Bantam Books, an imprint of Random House, a division of Penguin Random House LLC, New York.

Bantam Books is a registered trademark and the B colophon is a trademark of Penguin Random House LLC.

ISBN 978-0-593-49732-6
Ebook ISBN 978-0-593-49731-9

Printed in the United States of America on acid-free paper

randomhousebooks.com

2 4 6 8 9 7 5 3 1

Book design by Alexis Capitini

To Danny.
I couldn't do any of this without you.

CAST OF CHARACTERS

THE GUESTS
(IN ORDER OF APPEARANCE):

BECCA WILSON

(playing ingenue Debbie Taunte)

Becca knows that she's been wound a little tight lately. But you know what they say: Just because you're paranoid, that doesn't mean you're *wrong*.

BLAKE WILSON

(playing newspaper heir Reid A. Daily)

You have to feel for poor Blake. After spending however many hundreds of dollars to whisk his wife away to a manor estate for the weekend, he's *still* stuck in the doghouse.

GABBY SCHULZ

(playing mob moll Dolly Diamond)

When you think about it, isn't *all* of life just an extended LARPing session? No? Well, you probably won't understand Gabby, then.

DREW SCHULZ

(playing gangster Bugsy Slugs)

Don't let the oversized fedora and the wise-guy accent fool you: This is much more than a *game* to Drew.

PHIL ARMUNDSEN

(playing oil tycoon Peter Oleum)

Looking at Phil, it's impossible not to notice his spokesman-ready smile, easy confidence, and all the trappings a highly successful career in finance can buy . . . and he'd prefer you not look past them, thank you very much.

HEATHER ARMUNDSEN

(playing society wife Maria Richmann Oleum)

The only thing tighter than suburban mother-of-three Heather's schedule is her athleisure wear. And her smile. And her forehead (Botox works wonders).

JESSICA PHILLIPS

(playing Hollywood starlet Lulu Larksong)

Some women as objectively beautiful as Jessica have a hard time connecting with other females. That's *never* been a problem for Jessica, though.

JOSH BERGMAN

(playing beat reporter S. Cooper Mudslinger)

Wry, perpetually amused Josh would be the first person to tell you that when he wound up with Jessica, he got more than he bargained for. Much (or is it many?) more.

THE STAFF:

JENNIFER MAROTTA

(playing the housekeeper, Miss Ann Thrope)

As a hotel manager who also runs and stars in regular theme weekends, Jennifer's used to having to be able to turn on a dime . . . and *very* sharply on her heel.

BETHANY BURGESS

(playing the housemaid, Miss Terry Yuss)

Bethany's always been really committed to her acting career. But she may have gone a bit too "method" for her current role. . . .

MIKE DOHERTY

(playing the butler, Wynnham)

Not an actor by nature, Mike is nevertheless deeply committed to making sure the guests' wines are never poisoned.

MANNY RUIZ

(playing the footman, Scuttles)—

When the gloves and tails are on, he's nearly as cringing as a grand estate demands its low-level staff to be. When they come off, though . . . let's say it's not just Manny's outfit that changes.

LARA PHIPPEN

(playing the hostess, Ida Crooner)

If you thought a theme weekend would interfere with Lara's drink-slinging skills, you'd be *dead* wrong.

BRANDON IKOLA

(playing the chauffeur, Putters)

Old high school athletes never die, they just thicken through the middle and wind up picking up side gigs like this.

All Dressed Up

SATURDAY, 1:30 A.M.

The mansion changed at night, all the rigid lines and hard surfaces of the daytime melting into something softer, more secret, a little strange. Spotlights hidden around its base shot dreamy fountains of soft yellow light over the heavy grey stones, catching the tiny flecks of mica and quartz sprinkled through their rough-hewn sides, the whole surface shimmering as you moved past it, as though it were trapped behind a veil of rain. Tiny lanterns had been buried around the border of the drive and along the paths that crisscrossed the grounds, fairy trails through tamed forests. Even the shadows of the trees seemed to come alive, the night breezes blowing them out to impossible lengths, the bony echoes of the branches stretching into corners they were never meant to reach.

A small wooden door at the very edge of the building opened soundlessly, spilling a puddle of light onto the flagstone path that huddled up against the building's broad shoulders. A woman emerged, features smudged by night, and moved quickly across the lawns, turning back every few seconds to check behind her. The night air was crisp, a faint hint of far-off smoke weaving through the heavy, dusty scent of crumbling leaves. She wrapped her arms around her body, shivering slightly, and started walking faster, making for a small stone building tucked against the edge of the forest that surrounded the tiny, ordered island of the mansion and its grounds.

When she reached the door she stopped, sucked in a whole-body breath, and ran both hands through her hair, lips moving silently. After a few moments she straightened, shaking both hands out at her sides, and opened the door.

Inside, the air was close, the heat of the day still trapped between the heavy stone walls. A broad, rustic hearth dominated the main room, heavy candlesticks anchoring either side of the mantel, and in front of it the chairs and couches huddled together beneath capacious white shrouds, ghosts of themselves. To the left, you could make out the dim outlines of butcher-block counters, a monstrous gas stove, even the shiny surface of a fridge that seemed to have been ported in from the future.

She squinted against the darkness.

"Hello?" Her voice seemed to disappear up the gaping maw of the hearth. She bit her lower lip, taking a tentative step forward. "Are you here?"

From the shadows beyond, a voice emerged, low and rough.

"I wasn't sure you'd come." The girl went still as the speaker stepped out from the shadows. "But I'm glad you did. It's time you and I had a talk."

"Does this mean . . ."

"Oh, yeah. She knows."

ONE

FRIDAY, 4:15 P.M.

The scene out the passenger side window was like something off a New England postcard: trees rolling away in every direction, a patchwork quilt picked out in a cornucopia of fall shades, drawn up around the necks of the distant hillsides against the chill in the air. I cracked the window slightly, hoping for a hint of that fall scent, part woodsmoke and part decay. Which makes it sound morbid and terrible, but I'd wear it as perfume if someone could figure out how to bottle it. That, and whatever they use in those fir-tree candles you find at the seriously overpriced boutiques around Christmas—not the cheap Yankee Candle crap, the expensive soy ones by companies named after herbs. I want to live *inside* those candles.

"Remember the time we went camping around here?"

I glanced across the console at Blake. He pulled his eyes away from the road just long enough to flash his wry half-smile at me, the one that brought out the dimple in his left cheek. The imbalance always made him look mischievous, as if he was plotting something he knew the powers that be would disapprove of. I used to get all melty describing his dimple to girlfriends, the feature that turned his boyishly handsome face interesting.

I thought back to that first camping trip, years ago now, just after we'd started dating. Blake had just started at Playpen, and the entire staff was on ramen-subsistence wages, "one step below ramen-profitable," according to Blake. He was still in that decrepit walk-up in Bushwick, we both still had roommates, and the need to fuck each other's brains out was still at that semiferal level that only lasts a few months, maybe a year if you're lucky. It had seemed like such a good idea—a campfire, stars twinkling overhead, miles and miles of empty woods just waiting for us to defile them . . .

I raised an eyebrow, mouth twisting into a small smile.

"What was it the doctor said?"

"I believe his exact words were 'Never seen poison ivy *there* before.'" Blake turned to me again, blue eyes sparkling. "But it was more his tone. Actually *calling* me a degenerate scumbag would have been redundant."

"Well, you disappointed him, obviously." A laugh burst out of me. "Remember the look on his face when I asked him to check me out? I don't care how ancient the guy was, you'd think a doctor would be able to hear the word *vagina* without having an aneurysm."

"To be fair, when he went to medical school, the preferred term was 'portal of shame.' I'm just lucky he prescribed calamine lotion instead of penance."

"Clearly he didn't know you well enough."

Blake's smile faltered for just a second, eyes narrowing, and just like that, there it was again, rearing up between us with a malevolent grin, *Remember me?* Of course I did, I couldn't forget about it for more than a few seconds, the mass of everything we weren't saying was so damned hulking I was surprised we'd been able to squeeze into the Prius alongside it.

I turned back to the window, jaw tightening in a way so familiar that lately it was starting to give me headaches.

"Don't worry, I asked when I booked the room, genital rashes are not included with our package."

I could almost hear the hopeful look in his eyes. With a monumental effort of will, I prised my jaw open wide enough to slip out a noncommittal "That's good."

A few minutes later, we pulled off the highway. A McDonald's and a smattering of gas stations had sprouted around the exit ramp, but within a few blocks they gave way to folksy-looking shops with hand-painted signs advertising car repair prowess, hot coffee, or in one case, antiques and live bait. The obvious combo.

"I bet their milkshakes are good," I said, pointing across the intersection. "Towns like this always have the best ice cream."

"We don't really have time to stop," Blake said, mouth screwing off to the side. "We're running late."

Fury shot through me like a flame.

"Fine." I huffed out a breath through my nose.

"I mean . . . if you really want one . . ."

"Did I *say* I wanted one?" My voice was getting noticeably tight. I could actually feel the pressure building behind my eyeballs. That couldn't be healthy. "Anyway, we would have been on time if you'd grabbed the lunch I made us out of the fridge. Like I *asked*."

"I already said I was sorry for that."

"It's *fine*. I don't need a milkshake anyway." Then I tilted my whole body toward the window, as though a wall of ribs and spine would somehow protect me from the curdled atmosphere in the car.

"Okay . . ." I could hear the defeat in his tone. An apology shot up like a gag reflex, but I swallowed it, relishing the acid burn at the back of my throat. I was not going to give in that easily. I *always* gave in. This whole weekend was me giving in, really.

And then, of course, came the guilt. Which was asinine—*I* wasn't the one that invited that foul, oxygen-hogging monstrosity of *what happened* along—but when has marriage ever been built around logic? Lately ours seemed to be built mostly on shared

Netflix tastes, perched delicately atop an ever-shifting sea of eggshells.

"Do you want to listen to a podcast?" My voice was barely a mumble.

"Sure. That'd be good."

Jesus Christ, how were we ever going to make it through this weekend if we couldn't handle a four-and-a-half-hour car ride?

I pressed my forehead against the window as the soothing, vaguely nasal NPR cadences filled the dead space in the car, letting the colors outside blur together, go abstract.

It will be okay. You *will be okay. You can't expect everything to bounce back to normal immediately. You need to try harder, give him more space if you want this to work.*

The little therapist on my shoulder sounded so reasonable I almost let myself believe her.

"Almost there now."

"Mmm." I felt too wrung out to trust myself with more words at the moment.

But as we made our way farther and farther from what passed for civilization this far upstate, I could feel myself lightening, my shoulders unslumping slightly. Every so often a thin gravel road would snake off through the trees, the tiniest bit of clapboard visible at the end of it. The mailboxes started getting more and more folk-arty, their sides studded with moose and loon and canoe silhouettes. One was even held up by a miniature grizzly, his cheery face carved—poorly—out of an old tree stump. Anywhere else, they'd be tacky, but out here, they were . . .

Well, still tacky, but also kind of charming. A not-small part of me would be thrilled to sink into a life of woodsy tastelessness, swathing my body and home in chunky cable knits so thick nothing bad could penetrate them.

Ahead of us, a giant carved wooden sign proclaimed MILLINGHAM HOUSE. Blake nosed the car down the winding drive, the boughs of century-old oaks and maples holding hands above our heads. After about a half mile, he turned around a final bend and the house appeared.

"Holy hell," I murmured.

"Apparently the other half lives very, very expansively," Blake said, grinning at me. I let myself return the grin, let my shoulders loosen further. *You're here to enjoy yourself, Rebecca, stop trying to ruin it for at least a minute.*

He pulled up to a booth just outside the gates and chatted with the attendant as I gazed at the mansion.

It was a behemoth in grey stone, U-shaped, its stubby arms reaching out to us on either side of a blocky central wing. The drive—drive*ways* are for plebes—ran straight toward the center of the main building, curling around a small island of garden, complete with tiered fountain, just in front of the entrance. Ivy scaled the walls, tendriling around the leaded glass windows, leaves poking between the slots of the wrought iron balconies that jutted out from a handful of the second-story rooms.

Really, it was more castle than mansion.

"How'd you find this place?" I asked him.

"Oh, umm . . . one of the guys at work recommended it. Said he'd been here before."

"Was that a theme weekend too?"

"Maybe? I didn't ask. I think most of the year it's just a normal hotel. Or, you know . . . *this* hotel."

The "Roaring Twenties" getaway had been Blake's idea—credit where it's due—and clearly for my benefit. Blake might occasionally read nonfiction bricks about World Leaders or Important Historical Moments from around that time, but dressing up for a three-day Gatsby theme party definitely wasn't his idea of fun, it was a peace offering. One of many that I was trying desperately to accept.

Gazing up at the peaked slate roof, where tiny gargoyles watched over especially critical sections of gutter, I couldn't help but hand it to him. You couldn't have found a more fitting spot to wrap a few ropes of fake pearls around your neck and sip booze out of coupes. He wouldn't tell me the name of the hotel before we left—I'd been especially annoyed with our therapist for backing his play that week—but now that we were here, I had to admit it was better as a surprise.

"So this place was just . . . someone's house once?"

"Someone's *summer* house. Jeremiah Royland O'Malley's, to be specific." Blake turned the car off the main drive down a narrow tributary that shot off to the west—well, "left," at least—wing and around to the back of the building. I raised an eyebrow at him, signaling for him to continue. He grinned, warming to the subject. "He was one of the robber barons around the turn of the century, made a fortune on steel mills, then patented a special alloy that multiplied that fortune a few times over. Apparently his wife's maiden name was Millingham. Romantic, no?"

I glanced up at the gargoyles.

"Sure."

We pulled in to a drab asphalt parking lot jutting out from the back of the house, a more modern addition to the storied manse. Acres and acres of gardens spread out all the way to the tree line, carefully trimmed hedges dividing them into neat geometric patches. In the distance, a couple in silhouette were picking their way around a largish pond dappled with water lilies, glimmering golden in the late afternoon light. I shook my head a bit to clear the glitter.

We'd barely managed to stretch our legs and pop the hatchback when a young man in a full tux with tails hurried over from a side door, smiling anxiously as he moved up next to Blake to reach for the luggage. He was wearing spotless white gloves. God, old-fashioned laundry must have been an absolute nightmare.

"Please, sir, allow me."

"Oh, it's no—"

"*Scuttles!* I take it you're not allowing the gentleman to carry his own luggage like some kind of common porter."

A middle-aged man, his grey hair swept straight back from his high forehead in a slick of pomade, strode through the same door, nose tipped up imperiously as he stared down the now cowering . . . *Scuttles,* apparently. The vest of the older man's tux puckered at the buttons, the fabric straining to contain his formidable belly, but somehow it added to his air of gravitas.

"No, sir. 'Course not. I was just telling the gentleman . . ."

"Telling him? Don't tell me you were speaking to your betters." He sniffed exaggeratedly. "Sir, Madam, please forgive Mr. Scuttles's insolence. He's new to the household and hasn't yet learned his place. Good valets are so hard to find these days," he added, raising his eyebrows in commiserative exasperation. "I'm Mr. Wynnham, Ms. Crooner's butler. I assure you, there won't be any such *breaches* again."

Blake glanced at me, mouth twisting in a wry grin as the young man nodded furiously, face purpling.

"Think nothing of it," Blake said, enunciating the words exaggeratedly. I tried not to laugh. Blake had told me it was a theme weekend so I'd know what to pack, but it hadn't really occurred to me what that would mean in real time. Specifically: forty-eight hours of interactive dinner theater. I felt a surge of warmth for my husband. Whatever might have motivated it, he really had picked an apology that was right up my alley . . . and several blocks over from his. That had to count for something. Maybe I could let it be enough.

"So kind of you, sir. Though I'd expect no less from friends of Ms. Crooner. And who shall I tell her has arrived?"

"The Wilsons. Blake and Rebecca."

"The Wilsons . . . hmm," the man frowned, considering. "The only guests she's still expecting are a Miss Taunte and a Mister Daily, but perhaps I'm mistaken . . ."

"Oh, right . . . I umm . . ." Blake held up a finger—*pause, please*—as he swiped through his email. "Yes, right, that's us. Sorry, I explained to Miss . . . what was the name she gave me?" He stared at the screen, tapping a few times. "When I booked this, she told me . . ."

"No need to worry yourself, sir, I believe we understand each other." The butler's lips curled the slightest bit at the corners, a golf clap of a smile. "If you'd be so kind as to follow me, I can show you to your suite for the weekend. Ms. Crooner has you in the lavender room, yes?" Blake blinked, then, taking the cue, skimmed his email again and nodded. "Excellent. Scuttles can manage your luggage."

"Should I leave my keys with him, or . . ." Blake glanced over his shoulder at the slim, dark-haired young man gamely pulling our luggage from the trunk.

"Your keys . . . ahhh, you mean to this fine automobile? Quite modern, by the way, sir. I'm sure Putter will want to speak to you about its manufacture. Ms. Crooner's chauffeur, of course. Such a *unique* fellow." He pursed his lips demonstratively. "But no, no need for that. Your automobile will be safe here for the weekend."

As if on cue, "Scuttles"—bit on the nose, theme weekend—closed the hatch. Blake clicked the automatic locks . . . then again . . . then again. I rolled my eyes at the familiar tic.

Did she *know how many times he had to click the car locks? The way he'd repark five times to get half an inch closer to the curb?*

I swallowed the wave of bile. *You need to stop dwelling. This weekend is about moving forward. Try. Harder.*

Then the butler cleared his throat and pulled the door wide, sweeping a hand toward the opening with a slight bow.

When I glanced at Blake, he was already looking my way, barely repressed glee widening his eyes.

I turned toward the door, peering in at the darkened interior. Polished wood and brass fittings glinted in the late afternoon light, dust motes traveling down a beam to rest in the thick pile of a blood-red oriental rug. I could almost feel the glamour of the place reaching out for us, beckoning with an elegant curled finger, *Right this way, let me make it all better.*

God, I so needed something to make it all better.

I sucked in a deep breath and stepped through.

TWO

"We'll be serving cocktails in the lounge at five," Wynnham said, actually clicking his heels like some kind of Mary Poppins extra. "Ms. Crooner prefers that her guests dress for dinner."

And with that, he turned and marched down the hall, belly thrust out in front of him like fleshy, tuxedoed armor.

Blake barely had the door closed before we both burst out laughing.

"Okay, when you said theme weekend I had no idea—"

"Trust me, if I *had* known, we'd have been doing the spa package in the Berkshires."

"Did you see the way the valet— Are we really supposed to call him *Scuttles*?"

"I mean, he didn't give another name."

"But did you see how he cowered when Wynnham pointed out where the luggage should go?" I giggled even more, remembering. "Do you think it was a set piece?"

"I'm absolutely *certain* it was a set piece." Blake rolled his eyes, plopping down onto the bed and propping a shoe over his knee, carefully untying and loosening the strings before easing it off.

I tugged my own shoes off with a foot pressed against each heel and collapsed onto my back on the other bed, heaving in a deep breath. Maybe this would be okay. Maybe it was exactly what we needed.

Overhead, ornate gold molding crept over the edges of the wall and curled toward the center of the ceiling, an empty frame for a blank expanse of plaster. I sat up on my elbows, taking in the room a bit more thoroughly.

Jesus, they weren't kidding about the lavender.

The entire room was papered in an elaborate two-toned brocade, thick enough that it almost looked like fabric. A gigantic peaches-and-cream marble fireplace dominated one wall, a pair of large brown-and-white china dogs facing each other across its mantel. Actually, they faced us, their yellow eyes staring outward with a glazed—literally and figuratively—lifelessness. Creepy things probably cost more than our rent; they had that "big winner of *Antiques Roadshow*" look. A mahogany writing desk dominated one corner, simultaneously ornate and spare, studded with dozens of drawers far too small to serve any practical purpose. It was the kind of thing you could imagine Dickens bending over, the effect marred only slightly by the blocky plastic phone and fan of hotel information and local attraction pamphlets on the artfully worn leather blotter. Two Victorian-looking chairs, their chintz fabric buttoned and nipped into ornate dark wood frames, created a little seating area near the leaded glass windows, the view through the aging geometric panes pleasantly distorted, a Van Goghian version of the gardens we'd seen flowing out around the house. A tiny marble-topped pedestal table hovered between their arms, fighting for its share of wavering, distorted light.

"What time is it?" Blake said. He had fully melted into the duvet, a thick down affair in brilliant white, like a signpost proclaiming "Don't worry, *some* things have changed since 1882." I pulled out my phone.

"Dammit! It's already four-forty." Stomach pulsing with anxiety—yes, I, and all the therapists I've ever been to, know it's out of proportion to almost every single occasioning factor—I bounced off the bed. "Do you need the shower? I feel like I should shower."

"Didn't you shower this morning?"

"But then we sat in the car all day. Do I smell like fast food?" I lifted an arm and sniffed tentatively. "I'm gonna shower. Do you need it?"

"All yours." He was flat on his back again before I even reached the bathroom, the heavy wooden door with brass knobs belying the glistening subway-tiled interior. A mirrored vanity tray hinted at the mansion's history, but everything else in the room—suite almost, it was at least the size of my first college dorm—was aggressively modern: a glass-walled shower, jacuzzi tub, various personal appliances in cloth bags (why does putting a hair dryer in a bag somehow make it classier?), and an array of spa-quality toiletries that I immediately scooped up and dropped into my bag. Honestly, there's something affected about *not* taking hotel toiletries.

I bent toward the mirror, squinting as I fluffed my thick dark curls, bobbed just too long ago for me to still be riding the post-salon good-hair-days wave. It had been so long since I'd tried to pull myself together for anything, or seen anyone but my own ghostly reflection in the corner of the television screen, the uncredited extra in whatever cozy mystery show was numbing my brain for the night. Still, I looked mostly decent, plus a little bit of frizz on the sides felt period appropriate. A quick rinse later, and I was ready to slip into the knee-length gown I'd bought for the weekend. On the joint bank account, because I *dare* you to say anything, Blake.

I belted my hair with the little band of velvet and rhinestones I'd bought to match, touched up my makeup, then took a step back to admire the effect, twisting back and forth so the gold and silver beads winked in the light, reveling in the silken swish of fringe around my knees. A tiny flutter of excitement awakened in the middle of my chest. Playing someone else, burying myself in an impossibly luxe, throwback, *simpler* version of life, if only for the weekend, would be fun.

I tapped my phone again: 4:58. *Perfect.*

"All right, hon, I just need to dig out my heels and then we can . . ."

He was asleep.

"Blake."

Nothing.

"Blake." I moved over to the bed, shaking one shoulder hard. "We have to *go.*"

"Oh . . . right. Just give me a minute."

"What about 'It's four-forty' wasn't clear?" I could actually *feel* my nostrils flaring.

"I'll be quick." He blinked hard, licking his lips as he unzipped his bag, extracting the black tux he'd worn at our wedding. "Dang, is this too wrinkly?"

"Why would you stuff it in your suitcase when we *drove* here?"

"Calm *down,* Becks." He crossed to a dresser, tugging open drawers, then moved to the wardrobe across from the bathroom, craning his neck to see to the back of the top shelf. He pulled out a steamer, hung the suit over the open wardrobe door, wandered into the bathroom to fill the water receptacle . . .

For the love of—was he *trying* to move as slowly as possible?

Blake blinked owlishly as he emerged, poring over the purple-papered walls in search of an outlet.

"It's right *here,*" I huffed, bending to plug the stupid thing in, gritting my teeth at the sound of a bead popping free from my hip and bouncing against the baseboard. This was supposed to be *my* weekend and already he's taking it over, the way he always does, which is probably my *fault,* since I usually just sigh and wait for Blake to take however long he needs, *that's what a marriage is, compromise,* and of course customer projections and multipronged marketing campaigns and massive investor presentations he can handle but somehow the concept of *time* is beyond his capabilities, but *patience, Rebecca,* because it's always only me who's supposed to mold myself into some better, more perfected, beatifically smiling zen-goddess-on-a-bottle-of-oat-milk form . . .

Deep breaths. Don't ruin things, Becca. This doesn't have to be a fight. *The goal isn't to control your feelings, it's to control your reactions to them.* Another thing many, many therapists had told me to no useful end. Who gives a fuck how you express yourself when the alternative is feeling like someone slipped a vise around your chest when you weren't looking and just kept twisting the handle tighter and tighter and tighter?

Slowly he began dragging the steamer over the suit, moving over it inch by inch. Exhaling sharply, I plucked the suit off the wardrobe.

"You'll damage the *wood.*"

"Okay . . . thanks." Blake raised his eyebrows sky-high but didn't say anything else.

Finally he finished his meticulous steaming routine (Wynnham would be so proud) and replaced the steamer in the closet, tugging his shirt free from his pants and pulling the whole thing over his head in that way all men seem to learn as part of puberty.

It was 5:12 by the time he finally had the tux on.

"How do I look?"

Late.

"Great. Can we go now?"

He laughed. *God, isn't it* hilarious *how Becks likes to be on time to things?*

"I'm just waiting on you."

"Make sure you grab the room key," I said, brushing past him toward the door, trying to exhale heavily enough to release some of the pressure building inside my skull. By the time we'd turned the corner back into the gallery that joined the three wings of the house, an expanse large enough to cram dozens more pieces of incidental furniture into, I felt . . . less aneurysmy, at least.

Things like Blake's flexible understanding of time never used to bother me this much, but lately my brain was all tinder, ready to burst into flames at even the slightest spark. It was exhausting. And guilt-inducing. *Was* I being too hard on him? How do you know when you're being too hard on your partner versus accepting less than you deserve? *Or was the real problem thinking I'd ever be able to get past his cheating in the first place?*

Luckily, I was saved from that train of thought by the appearance of a woman dressed in a long, plain black dress at the top of the opposite staircase. Her mouse-brown hair was drawn back into a tight bun, which gave her face a slightly pulled look. Starched white lace burst out of her collar in a geyser of pleats and trickled out from wide cuffs over her short, plump hands, the kind that rings always seem to slice into. A loop of ornate-looking keys hung from a tight velvet belt at her waist.

She nodded slightly and started a rigid descent, pausing at the central landing—where the two tributary staircases joined to form the grand river of wood and burgundy carpeting that flowed down to the main entrance—to wait for Blake and me. I took one more deep breath and started down, smiling broadly as we approached.

"Hi, there. We're . . ."

"Miss Taunte and Mr. Daily. So pleased you could join us." She spoke with a vague, unplaceable English accent, of the generally arch but regionally nonspecific variety that proved she was American. But points for effort. "I'm Miss Ann Thrope, head housekeeper to Miss Crooner. Can I show you to the lounge? I believe cocktail service has just begun." She smiled tightly, in a way that pinched her already small eyes smaller.

"That would be great, thank you," I said. With a clipped nod, she turned on her heel—I think she actually left a divot in the pile of the carpet—and continued her stately descent to the ground floor. I fell in behind her, glancing over my shoulder briefly at the dozens of paintings lining the walls overhead, a gallery of ghosts from decades and centuries past. Their eyes seemed to follow us down the stairs. I repressed a gleeful shiver at the thought. I'd always loved that kind of movie.

"Wow. Should've come in the front way," Blake murmured as the grand hall came into view, an absolutely ginormous expanse of creamy marble, gilt-edged furniture, and gleaming wainscoting, all of it presided over by the largest chandelier I'd ever seen in my life. I tilted my head upward, gaping.

"Do you think those are real crystals?"

"Ms. Crooner would accept nothing less," Miss Thrope murmured with another tight smile. "She had it imported from Austria after her most recent tour of the European capitals. I believe a Miss Millingham recommended it to her? Matched the style she had installed in her own summer home."

"Impressive," Blake said, raising his eyebrows at me, dimple popping out as he tried to repress a laugh.

"Miss Crooner *is* one of the best-known performers of the era," the housekeeper said, turning sharply to the left. All her movements had a jerking abruptness to them. She seemed like she should have been carrying a ruler to swat us with. She skirted the edge of a giant wooden desk that fit into the overall aesthetic of the house . . . except for the massive sign across the front proclaiming *Reception* in twirling script. "Cocktails will be in the lounge. Just this way."

She continued across the floor, the clicks of her heels echoing in the vaulted room, until she reached a narrow hallway. About twenty yards down it she stopped, nodding to an open doorway. A brass sign to the left of it proclaimed BAR HOURS: 11 AM—1 AM.

"Just through here. And please, let one of the girls know if there's anything I can do to help make your stay more comfortable."

With that, she turned and continued past the doorway and into a room beyond, the thick dark carpet muffling the sounds of her steps.

Blake looked at me, raising his eyebrows impishly, and ducked inside.

Late afternoon sunlight poured in through the windows at the opposite side of the room, shining softly on the dark wood of the imposing bar that ran along much of the left-hand wall, elaborate Victorian mirrors behind it reflecting the scene. A middle-aged woman in a giant fluffy white stole clutched a martini glass at the edge of the enormous black marble fireplace that dominated the opposite wall. She smiled nervously at me as we entered, lifting her glass slightly. Noticing the gesture, the man she was with, his face obscured by his oversized fedora, turned toward us. His face had a scrunched feel to it, as though the features had been designed for a less broad background and no one had bothered to resize them to fit. I was fairly certain these were the people I'd seen walking around the gardens before, bending over the planters and benches, no doubt to inspect all the lavish detailing turn of the century money could buy. There couldn't be *that* many hats that size around the place, no matter how much everyone got into the theme. Another couple stood near the windows, gazing out at the lawn as they spoke quietly to each other, their backs to us.

"Ahh, Miss Taunte and Mr. Daily, so lovely to see you again." Wynnham bowed slightly to us from behind the bar. Blake moved over to lean against it, probably grateful for the excuse not to have to introduce himself quite yet. "Can I get you something to drink? Champagne, perhaps, or a martini? I hear they're all the craze in the city."

"I'd love a scotch." Blake craned his neck to look over the bottles on the back bar. "Macallan's 12, if you have it."

"Of course, Mr. Daily. How do you take it?"

"One ice cube, thanks."

"And for the lady?"

"A martini sounds amazing, actually. Vodka, a little dirty?"

"I'll have it ready shortly," Wynnham said with another small bow. Blake reached for his wallet. "No, no, sir, that's not necessary." He raised a hand. "Miss Crooner wouldn't dream of it."

"Oh, well . . . for you, then." He pulled out a five and slid it across the bar.

"You're most generous, sir."

While Wynnham made a show of shaking my martini, the woman took a step toward us, smiling shyly. So much for Blake's strategy.

"I figure we might not have another chance to introduce ourselves for a while," she said with an awkward giggle. "I'm Dolly, this is my fella, Bugsy." She squeezed the man's forearm, swimming slightly in the boxy, oversized suit he was wearing, somehow loud despite its fairly simple chalk-stripe style. "You mighta heard *his* name before."

"Nice to meet youse," he said, lip curled exaggeratedly as he tipped his hat in our direction. "This your first time at Ida's joint?"

"Oh, umm . . . yes, first time," I said, smiling more brightly, my default defense against awkwardness. I turned to Blake, unsure how to play this. I hadn't expected to be making introductions "in character," but of course that was part of the fun for people, and the couple in front of me had that overeager, voice just-too-loud air of community theater performers. "I'm Miss Taunte," I added, sticking out my hand, mildly proud of myself for remembering what the bartender had just called me.

"A dame that shakes hands? How *modern,*" the man said, raising his eyebrows exaggeratedly as he took my hand in his. "But then Ida never has stood on ceremony. We wouldn't be here otherwise, right, baby?"

"That's right, Bugs," the woman said, moving her hand to his shoulder and fluttering her eyelashes at his large, flat face. Up close, it was clear the stole was the sort of stiff faux fur you found in the accessories aisle of Halloween shops. "Most folks'd eat their hat before they'd invite a guy like *you* to a place like this." He nodded agreement.

"I'll say this for the joint, they don't stiff you on the booze," he said, lifting his glass and taking a big swig, wincing slightly as he did. Presumably he'd ordered in character, too.

"Speaking of, I think we're going to sit down to enjoy our drinks," Blake said with a polite smile, holding up two glasses. "Nice to meet you."

"Youse too," the man said, tipping his hat again. I tried to repress a giggle. We were in for a *lot* this weekend.

I gave a small wave goodbye and followed Blake to one of the tables at the opposite end of the bar, sliding into two of the club chairs tucked up around it. We'd only just gotten our drinks when the couple from the windows came up.

"Wait . . . Phil?" I blinked, not quite believing my eyes.

Phil—one of the earliest investors Blake had convinced of Playpen's merit—slid into an empty chair, long legs kicked out in front of him. I always seemed to forget just how tall he was. Though, to be fair, it's not as if we saw Phil and Heather *all* that often. He smiled amiably, the skin at the corners of his eyes crinkling just enough, his teeth white and straight and shiny. His brown hair was salted throughout, especially at the temples, but it was still thick, and he was trim in the tuxedo he was wearing. I'd told Blake the first night I met Phil, at a summer barbecue in their expansive, exquisitely landscaped backyard however many years ago—Phil presiding over the grill with that same drank-my-milk smile, Heather flitting around, the consummate hostess—that he should have been a spokesman for insurance. Phil showed his age just enough that you trusted him, but he was still dad-hot. After that evening, Blake found a way to drop the term "dad-hot" into at least one exchange for *months* whenever we'd meet them for drinks in the city, or dinner at their place. It always threw off that spark of intimacy you get when you're still early in a relationship and every inside joke feels thrilling, a daring concept the two of you have invented and solely possess.

"Wait . . . so that means . . ."

"I was wondering when you two would get here." Heather grinned devilishly as she moved into view, accepting Phil's seated attempt to pull out a chair for her. She looked impeccable. But that was no surprise, Heather *always* looked impeccable. She was wearing an obviously expensive calf-length gown, burgundy satin with jet beads carving elaborate diamond patterns across the front that emphasized the narrowness of her waist. Of all of her, actually. Heather was very into fitness, and she had that ropy, taut look thin women sometimes got in middle age. Probably her navel-length double rope of pearls was real. She perched on the edge of the chair, eyes glittering, thin lips pulled into a smile, as she cradled her glass of white wine in a hand gloved in elbow-length black satin.

"So? Did you pull it off?" She turned to Blake expectantly, widening her large, precisely lined eyes.

"TBD," he said raising his eyebrows meaningfully. Heather sat back, nodding, then turned to me.

"Have you two had a chance to poke around the place yet? Oh, speaking of, what are we supposed to be calling you?" She clicked her phone on and squinted at it narrowly—her vanity definitely extended to the concept of reading glasses. "I have our names in one of these emails somewhere . . ."

"We're Peter and Maria," Phil said, taking a swig of the brown liquor in his cut crystal lowball. Heather drew her chin down in a way that emphasized its weakness, trying to confirm Phil's statement. Finally, she poked a thin finger at the screen.

"That's right. The 'Oleums,' if you can even stand it. Though I suppose we don't have to start in on all that *quite* yet," she said as she slipped the phone back into her tiny clutch. I smiled.

"Good, because I already forgot whatever that woman in the hallway called us."

"Was it the housekeeper?" Phil's lips twisted in a knowing smile as I nodded. "What did she call herself?"

"I believe you're referring to *Miss Ann Thrope*." Blake's lips curled with amusement.

"That's the one." Phil finger-gunned Blake. "Looks like she's out for blood, doesn't she? I bet she's got a riding crop somewhere in that getup." Heather slapped his arm in a faux scold and he grinned even wider.

"I'm sure she's trying to make the experience more fun for all of us." Heather sipped her wine. The diamond over her glove looked like the inciting event in a heist movie. Phil had done very, *very* well in finance before he switched over to teaching.

"For the record, Becks, we're . . . Mr. Reid A. Daily and Miss Debbie Taunte," Blake said.

"Oh my god, I don't think I registered that they were *that* cheesy." Vodka burned the back of my sinuses as I stifled a laugh, turning back to Heather. "I guess you two must know already, Blake surprised me with this weekend. In more ways than I realized, clearly."

"I know how much you love puns," he said. I sniffed out a laugh. Work in marketing long enough and they're practically a second language. Blake knew *exactly* how much I "loved" speaking it.

"Phil *might* have nudged him toward it," Heather said, laying a hand on her husband's arm, smiling lovingly in his general direction. "I'm guessing he was after safety in numbers. We have a big anniversary this year, and he knows what a fan I am of this sort of thing, especially since it's happening in a massive Gothic mansion, so he *very* thoughtfully arranged the whole thing." She squeezed his arm once before turning to me again. "So *And Then There Were None,* don't you think?" I nodded. Heather and I had discussed our shared love of mysteries on several occasions.

Phil raised an eyebrow rakishly.

"If I hadn't picked up on all the hints you were dropping over the last few months, I think this anniversary might have been our last. I found not one, not two, but three different brochures about this weekend in places I'd just *happen* to see them. Not to mention the several reminders on my Google calendar to 'book Millingham House weekend for my beautiful wife.'"

"But it was so lovely of you not to force me to make the reservation myself!" She pinched his arm playfully. "Anyway, you know me, I'd rather have a plan than a surprise. I did all the research on weekends like this, and I found the absolute best one. Besides, I could have requested something from Cartier, so all in all, I think you came out ahead, mister."

We all laughed, and I could feel something that had been coiled tight on the drive loosening in me. Phil and Heather weren't close friends, by any means. The relationship had started through business, after all. Blake had been so thrilled after that meeting. Phil had pulled him aside to say that he was excited about the technology, but really, he was investing in *Blake*. That picking the right horse to tie his wagon to had always served him well in the past and he could tell Blake was a stallion (or some other macho analogy that Blake probably still remembered word for word). I still remembered the look in his eyes, like a kid who got picked first for kickball, as he recounted Phil's assessment of him. After that, the two of them hit it off quickly, developing one of those easygoing, surface-level male friendships that required nothing more than a shared appreciation of scotch, a willingness by Blake to let Phil play the sage on occasion, and mutual interest in sports to survive. It hadn't been long after that they'd asked us up to Pine Haven for that barbecue. Since then we'd been getting together once every few months, usually somewhere in the city, but a few times at their absolutely stunning home on nights Heather had to help one of their three unfairly attractive kids with a tough homework assignment, or was on the hook for too many carpools to make it in to the city by a reasonable hour.

Phil and Blake were closer, obviously, but Heather had clearly enjoyed taking us under their collective wing as well. More than once she'd whispered to me, at some gathering of dozens of suburban couples, all the women as well turned out as she was, that Blake and I *gave them cred.* I'd never told her in so many words, but she and Phil gave me . . . not *hope* exactly, but something nearby. A vision of the future? Yes, Pine Haven was still way out of our budget, and a little Stepfordy, but when we were all sitting in their beautiful dining room, enjoying some clearly complicated recipe Heather had "wanted an excuse to try," I'd sometimes catch one of them looking so tenderly at the other, like they were still college sweethearts, that it made *me* a little swoony. I wasn't ready for all that yet, but . . . maybe it wasn't so bad. In fact, maybe part of me wanted it. Back when we were still trying to get pregnant, a prospect equally tantalizing and terrifying, I'd sometimes imagine us into Phil and Heather's home, a high chair attached to the marble-topped kitchen island, all the things we struggled to find room for in our tiny New York apartment placed neatly into tasteful, oversized, doubles-as-storage furniture, our frankly profligate number of closets each dedicated to a specific purpose, subdivided with neatly labeled wicker baskets, and the fear would steadily drip away, leaving only the firelight glow of the vision.

Though these days that was looking like a distinctly rosier outcome than Blake and I could ever hope to achieve. I blinked, took another sip of my martini to center myself, and turned to Phil.

"How's teaching going, Phil? You're still at Columbia, right?" I twirled the olive in my glass, glancing up at him. He leaned toward me, smiling in a wolfish way that probably made all the undergrads go damp. I could already feel the martini hitting me; it had been hours since we'd eaten. Had it come out flirty? Instinctively I leaned back, though I'd spent enough time with Phil to know that flirting was almost reflexive for him, like breathing.

I could half-see Blake's smile in my peripheral vision. He was better at remembering the sorts of details that smoothed small talk along than I was. And apparently either unaware of, or untroubled by, the way Phil's stare had sharpened. Disappointment flickered through me. Not like I wanted Phil, but Blake could at least *notice.*

"That's right. Actually, I've recently become the darling of the theater department," Phil said with a smirk.

"For your Hamlet, I'm assuming," Blake said. Heather sniffed loudly and Phil laughed, taking another swig of his drink.

"That's a hell no. Heather will tell you, I don't have a creative bone in my body."

"That's not true. You come up with the most impressive reasons you can't get to your honey-do list." She smiled exaggeratedly at him, squeezing his forearm and batting her eyelashes before returning to her wine. The lines at the corners of his eyes tightened slightly, then he laughed.

"That's just cost-benefit analysis." He turned back to Blake. "As I was *saying,*" Heather widened her eyes playfully as he continued, "one of the classes I teach is on successfully structuring small businesses and nonprofits. A theater professor started recommending it to his students last semester. A lot of them wind up trying to start little off-off-off-Broadway theaters, or forming some sort of collective, and believe it or not, they tend not to have too much experience with the practical side of things." He leaned back, hitched his ankle up over his knee, and took another slow sip of his drink, eyes never leaving mine.

"And how are the kids?" I said, deliberately turning to Heather. She smiled warmly. Clearly Phil's flirting didn't bother *her.* I was just . . . more acutely attuned to that sort of thing at the moment.

"Really great, actually. I can't believe Ryan's applying to colleges, though. It'll be such an adjustment when he leaves next year." She blinked rapidly, smile wobbling a bit, and Phil took her hand.

"He'll do great, hon. You've done such a good job with him," he murmured, and she nodded, still a bit overcome at the idea of her oldest leaving the nest.

Wanting to give her some privacy—Heather was the kind of

self-contained that would much rather help you through tears than have you see hers—I glanced over her shoulder as another couple around Blake's and my age entered the bar. The woman was pretty—the soft finger waves in her light brown hair suited the heart shape of her face—and dressed in a slinky floor-length gold satin gown and heaps of costume jewelry. The man at her side was slim, almost slight, in his tweedy three-piece suit. His curly dark hair was just this side of unruly, and his prominent nose balanced out otherwise feminine features, like the full lips currently twisted in an amused smile. The woman met my eyes and I raised my glass slightly—tragically near empty. She smiled, pinching her lips in a moue of excitement that made me want to wave them over. Unlike "Bugsy" and "Dolly," they looked like the sort of people we'd actually seek out in the real world.

"Looks like we're about to get started." Heather raised her thin eyebrows conspiratorially.

Blake could read my confusion before I even opened my mouth. He leaned closer, lowering his voice.

"The weekend is limited to eight guests. That must be the last couple." He reached out absently to squeeze my hand. I glanced over at the new couple again. They were listening attentively to Wynnham's spiel at the bar.

"Do you think we should ask them to join us? If there's only eight of us, it might be nice to—"

I was cut off by a high-pitched, terrified shriek echoing down the hallway.

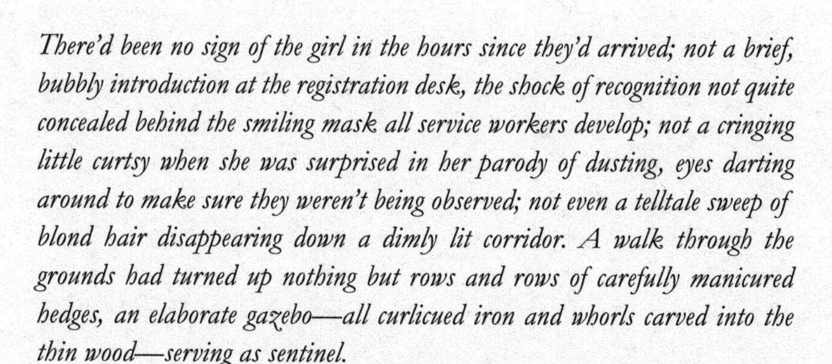

There'd been no sign of the girl in the hours since they'd arrived; not a brief, bubbly introduction at the registration desk, the shock of recognition not quite concealed behind the smiling mask all service workers develop; not a cringing little curtsy when she was surprised in her parody of dusting, eyes darting around to make sure they weren't being observed; not even a telltale sweep of blond hair disappearing down a dimly lit corridor. A walk through the grounds had turned up nothing but rows and rows of carefully manicured hedges, an elaborate gazebo—all curlicued iron and whorls carved into the thin wood—serving as sentinel.

It was absolutely vital that she be here. In a way, she was the whole point of this entire thing. And it was beginning to look as though she might not appear at all.

But then that scream split the air, prickling the hairs on the back of the neck with its echoing intensity, and strangely, instead of a rush of anxiety, or surprise, or that old fallback fear, the emotion it brought up was anticipation, spiked with a dram of relief.

They were the only people in the mansion this weekend, and the girl was there specifically to help entertain them.

Which meant there would be no way for her to avoid this. Nowhere for her to hide. The only thing to do was find the right moment. . . .

THREE

For a moment, all of us sat frozen by the banshee cry, then everyone burst into action at once.

"What in the . . ." I blinked at my hand, resting in a widening puddle of briny vodka. I righted the glass, shook my hand absently in the air, then turned to Blake. He was already standing, holding a hand out to me.

"We should see what's going on." His nostrils flared and he glanced over his shoulder. Wordless, I let him tug me up and after him toward the door while Phil grumbled his way out of the deep club chair behind us. It occurred to me that this is what they always did in horror movies—"they" being the people you scream at through the screen for basically choosing to die violently.

The other couples moved aside as we joined them in the hallway, Phil and Heather just behind us. I could just hear Wynnham calling out over the sound of my thudding heart.

"Ladies, gentlemen, there's no need for you to put yourselves out, I'm sure some scullery maid was just scared by a spider . . ."

Then the next door over whipped open so hard the brass knob thudded against the wainscoting. The dark hallway seemed to leach the sound away like water on cracked earth. A young woman in the black dress and white apron of a housemaid stood in the doorframe, blond hair spilling out wildly from beneath her starched white cap. Her eyes darted between us frantically, unseeing, throat working as if she might either scream or vomit at any moment.

"Please, I was just cleaning up and she . . ." Her whole body started to tremble and she took a stumbling step backward, knuckles going white where she gripped the doorframe for balance. "I think someone . . . saints preserve me . . ."

And then she went boneless, thudding to the floor heavily in a dead faint.

Instinctively, I rushed over to kneel beside her. I always had been the mother hen type, Blake used to make fun of it when we met.

The maid took shallow breaths. But breathing had to be good. I bent lower.

"Are you okay? Can you hear me?"

She lay there motionless, skin pale in the fading evening light that spilled in through the windows. I reached for her slim wrist, tried to find a pulse . . . there, it was steady . . . maybe fast, even? Could that mean something?

I reached for my clutch to pull out my phone—a vague memory of counting heartbeats and multiplying was coming back to me from some elementary school gym class—when I remembered I hadn't been able to fit my phone inside. That martini had gone *right* to my head. I scrambled to my feet, stumbling as my heel stuck in the carpet.

"Blake, I can't tell if she's okay, do you think you could—*AAAHHH!!!*"

I staggered backward, my hip bumping into something, then someone's arms were around my middle, making it impossible to breathe, to move, and then a thud of something falling to the ground, my feet catching in the carpet, but *what the fuck there was a dead woman in the middle of the floor I just needed to get away from the dead woman on the floor.*

At least I assumed she was dead. She was lying on her stomach, blood oozing around her head and over the knotted wood floor in a sticky, viscous pool, clumping her short straight hair into gruesome red-brown tentacles. Her skin had a grey, waxy look to it, and her flapper-style beaded dress was pulled up awkwardly around her knees, revealing a scrap of silky slip beneath.

I swallowed convulsively, hand over my mouth, trying to move farther away, but my feet wouldn't obey me—why wasn't anyone else *moving*?

"Becks. Honey, are you okay?" Blake twisted me around, gripping onto my shoulders, staring into my eyes. "It's okay, honey, everything's fine. This isn't what you think."

Behind me Phil burst into a bellowing laugh.

"I think we can all agree that you pulled this one off, Blake."

I blinked at him, confused. Below me, the maid groaned weakly. When I glanced down, her eyes were fluttering open. A pile of books had spilled across the floor from a side table I'd apparently upended.

"Terry? What's the meaning of this?"

The housekeeper—Miss Thrope—was pushing past the other couples and into the room. She planted her hands on her hips, glared at the housemaid, struggling to her feet . . . then gasped.

"Oh dear lord . . . Miss *Crooner*!"

With a yelp, she hurried over to the dead woman, moaning loudly as she leaned over the body, shoulders shuddering with sobs.

I frowned. *Wait a second.*

Why was she calling her Miss Crooner—hadn't that been part of the theme? The buzzy, skittery feeling of shock was dissipating now, leaving only the buzzy martini feeling behind. If they were all still in character . . .

Oh dear lord. I turned to Blake, eyes wide with the question that—judging from the casual way they were leaning against tables and bookshelves—had been answered for all the other guests well before they got here. He grimaced, mouthing "Sorry" as the woman continued her hammy show of sorrow over the "murder."

My chest went tight as all the eyes in the room seemed to crawl over my skin, insect-like. *Wonderful, just the way to kick things off, by acting like a complete and utter idiot.* And with just eight guests, there was no way to avoid everyone . . .

But I didn't have time to dwell on that, the show must go on. The housekeeper stuffed a fist into her mouth, shook her head, and rocked back . . . then tilted her head to one side, quizzically, and reached down to grab something small and round. It glinted as she held it up to the fading light.

"What's this? Miss Crooner didn't own anything of the sort . . ."

She thrust the object forward. Three slender diamonds of gold wire nestled inside one another, twisting back and forth on the delicate gold chains binding them together in lazy, perpetual orbits.

I could feel every single drop of blood in my body geysering into my cheeks. Of course I'd be the first to have the *joy* of participating. Smiling awkwardly, I took a step forward, half-raising my hand.

"That would be my earring. Which was in my jewelry bag last I looked . . ."

"Are you saying this belongs to you, Miss Taunte?" The housekeeper's eyes narrowed. She took a step closer, thrusting the earring toward me. I recoiled instinctively.

"Yes, but again, I wasn't even wearing it tonight. I'm really not sure how it got here."

"*Innn*-teresting," the woman said, narrowing her eyes. "Can you confirm this woman's claims, Mr. Daily? You two were together most of the evening, if I recall."

"Oh, uhh, yes, that's right," he said, flashing a squeamish "brunch with the in-laws, don't let them know you're hungover" sort of smile. "She hasn't worn those earrings since we arrived together."

"I wonder what that could mean." Miss Thrope's head whipped around toward the body. *Was everyone in the room still watching me, or was it just the fabric of my new dress making my skin itch this way?*

"It were me who found her, Miss," the housemaid said, voice tremulous. "I was just coming in to stoke the fire, like Miss Crooner asked, but when I got here she were . . ." She turned her head to the side with a whimper, a single tear sliding over her smooth cheek.

"Terry, please lead our guests back into the lounge, I'll handle this," Miss Thrope said.

"But Miss . . ."

"That's not a request, Miss Yuss."

The housemaid nodded, pale and mute, and stumbled out the doorway and into the room we'd just come from, zombie-like. I glanced back at the scene one more time. Now that I was prepared for it, the corn-syrup texture of the "blood," the artfully posed body, even the lack of any obvious head wound, were all apparent. But who would notice that when seeing what looked like a dead body with *zero warning*? Blake tugged gently on my arm. I glared at him so hard he dropped it like a hot iron, but I followed him out of the room.

Back in the lounge, Wynnham was waiting with a tray of glasses and a bottle of something brown, the maid standing next to him, eyes wide with lingering "shock."

"Spot of brandy? It sounds like you've had quite the scare," he said, forehead corrugated with concern.

"That'd be good," I nodded, forcing the "dumb ol' me" smile onto my face again. "If nothing else, it'll help me forget how much of an idiot I looked like just now."

"Uhh . . . two, please," Blake said, licking his lips anxiously.

The butler poured us each a finger of liquor, passing us the cut crystal glasses before turning obsequiously to the couple trailing behind us, the glamorous pair who'd come in just before everything went sideways.

"Spot of brandy? It sounds like you've had quite the scare," I could hear him saying as Blake led me to our table in the back corner. Right, just another set piece. Which should be reassuring—*it's not all about you, Becca, no one cares how you reacted*—but somehow just made me more angry. How didn't I guess it *earlier*? I gripped the tumbler in both hands as I settled into the seat, barely tasting the warm, sweet liquor as it passed my lips. Blake leaned over the arm of his chair to squeeze my forearm.

"Listen, Becks. I probably should have said something before . . ."

I caught movement at the door out of the corner of my eye. The housekeeper was entering, back more ramrod-straight than ever, a small stack of booklets in her hands. The attractive woman with the finger waves and her mischievously handsome partner moved toward us to let her through.

"Just . . . don't."

"You have to understand . . ."

I silenced him with a raised hand, turning my head as far as it could go until just the housekeeper and the butler were in my line of vision. From across the room, I could feel the eyes of the fedora-and-stole couple drilling into me. I swallowed hard, trying to ignore it. *Just . . . act like you were playing along, Becca.*

"Have our guests been served?"

"Yes, Miss. Please, proceed."

She gave a swift nod of approval and took a step forward, crossing her hands behind her back.

"I'm sure all of you were as horrified as I was by tonight's events. I've rung the inspector, but it's too late for him to drive here safely, you've all seen the state of the roads south of the fork, he'd be likely to go off into the ditch." She shook her head sorrowfully. "He's instructed me to keep you comfortable until he and his deputies are able to reach the estate. And he's also informed me that none of you are allowed to leave the property until then."

"Not even for a booze run?" Phil was leaning against the mantel, grinning rakishly. Oh Jesus, I'd briefly managed to forget *people we actually knew* were here. I glanced over at Heather, back in her seat, but couldn't catch her eye; she looked pale, lips pinched tight, gaze darting back and forth between the staff members anxiously, hanging on their every word.

"Sir, I assure you, we'd be happy to supply any of your needs in that or any other department," Wynnham said with a small bow.

"And to answer your question, Mr. Oleum, the inspector was very clear: None of you are to leave under *any* circumstances. As of this moment, I'm afraid each of you is considered a suspect in Miss Crooner's"—Miss Thrope pinched her eyes shut, turning her head to the side and pressing the back of her hand to her mouth—"*murder.*"

"Oh, Miss Thrope, you don't ever think . . . ?"

The maid's pretty features twisted with terror and she stumbled, propping herself up against the bar. As Miss Thrope shuddered dramatically, Wynnham reached out to pat the young woman on the shoulder.

"There, there, now. You're safe, love."

"But . . . Miss Thrope just said that one of them—one of *you,*" she raked her eyes over the room, "is a *murderer*!"

Who even *had* twenties-themed weekends? I should have been on to this before we even left the city.

"Chin up, we'll sort it, I promise," Wynnham murmured, reaching out an arm. She folded herself into him gratefully, burying her face in his chest. The housekeeper seemed to have gathered herself. With a stiff little shake, she turned back to us all.

"As we're all stuck here until further notice, I have a proposition. I suggest we all attempt to work out who could have killed my mistress together. I'm sure none of us would like to see a murderer go free."

"I like the cut of this dame's jib," "Bugsy" said in the same exaggerated wiseguy accent he'd been using on us, jabbing a thumb at the housekeeper. This time I couldn't help but feel grateful for the effort.

"With that in mind, I've drawn up a quick summary of the important details." She moved over to the man—still doing his best "Ya filthy animals!" twenties-gangster face—flipped through the booklets in her hand, and extracted one to hand to him. "Mr. Slugs, this is yours. And Miss Diamond . . ." She gave another to the woman with him.

"Maria Richmann Oleum, this is for you . . . and Peter Oleum . . ."

Heather and Peter each took the proffered booklet. The housekeeper moved over to us, plucking a booklet off the top.

"Let's see here . . . Mr. Reid A. Daily, I believe this belongs to you." She passed Blake a booklet. "Ahh, and Miss Debbie Taunte, here's your dossier."

I swallowed, taking the slim booklet from her.

All That Jazz . . . A Murderously Delightful Weekend

Heather leaned over the arm of her chair.

"Are you alright?" she whispered, eyes darting back to the black-clad figures at the door. "It *was* pretty gory, wasn't it?"

"Fine, thanks." I tightened my lips further, stomach curdling at the pitying tone in her voice. Of all the people I'd want to see me make a complete fool of myself, Heather—with her perfectly manicured lawn, nails, children, *life*—was pretty far down the list.

The housekeeper moved to the last couple, tucked up against the near side of the bar. "Miss Lulu Larksong, for you . . . which leaves this for Mr. S. Cooper Mudslinger."

Out of the corner of my eye, I saw Blake duck lower, trying to get my attention. I clenched my jaw—*Welcome back, headache!*—and kept my eyes on my lap.

The housekeeper resumed her position at the front of the room.

"In this booklet, you'll find everything you need to know. Please take the next half hour to apprise yourselves of the relevant facts. Please do *not* turn the page marked 'Round One.' I think we all need a bit of time to process what's happened before that, don't you?" She pulled a sorrowful face, folding her hands in front of her as she caught Wynnham's eye. He nodded somberly.

"We'll reconvene in the main dining room at seven o'clock. It's in the opposite wing, just after you turn off from the great hall. You can also refer to the schedule and map provided with your check-in materials. Until then . . . please pray for poor Miss Crooner's soul."

She closed her eyes, shaking her head slowly, then turned on her heel—she probably practiced it, the sharp little twist in the carpet—and strode off down the hall.

"The game's afoot, eh?" I glanced over at Phil, who was raising his glass to Blake. And Blake, that traitorous shit, was raising his back, *smiling* at him. When he'd known this would happen. Had *planned* for it to happen.

"Upstairs," I somehow managed to squeeze past my tooth-barricade. I glanced over at Blake, who was deflating into the chair, eyes pinched closed, teeth bared in a grimace.

"Becks, nobody really . . ."

"Now."

I stood, breath fiery in my nostrils, and stalked out of the room, not quite sure whether I was hoping my husband would follow or whether I'd rather never see him again.

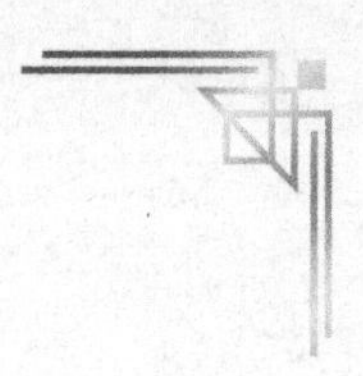

THE SCENARIO

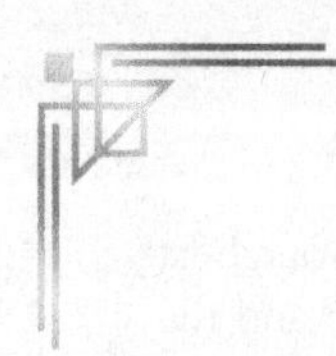

It's 1925, the height of the roaring twenties, and the celebrated jazz singer Ida Crooner is hosting a weekend at her lavish country estate for society's best, brightest . . . and richest. It'll be the cat's meow!

She's busy preparing the evening's entertainment for her guests (of course she'll be serving plenty of giggle water, and singing her worldwide smash hit "Charleston, Choose Me"), but in the meantime, freshen up, enjoy the grounds of Miss Crooner's stately manor, and feel free to ask anything of the five-star staff she employs. Just make sure you're decked out in your ritziest rags and ready to meet downstairs at *five p.m.* sharp for cocktails, dollface. This wingding is just getting started . . .

THE RULES:

One of you is guilty of a murder . . . but who? The only way to find out is to work with your fellow guests (and suspects) to solve the mystery.

This dossier contains several pieces of information you should **confide,** and others you should do your best to **hide** (after all, it's possible the murderer is *you*). Each round, you must share all the information you know about other suspects, the victim, and the staff. You should do your best to keep incriminating information about you from coming out.

You can change the subject, try to shift the group's focus, or simply fail to mention more damning tidbits about yourself. However, if you're asked directly about a piece of information in your "hide" facts, **you cannot lie.**

The game has been divided into several rounds. Do not look ahead in your manual. Your host will instruct you when to proceed to the next round. In the meantime, put your best sleuthing skills to work questioning the other guests and the staff, and examining the scene and provided clues. You can even go exploring between rounds; you never know what you might come across, or what piece of information might prove vital!

Can you and your fellow guests solve the mystery before the authorities arrive? Only time will tell . . .

FOUR

I didn't even wait for Blake to close the door behind him before rounding on him, waving the booklet in his face.

"What the *hell,* Blake?"

"Becks, I'm sorry, I should have told you—"

"You think?" I sniffed out a thin laugh. "You think maybe I might have liked to know that our 'theme weekend' was a murder mystery game *before* I saw a dead woman on the floor? And Heather and Phil were there watching . . ."

"Okay, in my defense—"

"No, *fuck* your defense." There was so much pressure inside my skull it felt like my eyes might splatter all over him. "Believe it or not, it's *scary* to see a dead body. It's not something where you mentally take a step back and say, 'Wow, that's unlikely, probably the pool of blood is just corn syrup and food coloring, what a neat piece of interactive theater' and then go back and enjoy your snifter of brandy. I mean . . . Jesus, Blake, what were you *thinking*?"

His body slumped and he shook his head.

"I wasn't. I wasn't thinking. I just know how much you love mysteries—you're always watching those British shows—and I didn't realize . . ." He looked up at me, eyebrows tented sorrowfully over drooping, miserable eyes, a perfect puppy-dog look.

Goddammit, of course he had to go and do something sweet like file that fact away. I could feel my rage flickering . . . but no, no way. So Blake managed to notice the *hundreds of hours* of mysteries I'd been grief-watching. He said it himself just now, he *wasn't* thinking, not where it counted, not about me, the real person he married.

"So you're telling me it never occurred to you that I might not love being made a fool of in front of a bunch of strangers and our only couple friends who have an actual adult life?" I laughed sharply. It felt like the brittleness in my voice was spreading over my body like ice on water, encasing me in a hard, glittering shell. "Or was that the point? 'Haven't gotten enough laughs at Becca's expense lately, better find another way to make her feel like a complete idiot.'"

"Becca, of course I didn't want that." He reached for my hand, but I snatched it away. I could see the muscles in his throat working as he fought to keep calm. "It was supposed to be a surprise, okay? Phil was doing it for Heather, and you two are always talking about mysteries when we get together. It just sounded like . . . something fun, something you'd enjoy. I guess I thought you'd . . ."

"Catch on sooner? Sorry, your wife's just too stupid to figure it out." My throat tightened. *Just like always, huh, Becks?* It was harder to control my breathing now.

Blake raised a hand and looked up at me, his whole body tense. He leaned back on the bed, physically shying away from what we could both see coming, the backseat passenger we'd brought along to this stupid, ill-conceived *surprise.* My hands clenched around empty air, fingers so rigid they were starting to shake.

"I get that I should have told you before things started. I'm sorry, okay? I promise, I wasn't trying to embarrass you. I just thought . . . it might be more fun for you this way."

I could feel it now, crawling up from the pit of my stomach where I'd tried to stuff it in a rickety little bamboo cage—why did I think that would hold anything? Too late, its claws were tearing through my middle, its mouth open in a snarling, slavering roar.

"Pretty sure I've had enough surprises from you to last a lifetime, Blake." The words tasted like venom, bitter and thick, coating my tongue. "Maybe focus on *not* keeping things secret from me for once."

The air seemed to suck out of the room all at once, leaving us suspended there, breathless, two astronauts shot out into the vacuum of space.

"This has nothing to do with that, Becca." Blake's voice was low and even, but I could see the muscles in his jaw contracting, his hands digging through the duvet.

"It has *everything* to do with it," I said, feeling more in control than I had in weeks, a surgeon drawing a scalpel through the patient, enjoying the wake of blood it left behind. "We wouldn't be here otherwise, would we?" Blake's shoulders hitched around his ears. "I'm just trying to figure out if you really believed that a weekend getaway would be enough to make me forget that you spent the last six months screwing your secretary."

Blake looked carved from stone.

"She wasn't my secretary," he murmured. "She was a colleague."

"God forbid I get her *title* wrong." I strode across the room on a current of righteousness and pulled open the bathroom door. Suddenly I couldn't stand to share the air with him, couldn't stand to have him physically stealing space from me.

"You said you wanted to work through it." Blake's voice was barely a whisper.

"*You* said you were working late. Guess we both say all sorts of things."

"So . . . what, it's just gonna be like this now?" I glanced over my shoulder. Blake was staring at me, face a mix of pain and frustration. "Any time I screw up, you'll pull this out and we're back at square one?"

I could almost feel the blood draining from my body, a tidal pull. I started to feel a little light-headed.

"That's not fair."

"You're probably right," Blake shrugged, eyes pinched so tight the bridge of his nose was furrowing. "Did I think this weekend would fix everything for us? No. But after all the time in therapy, after what you told me, I guess I thought you were willing to try."

"Don't you *dare* turn this into my fault."

"Fine, it's not. It's my fault. Just like everything else."

"Fuck your self-pity, Blake, *you're* the one who stuck your dick in someone else, *not* me." I whipped the bathroom door wide. "You're the one who needs to make things right. And this?" I flung my hands up to take in the room, the mansion, the weekend where I was the butt of the joke, *again*. "This isn't gonna cut it."

Then I stepped into the bathroom, slamming the door so hard it shuddered in its frame. My eyes were going blurry—Jesus, was I going to cry *again*? I'd been crying so much in the last six weeks it was starting to feel tedious. Body puffing and pulsing with rage and tears and embarrassment and guilt—because was he right? Was I the bad guy here? Did I owe him more chances, more patience, just *more*?—I crossed to the shower, yanking open the glass door. I tugged at the top handle—I needed noise, didn't want him listening to my tears, didn't want his forced, exhausted comfort, because then he gets to feel like he's fixing something again and he's not fixing anything, he's not even trying, and why won't this stupid knob turn, just *turn* on, *you piece of*—

I stumbled backward through the shower door, losing my leverage as the knob—and whatever had been mounted around it—came away in my hands.

Right, the lower one pulled out to start the water flow. This one just turned.

Well, isn't that just fucking lovely.

GETTING STARTED

WELCOME TO THE CROONER ESTATE

WE KNOW YOUR STAY WILL BE *DEADLY* FUN.

The weekend has been split up into several rounds of play, spread across the rooms and grounds of the historic Millingham Mansion (excuse us, the Crooner Estate). While game play can't be entirely predicted, the following schedule should give you a good idea of what to expect:

FRIDAY:

5 P.M.—Lounge: Cocktails (and a deadly surprise!)
7 P.M.—Dining Room: Round 1 of play over dinner

SATURDAY:

8–10 A.M.—Dining Room: Continental breakfast
11 A.M.—Library: Round 2 of play
12:30 P.M.—Dining Room: Light lunch
1:30 P.M.—North Wing: Round 3 of play
3:30 P.M.—Various Locations: Round 4 of play
7 P.M.—Dining Room: Round 5 of play (and more bone-chilling surprises!)

SUNDAY:

7:30–9:30 A.M.—Dining Room: Continental breakfast
10 A.M.—Library: Final guesses and unveiling of the murderer

Remember, the game doesn't stop when each round concludes! Make sure to explore the mansion and grounds, compare notes with your fellow players, and inspect the evidence between rounds to ensure you catch the killer!

THE PLAYERS:

You'll need to keep a close eye on your fellow guests if you want to find the killer . . .

MR. PETER OLEUM: Texas born and bred, this tycoon has shot up to the heights of high society on a geyser of crude oil. Though he may not have the breeding of some of New York's finest, his money opens a lot of doors, including the ones to the speakeasies where Miss Ida Crooner, your hostess, often performs.

The role of Peter Oleum will be played by

Phil Armundsen

MRS. MARIA (RICHMANN) OLEUM: Unlike her husband, Maria (née) Richmann comes from one of New York City's oldest and most respected families. Though the Richmanns have fallen on hard times recently, they're a fixture in high society, and if Maria's daughter marries anywhere near as well as her mother did, they will be for some time.

The role of Maria (Richmann) Oleum will be played by

Heather Armundsen

MISS DEBBIE TAUNTE: Young, innocent, and dazzled by the big city, Debbie Taunte has been sent to live in New York with an aunt in an effort to find her a suitable husband. Of course, it didn't take her long to shake off her chaperone for the jazz scene where Ida Crooner reigns as queen, but this lost generation *will* have their fun.

The role of Debbie Taunte will be played by

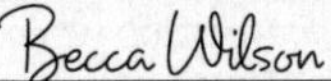

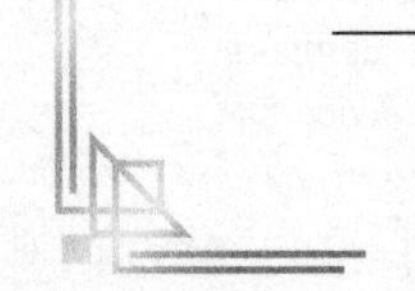

MR. REID A. DAILY: Heir to the *Daily News* newspaper fortune, Reid A. Daily is known as a playboy around town. One of the city's most eligible bachelors, Reid's hinted he might be ready to settle down. Though if his dalliances with Hollywood actresses and jazz club singers are any measure, married life won't be all that settled for him . . .

The role of Reid A. Daily will be played by

Blake Wilson

MR. BUGSY SLUGS: Racetrack owner, nightclub proprietor, and rumored mobster Bugsy Slugs is more than happy to help New York's upper crust part with their hard-inherited money. He discovered Ida Crooner back in his first Chicago club, and together they've risen to the top of New York City's seedy underbelly.

The role of Bugsy Slugs will be played by

Drew Schulz

MISS DOLLY DIAMOND: A former showgirl, these days Dolly's only job is being Bugsy's best gal. She helps out around the nightclub, but since she's hung up her sequins and feathers, she's started dreaming of a more domestic life . . . or as domestic a life as you can get when you're marrying into the mob, that is.

The role of Dolly Diamond will be played by

Gabby Schulz

MR. S. COOPER (SCOOPS) MUDSLINGER: A reporter at the *Daily News*, Scoops has quickly made a name for himself covering the glittering, glamorous world of New York's jazz clubs (and the boldfaced names who frequent them). Given his fawning coverage of Ida Crooner, it's no surprise she'd want to thank him with a weekend away.

The role of S. Cooper (Scoops) Mudslinger will be played by

Josh Bergman

MISS LULU LARKSONG: The mysterious star of the silver screen, reputed to be a deposed princess, has a history as romantic as one of her many films. Her star has faded a bit recently . . . but her friendship with Ida Crooner, formed on the set of one of her earliest films, has apparently stood the test of time.

The role of Lulu Larksong will be played by

Jessica Phillips

FIVE

I didn't even have a chance to get off my ass on the bathroom floor before Blake appeared around the door.

"Becks, are you alright?"

"I'm fine," I huffed, twisting around to show him the hardware in my hand. Genuine fear lingered around his eyes as he took in the scene. Seeing it pricked a tiny hole in the rage balloon that had been swelling inside me. Blake had always been protective. He'd hold an arm in front of me when we neared a street corner if he spotted a bad driver half a block away, as though I hadn't navigated New York traffic for half a decade without him. Whenever I nicked myself chopping vegetables (read: at least twice a week), his face would tug down with worry and he'd rush off to find first aid supplies, wondering aloud about whether I should get stitches, then insisting I let him finish the job. Whenever I traveled for business, or visited family on my own, he'd check to make sure my phone was charged, insist I text when the plane landed so he'd know I'd made it okay.

It was one of the things that drew me to him when we first

started dating, the almost old-fashioned way he was always taking care of me. More than that, he was the first person that I could really *see* as a father. Imagining scenes of first steps and bedtime stories and backyard campouts with our future child, I could see him not simply caring about, but caring *for* this tiny person. I could still see it, even though we weren't trying anymore. In a way, that had been a bigger blow than the cheating, him cracking the glass on all the family photos in my imagination, tearing up the pages of the story I'd built around the two of us, one I'd been so sure had a happy ending. Sure, I could have kept trying—he certainly wanted to—but how could I take the ultimate leap of faith with Blake when I couldn't trust him? How could we build such a towering castle in the sky on foundations I'd only just realized had rotted through when I wasn't looking?

I sighed heavily, lifting the faucet to him as I pushed off the floor with the other hand. He took it, frowning.

"The shower, on the other hand, is in pretty rough shape."

He stepped over to peer inside. It wasn't quite as bad as I'd feared; the tiles around the handle were intact, forming a neat hole around the now missing spout. Blake bent, peering at the mass of metal poking out from the wall, and slid the handle back into place.

"Good as new?" I asked hopefully.

He stepped back, turned the handle . . . then dived to catch it as it tumbled off again.

"Wonderful. So now I'm the idiot who thought the dead flapper was real *and* broke the shower." I pressed the heels of my hands into my eye sockets.

"I'm sure it was coming loose already," he said, laying the handle gently on the gleaming sink. "The face plate definitely wasn't mounted right. Probably an easy fix if you had the right tools and some heavy-duty glue. Whoever did the work on this bathroom definitely screwed this up."

"Yeah, maybe." I pulled the door open, holding it for him, feeling a surge of gratitude in spite of myself.

Blake was unfailingly supportive, especially if I was being "too hard on myself," as he put it. The most regular version of this was the Sunday morning eyes-pinched-tight hiding-beneath-the-blankets Q&A sessions in which, hangover already prowling my guts, I'd insist I'd said something dumb, undone a friendship, embarrassed myself irredeemably in the eyes of all our friends and favorite bartenders. Years of nights out were nowhere near enough to undo the guaranteed shameover that would rear up pretty much any time I had more than two drinks over the course of the evening, the tiny part of me that had always equated, and *would* always equate, letting loose and enjoying myself with evil *(Thanks, Midwestern upbringing)*. But even though we'd been through it a few hundred times—after all, we got together in our twenties, when nights like that were much more common—Blake was unfailingly calm as he'd look me in the eyes and insist that I hadn't done anything wrong, that no one was bothered, that I had nothing to feel bad about, *and anyway, Lauren was way drunker, do you suddenly hate* her? After my grudging *no,* I'd wallow in my blanket fort while he'd cook up a greasy feast and infinite coffee and "surprise" me with it in bed, kissing me gently on the forehead and insisting once more *You have nothing to feel bad about. Anyway, I love you more than ever, so who cares what anyone else thinks?*

Somehow it always seemed to help, at least a little.

"In the meantime . . . try not to sweat?" I said.

"I'm sure they can find us another room, it's their fault, after all," Blake said, then his head jerked up, eyes widening. "Or if you wanted your own . . ."

I pinched the bridge of my nose, eyes squeezed tight.

"No. I don't want that."

Part of me did, obviously, but it was the same tiny little gremlin-self that just wanted to punish him a little more, inflict another, and another, and another dose of pain until maybe, someday, our cosmic pain tallies would match again. But he'd probably just pass out with the TV on wherever he was sleeping—Blake had always been childlike in his ability to sleep whenever, wherever—and I'd be the one lying awake, lonely, staring at the ceiling and berating myself for wishing he was there next to me, his breathing, and scent, and the shape of him under the sheets comforting in a way that nothing else was.

Besides, he was right. I had said we could come back from this. He'd been so relieved when I did that he'd broken down crying right there in the therapist's office, racked by the heaving, snotty, unselfconscious sobs of a child. It just turned out that the feeling of superiority that gave me, the sense of my own beatific power for forgiveness, had a much shorter shelf life than the heavy mass of hurt fermenting at the bottom of my guts.

In a way, he wasn't wrong about *this,* either. At least, with the rage fog dissipating, I could see what he'd been going for. *Becca loves mysteries, I'll give her a mystery weekend, she'll know I love* her. Since the moment when I found out about the cheating and everything in the world suddenly tilted sideways, I'd been diving into my favorite form of escapism more than ever, losing myself in the worlds of Miss Marple, Luther, the Dublin Murder Squad, every book or episode ending with a neat resolution, the chaos safely hidden away, order restored. I'd always loved a good detective story, but in the last few weeks, when all I'd been craving was both literal and mental mashed potatoes, things had tilted over toward obsession.

I mean . . . he should have told me. Obviously. But the *thought* was there. I had to let it count for something.

He lifted a hand to my shoulder, squeezing tentatively, arm stiff and awkward, then crossed to the hulking wooden desk in the corner, squinting at the phone until he could find the number for the front desk.

"No one's answering," he said after a few minutes. I glanced at the digital clock between the beds. We had only ten minutes until we were meant to report for dinner. Probably the "cast" was busy setting up their next elaborate scene. Which reminded me . . . I picked up the little pamphlet the housekeeper had handed me from where it was lying on the bed. Beneath the title, the name *Miss Deb-*

bie Taunte was printed in flowing script. Maybe I could just convince the rest of the people there that I had been taking the part really, *really* seriously? *Except Heather and Phil, who knew I didn't know.* Did that make my ridiculous overreaction better or worse?

I glanced over to find Blake watching me, body rigid, eyes a little wary, *When's she gonna blow next?* My jaw tensed—I knew he wasn't *trying* to make me feel unhinged, but his whole kid glove demeanor felt like a new provocation.

"Let me see if I can find someone," I said, rolling the pamphlet into a cylinder and opening the door to the hallway, grateful for the opportunity to breathe air that hadn't been thickened with tension.

"Sure, okay. I'll meet you . . ."

"I'll come back, don't worry."

He nodded and I went out, both of us exhaling relief.

To the left, the hallway extended past a few more stately doorways, ending in yet another leaded glass window that overlooked the front drive. I turned right, heading for the juncture with the central wing. If I didn't find anyone, I could walk down to the front desk.

As I approached the end of the hallway, I heard a murmur of voices.

"What did you expect?" A pause. *"I've already told you—"*

"Hey. Calm down. I'm just asking if we can—"

I turned into the large hall slash creepy portrait gallery, coughing lightly to announce my presence. A few feet away from me, beneath a massive oil painting of hunting dogs murdering some poor bird, Phil and the housemaid were huddled together. She jumped as I walked into the room, flushing brightly and lifting a hand to her stiff little cap. Phil grinned, giving me a two-fingered wave over the rim of his brandy glass. Considering Phil's compulsive flirting, all evidence pointed to his saying the sort of thing men his age kept refusing to understand that women her age did *not* find complimentary.

"Am I . . . interrupting?" I put on my best "Whoops, sorry for existing!" smile, one I'd learned doubly well as a *Midwestern* woman—self-effacement ran deep in both blood and genitalia in the outer Chicago suburbs—stopping short a few feet from the stairs.

"Not in the least." Phil started toward me, his stride easy and languid. I could see the mix of embarrassment and relief on the maid's face. I—and presumably every other adult human with a vagina—knew that feeling *well.* "I was asking Miss . . . what did they call you, again?"

"Miss Terry Yuss, sir."

Jesus, could Blake not have found a less aggressively punny peace offering?

Phil sniff-laughed, rolling his eyes at me. I couldn't help but smile. Phil's charm had always struck me as a bit superficial, but it was pretty effective.

"Right, I was asking Miss *Yuss* whether it was possible to have a bottle of champagne sent up for me and my wife after dinner, since her idiot husband forgot to put a couple in the trunk, but I guess that's the *butler's* job."

The woman smiled apologetically, glancing up at him from under heavy eyelids. If her chin were a little stronger, she'd really be striking.

"Miss Thrope is very particular about who's meant to do what. But I'll be sure to let him know you were askin', sir," she said, dropping a curtsy. He laughed again and continued down the hallway, leaning in to murmur as he neared me, "If you find one willing to drop the act for a few minutes, let me know, yeah?"

I smiled over my shoulder at him as he passed. He was looking back at me with a knowing smirk, and for just a moment something sparked through me that I hadn't felt in god knows how long. Even though I didn't want Phil—to say nothing about the inadvisability of shitting where you eat—he *was* handsome. It felt good. Mildly intoxicating. *No wonder Blake likes it so much.*

By the time I'd managed to swallow the bile, the maid was bustling off across the gallery toward the opposite hallway.

"Sorry . . . do you have a minute?" I called after her.

She turned back to me, cheeks still flushed with anxiety.

"Anything for Miss Crooner's guests, Miss."

"Listen . . . if Phil was getting a little too friendly, let me know. I'm happy to say something to him."

Her eyes widened and she blinked a few times, the color draining from her cheeks.

"What would you say?" Her voice was very even. I frowned. Had I read it wrong?

"Just to dial it down. Flirting's practically compulsive with Phil, he probably doesn't even realize he's doing it. But I know it can get awkward."

She narrowed her eyes for a second, then nodded.

"No need," she finally said, eyes dropping to her feet. "He just . . . surprised me, I suppose. Of course a gentleman like him wouldn't understand servant politics."

"Totally," I said, nodding too emphatically. She tilted her head to one side expectantly.

"But I'm going on. You needed something?"

"Right. I was wondering if maybe you had another room available? We tried calling the front desk but no one answered."

"Another room? Is something wrong with yours?"

The pretty, absurdly young woman stared at me. She couldn't have been more than twenty-four; her skin had that smooth, poreless, *glowy* quality that no amount of makeup or Botox could fully re-create, no matter how hard the Pine Haven wives of the world tried. Suddenly I felt flustered. What was I going to say to her?—*My husband cheated on me with someone your age, so I Hulked out on your shower . . . fix it!* I could feel the heat creeping up my neck, probably turning me all splotchy.

"Yes, actually . . . the thing is . . ."

"It's my fault." Blake emerged from the dim stretch of hallway with a puckish look of embarrassment. "I dropped my soap in the shower, and when I bent to pick it up I caught hold of the handle and . . ." He spread his hands wide, shrugging. "I'm guessing it wasn't mounted correctly. But I'm pretty sure my wife is going to want a shower at some point this weekend, so . . ."

He smiled at her expectantly, his handsome face perfectly still, and for just a second I could see what he must be like with clients, convincing them that the partnership or venture funding or whatever else Playpen wanted right then was not only perfectly reasonable, but honestly, you'd have to be kind of a dick to say no. No wonder he and Phil had hit it off so quickly; Blake was quieter, more thoughtful, a much better listener even in casual conversations from everything I'd seen, but they clearly had this, at least, in common.

"I . . . I'm not sure . . . it's just that we close up the north wing for these weekends. Or . . . what I mean is, Miss Crooner's rooms occupy the, uh . . ."

"We don't expect an upgrade. We'd be happy with anything. But there must be at least a couple rooms available, considering how exclusive the guest list is, no?"

"Well . . ." She twisted her mouth into a tiny little bud. "We can probably sort something. Let me ask Jenn—uh, Miss Thrope."

"Thank you so much. We'll just get our things together so it's easier." Blake smiled, genuine gratitude in his eyes, and the pretty maid unconsciously mirrored it before remembering he was making her life harder. With another quick curtsy, she hurried down the staircase to the entrance hall.

"Do we have time to pack? I don't want to make us late again," Blake said, hunching slightly to meet my eyes.

I sighed, gratitude at the rescue welling up in me, blurring the rocky shoreline of our fight. It was still there underneath, I could feel it scraping my hull, but it wasn't the only thing.

In a way it would just be easier if Blake could be more *consistently* an asshole, not just in the one ridiculously *major* way, but in the little everyday ways that would make all the anger still swirling around me feel justified. I wouldn't get so nauseated from the pendulum swings . . . and wouldn't have to wonder whether maybe I was the one to blame for them. But no, most of the time he *was* lovely, if you didn't count the fucking other people. Jesus, why did everything have to be so confusing?

"Sure. It's not like there's much to pack, anyway."

I took his hand, feeling his entire body relax as I followed him back to the room, both of us silent, unsure how sturdy the truce was, how much weight we could put on it. As Blake worked the door open, Heather and Phil emerged from a room farther down the hall. She smiled at us as they passed.

"See you down there? I've been practicing my mid-Atlantic accent for the last twenty minutes so you won't show me up."

"Yup! Just realized I forgot my lipstick," I added unnecessarily. Amy always used to make fun of me for it when we were kids, the way I'd chatter when I was nervous, as though I could bury whatever was bothering me beneath a big enough heap of small talk. Sure, it didn't fix anything, but I saw it as the verbal version of "Dress for the job you want." Pretend things are okay long enough, and well enough, and eventually reality would have to catch up.

At least I used to think that.

"I'll save you a seat," Phil said, winking at me as they passed. Heather rolled her eyes indulgently my way—*He's incorrigible, but I love him anyway!* My lungs ached as I watched them go. How did you get from where we were to a place like that, aware of the other's flaws but tolerant of them, moving through the world as a unit, confident that the life you've built, the choices you've made, were, if not objectively right, then at least right for *you*? I wasn't stupid, I knew other couples had fights, rough patches, stresses that brought out one or both partners' worst qualities, but some people just seemed built to withstand them somehow.

Or maybe they just didn't make the kinds of mistakes that we had.

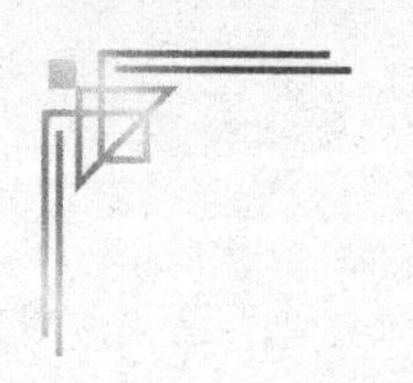
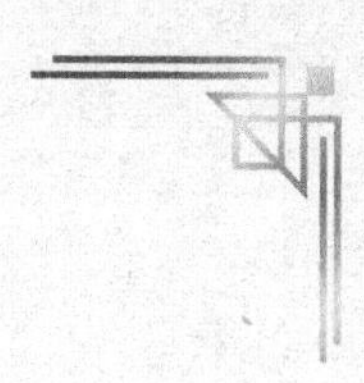

ROUND ONE

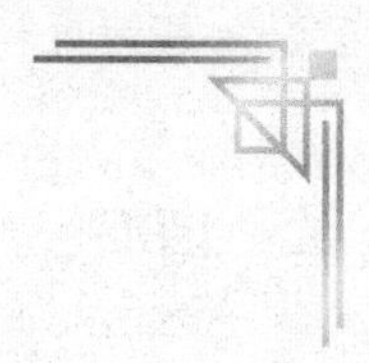

MISS DEBBIE TAUNTE

BACKGROUND INFORMATION

CONFIDE:

Young, innocent, and dazzled by the flash and glamour of New York, you're eager to make your way in the world (and maybe land yourself a suitable husband while you're at it!). But you can only hope to do that if you get to know the right people, and with an upbringing like yours (you always tell people that your father was just about the biggest fish the pond of Lincoln, Nebraska, ever saw . . . but it's not such a big pond), that's no small task!

Luckily, life with your elderly aunt in New York is about as free as can be. She's too ill to attend social events, which means you get to go unchaperoned . . . and flirt to your heart's content! This year, your first official season, has been a whirlwind to say the least. With half a dozen suitors mooning over you, you could be settled down (and set up!) in no time flat, but for now you're enjoying the fun of it all: meeting interesting people like Ida and her chums, dancing until your feet are sore at society balls and Harlem jazz clubs, it's all just ducky! You're sure Daddy will be expecting you to write home with news of a special someone soon . . . but oh, you hope you can have a lot more fun first!

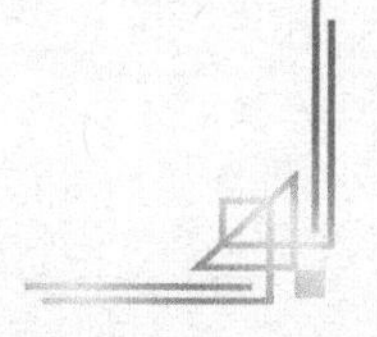

HIDE:

You and Ida go back . . . *way* back, to her earliest days as a Chicago lounge singer. Back then you were living a different life (with a *very* different sort of career), but the two of you hit it off immediately. She's been open with her fans about her rough upbringing. You, on the other hand, are trying to re-invent yourself, and Ida's been helping any way she can.

Unfortunately, you're not the only one who's known Ida a long time. Coming to this weekend's party poses a serious threat to your long-term goal of settling down with the right sort of man and getting to the end of the fairy tale you've been building up in your mind. You've decided it's worth the risk . . . but be careful, if your past comes out you might have to start all over . . . *again*.

SIX

I gasped as we walked into the dining room.

"It's like something out of *Downton Abbey,*" I murmured, mouth dropping open as I took it all in. Mysteries were definitively my primary escape lately, but period porn was a close second in my choice of self-care genres.

"Thought you might be into that," Blake said, his self-satisfied smile pulling his dimple out.

Weirdly, the first thing I noticed was the dark wooden beams shooting up the walls and across the ceiling, meeting in dozens of intersecting diamonds, like a beautifully designed, expansive cage around the room. The plaster between had been painted into a fanciful garden, vines snaking up along the beams, profusions of flowers and leafy tree branches bursting out into all the perfect geometric frames before giving way to blue sky overhead, dotted with butterflies and hummingbirds, their colors sharp and bright against pillowy white clouds. The massive crystal chandelier in the center of it all almost looked like falling rain, another carefully chosen detail in this extremely designed ode to the natural world.

Closer to earth, the wall panels were covered in a rich forest-green paper, every third or fourth panel given over to giant murals of bamboo, a cherry tree, and, on either side of the massive marble fireplace—clearly that was a bit of a *thing* for J. R. O'Malley—two larger-than-life geishas (or courtesans, depending which culture he'd appropriated them from), bowing at each other across the expanse of green-veined stone. There were various chinoiserie objects on high shelves, and a gigantic vase in one corner in distinctive cobalt and white that had probably been pillaged from some long-gone dynasty, but there was less by way of ornamentation than you'd expect in a room built on such a ludicrously grandiose scale. It was clear from the wear pattern in the massive central rug that at least a dozen tables usually filled the space; probably the hotel had cleared out some of the embellishments to make way for a more modern seating plan.

Currently, though, there was just one largish oval table, placed dead center in the room, eight chairs spaced generously around it. It would have been perfectly sized for Heather and Phil's spacious formal dining room . . . which meant it was dwarfed by the scale of its ornate surroundings.

Heather and Phil were already seated at the far end—it didn't surprise me that he'd claimed the head—with the glamorous couple filling out Heather's side of the table. Phil waved us over and I slid into the seat at his left.

"Blake, Rebecca, this is Josh and Jessica," Heather said, gesturing to the pair seated to her right. "City kids like you." She smiled between us, almost as though she'd planned the dinner party specifically to bring us together.

"Nice to meet you," I said, smiling at the woman in the floor-length gold satin gown. "I love your hair, by the way. I feel like that's what my hair wishes it could be when it grows up." She laughed, raising a hand to the perfect old-Hollywood waves.

"See, Josh, I told you it was worth the extra effort."

"Excuse *me* for thinking you're beautiful without so much work."

"Ooh, very smooth." Blake raised a fist to give Josh a pound. "My lines want to be as good as yours when *they* grow up," he added with a grin.

"I know when I'm punching above my weight," Josh said with a sly smile. He leaned across the table, raising a hand to his mouth to stage whisper. "Plus, *two hours*." His large, deep-set dark eyes sparkled mischievously. Probably Jessica had described *that* look to all her girlfriends back when she and Josh first got together. Or maybe she still did; they had that infatuated air that certain couples seem to keep indefinitely. She leaned across the table, smiling conspiratorially.

"Isn't it cute how he still thinks I do my hair for *him*?"

"Jessica, weren't you telling me that you live in Brooklyn? Close to Becca and Blake, from the sound of it." Heather smiled tightly, turning an expectant gaze on Jessica. She blinked, clearly a bit startled at the slightly schoolmarmy note in Heather's voice, then nodded.

"That's right, we're in Carroll Gardens."

"Oh, just around the corner," I said. "We're in Prospect Heights."

"Thank god. I was worried you were going to say somewhere with way more cred than *Carroll Gardens*." Josh dragged the words out into a verbal eye roll. "Then I'd have to get all defensive about how tragically bougie we've become." He sighed dramatically and Jessica laughed a bit.

"Josh likes to pretend he'd rather still be living in that horrible walkup in Bushwick from grad school."

"I just want people to understand I have *layers,* Jess." He pulled a faux exasperated face. "As an *artiste*."

"I had a place in Bushwick just after college, I've never seen roaches that big before or since," I said, laughing. "Except maybe at

Marty's, did you ever go to that bar when you lived there? Blake swore by the pizza, but the bathrooms skeezed me out so bad I couldn't make myself eat it."

"Oh man, I'd forgotten about Marty's. Jess, can we take a field trip to Marty's? They keep saying we need to get used to insect protein, right?" Jessica wrinkled up her nose in disgust, shaking her head as Josh turned widened eyes on her.

"I said it before, I'll say it again, they don't make the pizzas in the bathrooms," Blake said, a genuine grin stealing across his face.

"See, honey? I told you we weren't missing out on anything in the city," Phil drawled, smirking as he took another sip of his scotch. Heather sniffed out a small laugh, but out of the corner of my eye, I could see her forehead tightening with repressed annoyance. I had a feeling she'd been hoping to play hostess, running the conversation the way she did at her parties in Pine Haven, but then we'd gone and spoiled it by clicking a little *too* quickly.

I was half-reprimanding myself for the unkind thought—Heather was just trying to smooth things over for me, I should be grateful for the assist—when "Dolly" and "Bugsy" bustled through the door, both a little red-faced.

"Are we late? Sorry," the woman said, smiling apologetically as she shuffled over to the seat next to Blake. "It's my fault, I'm terrible with timing."

"We just got here," Blake said with a smile. "I'm Blake, by the way. In real life, that is."

"Gabby, and that's my husband, Drew," she said. He lifted both hands in a jazzy wave. His fedora had slipped back on his head, and I could see wisps of reddish hair peeping out. "Though I guess the game's officially afoot." She let out a nervous little titter. "In case you missed it earlier, I'm Dolly Diamond. And this is Bugsy Slugs."

"She's my best gal, see?"

We all laughed politely at his continued use of the terrible accent. The forced jollity seemed to have cut through the easy camaraderie we'd been building with Jessica and Josh.

"We're still working out when we're expected to be in character, we've never been to one of these before," Gabby continued, smiling apologetically. "Though we are *very* active in our local rennie scene." I nodded along, as though I had any idea what that meant. Some sort of LARPing, maybe? She had a dorky-kid-sister quality that was probably annoying in large doses but that made me feel vaguely protective.

"Us either." Here goes. I sucked in a deep breath. "In fact . . . Blake brought me here as a surprise—he knows how much I love mysteries—so yeah . . . in case it wasn't already obvious, I *definitely* didn't expect the body in the library. Expect a noticeable downturn in the quality of my acting from this point forward."

Everyone laughed politely again. Gabby turned to Drew, raising an eyebrow in some sort of private communication.

"Don't worry, Becca, it can't *possibly* be worse than that maid's," Heather said with a sharp little smile. "Like . . . don't worry, sweetie, we get it, you were *so scared.* And she actually had a chance to practice!"

"Really? I thought she was pretty good," Jessica said with a shrug.

"Different strokes, I suppose." Heather shrugged, lips pursed. "Phil and I have season tickets at a few theaters in the city, maybe I'm just spoiled." Jessica made a noncommittal noise and turned away, feigning fascination with the decor. It was all a bit cattier than I was used to from Heather; she was usually the picture of good manners. Phil's eyes darted over to her, but she didn't seem to notice. Apparently he wasn't the only one who was being overserved.

Just then the housekeeper appeared at a side door, followed closely by the butler, a decanter of wine in each of his broad, stubby hands.

"I see you've all made it. I'm impressed by your fortitude, especially considering the . . . *circumstances* of the evening," she said, pinching her lips tightly and lowering her eyes. "Wynnham will be coming around with your choice of wines. As we start the dinner service, why don't we all take the opportunity to get to know one another?" She raised a hand to her black-swaddled bosom. "As some of you know, I'm Miss Ann Thrope, head housekeeper and personal attendant to Miss Ida Crooner—or at least, I *was*." She tilted her head to the ceiling, blinking rapidly as though trying to get her emotions under control. "Please, if you wouldn't mind, sir . . . I need a moment to gather myself," she gestured to Phil. "Perhaps you could start us off."

He lifted his eyebrows and reached into his breast pocket to pull out his booklet and a pair of reading glasses that he settled on his nose.

"Gladly. I'm . . . Mr. Peter Oleum, I'm sure most of you have heard of me. I struck oil when I was twenty-three, made some smart business moves since, and now me and my lovely wife brush elbows with New York's finest. Which I still get a kick out of—Maria will tell you, I was pretty rough when we first met. Nothin' a few million won't gloss over though, right, honey?" He turned to Heather, waggling his eyebrows playfully, then turned back to the housekeeper. "Is that what you meant?"

"Precisely, sir," she said. "Perhaps your wife will continue the introductions."

The butler leaned over my shoulder, murmuring in my ear, "Red or white, Miss?"

"Oh, umm . . . red, I guess." He unbent to pour as Heather quickly scanned her booklet.

"Right. I'm Maria Richmann Oleum, and my job is being a society wife." Heather smiled graciously at everyone, about two shades more ingratiating than her *actual* hostess smile. "As my husband said, we move in some of New York's best circles. My family always *was* respected in the city, even if Daddy had a bit of a gambling problem. And really, what gentleman of quality doesn't spend some time in the betting parlors? Anyway, my marriage fixed all that for us. Now it's my daughter's turn to get married, presuming I can find a gentleman worthy of her *considerable* charms."

We continued around the table. Jessica was "Lulu Larksong," a famous Hollywood actress; Josh was "S. Cooper Mudslinger, but everyone calls me Scoops," a reporter rapidly rising through the ranks at the *Daily News*. Drew as "Bugsy Slugs" was—surprise, surprise—the notorious gangster who ran both the city's most popular racetrack and its most scintillating jazz club, and Gabby, aka "Dolly Diamond," had caught his eye when she worked as a showgirl in his first club in Chicago, after which they moved to the Big Apple together.

I could feel the fug of anger lifting. It was all a little ridiculous, but everyone seemed genuinely happy to be there, gamely getting into the spirit of the thing, which allowed me to lean in as much as I wanted. In fact, they'd all paid what I was starting to guess must have been a small fortune for the privilege. I took a small sip of the wine. It was jammy and fruity and dangerously drinkable. I could feel it moving through my body, loosening my muscles with a pleasant ache . . .

"I'm Reid A. Daily," Blake said with a small chuckle. "Heir to the *Daily News* newspaper fortune. Scoops works for us, of course." He nodded across the table at Josh, who doffed an imaginary cap. "My father has been pushing me to learn the family trade, but after the time I had in the Great War, I think I deserve a bit of fun. What's the point of inheriting if you don't take a few yachting trips around the Mediterranean?"

"To the high life!" Gabby said, raising her glass of white wine with a lascivious grin. If she hadn't been a theater kid at *some* point in her life I'd eat my hat.

Annd . . . apparently the twenties slang was starting to work its way into my actual thoughts.

"Really, though, I'm ready to settle down . . . just as soon as I find the right woman. Maybe she's here tonight?"

Blake raised a rakish eyebrow. Jesus, no wonder he had coworkers throwing themselves at him, I could practically *smell* the pheromones all the women were flooding the room with.

He nudged his knee into mine, lowering his voice.

"Just you, hon."

"Right. I'm, umm"—I bent to grab my booklet, flipping it open and scanning it again quickly—"Debbie Taunte. My father was a bigwig back in Nebraska." I fluttered my eyes a moment and affected a bit of a twang. Amy always joked that accents were the easiest acting hack around—when she was still auditioning actively she'd spend hours practicing them on me. It certainly always seemed to work on my favorite mystery shows; Benedict Cumberbatch's elocution made Sherlock's glittering-cold brilliance feel that much more indisputable, and the opposite effect seemed to hold any time an American Southern accent came into play, no matter how garbled. "But there aren't *nearly* enough eligible young men there, so he sent me to live with my aunt in New York City. And maybe find a match?" I turned to Blake, pursing my lips and widening my eyes hugely, batting them fast. After all, my character was *supposed* to flirt. "But there are so many parties, and so many fun jazz clubs where you can dance all night, it's just the *bee's knees*!"

"Careful, fellas, we've got a regular flapper in our midst," Josh said, flashing his sultry grin at me. I took another sip of wine, feeling almost sparkly again. Blake still should have told me what we were getting into, but it was fun, and specifically in a vein that appealed to me and probably felt halfway to pulling teeth for Blake. He always had been a pretty incredible gift giver, picking up on hints you hadn't even realized you'd dropped, surprising you later with the perfect thing you would never have thought to ask for. But that only required thoughtfulness, the listening, attentive quality that he brought to everything he did. This was on another level; a weekend-long social event might be fun for me but it probably almost physically pained Blake. *It really had been generous of him, even if he flubbed the opening move.* And I'd tell him so . . . just as soon as he opened the conversation with a blanket apology for not realizing that gifts, however thoughtful, are only nice when they don't embarrass the hell out of you.

"Excellent. Now that we all know each other, Miss Yuss and Scuttles will come around with the first course," the housekeeper said. "Once that's complete, you may turn the page in your dossier marked 'Round One.' "

She jerked her head to where the two young people were waiting at the door near a tray of wedge salads.

"Please remember, anything you know about your fellow guests and the day's events, it is absolutely vital that you share. If anyone asks you a direct question, you *must* tell us the truth. Whatever you're hiding . . . rest assured, it will come to light."

SEVEN

"I just can't quite sort it. I report on all the society gossip, all the celebrities, all the news that's fit to print . . ." Josh said.

"At least fit for a *Daily* paper," Blake said with an appreciative tip of his head.

"Precisely. And yet I've never come across Miss Taunte until now. She and Miss Crooner were apparently thick as thieves, but . . . well, not to be rude, has anyone else ever *heard* of you, Debbie?" Josh smiled ruefully, glancing around the table for support.

I turned to the half-finished plate of strawberry shortcake in front of me, buying time with a bite.

"I suppose I can't speak to what a newsman might know about me. But yes, Ida's a friend. She's been so good to me since I made it to New York." I glanced up at Josh, batting my eyes rapidly. I'd pulled the move about fifteen times over dinner, but he grinned anyway.

"Bully for her," Blake said, clinking a fork against the side of his glass in laconic, silvery applause, "but I have to back Scoops here, I've never heard of you in my life."

"Oh? Did you get much mail on the yacht? Keep up on the latest news?"

"Fair point," he raised his glass of port and took a swig. "The open ocean *can* be a bit remote."

"But just to be clear, you *do* know Ida well," Josh said, leaning across the table, cheeks flushed. "Or did, I guess?"

"Yes." I scanned my notes again. The further we got into the night, the harder it was to keep track of what I was supposed to say or not say. "We're quite good friends. Though . . . I'm not sure exactly how you know about our friendship."

"Well, we all know Ida'd take up with just about anyone. Even gangsters," Jessica said, glaring pointedly at Drew, perfectly red lips puckered.

"Guess she must know which side her bread's buttered on, huh?" He grinned.

For a few seconds the conversation went quiet. Eventually the housekeeper stepped forward.

"I'm sorry to interrupt, but I must ask . . . is there *anything* that you were told to confide in the rest of us that you haven't yet? For anyone here?"

Everyone scanned their booklet and shook their heads.

"Then I think it's time we all called it an evening. Please feel free to look over the note I found on Miss Crooner's body at your leisure, as well as the crime scene. Perhaps you'll be able to make more sense of them than I could. Otherwise . . . we'll officially reconvene after we've all had a chance to rest."

Scuttles moved up to Wynnham, fake-dozing in a chair in the corner. The butler startled as the younger man gently touched his forearm, harrumphing himself "awake."

"Yes? What do you need, boy?"

"I just wanted to be sure, sir. I'm to set up the *library* for the guests tomorrow?"

"That's right, the *main library,* just next door. How many times do I have to tell you?"

"And what time was that for, sir?"

"Eleven o'clock sharp. They all deserve to enjoy their breakfast in peace, after all. Which will be served in this room, from eight to ten o'clock."

"Right. Thank you, sir."

Then, true to his name, he scuttled out the side door.

One by one everyone stood, stretching arms overhead. I bent to look at the note the housekeeper had presented to us earlier in the "round," handwritten in flowing script:

I'll leave the door between our rooms open. xx

We'd wasted a solid twenty minutes trying to map out where we were all staying, and which doors *could* be left open, only to learn, when the staff came back with the entree, that "accommodations have been rearranged since the death, out of respect for Miss Crooner," and we were presented with a map of where we were all "staying" in a blocky building that didn't even share the same physical layout as our hotel.

Still, even with the pointless detours and awkward "acting" on all sides—Heather and Gabby seemed to be having a pearl-clutcher-versus-mob-moll bad-acting standoff—the night had been so much *fun*. I turned to Blake, grinning widely, effervescent with the silly game (and the regular drink refills).

"So? Who's your top suspect?"

He laughed. "So far we know what? That some people gamble, some people sleep around, and a lot of people just *happened* to bump into each other at opportune moments?"

"And that Maria's got a secret bank account!" I widened my eyes meaningfully. "Maybe she and Bugsy are going to run away together."

"Just as soon as they murder an irrelevant mutual friend."

"Right . . ." I screwed my nose up. "Probably the clues get better later on." I reached for my glass of red wine, taking a quick sip, not realizing a drop had been clinging to the base. It landed perfectly on the tiny patch of lacy white collar circling the top of my fancy new dress. "Dammit . . ." I dropped the glass on the table, reaching for a napkin to dab at the spot, but the little splotch of burgundy refused to budge.

"Don't worry about it, babe. They'll get it out at the dry cleaner's." With an affectionate squeeze of my shoulder, Blake took the last swig of his port and started patting himself absently, his regular check for wallet, keys, cellphone. I couldn't help but smile. There was something nice about knowing what your person would do next.

"Excuse me, Mr. Daily? Miss Taunte?" When I turned, the pretty maid was just behind us, smiling a little anxiously. "I wanted to let you know that we found you another room."

"Oh, fantastic!" I smiled wide, trying to prove to her—really, to myself—that she wasn't a threat. I'd always hated women who treated other women as automatic threats.

"I can make you key cards now if you have a moment?"

"That'd be great," I said, turning to Blake. "Do you wanna go get our things together? I'll get the keys."

"Works for me." He bent to plant a light kiss on my lips. "Don't be long."

I watched as he made his way along the hall to the staircase tucked at the back corner, the smile lingering on my lips. Once we got past the rough bit, tonight had been almost normal. It wasn't a fix, but at least it was a start. Proof that *we*—not Blake and Becca, but the whole that had, until fairly recently, seemed like so much more than the sum of our parts—still existed, somewhere beneath the eddies of hurt.

"It's just this way," the girl said, heading toward the concierge desk huddled near the front entrance to the cavernous main hall.

"You wouldn't happen to have a Tide pen in there, would you?" I gestured at my collar. "I almost made it through dinner without making a mess."

She rummaged around in the drawers. "Sorry"—she flashed an apologetic smile—"I don't see one. But I think I have one in my room."

"Oh, that's okay."

"It'll only take a second. You don't want it to set." She tilted her chin down sharply, a "no arguments" gesture that was *pure* Amy. Affection bloomed in my chest at the familiarity of it. Before I could protest, she darted up the staircase, returning a few minutes later with the Tide pen. I bent, trying to get a good angle on the spot.

"I think it might be easier if I did this in the room. Could I bring it back to you later?"

"Totally. Just drop it by my room in the morning, I'm off after this. And once, uhhh . . . *service* starts, Miss Thrope likes us to remain focused on our duties." I nodded. "I'm in 208, by the way, in the north wing. If no one answers, just go in, Manny and I don't leave it locked during the day."

"Great. Thanks again."

"Alright, now the hard part . . . keys." She pulled out a pair of blank plastic cards and frowned at them. "Sorry if this takes me a minute, I'm new at it."

"Really? I'm surprised." I leaned forward, lowering my voice. "You're a natural. You're the only one who can actually *act,* you know."

She giggled appreciatively, face lighting up in a lovely, shy smile.

"I meant the keys, not the show. I've actually done a few weekends like this before. Anyway, I'm not sure everyone here would agree with you even on that," she said, cheeks falling a bit.

"You mean Heather?" Her eyes darted up to mine. One small nod. My stomach twisted. Heather would absolutely hate knowing her snippy comment had been overheard. "Don't worry about her, she's in community theater, it's just . . . semiprofessional jealousy."

The girl sucked her lips in, eyes dropping to the counter in front of her, then drew in a heavy breath, shaking her head a little.

I resisted the urge to reach out and take her hand—*She's not Amy, Becca, she's just a girl working at this hotel.* Still, I knew firsthand how fragile performers could be, how quickly even the slightest hint of criticism cut through all the praise.

"Maybe. Anyway, Manny's good. I mean *Scuttles.* His part's just overwritten." The smile she forced back onto her face looked pained, but I nodded as though I believed it.

"I haven't seen much of him yet. All I'm saying is you were seriously convincing in the lounge earlier. Though obviously *I* thought that."

"I was gonna say you should try out!" She turned to the computer screen, eyebrows furrowing as she concentrated on it.

"I'll leave that to the professionals. I'm only capable of such a bravura performance when my husband surprises me with murder."

"That's nice. That he surprised you, I mean. I need to find someone like that. Someone nice." A sad, gentle smile stole across her face, transforming it from mostly pretty to magnetic, a girl in a Dutch Master painting. "Dammit. Sorry, just a second. Okay . . . I think I've got this now."

She slid the key cards into the small machine next to her keyboard, clicked the mouse, then glanced at the machine. The key cards remained inert. She really didn't seem to have any idea what she was doing.

"So . . . did you grow up around here?" I hated this kind of silence, the *I'm waiting for you to work for me* silence.

"*God,* no." Her eyes went wide in an embarrassed "Oh, no, did I say that out loud?" face. "Sorry, that sounds mean. I just meant . . . it's kinda middle of nowhere, you know?"

"I'm with you. Cities for life."

"Exactly." She nodded rapidly. "I grew up in Iowa, but I moved to New York, like, sooner than humanly possible."

"And you moved here recently? Or . . ."

"It's . . . sorry, is it okay if I break character?"

"Please." She laughed at that.

"Manny—he's Scuttles—is a friend from undergrad. He told me about weekends like this. Which are pretty much the only gigs I've managed to land, actually." Her face crumpled slightly.

"I'm sure more things will come through. It takes time."

"Right. You're right." She nodded, mouth set, as though trying to believe herself. "And right now I'm just really focusing on this, you know? Treating it like . . . workshop. A lot of actors would kill for a chance to focus this much on their craft."

She jutted her chin out and my heart squeezed—for the second time that night she looked just like Amy. She'd given herself almost a decade after college to really go after the acting thing—she'd always been the more artistic of the two of us, and the more determined. By the time I moved in with her, after I graduated (we'd binge all my favorite monster-of-the-week shows together as "research," *after all, they're always hiring extras*), she'd managed to book a few commercials, land an agent, but still the clouds-parting "Now you've arrived" *break* kept eluding her. After every failed audition, she'd go quiet and pale for a few minutes—up to an hour if she'd been really set on the part—and when she'd come out of it she'd put on that same jaw-jutting face and say something similarly, heartbreakingly determined. She only gave it up after Aaron got the tenure track position in Vermont, and the only argument for staying in New York was the career she'd never quite managed to scrape together. I'd introduced her as an actress once a few years back, to a colleague we were grabbing lunch with during one of her regular city weekends, and she looked genuinely angry. *Failed actress, she means. I work in HR now.* I think I only realized then how much it still hurt her, how hard it must have been to let go. God, I missed Amy. Ever since . . . the *thing* with Blake, I'd been keeping my distance. I hadn't trusted myself around someone who knew me that well.

"Is this part of your method, then?" I gestured at the key cards, still inert in the little machine, the *Let's talk while you serve me* need even more acute.

"Actually, a girl quit last week and Jen said I could pick up her shifts. Just for extra cash, I'm not like, moving here *permanently*." She fixed me with an intense stare, and I nodded solemnly. "It's just right now my apartment situation in New York is kinda"—her eyes darkened for a moment—"I mean, I guess I don't really *have* a place there. I was living with the guy I was dating, but things ended pretty suddenly . . ." A shiver went through her, clearly unconscious, and her eyebrows crept lower. When she spoke again her voice was low, barely a murmur, and I had a feeling she wasn't talking to me as much as to herself. "I needed to get away. Not that he's letting me." She closed her eyes, sucked a deep breath through her nose, clearly hoping to recenter herself. "But I have a place to stay during the week here, so I figured until I can save enough for a deposit . . ." She trailed off, shrugging. "Sorry, I trained on this, but it's the first time I've done it on my own." She forced a desperate smile, blinking a few times and swallowing hard.

"No worries. I'll shut up so you can focus."

She nodded and started clicking again, mouthing words to herself. Her head moved a little as she ticked through each stage, the stiff maid's cap tilting back and forth as she did.

"Okay, now I just click this . . . Oh, yes! That's it!" She grinned as the machine finally whirred to life, dragging the first card through.

"Nailed it!" I held up my hand and she slapped it five, giggling.

"Anything else I can do for you?" she said, still flushed with the tiny triumph. My heart squeezed again. I could remember the painful, all-enveloping *need* of being her age, the sense that everyone else had figured something out that you didn't even know existed, the constant, unending yearning without even a tangible goal to affix itself to. When Blake and I got together, tilted headlong from first dates into romantic weekends into practically living at each other's apartments, all of it so sparkling and vital that it had allowed me to finally stop putting the rest of my life under a microscope every single moment, to just settle into the unfamiliar feeling of *knowing* something was right, I'd been almost as overjoyed at being able to shed that sense of *What am I missing?* as I'd been at specifically finding him. It was the first time I'd had a sense that I was making the right choice, that I wasn't forgoing some other, better option.

I couldn't imagine how hard it must feel for someone like Amy. Someone who *knew* what they wanted but couldn't find a way to force the world to give it to them.

I swallowed against the prickling sensation in my eyes and nose. *She's not Amy, Becca. And there's nothing keeping you from calling your sister.* Which was almost true, if you didn't count the overwhelming need for Amy to keep seeing me—us—in our best light, for her not to tell me I was making the absolute wrong decision by staying. Because once she did—and I knew she would—it would become almost impossible to stick to it. I swallowed hard. *Force it back down.*

"Is there somewhere I can get a nightcap?"

"The bar in the south wing is open until midnight," she said, shoulders lowering as she launched into her recitation. "Just past your new room—oh, sorry, it's room 102, did I say that? I wrote it on the envelope. Anyway, your room is just around the corner, there, and the bar is farther down the hallway. Where cocktail hour was held earlier?"

"Perfect, thanks. You've been a huge help."

She smiled widely, clearly genuinely pleased by the praise, and I made my way to the large central staircase to meet Blake, feeling a weird mix of pity and nostalgia and slightly misplaced affection. Sure, I didn't really know the girl, but to be fair, my emotional compass had been a *little* uncalibrated lately. Last week, I'd started bawling at the elderly-but-sprightly couple dancing in a *Viagra commercial.*

Back in the room, Blake had changed into an old Playpen T-shirt and was closing his suitcase.

"I was starting to think I should come after you. After all, there *is* a murderer on the loose." He flashed me a sneaky little grin, as if he'd gotten away with something. I'd always liked how Blake couldn't seem to help acknowledging his own jokes that way.

"She's new, it took her a little while to figure out the keys." I tossed them onto the dresser and flopped onto the bed, handing him the Tide pen and pointing at my collar. Blake smirked, then bent to dab at it. "Forget packing, why don't we go get a nightcap? I bet people are still up."

"You go," Blake said, still dabbing. "I still need to decompress a little. Anyway, I'd rather move this stuff now than later." He stood, squinting at his handiwork. "I think that's good. But we should maybe do another round once it dries."

"A drink will be fun! You're almost done packing."

"I still need to do the bathroom stuff. But this is your weekend, I don't want you to miss out. Maybe once I'm done, I'll feel more social again."

We both knew he wouldn't. A multihour meal with a bunch of strangers? It was frankly remarkable Blake was still standing. Sometimes he was so good at the whole social thing it was hard to remember he found it draining.

"Sure, okay." I licked my lips, trying not to let my disappointment show. "Just . . . keep me posted, I guess."

I headed back down the central staircase, hand trailing along the heavy carved banister, footsteps soaking into the rich red carpet, then crossed the rest of the hall alone, heels punctuating my journey with tiny, sharp stabs of sound. At dinner, when Blake had been playing along for me, exaggerating every reaction and laughing at all my over-the-top bits, it had almost been like before. Like nothing bad had happened. I swallowed against the thickness in my throat as I rounded the corner to the lounge.

Inside, Josh and Jessica were seated at the far end of the bar, Phil and Heather standing a few seats away, clearly about to leave. Apparently her matchmaking plan hadn't extended to herself. Drew and Gabby were nowhere in sight.

"Aww, sorry we missed you," Heather said with a faux pout. "We were just going up. You're all young, but it's past our bedtime."

"Besides, you have that bottle of champagne waiting, right?" I grinned at Phil. He looked startled.

"What are you talking about?" The faintest hint of a frown made it past Heather's forehead Botox. I grimaced, looking between them.

"Sorry, that was stupid of me, of course it was supposed to be a surprise."

"Actually"—Phil gave me a tight half-smile, then licked his lips—"they couldn't find any extra. So much for my brilliant plan."

"Oh. Probably for the best. I'm sure I'll pay for this in the morning." I forced a laugh. *Classic me, get a little tipsy, say something stupid.* "Anyway . . . have a good night."

"You too," Heather said, taking Phil's arm as they exited the bar.

I exhaled heavily, rolling my eyes skyward.

"Okay, now I *need* a drink to get the taste of my foot out of my mouth," I muttered, reaching for a cocktail menu. My eyes glazed as I stared at the cutesy names: the Millingham Twist, the Summer Retreat. The bartender moved toward me, waiting quietly as I made my selection. "Can you do a Manhattan on the rocks?"

"Absolutely. Rye or bourbon?" I glanced up at her, then startled backward. It was the dead woman. She'd taken off the heavy eyeliner and bright red lipstick, and she was dressed in the standard-issue hotel restaurant uniform, black collared shirt and black pants, but it was definitely her.

"Uhh . . . rye, please." My eyes darted up to her skull. She flashed a crooked half-smile.

"Don't worry, all better." She leaned over the bar, tilting her head so I could see all the way around her shiny black hair. Sure enough, it was completely blood- and gaping-head-wound-free. Which the logical part of my brain knew it would be, obviously, but that was nestled under several thick quilts of wine. "For the record, I told Jennifer they should have let you know what you were in for once you two arrived. But she was adamant." The woman rolled her eyes, picking up a beaker from behind the counter and dropping a scoop of ice into it. She reached over her shoulder to grab a bottle of rye, looking back at me. "This is what the guest *specifically* requested, blah blah blah." She shrugged, half-smiled again as she started pouring the liquor. "Jennifer is *really* invested in these weekends." She tilted a bottle of vermouth over the jigger, just managing to fill it, then toppled it in, grabbing an elongated spoon and stirring rapidly.

"Jennifer's the . . ."

"Concierge, usually. Head housekeeper 'Miss Ann Thrope' to you." She strained the drink into a cut crystal glass, a giant ice cube taking up most of the space inside, and handed it to me. I took a long, appreciative sip. It was only as she bent to peer under the bar that it finally hit me.

"Wait, so . . . aren't you supposed to be in character right now?"

"You mean dead?"

"I suppose not. But everyone else was so . . . *on* all night."

"The main cast gets pretty into the act, but once the events are done, the rest of the staff is in the clear. Especially those of us who were cast as the dead body due to *very* serious acting limitations." She smacked her hands on the bar. "I'm apparently out of vermouth. I will be *right* back." With that, she moved through a hidden door in the wall of mirrors behind the bar.

I gazed around the room, taking it all in. Through the French doors that led to the small stone patio, the grounds were visible, silvered by moonlight. A velvety stole of night wrapped around the shoulders of the trees and hedges, statues and stonework, hundreds of stars threaded through the rich fabric like sequins.

The room was distinctly less fussy than the dining room, or even our suite, the rows of leather-bound books weighing down the dark wood built-ins punctuated by more masculine touches—a stuffed pheasant here, a faded globe that was probably full of Rhodesias and Siams there. Now that I looked at it, the bar itself was clearly the thing not like the others. All the details matched the feel of the space—scrollwork and brass, mirrors and marble tops—but it was too sparkling-bright to be original, the wells too perfectly cut for the branded rubber mats that lined them. Come to think of it, I was pretty sure I'd seen the same model in multiple Brooklyn "speakeasies."

Probably this had been a private study, or maybe a smoking room—god, think of living in an era where you needed an entire room dedicated to the leisure pursuit of lung cancer. I could feel the magic of the house starting to wash over me . . .

"Aren't you going to join us?"

I glanced up, startled out of my reverie by Jessica's slightly husky voice. She smiled at me from her perch a few seats down. "I mean, we *are* basically neighbors, right?"

"I'd hate to be unneighborly." I smiled, taking a sip of the drink. It was rich and caramelly, the sort of thing you should be drinking in a smoking-or-maybe-study-or-what's-a-drawing room? "You know, since New Yorkers are so known for their friendly, welcoming nature."

"Thank god." Jessica patted the leather cushion of the stool next to her. "I'm one drink past the point of staying in character, and Josh and I have run out of things to say to each other." She grinned at him, raising her eyebrows. "Years ago, actually."

"That's not true, I haven't even *started* discussing all the idiotic decisions the Raptors have been making since the start of—"

She slapped a hand over his mouth.

"No sports! *Tssss!*" She pinched the air with her other hand as Josh widened his eyes at me mischievously, then she whipped her hand away. "Oh come on, *gross*. Are we twelve?" She grabbed a bar napkin, laughing as she wiped away his spit.

"I regress when I drink."

"Clearly." She waved her hand through the air another moment, lowering her heavy-lidded eyes at him in a private look of loving exasperation.

Smiling, I moved over next to them. They were so easy together, like Blake and I had been when we first started dating. The thought clenched around my heart for a moment and I took another big swig of my drink.

Jessica leaned on the bar, swirling her drink with a cocktail straw and sipping through it slowly, eyes never leaving mine.

"Where's your other half? The two of you were hilarious at dinner, by the way. Like . . . I think the faces you were making were the only reason I got through that bit where Scuttles 'discovered' the note without suiciding."

"Blake's moving us into a new room," I said. "Our shower broke. But by now . . . honestly, he's probably passed out. Blake's got a lower social threshold than I do."

"I knew he and I were star-crossed," Josh said, mouth twisting in that same startlingly intimate smile.

"How long have you two been together?" Jessica asked, tilting her head to the side.

"God . . . nine years now? Married for five." I spun my engagement ring around on my finger, its delicate twists of filigree suspending a single princess-cut diamond. I still caught myself staring at it sometimes; it was objectively beautiful, with a vintage vibe unlike anything I'd seen in the dozens of clockwork-regular social media posts through our twenties, announcing that most of the people we knew were in fact the happiest, luckiest people on earth. I'd pointed it out one day after we'd been dating maybe six months, way too early to even think about moving in, let alone engagement. But I'd told Blake we were playing the "jewelry store window" game my mom used to play with me and Amy: *You have to pick one thing out of every window, and you have to tell me why that's what you want the most.* Half the time I'd pick the gaudiest, ugliest things I could find *just to melt down the gold,* but the tiny window box stuffed with engagement rings was different, an array of glittering shards of hope, not just hunks of rock and metal. Blake had grinned and pointed at a gigantic solitaire. *Let me guess, you'll hock it and retire young, right?* But I'd shaken my head and pointed to the ring that was now on my finger, all tiny twirls of platinum and chips of diamond in just the right places. *It looks like something out of an old movie. The kind where you get swept off your feet.* When I'd opened the box almost two years later I was speechless. Not at the question—my friends and I had been predicting which night would be *the* night for weeks. Because he'd remembered . . . and until that moment *I* hadn't remembered. When I'd been able to catch my breath enough to ask him how, he'd seemed genuinely baffled. *Of course I remembered. I mean, you already knew then, right? That this was it?* I shook my head and he shrugged, smiling softly. *Well, I did. I knew right away.*

God, it felt like so, so long ago. I inhaled sharply, smiling wide. "What about you guys? How long have you been married?"

"Oh, we're not." Jessica cupped Josh's cheek with a hand, pulled him in for a quick peck. "Maybe someday, who knows. But we've made it five years without that, so . . . maybe not."

"Jess is untamable."

"It's what you love best about me." He shrugged agreement and she turned back to me. "Sorry, we're being annoying. I always get this way when I'm drinking. Anyway, I want to know more about *you*. What do you do?"

She touched a hand to my shoulder as she said it, the sort of affectionate gesture you made with old friends, gazing at me interestedly with her wide, long-lashed eyes. The waves in her hair had loosened over the course of the meal, and they felt less polished now, more chic. I felt a thrill go through me. It was shallow, yes, but it just felt *good* when pretty people paid attention to you. I took another sip of my drink, feeling my energy rebounding. Who needed Blake? Honestly, it was probably better he *hadn't* come with me, otherwise I'd have spent the whole time watching for signs that he was fading, that it was time to call it a night, instead of just enjoying talking to attractive, funny people. It had been so *long* since we'd done anything different, met anyone new.

Well, for me at least.

"I'm boring." I smiled. The flapper headband was starting to itch, so I reached up to pull it off, running a hand through my hair to fluff it out. "I'm a freelance writer. Mainly in the personal wellness space?"

"That hardly sounds boring." Josh leaned on the bar, swirling his drink in one hand, eyes locked on mine. "I'm a lawyer. *That's* boring."

"I thought you were an *artiste*." I grinned.

"I'm a lawyer for architects. That counts by association, right? Though you clearly have the better claim to the *artiste* mantle," he added, flashing that intimate, sly smile.

"I mean . . . occasionally I place a cool article."

It wasn't where I'd planned to wind up. Not even adjacent, really. For a brief, shining window just before I graduated, I'd toyed with the idea of capital-*w* Writing. I sketched out a painfully dull coming-of-age novel peopled with characters that looked far too much like my actual friends and bought a cheap bartender's guide, thinking I'd brush up on some basics and easily snag a job that would support me for the few months it would take for me to finish said novel, wow dozens of editors, and be spirited away from the "dues-paying" portion of my soon-to-be-storied writing career.

That was before I'd fully processed what my parents meant by "You're on your own now" as it related to New York City rents. By the time I hit the middle section, the book was boring even me, I couldn't pay my cellphone bill, and the romance of adding "personality" to the grubby Bushwick apartment I was sharing with three Craigslist randos had disappeared under a thick layer of sticky dust. I had a full-time, soul-sucking marketing job for a local travel agency by September. It was only in the last couple years—after almost a decade of picking up marketing projects here, placing the occasional magazine article there—that Blake's Playpen salary had gotten stable enough for me to take the leap into full-time freelancing.

"Usually I'm just writing marketing copy for Amesha, so . . ."

"Like the yoga pants?"

"Yup, they've been a client for . . . god, almost two years now." I smiled ruefully, lifting my glass. "Any time you wonder 'Who *is* this brilliant human capable of so lyrically describing leggings' butt-sculpting qualities?' I'm your girl."

"That's still pretty cool, if you ask me," Jessica said, lowering her voice and leaning forward, delight dancing in her eyes. "Do you get awesome swag?"

"Infinite swag. Which works well, since freelancers live in yoga pants regardless of who they write for."

She laughed, a surprisingly throaty sound, and pulled back to return to her drink, glancing at me sideways with a conspiratorial smirk.

The bartender had reappeared at some point. She moved closer, pointing at Josh's near-empty glass.

"Need a refill?"

"Actually . . . it's probably time we head up, right, babe?" He and Jessica held each other's gaze for a moment before she turned back to me, smiling softly.

"Let us get your drink," she said, "it's been so nice talking to you."

"Oh, well . . . that's lovely of you, thanks." I lifted my glass to them. "To new friendships."

"Cheers to that," Jessica said. The bartender moved to the counter to print out their bill. "Speaking of, would you want to join us for another drink back in our room?" She glanced back at Josh, who nodded encouragement before turning his hooded gaze on me. Jessica's mouth twisted in a small half-smile. "We brought along cocktail makings. And we're all the way at the end of the hall, so no one can get mad if we're too loud. You could call Blake and tell him to meet us there if you want?"

"Oh, that sounds really fun . . ." I bit my lip. Right, *Blake*. I was just remembering—for the second time that night, thanks, alcohol—that I hadn't been able to fit my phone into my bag. If I went up without him and he tried to find me at the bar . . .

I was just a hair too sober to say "screw it" and go anyway.

"Can we do tomorrow instead? I know Blake's worn out from the drive, but I'm sure he'd want to join." He was always better about social things if I prepped him in advance, so he could . . . I don't know, gird his small talk? I understood the theory of introverts, but the practice seemed almost mystical to me.

"Absolutely." Jessica leaned forward to slide the check back across the bar, far enough that I could see down the top of her slinky dress. "It's a date."

Then, with one last smile, the two of them got up and left the bar, his arm slipping easily around her waist even before they reached the door. I finished the last few sips of my drink in silence, shaking my head when the bartender pointed at my glass. A wave of melancholy swept through me and I sighed. Somehow pulling the plug on the night now felt infinitely more disappointing than if I'd just stayed with Blake in the first place.

"Thanks again," I said to the bartender. "I'll probably be seeing more of you over the next couple days. We *didn't* pack cocktail makings."

As always, we'd been in a rush—Blake insisted he'd pack in the morning before we left, *I'm too tired, stop worrying,* and then, predictably, hadn't been able to find half the things he wanted. Which meant that even though I *had* finished packing in advance, I spent the morning running around for him, harried, and we didn't realize we'd left the lunch (and drinks) on the counter until we were past Scarsdale. Leading to our *first* bickering match of the day.

The bartender raised her hand in a two-fingered salute.

"I'll make sure to keep the vermouth stocked."

Out in the hallway, a rectangle of light wavered on the carpet to the left. I could hear voices from the room of the . . . well, *murder* certainly seemed melodramatic, especially since I'd just been speaking with the "victim," but nothing else seemed to fit.

"This always happens . . ." The voice was female, a bit breathy. Was it part of the game? The housekeeper had said we might find more clues if we poked around the house between rounds. Curious—I wouldn't admit it to Blake, but with the embarrassment of my overreaction wearing off, I really was enjoying this thing—I wandered over.

The maid was standing in the middle of the room, and she'd changed from her costume into a cropped T-shirt and yoga pants, probably some of ours. Or maybe twentysomething butts just look that good naturally. She was bending down to peer along the edges of the bookshelf, and just behind her, inches away from her likely unenhanced rear end . . .

"Blake?"

MR. REID A. DAILY

BACKGROUND INFORMATION

CONFIDE:

Forget a silver spoon, you grew up with an entire set at your fingertips. Only son of Winston Daily, the notorious newspaper magnate, you've always been one of the most sought-after young bachelors in New York. A lifetime filled with the finer things—summer homes in East Hampton, yachting trips around the Mediterranean, a Harvard education, and, once you turned 21, your own staffed townhome off Central Park—hasn't exactly made you eager to buckle down. The old man has started making some rumblings about your playboy ways, but you're having none of it. The one time you *did* try to impress your father, you wound up in a trench in the middle of the French countryside. Let him worry about profits and losses, circulation figures and headlines. These days, you're more worried about squeezing the most out of life.

By far your most enjoyable pursuit is of all the Bright Young Things that seem to spring up in your path like so many flapper flowers. You know it would please the old man if you could settle down with one of them—ideally one from a good family, with as much money as possible (as if the wretched miser hasn't got piles of the stuff already), but you're not quite ready. After all, country weekends are far more fun when you're hunting more than just pheasant. And you are *such* a good shot.

HIDE:

You've hinted that you might be ready to settle down . . . but the reality is you don't have much choice in the matter. After the little . . . *incident* with your younger brother's governess, the old man made it very clear: Shape up or life will get much harder, and *fast*.

So far, your father's allowed you to maintain the status quo, but he's made it clear that he might cut you off at any minute. In fact, just before you left, he told you in no uncertain terms that you should come back from the weekend ready to be a man, or he'll turn you out in the gutter.

You could show him your mettle by going to work at the paper . . . but that sounds like such a bore. Much easier (and more pleasant) to find the sort of wife that will pass his rigorous muster. It's not as if any of the married chaps you know have stopped having their fun with the ladies just because they have a dreary *wife* at home.

You'll tie the knot for appearance's sake. But when no one's watching . . . Let's just say you're used to getting what you want, when you want it, from whomever pleases you most.

EIGHT

Blake glanced over his shoulder, clearly startled to see me there.

"Hey, Becks. I was just about to join you."

"Well, I'm here now," I said, blinking rapidly at the scene. "And I'm tired. I'm going to head back to the room." The maid's blond hair was loose now, falling around her shoulders in the sort of perfect, beachy waves Housewives spent hours trying to achieve. She smiled easily at me, the friendly, unselfconscious smile of someone young enough not to care that her nipples were visible through her T-shirt. My jaw pulsed with tension, lips practically glued together in their pinched approximation of her expression. Growing up in the Bloch household, our two most sacred texts had been the gospel of *Always be on your best behavior in public,* and its close cousin *Do not put me on the spot,* and no way was I going to break with my religion for Miss Cut-rate Community Theater. Heather was right, the girl was just a warm body in crinoline. The thought only stoked my annoyance further. Dammit, *I am not one of those women who see other women as a threat,* and now Blake had me mentally trashing this person who'd been nothing but sweet, who I didn't even *know,* for the crime of being born later than me with amazing ass genes.

He frowned, fished the key card out of his pocket, and handed it to me.

"We were just—"

"Tell me about it when you get back, if I don't leave now I won't even make it out of my shoes before I pass out." I smiled even tighter—it felt like twisting a coiled spring past where it was meant to go—and stomped down the hall, making it halfway across the massive marble-tiled entryway before I realized I'd passed our new room. But *very* indignantly. Coz that helped.

I backtracked to the end of the hallway I'd just exited, teeth sanding each other down in my head. I'd barely managed to slip into the bathroom—a perfect mirror of the one from upstairs, almost blinding in its spotlessness—when the door opened. I kicked the bathroom door shut, turned the tap on, and leaned on the sink, heaving breaths in and out as I waited for the water to heat up. There was a timid tap at the door.

"Becks? Can I come in?"

"Fine." I snatched a washcloth up, running it under the stream of water just to have something to focus on. Blake pulled the door open and watched me in the mirror. His whole stance screamed *wary*. Which was even *more* annoying. I let the water scald my hand before flipping the tap and wringing the cloth out, furiously, as though I wanted to break its tiny terry neck.

"Is . . . everything alright?"

"Great," I said, swiping it across my face viciously. "Why wouldn't it be?"

"I don't know . . ." He licked his lips slowly. "Just seemed like something might be up with you."

"Why would anything be up with me?" My voice was growing manically tight. I reboiled the cloth, rewrung it. "I went for a drink alone; you went to find the girl playing the housemaid to have some private time."

"Wait . . . really?" His face twisted in disbelief. "Becca, we were looking for your earring. The housekeeper was supposed to give it back after the reveal but she forgot. I called the front desk and Bethany was the one who answered. That's *it*."

"I'm sure Bethany was *extremely* helpful." Gouts of fire shot from my nostrils, because dammit, *she* wasn't the problem and we both knew it and yet somehow I was becoming that worst of wifely clichés, laying all the blame at her feet. I dumped makeup remover on a cotton ball, swiped hard at my eye. *Wonderful, now you'll have more fine lines to worry about.*

"Seriously? You think I was . . . what, trying to screw around with one of the maids while we're here together?"

"I wouldn't put it past you."

"For god's sake, Becca, *nothing happened*." Blake's body was rigid with repressed anger, fists clenched at his sides.

I could defuse this right now, back down, apologize, blame my insecurities, even just cry, and it would all be over.

But instead I pictured the girl from Blake's work, willowy in a sequined dress, long dark waves cascading over her shoulders, the photo negative of Bethany's beachy locks, smiling at us at the Christmas party before she wrapped her hand around Blake's arm and leaned into me, conspiratorial, *I just need to steal him for a second,* then drew him away. Pictured the nights I'd spent alone on the couch, desperately lonely but refusing to tell him because making Playpen a success was everything to him, good wives support their husbands, this was the part I had to play in the story of our lives, that's what marriage *was*. Pictured the messages she'd sent, the photos, the moment I realized that it wasn't just a second she was trying to steal from me, it was *all* of them.

"Yet," I said, catching his eye in the mirror, eyebrow raised in vicious defiance.

Blake's nostrils flared as he tried to control his breathing.

"I think maybe you've had too much to drink."

Oh no you fucking didn't.

"God forbid I actually be *honest,*" I spat. I could feel us spinning out, could see the DANGER sign ahead, but I couldn't seem to help putting my foot on the gas.

"I'm going to bed." He swallowed hard, throat working. "Do you want me to take the couch?"

"Why not just head upstairs. The entire lavender *suite* is open. Maybe *Bethany* can join you." And now it was too late, the car was pinwheeling through space, no way to avoid the rocks below anymore.

Blake leaned forward, face red, the vein in his forehead pulsing, and practically shouted.

"I told you, *nothing happened!*"

"Then now's your chance," I muttered, tears already prickling at my eyes. I sucked in a shallow breath through my nose. I would *not* let him see me cry again, I would *not* give him the satisfaction.

Blake heaved out a massive sigh, shaking his head.

"Fine. If that's what you want." Finally I caved, glancing at him in the mirror, his face blurred by the film of tears, but he was already turning around, shoulders tight as he stomped across the room. "You know . . . you don't have to make it this way."

There were so many things I wanted to say. That I was trying—honestly, desperately trying—to put things back on track. That I'd never prepared for this part, the bit you usually see in muted montage, a series of pained gazes and heavy sighs between the conflict and the resolution, and so I didn't know my lines, couldn't figure out how to get us out of the scene we were stuck in and on to the next. That no matter how many times I told myself to let it go, get over it, move forward like I said I wanted to (did I really want to?), it would reappear, claws out, and slash through the tender, whisper-thin layer of skin I'd built up over the thing, and I'd be gasping, bloody on the floor, and I couldn't shield Blake from the backlash because every single ounce of me was going into the effort of just keeping all the torn, mutilated shreds of me together. That I wanted to be okay so, *so* badly . . . and I didn't know how.

Instead, I just focused on breathing, on blinking.

"Good night, Becca," he said, the acid in his voice splashing from the doorway all the way across the room.

Then the hallway door slammed, and the tears burst forth in huge, racking sobs, and I sank to the bathroom floor, wrapping my arms around my knees, rocking back and forth on the tiles and wishing desperately, futilely, that I could take it all back.

NINE

Thump, thump, thump.

My eyes shot open. Or sort of . . . squooshed open. Once the sobbing fit had passed, I'd crawled into bed, not even bothering to finish my nighttime routine, slipping out of the flapper dress—god, I'd been so excited to wear the stupid thing—and leaving it on the floor. I could see it a few feet away, a puddle of deeper black with just a ghostly whisper of white lace at the top, the beads and sequins turning its surface oily.

Thump, thump, thump.

The door rattled in the frame. I fumbled my phone off the nightstand, clicking it to life to see the time.

12:13 A.M.

A text notification hovered just below. I opened it to see the series of messages from Blake.

Blake

(10:13)

Got everything to the new room, do you want me to join? Kinda tired

(10:20)

Just remembered—did they ever give you back your earring?

(10:24)

Called the front desk, they think it's in the small library.

(10:27)

If you see any of these, I'll be there

(10:27)

Pop in and help if you want or I'll just scoop you after

Shame slithered through me. He'd been telling the truth about the earring—of course, it seemed stupid that I'd questioned it now, a by-product of the sort of peevish, brittle anger that I'd always liked to think was beneath me. Which meant he'd likely also been right about the other thing: I *had* been drinking too much.

"Open up! You can't avoid me forever."

The door handle rattled. Was it Blake coming to make things up? He might have thought I'd turned my phone off.

I slid out from under the downy duvet and padded to the door, pulling it open a few inches. But it wasn't Blake on the other side.

"Phil?" I squinted in the light from the hallway. I could feel it squeezing the skin of my inflamed eyelids up over the ridges of my cheeks. His eyes slid over my body slowly, and I realized that while he was in a rakishly rumpled version of his tuxedo, bow tie dangling perilously around his open collar, I was just in a T-shirt. I folded an arm over my chest, slipping behind the door a bit more. "Do you need something?"

"You're not supposed to be here," he mumbled, sticking his lower lip out in a childish frown, then pushing past me into the darkened room. "What room is this?"

Whoa there, scotch-breath. He may not have packed champagne, but clearly Phil hadn't forgotten all his supplies. My stomach roiled as he squinted around the room, rocking a bit on his heels, then bent to peer under the mattress, as though maybe I were hiding . . . what, Heather? I crossed to the hallway near the bathroom, shrugging into one of the hotel robes before I flipped on the light. He blinked owlishly, throwing a hand up to his eyes and leaning on the bureau for support. Keeping my eyes on him, I reached behind me, fumbling for the porcelain statuette I knew was perched on the vanity. Phil's flirting had never struck me as anything more than casual, and I'd certainly never worried that he'd cross a line, but I knew better than to assume that that meant anything. Slowly I drew my hand closer to my body, pleasantly surprised by the heft of the thing. Give this to the Victorians, even their tchotchkes were made to last.

"Do you need help finding your room, or . . ." I licked my lips, not sure how to defuse this, exactly. Not sure exactly what *this* was. My brain still felt foggy after the thunderstorm of booze tears that had rolled through earlier. *Just watch for any sudden movements.*

Thankfully, that seemed unlikely, considering how sauced he was. He tugged open his suit coat, peering into the inside pocket, then patted his front, his pants pockets, face set in a half-frown as though he were working out a puzzle. Hopefully that meant he hadn't noticed that Blake wasn't here? He closed his eyes tight for a moment, then took a few slow breaths through his nose, ran a hand through his hair. When his eyes opened again he seemed . . . well, not sober, but like he was at least trying to grasp the tail of it.

"I'm sorry, I got turned around. Too much of this, I guess." He grinned ruefully and raised the tumbler he was clutching. A thin film of scotch swirled around the bottom. "I'll see you in the morning?"

"Sure, sounds good," I said, smiling blandly as he opened the door. I followed, peering through the crack after him. A dozen feet away, he paused and turned back.

"You haven't seen . . ." His eyes narrowed. "What I mean is, no one *else* has been by your room tonight, have they?"

"Not that I know of." *What the actual fuck?*

He held my gaze, nodding slowly, then turned and, without another word, made his way across the entry hall, steps slow, but sure and straight. I couldn't decide whether it was impressive or a little unnerving how much the guy could put away without really showing it.

As soon as he was out of sight, I pushed the door closed, throwing the hasp lock across, then adding the chain for good measure, before returning the statuette to its place and crawling back into bed.

I closed my eyes and tried to focus on my breathing, to trick my body into thinking it was just on the edge of sleep, but the booze's soporific effect was long gone. Without Blake there next to me, just the warm solid *presence* of him a line of defense, I grew more and more anxious, until I was startling at every step in the hallway, every whoosh of water through the pipes, every chirp or squawk or cry of the woodland creatures that had clearly had enough of New York City and opted for the sprawling country life instead.

Just as I was drifting off to sleep, I heard a wail that, through the exhaustion and the jumpiness and the still-lingering fug of the drinks, sounded exactly like a woman screaming.

TEN

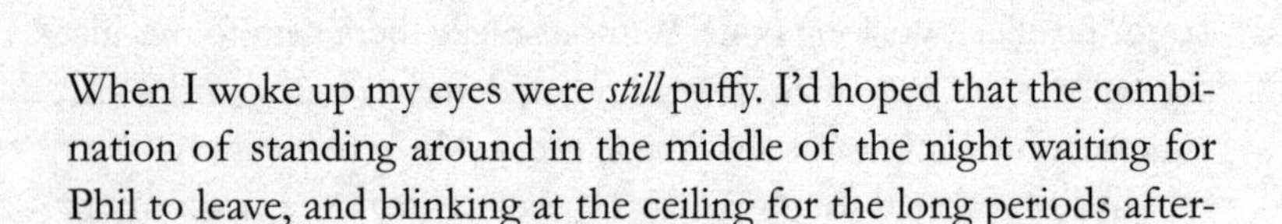

When I woke up my eyes were *still* puffy. I'd hoped that the combination of standing around in the middle of the night waiting for Phil to leave, and blinking at the ceiling for the long periods afterward that I wasn't sleeping, would have taken care of that.

I rolled over, half-expecting to see Blake there. But no. Another thing I'd dialed up past the point of return.

Before I could talk myself into circles about it, I tapped out a quick text.

Becca
(7:03)
I'm sorry
Come back? Promise not to kick you out again.

Blake
(7:04)
Glad you sent this coz I just realized
how much I didn't shower yesterday

I exhaled, stomach going liquid with relief. Blake could be even more conflict-avoidant than I was—which definitely made therapy, or talking through things when I *did* feel up to addressing an issue, challenging—but the upside was occasionally we just got to take a mulligan and move on. If "Pretend it didn't happen" was within several feet of the table, Blake was almost *always* going to pick it. Especially when "Really dig into our feelings" was the alternative.

I checked the time on my phone—barely seven, which felt like a deserved punishment for allowing myself to actually *enjoy* that much wine—and stumbled over to the coffee maker . . .

. . . which had no pods. Jesus *fuck* of all the things I needed right now. And the front desk wasn't answering. Which was starting to be par for the course.

I tapped out another quick text to Blake to let him know I was venturing out for dire caffeine purposes, threw on an old pair of pajama shorts and flip-flops, and avoided the mirrors on the way out the door.

"AAAH!"

I jumped back at the sharp squeal, banging my elbow into the doorframe. Because I needed injury on top of the acid-filled sponge of hangover I could already feel swelling my stomach.

Heather was standing a few feet away, eyes wide, face frozen in shock. Her face slowly settled as she stared at me.

"Are you okay?" I said, trying for a smile. She shook her head a few times, breathing shallowly through her nose.

"Sorry, you just . . ."

"Scared the crap out of you?"

She sniffed.

"Yes, actually. I wasn't expecting to see anyone down here. Didn't we find out that all our rooms were on the second floor of this wing?"

"Our first room had . . . plumbing issues, so they moved us down here after the round finished. They did not, however, move the coffee supply."

"Ahhh. Cruel and unusual."

"My thoughts exactly." I glanced down at Heather, dressed head to toe in grey Spandex, a nylon tote slung over one shoulder. The dark circles under her eyes were heavy, though whether that was thanks to her husband waking her up in the middle of the night or just a constant pre-makeup state of affairs, I couldn't be sure. Frankly, I was surprised Heather had left her room without putting on a full face. "Please don't tell me you're exercising this early."

She smiled distractedly.

"Just taking a quick walk around the grounds to clear my head, maybe see if I can turn up a clue to the mystery. Fair warning for the future, once you have kids, sleeping past six A.M. is . . . not a possibility." She rolled her eyes. "Unless you're Phil, that is. That man can sleep through anything." She tapped a finger against her thigh rapidly, glancing over her shoulder. "Listen, there's something I should ask you . . ."

Then she stopped short, frowning. I followed her gaze to where Blake was just starting across the great hall.

"Looks like your husband's an even bigger fitness freak than I am."

My face went hot as he drew nearer. I could almost *feel* her noticing his rumpled pajamas.

"Actually . . . Blake slept in our original room last night." *Just keep your smile neutral, this is none of her business, and Heather would be the* last *person to pry, besides, what does it matter if she notices everything isn't perfect?* "The hotel offered it to us as an . . . apology, and . . ." I glanced off to the side, grimacing, "and he . . . snores."

"Mmm." Heather's eyes narrowed as she looked me over, then, seeming to remember herself, she smiled brightly. "Well . . . I'll leave you two to catch up."

With that, she strode off down the hall to the side door, ducking through it before I could think of anything else to say.

"Was that Heather?" Blake said as he approached. I ushered him inside, pulling the door shut tight behind me and leaning against it with a low moan.

"Yes. And now she knows you didn't stay here last night."

"So?"

I widened my eyes meaningfully at him.

"Seriously, who cares? Even if she wants to gossip about it, it will be with a bunch of Pine Haven wives we barely know, and she's really never struck me as the type. Besides, Phil was . . ." He twisted his lips to the side, searching for the word.

"Flirtatious? Loud? Drunk?"

"All those things, in *spades*."

"That's definitely true." I glanced toward the gardens. Even with the gauzy daytime curtain drawn, I could easily make out Heather's sharp, angular figure marching across the grass toward a gazebo. "He actually came by here in the middle of the night."

"Wait . . . what?"

With effort, I pulled aside the thick, woolly coating on my brain, dug up the right words. Nothing had happened, and a lecture on my safety carried a *strong* risk of becoming another fight right now.

"He was drunk and got turned around. I'm pretty sure he didn't realize it wasn't *his* room. Either way, he stood at the door for all of two minutes, looking baffled, then headed back to bed."

Blake sniffed and crossed to the bathroom.

"Hopefully his own, for Heather's sake."

"Thankfully he had pretty limited options." I squeezed my eyes shut, pinched the bridge of my nose. "Alright, on that note . . . I desperately need coffee."

Blake grinned, reached into his pocket, and pulled out a handful of pods.

"Who do you love?"

"God, *you*. More than you can possibly imagine."

He stared at me for a moment, sucking first his upper, then his lower lip beneath his teeth . . . then nodded once and turned away. If there was something he'd wanted to say, he never did.

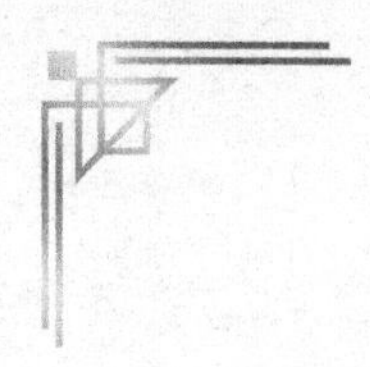
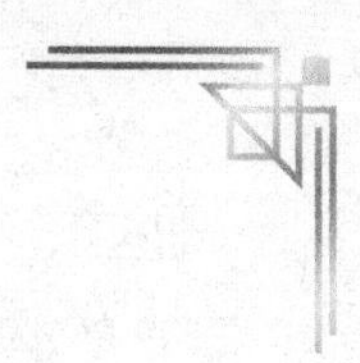

MR. PETER OLEUM

BACKGROUND INFORMATION

CONFIDE:

The son of a farmer (primarily of dirt), you struck it rich at just 23 years old, when you discovered oil while tilling the land your father left you (no one missed the man after that mysterious heart attack took him—consensus was he was pure mean).

A loan from the bank, a few purchases of neighboring parcels, and before you knew it you were one of Texas's wealthiest oilmen. You now oversee your concerns from your mansion off Central Park, which you share with your wife, Maria (née Richmann, from one of New York's best families), your son (Chip, about to start his first year at Harvard), and your daughter, the apple of your eye (but somehow still single two years after her society debut—you can't see why, Cady's a spitfire!). You can't wait to meet all the interesting folks Ida's pulled together for the weekend—you're still a small-town boy at heart, and when you think about brushing elbows with film stars, you feel like pinching yourself. You just hope it will appease your wife, who's been a bit . . . testy since you told her you wouldn't be summering in East Hampton this year. She oughta be more understanding, but you know what they say about women: Can't live with 'em!

HIDE:

You play the part of the aww-shucks country boy who struck it rich through sheer dumb luck, but there was more calculation to your rise than anyone realizes. In fact, your move to New York was partly to escape your cutthroat reputation on the Texas oilfields. Some of your business rivals spread rumors that you killed your own father. You didn't, but you suspect his heart attack had something to do with the land grab you made on him when he was in his cups. You've always played to win. And if someone else has to lose in the process . . . well, it wouldn't be a game otherwise, would it?

Recently, though, your "success at any cost" attitude is catching up with you. You've paid a lot of money to shut a lot of mouths, but lately, all your bad deeds seem to be coming home to roost. If any of them got out it would ruin the reputation your wife has fought so hard to spitshine . . . and take your marriage down in the process.

You need to make sure the dead stay buried. Otherwise the biggest casualty could be you.

ELEVEN

Between my hangover and Blake gamely waiting for me to finish my entire routine before claiming the shower—not to mention our mutual tiptoeing around each other—we didn't make it to breakfast until nearly nine. The dining room was less impressive in the daytime, the gilding and brocade and ceiling fresco shading toward tacky without the glamour of dim lights winking off polished surfaces. Last night had been a little like a private dinner at Versailles, but by morning it felt more . . . your fussiest aunt, the one who paints watercolors of children on beaches or fairies sleeping inside the cup of a flower.

An array of breakfast food was spread out along the buffet, the waxy muffins, plastic yogurt containers swimming in a tray of half-melted ice, and mini-boxes of cereal only adding to the overall sense of un-self-aware kitsch. Drew and Gabby sat at one end of the table, four plates spread between them. I wanted nothing more than to take the seats at the opposite end, say nothing to them beyond hello, and eat my breakfast in near-silence, but already she was raising her hand to wave at us, smiling broadly, and my programming took over.

I pulled out the chair across from Gabby and slid into place.

"I'll get us coffee," Blake said, flashing a perfunctory smile at the couple before escaping to the urn.

"Thanks, babe." Of course, strand *me* there. Not that I could really blame him. I turned back to Gabby, whose eyes were wide.

"Babe? Are the two of youse an item now?"

I blinked, unsure how to respond. It took me a full second to realize she was playing the game.

"Um . . . no, sorry, just . . . misspoke."

"If you say so."

"So . . . what's good?" I pointed at her main plate, piled with potatoes, eggs, pancakes, and various breakfast meats.

"I must look like such a greedy Glenda!" She moued her lips and glanced up to one side. "It's just fun to sample everything, don'tcha think?"

"Sure . . . yes."

"Though . . . these fritters tasted a little *off* to me. Here, you try, tell me what you think."

She pushed a small plate with a deeply beige apple pastry on it, the whole thing glistening gelatinously. Leaning forward, she lowered her voice.

"Go ahead . . . try a bite." She raised an eyebrow, watching me expectantly. "Promise it's not poisoned."

"Oh, uh . . . that's okay. I . . . don't really like sweets at breakfast."

She shrugged.

"Suit yourself."

I smiled, pushing away from the table, plate in hand. As far as I was concerned it was still *much* too early for such a full-on assault of character.

After staring at the buffet for a solid three minutes, trying to convince myself I should have something vaguely virtuous like oatmeal, I piled up all the ingredients for a bacon, egg, and cheese croissant and went back to my seat. It was vacation.

"So what are you thinking of the weekend so far?" Gabby said, leaning forward with an interested smile, eyes skipping between me and Blake. "Pretty nice digs, don'tcha think?" She gestured around the room.

"I mean . . . so far so good." I shrugged and turned to Blake. He nodded agreement. "Honestly, I don't have anything to compare it to. But last night was fun." She frowned at me, feigning confusion. "Sorry, I'm not quite up to staying in character before coffee," I said with a weak smile. "But I understand if you don't want to break."

She stared at me a moment longer, then sat back with a laugh.

"I'm surprised to hear *you* of all people say that, after last night's performance." She smirked at Drew. "But why not. We won't really have another chance today, will we?"

Unless the hangover abated, that level of commitment was not part of my *personal* plan, but whatever works.

"We were just trying to sort out which things were part of the game and which ones weren't," Gabby added. "It feels a little unclear, don't you think?"

"I'm not sure what you mean, actually." I stuffed a massive bite of carbs and grease into my mouth, raising my eyebrows in a show of interest. If I just constantly ate, maybe I wouldn't even really have to participate in the conversation. Honestly . . . I'd been half-hoping she'd say something like *What a dozey dame you are!* and just leave me alone.

"Well, for example, breakfast is obviously out-of-world," Drew said, leaning forward. "I mean, you two didn't even dress for it."

"Were we supposed to?" I glanced down at their outfits. Gabby was in a dress that might have passed for twenties daywear with the right accessories, but Drew was wearing a T-shirt that said ROLL FOR IT. He laughed.

"No, sorry, that came out wrong. We didn't either. Though a

good player can always find a way to spin that. I just mean . . . we're assuming there's nothing happening in the game right now since there weren't any instructions."

"And because of the staff," Gabby added.

"True," Drew nodded along with his wife. "The people stocking the buffet are definitely *not* in character." He pointed with a fork at a woman emerging from a side door to check the food levels, dressed in hotel-issue black. "Which honestly feels like something they could have done pretty easily, they wouldn't even have to improv." He rolled his eyes sideways, sniffing.

"But clearly all of yesterday afternoon was in-world. Everyone we talked to was in character, even when they were doing regular hotel work . . ."

"You mean like . . . Wynnham getting our bags?"

"Exactly."

Blake leaned forward.

"Didn't the in-character stuff end after dinner?" He glanced at me anxiously. "I . . . left something downstairs and one of the actresses helped me, but she was in street clothes."

"Okay, *that's* what we were arguing about!" Gabby stutter-laughed again. "Well, not that exactly. If she was in street clothes I think it was pretty clearly out of game. Actually . . . it seems a little sloppy, honestly, they should at least *try* to avoid the guests if they're not in character." She grimaced and pulled out her phone, tapping at it as she continued. "Anyway, Drew thinks it ended right after dinner, but I think it was still going on for a while. Maybe you can clear it up for us?" She looked at me with that same expectant stare.

"Sorry, 'fraid not. What made you wonder, though, if you don't mind my asking?" Head tilt, eyebrows up, stuff the croissant in.

"Okay, so after dinner, Drew and I decided to take a walk outside to clear our heads—I'm not used to drinking like that." I winced sympathetically. Good thing she hadn't swung by the bar. "And when we came back in, Miss Thrope and Miss Yuss were in the hallway just there"—she pointed through the wall and to the right, off toward entrances to rooms unknown—"having an argument."

"What about?" Blake sounded genuinely interested. I turned to him, a question in my eyes. "You heard the housekeeper. You have to spend as much time as you can exploring the mansion if you want to find all the clues. I guess there are all kinds of things hidden around. They make a big deal of it on the website, too."

I took a sip of coffee.

"I'm guessing I'm the only person here who *definitely* hasn't seen the website."

"Right," Blake reddened slightly. "Don't worry, I don't think you missed anything else," he mumbled, turning his gaze to his plate.

Gabby folded her arms over her chest, completely oblivious to our tension. Which . . . kind of a superpower, actually.

"I probably shouldn't tell you two about this. I mean, if it *is* a clue and you missed it . . ."

"It's not a clue, Gabs."

"Still, I think the game's more fun if we all know as much as possible." She grinned widely. "Okay, so, Miss Thrope and Miss Yuss were in the hallway, and they were still in uniform, which is why I'm pretty sure this was in-game, *especially* if they were interacting with guests in street clothes later"—she turned to her husband with a pointed stare. He rolled his eyes and grabbed an abandoned half a doughnut off her pastry plate. "And Miss Thrope was like, *That's not your job.* And Miss Yuss was like, *I don't mind, I'd even swap with Maria so I don't go over*—and then *No, I don't want to hear it. I'm your boss, I don't approve of it, and if you don't like it, you can pack your things.*"

She leaned back, opening her arms wide as if to say, *Elementary.*

"But . . . what does that even mean?"

"Precisely," Drew stabbed a sausage, pointing it toward his wife. "Plus, I'm ninety percent sure that one of them called the other Bonnie."

"She was saying *Ann*-ie, Drew. The housekeeper is Miss *Ann*—"

"Yeah, yeah, I know. Anyway, if it means anything we'll find out eventually."

It sounded to me like a classic wage-job boss refusing overtime, especially after the conversation I'd had with Bethany the night before, but it seemed unkind to ruin their fun.

"Speaking of"—I clicked my phone. "We should really get going, Blake and I both need showers before the game starts up." I stuffed a huge bite of croissant in my mouth, wincing as I forced it down. "See you guys soon!"

"No." Gabby tilted her chin down, lips pursed in a scolding little smile. "You'll be seeing *Bugsy* and *Dolly* soon. No more free passes!"

"Right. Totally." I laughed as plausibly as I could manage, stood, and crossed to the door, stopping briefly to refill my coffee and swipe another croissant. "Till then!"

Dear lord, was that what conversation felt like for Blake all the time?

If so, I really hadn't been giving him enough credit.

ROUND TWO

MISS DOLLY DIAMOND

BACKGROUND INFORMATION

CONFIDE:

A born fighter, these days you're usually sporting ermine and pearls instead of the shiners of your younger years. After running away to the big city of Chicago at 16, you started a career as a showgirl, wowing crowds with moves you'd still blush to tell your Meemaw about (she's a hard woman, she made you a hard woman, and you love her for it). But Meemaw's from a different time. You're a thoroughly modern dame!

These days your only job is to be Bugsy's right-hand gal. Which is no small potatoes; watching the guests, keeping track of who's planning to do him dirty—not just any broad could keep it all straight. But ever since he hired you as a dancer, he's known what a catch you are. Which is why, now that his mob ties have made him enough scratch to move to the Big Apple, he keeps you in the lap of penthouse luxury.

You two run in the fastest crowd in New York—who doesn't love the thrill of rubbing elbows with a big-time mobster?—and this weekend is your chance to get the inside dirt on Ida's fancy-schmancy friends . . . and take some notes about how she keeps this joint running. Before you know it, you'll be in charge of a heap just like this—better, even—and they'll all be dancing to your tune.

At least you hope. A girl can never have too many friends in high places, after all. And if this weekend doesn't help you climb another rung up New York's rickety ladder . . . then you can always drag the rest of these schmoes down to earth.

HIDE:

You tend to get jealous. After all, who wouldn't want your man? He's handsome, cultured, brings in the bread, and any girl would get a little hotsy-totsy for a rebel. That's why you're a bit more *watchful* than some other dames you know.

You and Bugsy both know Ida from way back, but lately you're wondering if their relationship isn't a little more than strictly professional. You know Bugsy would never do anything to hurt you, but if Ida's as wicked as she hints at in the press, she could be capable of anything! That's why you've been putting all those "observation skills" from Bugsy's clubs to good use, taking note of what's going on around you, what the servants are whispering about . . . and who's turning up where they shouldn't.

Usually all it takes for folks to fall in line is a stern talking-to from you and Bugsy. But if that doesn't work, a girl who's come up the way *you* have always has other tools at her disposal . . .

TWELVE

It's amazing what a midmorning nap can do for you. Physically *and* emotionally. When Blake and I walked over to the large library just before eleven, I actually took his hand and squeezed it. Touch had always been his love language. And right now, I wasn't even going to let the fact that he still seemed to mistake gifts for acts of service bother me. I just felt grateful that things finally felt peaceful between us. And that our real lives were very far away at the moment. Once the caffeine had kicked in, Gabby's full-tilt breakfast press seemed less annoying and more fun. Though that could just be distance talking.

Even though we were still a few minutes early, everyone but Heather and Phil was already in the large library, a grand, high-ceilinged room that smelled of the cracked leather, wood polish, and dancing, sun-spun dust motes that seemed to fill every corner. Gabby and Drew were poking through the lower levels of the floor-to-ceiling shelves, occasionally pulling down a book or tipping an *objet* over and whispering to each other as they tapped at their phones—apparently *they* weren't always perfectly in-world, either. Though I had to hand it to her: the cloche hat and matching drop-waist dress—both in a color I *wanted* to call écru, though I wasn't confident I really knew what that was—felt pretty spot-on, even if the overall effect was a bit . . . sausagey. Whatever the color's name, it was remarkably close to her skin tone, and she'd pulled her hair into a bun at the base of the hat; from the front, she looked entirely bald, and from the back, she looked like one long beigey tube that had split near the top. It was amazing how few people 1920s fashion flattered. I wondered if our grandmothers had looked back on the decade with the vaguely superior sense that they'd avoided a collective sartorial mistake, the way I felt about the eighties.

As one, Blake and I moved toward the empty couch near Jessica and Josh. She looked unfairly well rested, hair rolled into one of those elaborate false bobs, slim and elegant in a drop-waisted dress—evidently they flattered *some* people. I fluffed my curls, smoothing the pleats on the simple cotton print dress I'd packed. Back at the apartment, I'd thought the Peter Pan collar looked appropriately vintagey, but maybe I should have done more shopping before we came. Jessica leaned over the arm of the loveseat she and Josh were sharing, close enough that I could smell a hint of rose from her perfume.

"Ready for more intrigue?"

"That or more coffee," I muttered. She laughed easily.

"Right? They definitely weren't stingy with the booze last night." She glanced at Blake. "Tonight we'll have to pace ourselves a little better."

"Shit, that's right." I rolled my eyes skyward. What with last night's fight, I'd completely forgotten that I'd more or less committed us to an evening with Jessica and Josh. Which sounded slightly less fun now that the cocktails had curdled into hangover. "Clearly I had a few too many—I completely forgot to tell Blake about it when I got back to the room." I squeezed his knee and shot him an "I'm sorry" face. He glanced between us, pleasantly bemused.

"Do we have big plans? Besides all the murdering?"

Just then the door opened and the breakfast attendant pushed an elaborate scrollwork brass cart into the room, giant gleaming urns and a stack of mugs rattling genteelly on top. Gabby turned, frowning at the woman pushing it, still dressed in her thoroughly modern uniform. *To be fair, Gabby, we were told in-game play commenced at eleven, and it's only ten fifty-six.*

"Does anyone else want a coffee?" I stood, turning toward Blake to eye-communicate *Really, I'm sorry, but I promise it'll be fine.* "I feel like I should try to have at least half my brain functional before this starts up again."

"That'd be great. Cream, no sugar?" Jessica said.

"On it. While I'm caffeinating us, you fill Blake in on our grand plans."

"Gladly." She smiled easily as I crossed the vast room to the coffee station. I glanced back to see her patting my vacated cushion and leaning close to murmur to him. Probably didn't want Gabby and Drew to hear and invite themselves along. Which made me like her even more.

I was just balancing our cups on saucers—if my outfit wasn't *quite* as involved as it could have been, I could at least put a pinky in the air—when Heather burst into the room, Phil trailing several steps behind. I turned to smile at her, but she brushed right past, crossing to a pair of armchairs separated by an end table and perching on the very rightmost edge of the right-hand chair, rigid back to me. Phil flashed an embarrassed smile as he moved past, lifting his fingers in a waist-high wave. He looked disheveled, collar open beneath his tweed sport coat, the bright white shirt underneath wrinkled. In fact . . . it might have been the same one he was wearing the night before. He paused, licking his lips and lowering his voice.

"Listen, about last night . . . Did you . . ."

"Ahem."

His head darted reflexively to Heather, lips pursed as she tapped the seat next to her.

"Never mind. We'll, uh . . . talk later." Then he hurried over to sit next to his wife, head lowered like a scolded dog.

I felt absurdly relieved to have passed the bickering-couple baton. And more than a little gratified to know that even couples as seemingly in tune as Phil and Heather could occasionally be the ones to pick it up.

The housekeeper marched in just behind them, huffing as though she'd just finished a run, and I hurried back to my seat with the coffee cups, feeling caught out somehow. You had to give it to her—I couldn't speak to her range as an actress, but she had the "disappointed schoolmarm" vibe down *cold*. The cups rattled in my hands, but somehow I managed not to spill coffee everywhere.

"Thanks, lovely," Jessica murmured as I handed hers over, sitting up and turning to the table between her and Josh to find a spot for it. I slid into Blake's former seat and he turned to me, eyes narrowed as though he were deciding what to say.

"Listen," I said, voice as low as possible, "I'm sorry, I should have talked to you first, but we were all just in the moment . . ." I screwed my mouth to the side and shrugged. "I promise, if you're miserable, we'll leave."

"It's not that, it's just—"

At that moment the housekeeper stepped forward with a click of her heels. I squeezed Blake's hand and turned to her. Today would be a reboot, dammit. No more bickering, just enjoying the weekend as planned. If we could just focus on something other than ourselves for a while, things between Blake and me would have to start getting better soon.

"Good morning," she said loudly, as though to bring us to attention, though the entire room was already focused on her. One of her fingers wiggled anxiously just over the stiff fabric of her skirt until she clamped her other hand down to strangle it. "I hope you all slept well despite the . . . unfortunate events of last night."

She coughed, glancing over her shoulder toward the door. The coffee attendant, standing near the cart, shook her head once, and the housekeeper turned back, lips pursed even tighter. Anxiety tugged the fine webs of wrinkles around her eyes tight.

"I've just spoken to the constable and I regret to inform you that flooding near the crossroads has indeed made the road, you know . . . whatever, they can't get here." She heaved a sigh, twisted her hands around each other, and thrust her chin upward, throwing her shoulders back as if she was about to go into battle. "I expect they'll have a solution soon. With any luck, by tomorrow morning. Until then . . . I suggest we proceed with the investigation."

She glanced over her shoulder again, pausing for a moment, but the doorway stayed empty. Huffing out a breath, she continued.

"And as I'm sure some of you have noticed, Miss Yuss was . . . indisposed this morning." She swallowed hard, the color draining from her face. "Perhaps the grisly nature of the crime proved too much for her. I hope the girl I brought in . . . from the village"—she gestured at the woman managing the coffee trolley—"wasn't *too* uncouth." I glanced at Drew and Gabby, but they were simply staring at the housekeeper, stony-faced.

"Regardless, the rest of us must soldier on." Beads of sweat broke out on her forehead. Was this part of the act? If so, she was clearly better than I'd realized. "With that in mind, please turn the page in your personal dossier marked 'Round Two.' I believe you'll find more information there that may be pertinent to our investigation. We will begin the proceedings . . . now."

THIRTEEN

"I still say the negligee's important, *see.*" Drew leaned back in his chair, folding his arms across his chest. "What kinda creep steals a lady's drawers?"

"I plead the fifth," Josh pulled a faux-embarrassed face, turning pointedly away from the lacy slip spread out on the coffee table. Blake—or Reid, I guess—had informed us all that he'd caught Scoops stealing it from the dead woman's room the day before. "And anyhow, I still say Reid's just jealous."

Blake shrugged nonchalantly and threw a leg over his knee in a way that felt remarkably "old money." I smiled. It was sweet that he was getting into it for me. And especially sweet that he was clearly making the effort to connect with Josh and Jessica, playing off them the entire round, exchanging shocked looks and eyebrow waggles, generally acting . . . well, extroverted. Though of course *acting* extroverted had always been a skill of his. I was probably the only one who knew that beneath the easy smile, the effort was wearing on him.

Everyone subsided into silence for a few seconds. I flipped

open my booklet, checking to make sure I'd said everything I was supposed to. There were fewer clues this round, we'd all gotten better at finding openings for our own, occasionally developing a rhythm that felt almost natural, and, key feature, we were all *sober*. Or at least I assumed we were. Across the room, Phil coughed into his fist. He might be able to hold his liquor, but clearly it was punishing him. Finally he turned to the housekeeper—standing in the corner, clearly lost in her own train of thought—and raised his voice to grab her attention.

"Miss Thrope?" Her head jerked up. "Are we done, or . . ." He looked around at the rest of us. "No one has any more clues to share, right?" We all nodded. She shook her head once, as though clearing the cobwebs, and stepped forward.

"Excellent. Please proceed into the dining room. We've prepared a light repast to fortify you. Please do eat heartily, I think we'll all need our strength for what comes next." She jammed a fist against her mouth, turning to gaze out the windows, held it for a beat, then hurried out of the room without another word. Phil caught my eye and grimaced exaggeratedly. I couldn't help but laugh. If he was already drinking, he was firmly in what passed for his "charming" stage of tipsy.

"O . . . kay?" Gabby raised an eyebrow and gave her stuttering giggle, then Heather rose abruptly, marching out the door. By the time we all managed to gather ourselves and shuffle out, she was already rounding the corner into the grand hall. The rest of us headed to the dining room, where a spread of slightly wilted sandwich makings, various salads, a mountainous array of cubed cheese and crackers, and a grape-heavy fruit platter waited on the sideboard. A few minutes later, Heather returned, wiping her hands discreetly on the front of her dress, and made her way through the buffet, hesitating for just a moment before sliding into the open seat beside me.

"Were you in the bathroom?" I asked her. "Where is it? I swear, I'm surprised I haven't gotten lost in this place already."

She turned to me, frowning for a moment, almost as if she couldn't place my face, then blinked hard.

"Sorry, I always sleep terribly the first night in a new bed. I couldn't find it either, I just used the one in the room." With a shrug, she turned to Gabby, seated at her opposite side, and pointed to her plate. "Is that macaroni salad? I think I missed that."

Lunch continued in a similarly halting fashion. Gabby and Drew absolutely refused to break character, which translated to "projecting for the back row" for both of them. Heather kept feeding coins of in-game small talk into Gabby, never openly clashing with Phil but pointedly avoiding his gaze. For his part, he seemed distracted, and a few seconds behind, almost like he was experiencing the meal from the other side of an aquarium wall. *So maybe he* was *drinking, then. It would explain things.* The only time I ever remembered seeing Heather and Phil fight—if it even warranted the term—was at a cookout last summer, when Phil had been drinking more heavily than usual. After he'd gone to open his fifth or sixth beer, she'd taken his arm, voice carefully cheery as she asked if he *might want to slow down a bit? We haven't even eaten yet.* He'd brushed her off and taken a swig of the beer, but just after, he'd switched to seltzer for a while, and the tension had seemed to dissipate. Still, she was clearly aware of his hollow leg . . . and it probably wasn't her favorite thing about him.

Meanwhile, Josh and Blake were getting deep in the weeds about some "weird even for venture" guy they'd both met with (apparently Josh was in-house counsel for a green architecture firm that had developed some sort of new blah blah blah, he was just far enough down the table that trying to hear him over Gabby's regular crows of laughter was a strain). Jessica flashed faux-exasperated looks at me every so often, but between Josh's impressions of whoever this guy was (someone constipated, by the look of it), and Blake's play-by-play of the questions his team had been asked—*Did you get the one about which sea creature is superior?*—it was impossible to start a conversation with her.

I stared at the lone cube of pepper jack sitting on my plate, debating whether to go back for round two, when my stomach gurgled ominously. Apparently my hangover wasn't quite done with me. I stood, touching Blake on the shoulder and bending to whisper in his ear.

"I'll be right back, hon." He glanced up at me, face still wearing the traces of laughter at whatever Josh had been saying, and nodded, already turning back to their discussion of *wire frames dear lord have you ever seen someone so obsessed with wire frames?*

And I'd been worried he'd be gritting his teeth through drinks later. If anything, I'd probably be the one counting the minutes until bed.

I padded down the thick carpet of the hallway, looking around for some sort of sign pointing toward bathrooms, but there was nothing. My guts burbled liquidly again—the image of gases belching up through a tar pit came to mind—and I turned toward the juncture with the great hall. Our room probably wasn't the closest option, but right now I needed certainty. I was a few feet shy of the great marble expanse of the great hall when things . . . threatened. I stopped, a cold sweat breaking out over my entire body as I focused on clenching. I could hear the murmur of voices. They were low, angry whispers; I peeked into the near corner of the absolutely ginormous room, but no one was in sight. Some trick of the marbled surfaces and cavernous ceilings made sound echo across the space to my little corner of sweaty gut-churn. Jesus, god, please don't let them be a few feet away behind an urn and actually able to *see* me.

"Which room was it?"

"What does it even matter?"

"Just answer me."

"She didn't say, I swear. She just said it was supposed to be empty and she might be sleeping there. But forget the room, she's obviously not coming back, Jen. We need to make a plan for the rest of the weekend, otherwise—"

"I'm sorry, did someone promote you without telling me?"

"No. Obviously. I'm just saying it's probably better to cut our losses. Just . . . give them vouchers or something."

"Leave that to me. Just be honest with me, Manny . . . did Bethany tell you where she was going?"

"Of course not. We both know she's flaky. This isn't the first time she hasn't shown up for a shift. If you want my advice, cut your losses with her and try to salvage the rest of the weekend."

The wave passed and I exhaled, body shuddering slightly with the brief reprieve. But . . . I didn't feel like moving on quite yet. Whatever they were arguing over, it didn't sound good. A heavy sigh echoed through the room.

"You're probably right. Dammit . . . I'll think of something to tell the guests. Can you bring Mike up to speed? Bethany disappearing shouldn't change anything for him, but it's better if we're all on the same page."

"Sure thing."

"Thank you. If you need me, I'll be in the office. I need to see if Brandon can get here any earlier . . ."

I heard a door slam, then quick footsteps moving across the hall in the direction of the opposite wing of the house. I started across the great hall, trying to step softly, keeping my eyes straight ahead, *Nothing to see here, folks, didn't hear a thing, just popped out now because I am definitely not an adult woman who had to stand still for a solid minute in her struggle not to crap herself.*

I frowned as I reached the door to our room, what I'd just heard spinning around my brain. The girl who had been so earnest last night, so intent on doing a good job . . . why would she just up and *leave*? Forget that—*when* would she have left? She'd been in the house until at least elevenish . . . and where would she have gone? She'd said she didn't even have an apartment at the moment.

Were they really not even a little worried about her? When we'd talked she seemed so sweet . . . and so lost. She clearly needed the job. What could possibly have been worth abandoning it without a word to anyone in the middle of the night? Guilt slithered through me. *Maybe overhearing two of the guests fighting about her could have done it.*

And then I realized: *the Tide pen.*

It was still sitting on the dresser in our bedroom, I was sure of it. I could head upstairs to drop it off and see if . . . maybe she'd come back? Or at least left some clue to why she'd gone. From the sound of it, Jen was not going to be eager to talk about Bethany's departure with any of us, and besides, what reason would I have for being interested? *We had a nice conversation and also I'd rather not focus on the state of my marriage, so please, more staff gossip.*

Once my guts were finished with me, I washed my hands, snatched up the Tide pen, and, checking to make sure the hallway was empty, darted up the stairs at the end of the corridor, hurrying around the upper floor until I'd reached her room. I paused outside, swallowing hard. *Was I really doing this?*

Apparently the answer was yes, because without consciously willing it, I found myself knocking on the door, murmuring "Bethany?" When I didn't get an answer, I tried the handle. Just as she'd promised, it was open.

"Bethany? It's me, Becca. I just wanted to return this . . ." I craned my neck around, waiting for Manny to emerge from some corner of the room, but it was empty. With one last glance over my shoulder, I pushed the door closed behind me.

The room—rooms, really—were capacious, at least twice the size of the ones Blake and I had been in. A sitting room opened up to my right, the bay window at the back offering a view of the drive. Its low mahogany coffee table was cluttered with paperbacks and stacks of what looked like scripts. Off to the left, closed doors hinted at closets; another hanging open revealed one of the sparkling-white bathrooms all the rooms seemed to be outfitted with. A vanity built into the space between the closet and the bathroom overflowed with lotions, makeup, brushes, and hair supplies. A mirror hung above it, but someone had plugged a smaller, side-lit model into a wall outlet, a cheap plastic talisman that was nowhere near capable of transforming this into a real acting job.

Two queen beds sat on opposite sides of the long central room, one made, one a tangle of sheets and comforter, a long, prim occasional table with slender turned legs spanning the wall between them. The left-hand side of it was starkly tidy, with nothing but a single paperback (the spine perfectly parallel to the table's edge) and a framed photo atop it. It took me a moment to recognize the fit young man in shortish swim trunks and oversized mirrored sunglasses as Scuttles, Manny in real life, apparently—the tux and tails really changed his vibe. The man at his side, laughing and raising a tiki drink to the camera, wasn't familiar. In the drawer below were a cell phone and a neatly wrapped charging cord. Clearly Manny's side of the room, then.

The other side of the table was a riot of script pages, a half-drunk glass of water, a perilously balanced nail file, and on the floor below, a snowfall of what I assumed were used tissues. Clearly Manny and Bethany didn't share the same outlook on housekeeping.

I moved to her side of the room, glancing at the items on top of the table, but nothing jumped out at me. I bent to tug open the small drawer below. It was empty except for a riotous tangle of charging cord, the end near the charger frayed to the wires, and a keychain, the keys themselves disappearing under a thicket of frequent user, gym member, and discount minicards. The whole mess was attached to a large cursive letter *B*.

They were clearly her keys. If she'd left in the middle of the night . . . why not take them? There wasn't a car key attached, but it seemed unlikely that anyone who needed this job as badly as she apparently did could afford to keep a car in New York City. And if you were sneaking out of a shared room after midnight, you wouldn't waste time fiddling with removing a single key, right?

But then . . . how could she have even left the resort grounds? One thing you didn't need to suspend your disbelief for was the mansion's isolation. The tiny town we'd driven through was at least five miles away, and there was nothing but forest and a handful of homes, all set far back from the narrow strip of unlit country road, between here and there. There might be a bus stop in town, but who in their right mind would make the trek in the middle of the night, alone, on foot?

I was turning the keys over in my hands, trying to think of a reasonable solution to the puzzle of how she could have even left this place, when a wind-chime sound made me jump back, startled.

I lifted a few dog-eared script pages to find another phone, screen lit with the latest notification.

Sugar
2 messages

Manny
4 messages

She left without taking her *phone*? Leaving in the middle of the night without telling anyone was strange enough—why leave your phone behind?

I tried to scroll down the screen to see more, but a dot array showed up, urging me to unlock the phone. Maybe . . . a square?

Incorrect unlock pattern

Okay, rectangle?

Incorrect unlock pattern

A rectangle on the other half?

Incorrect unlock pattern

Well, shit. I checked the battery life—28 percent. Clearly Bethany's charging habits were as disciplined as her housekeeping. With a sniff of frustration, I clicked the phone dark. If there were any clues to where Bethany had disappeared to, they had to be locked inside.

A sickening, cold feeling started to pool in my guts as I stared at the blank screen.

Had something happened to her? Like . . . *happened* happened? Try as I might, I just couldn't imagine the twentysomething who'd been so proud to get the key cards made, dressed in nothing but that cropped shirt and yoga pants she'd changed into, walking a mile down a gravel driveway before she even reached the deserted woodland road, then however much farther to some backwoods bus stop, all while her entire life lay behind in a shared room. At least not unless she was running from something very, *very* scary.

I was still wondering what could have possibly been enough to drive her away when someone started fumbling at the door handle. Crap. Could I run for the bathroom? But if someone found me in there, what would I say?

The handle was starting to turn. Without thinking, I dropped to the floor and wriggled under the mess of Bethany's bed, her phone still gripped in one hand, the Tide pen in the other.

Jesus fuck, Becca, what are you even doing *right now?*

But it was too late for that question. Someone was walking into the room. From my spot beneath the bed, I could see two highly polished patent leather shoes. One of the drawers of the table jerked open, then slammed closed. Moments later a man started speaking. It was hard to recognize the tight, low voice as Manny's. When he was Scuttles he sounded much less . . . clipped.

"I finally got rid of Bethany."

I swallowed hard against a wave of intense nausea. *Please don't let him hear my heartbeat. How is it possible for a heartbeat to be this loud?*

"It was just like we talked about. If you ask me, she got what she deserved." A long pause. "Don't sound so shocked, you didn't want her around either."

Can you not breathe any softer, Becca?

"Well, she's gone, and no one's going to miss her . . . Of course not. I'm not stupid. Jen has no idea about . . . Fine. I have to go; Jen will get suspicious if I'm not back soon. We'll talk about this later. For now, just sit tight, I'll take care of it."

I almost banged my head against the bottom of the bed at the sound of the dresser drawer jerking open again. Manny dropped the phone inside, closed it, then stood there for a moment, motionless. *Could he tell I was here? Had I worn perfume this morning? Please, please don't bend over . . . please just walk away . . .*

A few more seconds—my heart was starting to feel like it might actually explode—then he turned and walked out of the room. The minute the door clicked, I wriggled out from under the bed, whole body shaking. What had I just heard? What had he meant he'd *got rid of Bethany*?

Whatever had happened, I couldn't stay here waiting for him to return. I briefly considered leaving Bethany's phone behind, then rejected the idea. It was the only chance I had at finding a clue to what had happened, and if Manny really had "got rid of Bethany," I couldn't leave it here for *him* to find. Heart in my throat, I crept to the door, pressing my ear against it, straining to hear anything over the sound of the blood orchestra crescendoing inside me. Finally, unable to stand it any longer, I jerked the door open and stuck my head out.

Empty. Thank every god and goddess since the dawn of everything.

I darted down the hallway and around the corner, only slowing when I'd reached the staircase, forcing myself to walk to the door of my room at a normal speed. I needed a second to regroup before I faced everyone around a table again.

Inside, I stared at the phone still clutched tight in my hand.

Now that I'd gotten it safely out of the room, I realized I still had no way of cracking it. So . . . what should I do with it?

Hide it, obviously, somewhere that Manny couldn't find it.

But . . . could he really have *murdered* Bethany? Or was I just spinning out? I thought back to the moments under the bed, and fear clawed through me anew; still, could I even trust my emotions anymore? Just last night I was accusing Blake of trying to hook up with Bethany, and arguably I had more evidence for that accusation.

I collapsed onto the bed, folding over until I was cupping my forehead with both hands. Blake. What would he say if he knew what I'd just done? What *had* I just done? Swallowing hard, I turned to grab the phone. I'd leave it in the pocket of my makeup bag until I could decide what to do with all this . . . or if there was even any *this* at all. I was just about to step through the door and head back to join the others—*Smile wide, Becca, nothing to see here!*—when I caught movement out of the corner of my eye.

I turned, frowning as I tried to puzzle it out.

My dress from the night before was draped over the back of the desk chair, fringe dribbling around the legs loosely, a few stray sequins dotting the floor nearby.

And it was *moving.*

Not much, just the lightest flutter, as if someone had run a hand along it as they passed.

I frowned, shivering slightly, then glanced around to see if anything else felt . . . off, but the room appeared to be just the way we'd left it, the bed still unmade, Blake's pajamas and underwear still in a tangled ball at its foot. I kept staring at the dress, trying to ignore the creeping feeling along the back of my neck. I hadn't gone anywhere near it, and I'd become very familiar with the hiccupping wheeze of the heating system kicking in during the sleepless hours of the night. The dress had moved on its *own.*

The fringe wriggled along the floor again and I yelped, the sudden flurry of motion bringing to mind spectral fingers. And then I glanced beyond it and saw something even more unnerving.

The door to the patio was open. Which meant that not only had Bethany gone missing overnight, but someone had broken into our room. But who? And why?

FOURTEEN

"Okay, let's lay this out methodically. So far, what do we know about the murder? It happened between four and five yesterday, possibly somewhere other than the small library, and it involved some sort of blunt object. None of the servants were nearby, right?" Josh looked up from the chicken scratch of notes he'd made on the inside cover of his booklet.

"That's right . . . although that does seem a bit convenient now that you mention it, don't you think, darling?" Heather laid her hand on Phil's sleeve, eyes widening. He glanced at it with a frown of confusion, as though he wasn't quite sure how it had gotten there. "I've always been shocked by the stories my friends tell me about *their* servants," she added, raising an eyebrow meaningfully.

"But isn't the point of the game that one of *us* did it?" Blake said.

"Game? What're you talking about, friend?" Drew tilted back, face contorting.

"I'm just saying, they might be involved somehow," Heather said with a shrug. "Servants have the most reprehensible morals, after all."

Conversation died for a moment, and Blake knocked his knee lightly against mine, startling me back to the present. For the last hour, I'd been watching everyone around the table, waiting for someone to say something really *off,* or break a sweat, or—ideally—tell us to forget the game, if we wanted *murder,* they've got the real deal.

But of course no one did any of that. If they were acting suspicious, it was impossible to sift out from the bad acting. Even Manny had disappeared back into the role of the footman; could he really pull that off so easily if he'd just *killed* a girl?

Maybe if he was an actual psychopath.

Not useful, Becca. Jesus, actually hearing the words, even inside my own head, made me want to give myself a stern talking-to. As of right now, the most suspicious thing that had happened was me breaking into one of the actors' rooms and stealing their personal property.

I cleared my throat, frowning at the packet in my hands.

"So . . . sounds like we still haven't narrowed it down much. And just about everyone was spotted either lurking around the gardens or Ida's rooms at some point yesterday." I leaned across the table to look at the map of the grounds, trying to sort through the thicket of chance encounters, suspicious looks, and hinted-at motives that were all we'd uncovered so far . . . and simultaneously trying to keep an eye on the other players. Any of them could be behind Bethany's disappearance, too. Not to mention the break-in of our room. But what would be the point of that?

"Whoa, there. I resemble that remark!" Drew folded his arms across his chest. "I don't needs to *lurk.*" I narrowed my eyes, trying to suss out guilt in his broad face. But if there was any, he'd squished it between the folds of his exaggerated frown.

"She didn't mean anything by it, baby," Gabby touched his arm.

"Everyone knows better than to cross a man with your connections, after all."

"They'd better," Drew said with a little *harrumph* sound.

"All I mean is that everyone has been acting . . . suspicious so far. So maybe we should focus on our more tangible clues. We have the negligee, and the note from last night," Josh said, frowning at his sheet. "Seems like sex is in play? How many lovers did Ida have?"

"More than one," I said, checking my notes to make sure I had it right. I should focus on the game, nothing *real* was going on, and if it was, rule one of every murder mystery was that acting suspicious would only put whoever was behind it on to me. "And at least one of them is a little . . . déclassé. Which could mean Bugsy . . ."

"Don't you *dare* imply my man would run around on me," Gabby spat.

". . . or her lover might not be one of the guests at all."

"Right," Josh confirmed. "We know for a fact that she and Reid have a past. I'm guessing the other lover is Peter."

"Why would you accuse *my* husband? After all, you were the one caught holding the teddy." Heather's back stiffened, her nose tilting up the tiniest bit. A bit of the tense watchfulness I'd been feeling dissolved at the ridiculousness of it. Her range was pretty limited, but I was pleasantly surprised by her willingness to throw herself into the mix. I knew Heather loved mysteries at least as much as I did, but she was always so *correct;* she'd literally sent a thank-you note the first time we had them over for cocktails. I was surprised to see her playing along so enthusiastically.

"She's got you there, old boy," Blake said, tapping his knuckles against the table. I stifled a laugh. Maybe there was nothing to be worried about. Honestly, which was more likely: that something terrible had happened, or that a twentysomething had flaked out on a corny part-time job? When I thought about it that way, my anxiety seemed a little ridiculous. Hysterical, almost. Definitely a word that applied to me lately . . .

"True. But we also know that Peter has a habit of sleeping

around. Isn't that right, Peter?" Josh looked at Phil expectantly, but he wasn't paying attention.

"Peter," he tried again. No response. Jessica—Lulu—leaned forward, looking straight at him.

"Phil." He jerked to attention, eyes darting between Jessica and Josh.

"Hmm?"

"You have a history of sleeping around, right?" Josh said.

Phil's eyebrows lowered, and he leaned forward in the chair.

"What in the hell is that supposed to mean?"

Josh drew his head back sharply, blinking, then started scanning his notes. I frowned. Was this the booze? Phil was usually so carefully laid-back, never fully shedding that boat-shoes ease successful men always seemed to wear like an extra layer of clothing.

"I could swear that came out . . . Who had that clue?"

"Oh, me!" Gabby said, eyes widening as she flipped through her booklet. "New floozy every week," she added, jabbing at the page.

"Ahh, well . . ." Phil sucked his lips in over his teeth for a long second, then flipped open his booklet and shrugged, a rueful schoolboy look on his face. "Fine, I admit it. What can I say? The ladies always have thrown themselves at me."

Heather flashed him an elaborate look of scorn.

"Which is why you need to try harder to *dodge* them, dear."

"Okay, so . . ." Josh frowned, reading over his notes again. "That still leaves . . . pretty much anyone." He sniffed out a sigh, mouth twisting into a smirk as he glanced over at Jessica.

"Ahem." Everyone's heads turned to where Miss Thrope was standing in the doorway. "If you're quite done with luncheon, I have an announcement." She closed her eyes for a moment, swallowing hard. Her stubby fingers were woven through one another like an undercooked challah. "I'm very sorry to say that one of Miss Crooner's staff has fallen ill and won't be able to join us for the rest of the proceedings."

"What?" Drew was so surprised he scared his accent into hiding. He turned to Gabby, his broad, lantern-jawed face going a bit grey. "I told you those oysters tasted off to me. Oh god . . ."

"I assure you, none of you are at risk from this . . . illness." The housekeeper's cheeks flushed as she struggled for words. "As it happens, Miss Yuss—the maid who found Miss Crooner's body—has a very weak constitution and is prone to, umm"—she pinched the bridge of her nose—"*hysterics*. She's quite prone to hysterics." *You and me both, girl.* "Which is why she's decided to stay at . . . her mother's for the duration of the weekend."

Gabby's eyes narrowed as she looked at the woman.

"This wasn't part of the plan, I take it?" The housekeeper shook her head. "Just tell us what's actually going on."

The housekeeper's shoulders slumped and her eyes pinched shut again. She spoke without opening them, voice lower.

"One of our actresses didn't show up to work today. We're making some modifications, but I promise it won't affect your ability to solve the mystery."

"It won't— Wait a second, she just didn't *show*? Don't you all stay here overnight? No, nix that, haven't you ever heard of a damned *understudy*?" Drew sniffed, looking around the table to find an ally in his disgust. The noise seemed to put a bit more steel in the housekeeper's spine, and she turned to him with a pale echo of the tight control she'd exuded last night.

"I'm sorry for any inconvenience it will cause you, but as I said, your gameplay won't be affected."

"But . . . if this actress was part of the weekend . . . won't we miss out on some of the clues?" Heather's botoxed forehead made a valiant effort to wrinkle. "We've all paid quite a lot of money to be here, I find it hard to believe that losing one of what, four cast members? Five? Anyway, the point is it *will* impact our experience. Don't you agree, Phil?" She turned to him expectantly, but he was just frowning, mouth slightly agape. "Phil?"

"What?" He turned to her slowly, confusion still heavy on his brow in a way that aged him more than the grey at his temples. The image of him leaning over Bethany in the hallway the night before flashed into my mind again. Could it really be that simple? He'd been pretty aggressive with the flirting from minute one; if she ran into him after he came by my room, he might have stepped more definitively over the line, made her feel too uncomfortable to keep up the act for an entire weekend.

"We paid a lot to be here, and this will make it less enjoyable. Don't you agree?" Heather folded her arms, the image of prim dissatisfaction.

"Oh, um . . . yes, that's right," he said, eyes going a little distant.

"It's not *just* about the solve," Gabby added, nodding her support for Heather.

"Of course," the housekeeper said. "And while I assure you that your weekend will still be highly enjoyable"—she raised both hands, cutting off further protest—"filled with all kinds of twists and turns—I'm personally ensuring any and all material related to her character will be dealt with elsewhere, so you won't miss out—still, we *do* want to make sure that you know how much we appreciate your understanding. Which is why all your drinks for the rest of the weekend have been comped. In addition to those included with your stay, of course."

Drew sniffed loudly.

"Lot of good that does us."

The housekeeper drew in a huge breath, chest ballooning against the confines of her tight black dress.

"Does anyone else have any questions?"

I glanced around the table. Heather's lips were still pinched in disapproval, and Phil had opened his mouth as though he was waiting for words to fill its reservoir, then eventually closed it with a small, wet slap. He looked like the dreaded afternoon second-wave hangover brought to life.

"I have a question," I finally said. The woman nodded at me to go on. "Is this normal? For an employee to just not show up, I mean. Are we sure she's alright?" I didn't want to press the issue *too* hard—both because there was no real reason not to believe the housekeeper's explanation, and because if my fever-dream version *did* have legs, I definitely didn't want to put a target on my back—but it at least seemed worth floating. Maybe someone would react in a way that was telling. Blake's eyes darted to mine for a moment, but he didn't say anything.

The housekeeper sighed, face going slack.

"This *particular* employee has a history of irresponsibility," she finally said. "While I'd hoped we'd moved past behavior like this, it's . . . not a surprise, no, though of course it's deeply disappointing." Her lips puckered. "However, I *promise,* the rest of the staff are fully committed to giving you a *murderously* fun weekend."

I nodded, smiling politely—it was a reflex—and everyone else seemed to accept the explanation. I shouldn't be feeling disappointed by her nonchalance. Or if I was, it was just because the game would probably be affected. *Sure, Becca. Tell yourself that.*

"Walking out on a job like that," Heather murmured, wrinkling up her nose. "I swear, that generation has no work ethic whatsoever."

"If we're all up to speed, then?" The housekeeper looked around again, then nodded, clapping her hands once. "Please follow me, there's something I believe you all deserve to see."

ROUND THREE

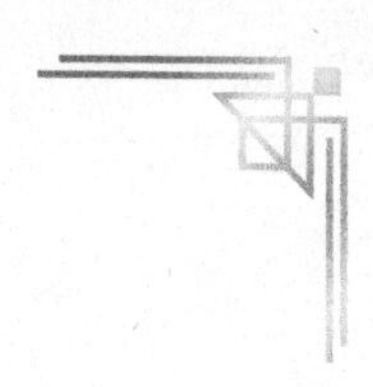

THE HUNT

By now, each of you has learned more about your fellow guests, none of it very flattering. But the only person who knew all of you—and all your secrets—was Miss Crooner. And in her case, dead women *do* tell tales.

At least they will if you're not thorough.

During your search of Miss Crooner's rooms, each of you will be looking for a particular object, one that could incriminate you. You'll know when you've found it because it will be marked with the symbol below. If you find yours before the time is up, you can choose to share it with the rest of the guests, or keep it to yourself. If you don't find it, Miss Thrope is likely to turn it up. And when a woman is as devoted to her mistress as Miss Thrope is to Miss Crooner, well . . . she's not likely to hold back anything that might help find the killer.

Be thoughtful. Be thorough. And above all, be smart. Remember, this could be the item that proves your innocence . . . or your guilt.

LOOK FOR THIS SYMBOL:

FIFTEEN

I lingered behind as everyone pushed back from the table, watching the rest of the guests. Drew's face was thunderous, and Gabby had a worried, ferrety look, head darting back and forth between her husband and the housekeeper. Josh murmured something to Jessica, who shrugged, her face briefly lighting up with whatever she was replying. Heather was efficiently pulling together her things, but Phil looked . . . stricken. She said something to him and he jerked his head her way, eyes still unfocused.

What the hell was going on there? Maybe he really *had* crossed the line. It wasn't all that hard to imagine him moving from a too-close chat to a casual groping in a late-night scotchy haze.

Seeing we were all more or less ready, the housekeeper set off down the hall. I tried to sidle up to Blake and catch his attention, but he'd fallen into conversation with Josh, so I drifted to the back. I didn't want to ask about the patio door with an audience. The phone I was . . . still deciding whether or not to mention. The further I got from the moment under the bed, the harder it got to imagine explaining to Blake what I'd done. He'd gotten used to my being a bit of a powder keg lately, but so far it hadn't crossed over into B&E.

"She *knows,* I'm sure of it." I stopped short; just as I emerged from the dining room, Gabby and Drew had turned the corner of the hallway that led toward the lobby. They'd stopped just inside the tiny alcove that led to the stairs, clearly not realizing I was still behind them. Gabby was whispering, but the narrow wood-paneled space bounced her voice right to me. I took a step back through the doorway just as Drew craned his neck to glance down the hall. Apparently he didn't spot me, because he quickly turned back to his wife. Gabby's whisper was ragged with strain. "Bethany must have told her. They're going to realize it's us, Drew."

"For god's sake, keep your voice down." Drew sounded harsher than I'd heard before, all the wiseguy yuk-yuk stripped away. "No one even knows that we recognized Bethany. And our rendezvous yesterday was private. They've already closed up the groundskeeper's house, and no one saw me go in. There's no reason to think anyone else will put it together."

"Unless Bethany *told* someone," Gabby whispered, so low I almost didn't catch it.

"If she did, they'd have said something. So just . . . keep it together, okay? It's just a couple more days."

With that, the muffled sound of hurried steps on plush carpet resumed. I swallowed hard, a cold, heavy feeling gripping my stomach as I emerged from the privacy of the doorway.

How did they know her real name? Worse . . . why were they hiding it? At breakfast they'd put on that whole show about Jen and Bethany's conversation, Drew made a point of noting that he'd heard the name *Bonnie.* He must have known it was Bethany. So why was he trying to make sure *we* thought they'd never met her?

The housekeeper wound up the stairs, crossing the gallery and turning sharply down the hallway opposite the one that held all the guest rooms, coming to a stop in front of a narrow marble-topped table. Overhead, a child in a white pinafore and giant, mushrooming bonnet, sausage curls trailing over her shoulders like blond snakes, stared balefully out at us, imprisoned forever in her gloomy oil-paint nursery. I shuddered, forcing myself to shift my focus back to the only slightly less dead-eyed gaze of "Miss Thrope." *Stop making up stories, Becca. A twentysomething flaked out, that's all that happened, so just enjoy the game.* I scooted up around Gabby and Drew, settling near the wall. She jumped, clearly startled, then turned to Drew, gripping his arm and tilting her head my way.

"Don't worry," I said, groping for some era-appropriate lingo. "I'm not, y'know . . . after your fella."

Gabby's eyes narrowed as she stared at me, then she sniffed, nodded once, and scooted farther away, darting occasional stares in my direction that I pretended not to notice. *Just don't look at her. She'll know you heard them if you look at her.* I folded my hands in front of me, keeping my eyes on the housekeeper, trying to project calm interest. Probably Amy had some theater trick for that, but if so, I'd never learned it.

When we were all spread out in front of her, the housekeeper cleared her throat, unhooking the giant ring of keys from her belt and gazing at it as she spoke.

"I've always protected Miss Crooner's secrets . . ." She bit her lip, gazing off into the middle distance, eyes not-quite-misting over, but her whole pursed, slightly gas-pained mien giving the impression of imminent tears. "It was my most important duty. 'Yeah, yeah, Ann, keep this old pile running however you like, just make sure no one's running their *mouth* off about yours truly,' she'd tell me." She sucked in a deep breath, thrust her chest out, and glared at us defiantly. "But what good is protecting her reputation if it means protecting her killer?" She turned to a small, ornate jewelry box perched in the center of the table and twisted a key in its front. The lid flipped up, revealing a tiny, faded ballerina, the velvet of her skirts worn with time. She pirouetted slowly as an eerie tune played, a sinuous glide down and up a minor scale, the tin cylinder plinking out each note a hair's breadth behind when you expected it, and just slightly out of tune. The housekeeper closed her eyes, swaying slowly to the mournful song. I knew it was all for effect—really, it was the first set piece she'd seemed fully *present* for all day—but still, the hair at the back of my neck prickled.

"Ooh . . . spooky!" Jessica grabbed my arm, leaning in to whisper in my ear.

I laughed, trying to stamp out the feeling scuttling around my stomach. Jessica, at least, seemed wholly unsuspicious. *But how would you know? You don't have any baseline on her. Or on any of these people.*

"Say what you will about the performances, but you can't fault the atmosphere," I murmured, gesturing along the dim hallway, taking in the various long-dead men, women, children, and pheasants dotting the walls. "Plus, pretty much anything sounds creepy coming out of a music box."

Finally, with another beleaguered sigh, the housekeeper pressed down on the velvet-lined platform at the ballerina's feet. A small drawer shot out, holding a single key. Key in hand, she turned to a door just behind her and, with a rustle of her stiff black skirts, fitted it into the lock. Or rather . . . pretended to. The way she was holding herself was *almost* enough to hide the electronic keypad behind her swirl of lacy cuff. The sight set the crawly sensation on my skin into overdrive, and it definitely wasn't thanks to the housekeeper's acting skills, or even the music box. Whether or not Bethany's sudden disappearance was as sinister as it seemed, why would someone have come into our room? If it was part of the game, how could they assume I'd have a chance to go back and notice before housekeeping swept through? And if it wasn't . . .

The more I thought about it, the more unnerved I felt. I looked around at the rest of the guests, the housekeeper intent on making this her Lady Macbeth performance. I didn't know most of these people, didn't know what they were capable of. If someone had broken into our room, it's not like I'd know their tells. I smiled tightly at Jessica, then moved over to Blake, tugging on his arm to pull him down to my level.

"When you have a second, there's something I want to talk to you about. In private." This, at least, I could share. Maybe I could decant at least some of my anxiety into him.

He turned, smiling vaguely at me, and raised a finger to his lips. "After this, okay?"

I nodded, and he loosed his hand, turning back to the housekeeper with his good-student face firmly in place.

"Before we go in to Miss Crooner's private rooms, please allow me to explain. My mistress was a wonderful woman in many ways, talented, generous with her friends, and very forgiving, at least with those closest to her." She bit her lower lip thoughtfully, pausing for a beat, *one*-one-thousand. "But Miss Crooner was rather covetous with information."

She narrowed her eyes and looked over us one by one. I glanced at Jessica, who was raising her eyebrows mischievously at me, lips pursed in a cherry-red *o* of faux surprise. I responded with what I hoped was a convincing smile and turned back to the housekeeper.

"Miss Crooner truly believed that knowledge is power, and that it's at its most powerful when you can back it up with evidence. I've come to believe that she had gathered some variety of . . . *'evidence'* on all of you. In fact"—she lowered her eyes, lifting the back of the hand holding the key to her mouth—"I'm afraid she may have intended to use it against you, given the chance." She shook her head sorrowfully, then gathered herself, stiffening again as she looked at us. "Perhaps whatever information she had on each of you will help us unravel the mystery of her death. At least that's my hope. If you'll turn the page marked 'Round Three' in your dossiers, you'll find further explanation of my suspicions. We'll be searching Miss Crooner's rooms for precisely thirty minutes. If, during that time, you find something with your personal seal upon it, please take a moment to peruse it privately. You can decide whether to share it with the rest of the guests later this afternoon. If you find another guest's marked item, please return it to its place. You're free to point that person to their clue or not. You may not, however, share it with the group." She tilted her chin down curtly.

"If any of you fail to find your items during the allotted time, I'm afraid I'll be forced to conduct a more thorough search of Miss Crooner's rooms myself, and to share whatever I find there with the group."

Drew let out what was probably meant to be a low whistle but sounded more like a sad fart.

"If you have any questions, I'll be waiting by the vanity. Please, take this opportunity to look high, low, over, under, and everywhere in between. My mistress's fate depends upon you." With one final, haunted gaze at the lot of us, she turned, fully obscuring the door with her black-swaddled back, and "turned the key" to let us in.

We trailed after her into a suite similar to the one Manny and Bethany had been set up in, at least in size and layout. The wallpaper was creamy, flocked with gold, and that, combined with the afternoon light pouring in through the French doors built into the opposite wall leading out onto a small private balcony, gave the room a cleaner, airier feel than the others. Built-in bookshelves were stocked with a combination of cut crystal decanters, porcelain figurines, and artfully arranged stacks of books, the autumnal hues of their leather covers brightened by the gilded lettering on the spines. To the left, an arched opening, about as wide as a double door, separated the bedroom from a large sitting area, its graceful button-tucked chairs and deep overstuffed couch covered in floral fabric seeming to grow toward the sun pouring in through some large, unseen window. A gigantic armoire, its drawers and cabinets festooned with intricate scrolls and knobs, huddled in one corner, and various occasional tables and dressers adorned the rest of the space. Off to the right, a short hallway lined with doors and a series of antique sconces presumably led to equally expansive closets and bathrooms.

"And I thought *our* room was nice," Josh murmured under his breath.

"Your clues could be anywhere in Miss Crooner's suite, so please don't hesitate to search thoroughly," the housekeeper repeated, looming behind us near the doorway. "Your time begins . . . now."

Gabby and Drew scurried over to one of the bookshelves and started pulling down each and every book and riffling through the pages, turning over the decorative items and poking into the dim, hidden corners behind, whispering to each other occasionally. Gabby's eyes darted over to me again as she raised a hand to cover her mouth. Was this them playing the game? Or were they using the game as cover for something darker?

Slowly, we all spread around the room, following their lead. I made sure to start off in the opposite direction.

I skirted around Phil—bending to peer inside an armoire drawer that had stuck at the halfway-open point—and made my way into the sitting room, slowly checking all the objects on a prissy whatnot shelf pressed up to the back side of the cut-through wall. Inside a small stained glass box, a false bottom easily came away to reveal an envelope, folded sharply in half and stamped with what looked like a tiny Eiffel Tower. *Someone's clue, but not mine.* I slid it back into place, working my way down the shelves until I found a black-and-white photograph of the bartender standing in front of a microphone in full flapper regalia. The back of the frame was marked with an inkpot, a quill sticking out the top.

Damn, I was awesome at this . . . if I were one of the other players, that is.

I unbent and walked across the room to a small end table topped with a fat-bellied porcelain lamp.

"Oh!"

Phil was just moving through the archway, and we both jumped back at once. My heart thudded dully in my throat, making it hard to squeeze out the words. Who knew it was possible for me to get *more* on edge?

"Sorry, I . . . didn't realize you were there." I tried a smile and he just stared. With the color drained from his face like that, you could see his age, the creases around his eyes deeper than before, his skin dull to the point of waxy.

After a moment, he licked his lips, nodded, and crossed to the corner shelf, turning away from me to examine each item.

"Not your fault," he said, back still to me. "I think the atmosphere has me a little jumpy. Plus, I'm always a little off my game when I've had a few too many the night before."

"Hah. Definitely."

"By the way, about last night . . ." He lowered his voice, leaning toward me. "I wasn't myself. I hope you know I had no intention of . . ." A pained look settled on his forehead as he searched for the right words. "I'm sorry if I upset you. I was just confused."

"No problem," I said, heart beating faster. Because my own anxiety wasn't enough, I had to soak up any excess spilling out around me like an emotional sponge. "I figured it was something like that."

"Mmm." He licked his lips again and leaned closer, voice almost a whisper. "Would you mind not saying anything to Heather?" He glanced over my head into the main room, and I followed his gaze to where Heather was carefully flipping through a book. "I know it was a mistake, but she doesn't like when I have a few too many, and I just . . . I don't want me being an idiot to ruin the weekend for her."

"Sure," I said, relief flooding through me. At least *Phil* I could trust. What was that expression? Occam's razor. Phil was drinking too much, Heather never loved it when he did, he didn't want the one person she knew here to embarrass her by pointing it out. Simple. Privately, I tended to think Heather might have a reason to worry. Drinking enough that you can't find your hotel room is champion level. But getting in the middle of someone else's marriage was never a good idea. Besides, nothing had actually *happened.* "I won't say anything."

He exhaled heavily, a bit of color finally returning to his face.

"Thanks," he said, turning back to the shelf. "Wouldn't want to end up in the doghouse again."

Flashing him a thumbs-up, I moved back through the archway to a nightstand, glad that the game gave me an excuse to definitively end the conversation. One thing, at least, was resolved, but the bigger issue still hovered at the back of my mind. *Phil might not have anything to do with Bethany, but that only makes her disappearance* stranger. I picked up a pair of binoculars from the shelf. They were gold-colored but were clearly modern, an anomaly in the period-heavy room. Idly, I lifted them to my eyes and glanced through the window, training them on a dark-clad figure moving slowly across the lawn. It was Manny, and in his hand was a vicious-looking saw, its teeth glinting in the afternoon sunlight. Seeming to sense that he was being watched, he glanced over his shoulder toward the house, and I stepped back, startled, dropping the binoculars. By the time I felt capable of risking another visit to the window, he'd disappeared.

He could have made a key to your room at any time.

The thought dumped an entire bucket of anxiety over me, the clammy cold of it leeching across my fabric inch by inch, setting ever more deeply as it spread. Bethany had done it just last night, and half the time we walked by the front desk it was empty. Hell, for all I knew Manny *already* had keys to all the rooms. Bethany might only just have started picking up shifts around the hotel, but he could have been working here for weeks, maybe longer. As soon as I could, I caught Blake's eye and tilted my head toward the French doors. He frowned, obviously confused, so I eye-communicated *Come on, Blake, I* just *told you I needed to talk.*

That seemed to get through.

Once we were outside, I slid the door closed and turned to him. He was already busily flipping the ashtray on the table, then, presumably finding nothing, he crouched down on hands and knees to see beneath the table.

"Can you just . . . stop for a sec?"

"Sure." He stood. "Sorry, I figured while we were here . . ."

"Right. Anyway . . . I know this is going to sound silly, but—" I craned my neck to look over his shoulder into the room. Everyone was either poking around or out of sight. Still, I lowered my voice. "Did you see anyone hanging around our room this morning? Maybe on the patio?"

"The patio?" He scrunched up his nose, crossing to a large stone urn planted with mums, glancing over his shoulder at me as he rifled through the flowers with one hand. "I don't think so. Why?"

"When I went to the bathroom earlier, the patio door was open, and I just . . ." I rolled my eyes, spreading my palms wide. "I think someone came into our room, Blake. I don't think they took anything, but it's *creepy*. Plus, don't you think it's weird that Bethany allegedly just left in the middle of the night? We both talked to her." I swallowed, eyes flitting to the side as my reaction to Blake's conversation floated up between us, ghostly in the daylight. Thankfully, he simply nodded—of the two of us, he would never be the one to take opportunities to rub in how right he'd been, a fact that I was supremely grateful for right now. "She didn't seem ready to run off to me, you know?" The anxiety of the last twenty-four hours—and of the weeks and months preceding them—started to flood my synapses, giving me a shaky, overcaffeinated feeling, the air around me turning brighter, sharper. I bent closer, lowering my voice further. "I think something might be going on. I'm not sure what, but everyone's acting weird, and breaking into our rooms is just *beyond*." I bit my lip, trying to work up the nerve to admit to visiting Bethany's room. *He'll understand, won't he? If you just explain it right?*

While I was struggling to find a way to phrase "Yes, I stole her phone, but I swear I had a good reason" that *didn't* sound insane, Blake stood, cheeks going pink.

"I don't know about Bethany, we didn't really say much to each other." He licked his lips. "But I'm sure her co-workers know her pretty well. If they're convinced she'd just walk out on her job . . ."

He let the sentence hang there. I could feel my jaw tightening, defiance rearing up inside me . . . but what if he was right? I'd had one conversation with the girl, and she'd admitted to being the sort of person whose thinking-ahead abilities hard-stopped at a bad breakup. *And you really haven't been yourself lately, Becca.* People were acting weird. So? We were at a period-themed murder mystery weekend in the Catskills, for Christ's sake, what about any of that screamed "normal"? Finally I managed a tight nod. Whether or not I actually agreed with him, this clearly wasn't the time to start spouting off about hiding under beds and swiping phones from relative strangers. Blake exhaled, clearly relieved.

"As far as the patio, I'm pretty sure that's my fault."

"What?" The sun seemed to be drilling directly into my brain, merging with the too-heavy thud of blood in my head.

"When you were napping earlier, I stepped out to take a call. Then I left the door cracked a little to let the breeze in through the screen. Unless you noticed and locked it back up before we went to the library . . ." I shook my head. "So yeah, that was me."

I exhaled heavily, trying to slow the freight train of adrenaline coursing through me.

"You need to pay more attention to stuff like that," I finally said, frustration rushing in to fill the void. Which only made me *more* annoyed. *Jesus, Becca, did you* want *it to be something sinister?* "Anyone could have gotten in."

"I know, I know." He moved closer to lay a hand on my shoulder. "It was stupid. But for the record, it was only open for a couple hours, while we were all in the library. There's no one else in the hotel—"

"There's the staff, and the actors—"

"True, but they all have keys to the rooms *anyway*."

How could I explain to him that that fact was exactly what was crawling over my skin at the moment? "Something still feels off . . ."

"Becks, no offense, but you were a little . . . *rough* earlier. I know sometimes hangovers make you more anxious. Do you think that could be part of this?"

I stared at him, rage bubbling up my throat, surging down to my fingertips, threatening to torch my hair . . . then forced myself to take a deep breath. Blake wasn't trying to use it as a weapon, he'd never once done that about a drink too many. He was just trying to calm me down. He saw my anxiety and his instinct was to reach his hand out until I sniffed, then slowly, methodically stroke my back until my hackles dropped and I curled up in purring contentment. Blake was just doing what he always did, what I usually loved him for: trying to make everything feel less scary.

How could I explain to him that this time, maybe *only* this time, I wanted him to agree there might be a big bad wolf hiding in some corner?

Let it go, Becca. The whole reason you're here is that you need to figure out how to just let things go. Finally, effortfully, I exhaled. "I guess that makes sense."

"Then on that note, I need to find whatever has this stupid Eiffel Tower symbol on it before the time's up or I might explode a vein in my eyeball." He slid open the balcony door. Blake had always been quietly competitive, possibly even more so than me. I whispered in his ear as he passed, "Try the corner shelf in the lounge."

He grinned widely and hurried off through the archway. I tried to let his glee be enough to dispel the sludge of anxiety and annoyance still clinging to my insides. Tried not to feel a new wash of guilt when—surprise, surprise—it wasn't.

About five minutes later, I'd turned up my "clue"—a scrapbook page with a piece of black construction paper neatly tucked into photo corners at the edges, a giant white eye staring out from the center (helpful instructions to "Please remove entire page from this binder as your clue" handwritten in glitter pen below it). I stared at the black-and-white photo hidden behind the homemade modesty panel: of the bartender, in costume, with her arm around a very scantily clad showgirl. Flowing handwriting beneath noted that it was taken at "Bugsy's Chicago club, the Pretty Kitty," and that the unidentified woman was "Pearl . . . though these days she's going by Miss Debbie Taunte," with a little winking proto-emoji for good measure. I wondered what they did if whoever was playing Debbie wasn't white . . .

I was just mulling over whether I should keep searching the room—between the hangover and the ebb tide of adrenaline, I was still moving slowly, but there could be clues besides the ones we were meant to find, and I did want to solve at least *one* mystery while I was here—when a piercing shriek split the air.

Jesus fuck, not again.

SIXTEEN

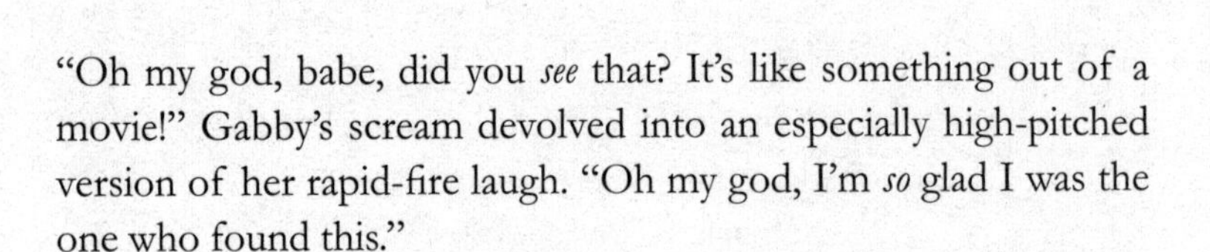

"Oh my god, babe, did you *see* that? It's like something out of a movie!" Gabby's scream devolved into an especially high-pitched version of her rapid-fire laugh. "Oh my god, I'm *so* glad I was the one who found this."

I stood, gazing down the hallway where Gabby was standing, hand still gripping one of the wall sconces, which she'd pulled toward her like a lever. A central section of the paneled wall at the end of the hallway had swung open slightly, revealing a sliver of some other room. Who would think to pull on the wall sconces?

The answer floated up to me almost too quickly: *Someone who knew more about all this than they were letting on.*

The housekeeper moved to place herself between the couple and the passage they'd opened, smiling frostily. She pulled a pocket watch out of her skirts, glancing down at it before turning to the rest of us, gathering around to glimpse the passage.

"I'll go through to make sure it's safe. In the meantime, please use the remaining five minutes to continue searching Miss Crooner's rooms for anything that might be relevant to her murder." She tightened her smile even more and slipped through the doorway, pushing it closed behind her. Drew grunted, then pulled his fedora off, making a show of fanning himself with it, one hand in his pocket. I was just turning away when I noticed him draw his hand out and pass it over the vanity tucked between the bathroom and closet. I frowned, trying to make out what he was doing without being too obvious about it—the exaggerated thrill of the sconce seemed to have overtaken Gabby's narrow-eyed watchfulness for the moment, but who knew how long that would last—when Josh moved up next to me.

"Find your deeply important clue?" His lips twisted to the side mischievously. I couldn't help but smile back. Josh wasn't the most conventionally handsome man, but he was viscerally *appealing* in a way I couldn't quite put my finger on.

"I did. Deeply disturbing stuff in here." I lifted the page, its black panel tucked back in place, for emphasis. "What about you? Am I chatting with a killer?"

Josh smirked and dipped two fingers into the chest pocket of his tweed blazer to tug out a folded envelope marked with the ink-pot I'd spotted on the back of the picture frame. "Honestly? You might be," he said, then tucked it back into place.

I laughed, and Josh flashed that same devilish smile before turning to glance through the French doors.

"Looks like our better halves are hitting it off."

My eyes followed his. Blake and Jessica were leaning on the balcony railing, bodies angling toward each other unconsciously as they chatted about something that seemed to be desperately funny. A vise started tightening around my ribs, but I forced myself to keep my smile in place. *He said it just this morning, he's not trying to cheat on you in* front *of you. Plus, Josh doesn't seem worried.*

Fortunately, I was saved by the reemergence of the house-keeper from having to find a way to respond without accidentally vomiting my bilious hurt onto Josh's shirtfront.

"Please, follow me through to the adjoining rooms. I'm certain this new discovery is relevant to our inquiries."

With that, I rose, crossed to the balcony door to rap sharply on the glass, and turned to follow the housekeeper down the hall before Blake could intercept me, trying to ignore the tender, swelling mass forming around my heart.

He hasn't done anything yet, he won't do anything, stop being threatened by every attractive human that breathes near you, it's really hurting your internal sense of cred.

I only just remembered to pause at the vanity, running my eyes over it rapidly as Josh slid past me into the next room. Silver tray with elaborate jars stuffed with cotton balls, jewel-shaped plastic toiletry bottles, an antique brush and mirror set . . . there, propped against the wall, a thick black business card with a weird abstract white swirl on the front. I snatched it up, glancing at it just long enough to recognize . . . a noose?

Heart beating fast, I slid the card into my pocket and hurried after Josh through the doorway—the wood paneling perfectly hid the seams, a neat trick I intellectually admired and emotionally felt completely numb to—and into a room more like the suites Blake and I had seen, the walls covered in burgundy fleur-de-lys paper, antique furniture propping up thoroughly modern conveniences, blah blah blah, right now this game was *not* enough to hold my focus, no matter how desperately I wanted it to be. Out of the corner of my eye I saw Blake walk through the door—no trompe l'oeil effects on this side of things—his head swiveling as he tried to locate me. I knew my hurt was irrational, but only intellectually, so I took a step closer to where Phil was leaning against the mantel, forcing a smile as I turned to him.

"Find your clue?"

"Only just." He plucked the corner of what looked like a handkerchief out of his pants pocket, then stuffed it back inside. By then, the housekeeper was clapping for our attention. I didn't want to think about how pathetic it was that my first thought was *Phew, safe for now.* Since when did I need to be safe from a conversation with my own husband?

"I'm certain this discovery is important. Even as Ms. Crooner's trusted head of household, I must admit, I had no idea these rooms were connected." I glanced over at the very-much-a-door leading back the way we came. "As I'm sure you've realized, this house is quite large. This is one of many rooms that are usually kept closed. But . . ."

She stopped, head pricking like a hound that's caught a scent. Eyes widening, she raised a finger to her lips and mouthed "Do you hear that?" as she scanned each of our faces for an answer. She cupped a hand to her ear, eyes darting sideways, and there, on cue, was a small thump.

Throwing her shoulders back, she took a deep breath, tiptoed across the deep-piled oriental rug to a gigantic armoire, and, with a final gesture at us to stay silent, whipped open the door, through which a large man somersaulted out, legs plopping in front of him with a heavy thump.

"*Mister* Putter," the housekeeper said, voice pinching up an octave in her indignation. "What in heaven's name are you doing here?"

The man stood, brushing off the sleeves of his black suit and turning to us with a rakish grin. Somehow, the jaunty black half-brim hat he was wearing had stayed in place. A ring of shaggy dirty-blond hair had escaped around the bottom of the band. He looked about thirty, with that puffiness through the chest and stomach of a former athlete gone slightly to seed, but even in his slightly-too-tight chauffeur's outfit, he was still handsome, in a laid-back, low-key-stoner way. Like . . . the less-hot alternate-universe Matthew McConaughey who never made it out of small-town Texas.

"Well, I *was* enjoying a little peace and quiet." He winked at Gabby and she tittered excitedly.

"The cheek of you! There's no need for a chauffeur to be anywhere near the private rooms. How would you even have gotten into this . . ." The housekeeper turned her eyes—and her head, just in case her acting was too subtle for us—toward the door leading into Miss Crooner's rooms. "Were you and Miss Crooner . . ."

"Lovers? You bet your bloomers."

The housekeeper gasped, covering her mouth with a horrified hand. Phil elbowed me, waggling his eyebrows exaggeratedly, and for a moment my anxiety melted away into the ridiculousness of the scene.

"What can I say? Ida had taste, but she was no hoity-toity type. At the end of the day, she could bring home her own bacon. All she needed out of a man was the *sausage*." He made a few lurid thrusts. Reflexively I glanced around for Blake. There he was, laughing and bending toward Jessica, whispering something in her ear that clearly *delighted* her.

I tried to blink away the red haze forming over my vision as I stared at the housekeeper's pantomime of shock. My jaw headache was threatening again . . .

"This is *highly* irregular."

"What can I say? I guess I'm no regular fella." He swept his hat off, bowing to the housekeeper, and something silver-shiny slipped out of the sleeve of his coat. "Oh, let me just . . ." He scrambled to retrieve the item, but the housekeeper was faster. She plucked it up and took a step back, looking between it and the chauffeur suspiciously.

"Where'd you get this?" Carefully positioning it between her thumb and middle finger, she held it out toward the group, arm swiveling slowly to ensure we all got a good look. It was a large rhinestone-studded hair comb, the kind a million Etsy bridal sites sold, in a vaguely Deco diamond shape. Next to me, Gabby gasped.

"Wait, that's mine!"

She darted forward, plucking the comb from the housekeeper's hand, bending to peer at it as she turned it over in her hands. "There, that engraving. That's the store I bought it from! It's definitely mine!"

She turned to catch Drew's eye, her eyebrows raised in a *Well, shit* look. He shook his head once, and she frowned, then shrugged, turning back to the scene.

The housekeeper fixed the chauffeur with narrowed eyes.

"Have you been *stealing* from Miss Crooner's guests?"

"Y'see, the thing is . . ."

She strode across the room, flinging the doors of the wardrobe wider, and started plucking things out—first Jessica's luxurious rhinestone-studded clutch, then a watch Phil identified as his, and on and on.

"Explain yourself. *Now*." The housekeeper screwed one fist into her hip, thrusting her opposite forefinger in the chauffeur's face.

The man drew his hands down his face, tugging it into a hangdog expression.

"Listen, I know this looks bad, but Ida—that is, Miss Crooner—was the one as made me do it. I just figured with her dead and gone, and I know a fella down the way who said he'd pay me good money . . ." He shrugged. "Seemed a waste to let these things sit here's all."

"Are you saying Miss Crooner *directed* you to steal from her guests?"

"Wow, aren't you a smart cookie." He rolled his eyes hugely. You had to hand it to the guy, at least he was playing it up in the right places. And unlike the inimitable Miss Thrope, he seemed at least *partially* in on the fact that this script was more Three Stooges than high gothic drama.

With another haughty sniff, she turned back to face us.

"Allow me to apologize for this unexpected turn of events. Please, take the next hour to gather yourselves while I deal with Mr. Putter. We'll reconvene for restoratives in the cocktail lounge at three."

With that, she pinched the chauffeur's ear between two fingers and, to a soundtrack of his comically exaggerated wails, tugged him back through the door to "Miss Crooner's" room, slamming it behind her. Drew moved over to try the knob, then turned to all of us, shaking his head mournfully.

I drifted after Phil and Heather to the exit, *feeling* Blake over my shoulder. My diaphragm pulsed in the effort to keep my internal organs from exploding out in every direction. *You are being ridiculous you know you're being ridiculous* why *the hell was he flirting with her?*

"*Scandalous,* huh?" Blake said. I glanced over my shoulder. Jessica and Josh were just behind him, and she lifted her eyebrows in commiseration. My return smile probably looked like some animatronic doll in a horror film.

"Definitely. Murder's one thing, but sleeping with the help? Disgusting!" I said.

Blake's eyes tightened briefly, like a dog picking up on a whistle out of the range of human hearing, but Josh and Jessica both laughed, and he quickly followed suit. We all made our way down the hallway, waving goodbye at the landing, and Blake and I continued down the stairs alone.

"Are you going to tell me what I did this time?" he said under his breath once we reached the door to our new room. The words crashed over me like a wave, stirring up a flotsam of anger, hurt, anxiety, even guilt, because he was right, wasn't he? I felt prickly all the time, like someone had sloughed off my skin and I could mostly stand it until the tiniest hint of breeze blew through and every nerve ignited again. I couldn't trust him anymore, couldn't trust myself, what I saw, felt, wanted . . .

I bit my lip, tried to channel the yoga videos I'd do a lifetime ago. *Imagine your breath reaching all the way to the bottom of your feet, to the tips of your eyelashes, to the entire spasming length of your trachea.*

"Nothing. Why?" I turned over my shoulder, quizzical.

"You just seem tense."

"Sorry. I guess the door being open shook me up," I lied as we pushed into the room. "Not to mention one of their main actresses just . . . *poof,* disappearing."

"Right, I forgot about the door."

He flopped onto the bed while I struggled with a new tidal swirl of *Of course you forgot about it, I only told you it completely freaked me out, but come on, Becks,* relax, *there's a hot chick to talk to.*

Breathe all the way from the tips of your clenched fingers to every single fold of your tightly puckered asshole.

Blake sat up on his elbows, grinning widely.

"You know what? Maybe it was for the chauffeur thing."

"Excuse me?"

"The patio." He rocked all the way up. "If I didn't leave it open, I mean. They had stuff from half the people here in the closet, right? I bet someone came in to find something from us."

"Then why didn't they take anything?"

He shrugged.

"Maybe they ran out of time. They're short-staffed, after all. Anyway, I don't think you need to be worried. I'm sure that if it wasn't me, that's what it was."

Tenderness bobbed to the surface briefly before sinking below the muddy swirl of everything else again. I nodded, blinking against the sudden stinging in my eyes.

"What about Bethany?"

He frowned, thoughtful.

"She was talking about her acting last night. When we were looking for your earring, I mean." He sucked in his lower lip, eyes darting to me. "Maybe she got a last-minute audition that was worth leaving this behind for."

And left her phone, and her clothes, and not even a note for her roommate behind?

But what was the point of even talking about it with Blake? He'd keep trying to make this okay for me, and part of me ached with tenderness for that, but the rest of me still just wanted him to say *You know, you're right. It's beyond weird.*

And until he said at least that much, I couldn't very well admit to how far beyond weird *I'd* gone.

"Are you sure you're okay, Becks?" Blake reached a hand out to me, forehead crumpling in concern. "If this is too much, we can always go."

"No, I'm fine." *Exhale all the way from the hole in your back where the knife went in, and place your hand in his.* "I think I just need a walk. Something to clear my head. Who knows, maybe I'll finally find one of those secret clues."

"Okay." Blake's eyes stayed on me, his eyebrows still tented, but he dropped my hand. "Be safe, alright? I'll be here when you get back."

"Sure," I said, forcing a smile until I could make my way back through the door and out into the narrow, dark hallway where I could finally, paradoxically, *breathe.* I started across the tile toward the entryway, moving faster and faster, hands clenching and unclenching as I went.

Sure you will.

SEVENTEEN

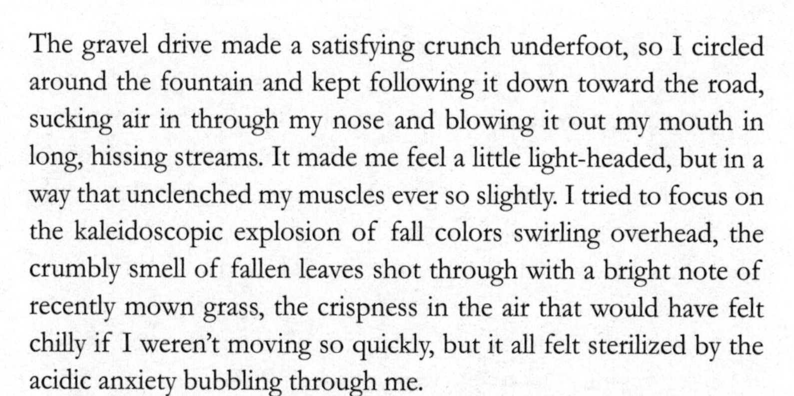

The gravel drive made a satisfying crunch underfoot, so I circled around the fountain and kept following it down toward the road, sucking air in through my nose and blowing it out my mouth in long, hissing streams. It made me feel a little light-headed, but in a way that unclenched my muscles ever so slightly. I tried to focus on the kaleidoscopic explosion of fall colors swirling overhead, the crumbly smell of fallen leaves shot through with a bright note of recently mown grass, the crispness in the air that would have felt chilly if I weren't moving so quickly, but it all felt sterilized by the acidic anxiety bubbling through me.

I slowed my pace as I reached the dappled shade beneath the trees—I didn't have another day dress if I completely pitted this one out—but my heart rate refused to come down, throat-gripping anxiety hammering away in exertion's place.

Dear lord, would it always be like this? The moments of connection and joy completely subsumed by oceans of anxiety and guilt and bone-deep hurt any time he smiled at someone pretty?

The worst part was the logical part of my brain was telling me I was creating phantoms out of dust, but I could barely hear it over the body-trembling bass thump of emotion pulsing through me. And there was no one I could talk to, no one I could turn to for insight.

The way I found out was so clichéd. We were supposed to be halfway to the Fourth of July party the Playpen founder was throwing in the Hamptons, had a room waiting for us at a hotel near the expansive beach house he'd rented out, but of course Blake's malleable sense of time meant that while I'd been ready for half an hour, he'd only just gotten in the shower. I was sitting on the bed, trying to keep myself from tilting into full-blown annoyance, when his phone lit up on the nightstand. A Slack message from "Lara." Probably whichever HR person was organizing the event wanted to make sure we had all the information, since everyone else was *probably already there.* I clicked on the notification to see whether it was important. Instead I was slapped in the face with

Gonna be hard to keep my hands off you all day

I could hear the shower turning off, so I dropped the phone back on the bed, wiping my hand on the duvet cover, as though that could rid me of contamination, and tried to ignore the churning in my stomach. It was probably . . . meant for someone else. Or an inside joke? Some Playpen thing? It was nothing. It had to be nothing. *Don't be paranoid.*

Less than three hours later, a dark-haired, sharp-featured woman in a string bikini, at least ten years younger than us, was standing in front of me, her hand out.

"Nice to meet you. I'm Lara."

The rest of the day passed in a haze of margaritas and small talk with colleagues of Blake's I barely knew, every moment crackling with static like a radio that's been tuned wrong, just shy of the place on the dial where the experience would snap into crisp clarity. As everyone else got progressively looser, my body just seemed to get heavier and heavier, sodden with suspicion and hurt and embarrassment. Now, looking back, it seems strange I didn't make a scene. Refuse to leave the city until we had it out. But I just felt numb, unable—no, unwilling—to wrap my head around the idea that he might really be cheating. And once we were at the party, some visceral need to keep everything pleasant kicked in, piloted me through all the cheery, insipid conversations, kept a smile on my face. *Do not put people on the spot, do not make a scene* . . . I could almost *hear* my mother in my head. In the end, it took me almost an hour after we slipped into bed—Blake too sun-dazed and half-drunk to realize how silent I'd been in the Uber—to get up the nerve to open his Slack app, to scroll through the proof of his betrayal, going back months, whole seasons of our lives that I'd thought were happy hollowed out in minutes.

I thought I'd scream, cry, hyperventilate, but the conversation felt bloodless, my body so, so cold. Blake's shock, his tears, his performance of contrition, only made me feel nauseous. Then extremely nauseous. Then like I might actually vomit at any moment. That was when I finally told him he had to leave. Blake had frowned, obviously startled.

"What? And go where?"

"I don't care. Anywhere. Just go." I could feel my gorge rising.

"Becks, it's the middle of the night, I don't think I'm good to drive—"

"Get the fuck out. *Now.*"

And beneath the wave of vomit that rushed out seconds after he left the room, the crippling, body-doubling pain. It wasn't just that he'd betrayed me, wasn't even the idea of them together, him bending over to kiss her tenderly while I sat at home on the couch thinking we were still a team. It was the *laziness* of it, the complete unoriginality. He hadn't just cheated, he'd made no real effort to hide it. Seriously, he left his laptop on 99.9 percent of the time, and he had the same PIN for his phone and *every card he'd ever owned.* Either he thought I was too thick to ever find out, or he didn't care if

I did. Or maybe he *wanted* me to find out. Wanted to let me pilot him out of this the way I took charge of most of the big-picture things in our lives, in which case *Jesus* could he really not see how needlessly cruel that was?

I'd called Eve, my college roommate, and poured everything out in a heaving, gulping, choking series of sobs, and she'd said all the right things, reminded me what a catch I was, that it wasn't my fault, that I was strong and fierce and independent and this would *not* break me and she could move into my apartment if I needed someone while I worked through this.

And then a week later, when we met up for coffee, the first question out of her mouth after the requisite *How are you, honey*s, was:

"Have you talked to a lawyer yet?"

It took me at least ten seconds to figure out what she meant. Another beat to find a way to respond.

"Not yet. I'm . . . not sure if that's what I want."

"Oh." And I could see it on her face, like a light switching off, that moment her empathy turned to judgment. After an awkward pause, she finally noted, "Anyway, there's no need to make a decision about that now. You're still processing," and we spent the rest of the coffee in the sort of strained small talk you have at holidays with the relatives you secretly think are monsters.

I never even told Amy what had happened, beyond a vague mention of a rough patch. I'd always known her take on cheating was monochromatic. She'd inherited our mom's view, saw the same bright line there that had left us splitting holidays through most of our childhood. Whereas all I could remember was how tired Mom always looked, how sad her face used to get when she didn't realize we were watching. The heartbreaking bravery of her chirpy "Nope, no one yet" to my grandmother's constant prods about new men in her life.

Once I agreed to therapy, I stopped pretending I'd be telling anyone else what had happened. It would take me weeks of visits to let Blake off the hook of "will we or won't we," but deep down I'd known, the moment I agreed to show up in that sterile midtown office and lay out our lives for a stranger, that I'd forgive him. Or at least I'd try. And if that was true . . . why give anyone else the chance to judge me for it?

I exhaled a shuddering breath, standing still and closing my eyes for just a moment, trying to ride out the discomfort the way my personal therapist (all the therapy practically felt like a second job these days) had told me: *You can control how much you let it affect you, Rebecca.*

Or maybe that was total bullshit and eventually you just got used to the particular shape of the shard of pain left inside you, skin growing back over shrapnel, layer by tissue-thin layer, until it was invisible to the outside world. God, what I wouldn't give for my sweatpants, my Netflix account, and a brand-new season of each and every one of the mystery shows I'd been watching over the last several months, so I could swap between the hard-boiled procedurals, the cozy throwbacks, and the only-this-genius-can-help options to my heart's content. The setting might change, but underneath they were all the same: Something terrible threatened, but every single time there was a solution. Closure. The good were exonerated and the evil was safely tucked away, episode after episode, the unchanging cadence of it pure mental balm.

When it became clear that my therapist was in fact *eminently* wrong about my capabilities, at least at this juncture, and the pressure of it all felt like it was going to pop some vital part of my inner ear, I dug my nails into the butts of my hands, scrunched up my face, turned to the sky, and let out a short, barking scream.

It felt remarkably good. Until I heard the footsteps running down the gravel.

"Are you okay?" Heather's eyes were wide with concern as she emerged from around the side of the house, her steps slowing as she approached me. She frowned, looking over my shoulder to where the drive snaked off between the trees toward a large outbuilding. "For a minute I thought . . ." She blinked, then turned back to me with effort.

"I'm fine," I tried to force a smile. God, of *course* it had to be Heather who caught me mid-losing-my-mind. "Sorry, didn't mean to scare you, I just . . ." I shrugged. The smile was starting to stretch too far even as my chin began to wobble perilously. The insides of my nostrils stung and I blinked rapidly, trying to get myself under control.

"Do you need me to get Blake?" Her frown was deepening into something like suspicion. Which . . . fair. I probably looked like the origin story of some murderous clown.

"No, no. I uh, I just . . ." I could feel panic rising in my throat as I flailed around for any sort of explanation. "I thought I saw a . . . skunk."

Then, to complete the picture, I burst into manic giggles while simultaneously bursting into tears. Almost instinctively, Heather moved over, slipping her nylon tote to her opposite shoulder and sliding an arm around me in one smooth motion, shushing quietly, huddling her body around mine in a way that reminded me that, despite the ultra-marathoner physique, Heather had always been a mother first.

Maybe because I'd already popped the cork with that stupid scream, or maybe because Heather had always seemed so capable, the kind of person who could make a schedule and an action plan for anything, even feelings, or maybe because I literally couldn't contain it anymore, the verbal vomit was coming up no matter who was there to bear witness, *better out than in,* just like my mom would say while she rubbed slow circles into our backs and held our hair over the toilet . . .

Who even knows why I started blubbering it all out, but I did.

"I'm sorry I'm such a mess. I know I'm acting crazy."

"That's okay."

"It's just Blake, he . . ." I inhaled deeply, eyes rolling heavenward. "He was cheating. For months. And we're trying to work through it, but I'm not sure if we can. And this is the first time we've tried to be like . . . *normal* in forever? But everything just keeps reminding me of it." I snot-choked out something between a laugh and a sob. "I'm not even a jealous person, but now I see him even just *talking* to someone else, and it's like . . ." I bit my lip, a dam against the next surge of tears.

"Oh, honey." She squeezed me a bit tighter. "You poor thing. I had no idea."

After a few seconds of heavy, rattly breathing, it felt like the storm had mostly passed. I swiped at my eyes experimentally, trying for a rueful smile.

"Clearly I'm dealing with it *extremely* well."

"Honestly, yeah. You are." Heather took a step back, smiling gently. "I mean, you've been a little jumpy, maybe a bit . . . *sensitive,* but I just assumed you were on your period or something."

"Have I?" She flashed an amused grimace, eyes darting off to the side. "Sorry about that. And this." I ran my hands through the air on either side of me, a game show hostess displaying herself, the absolute worst of consolation prizes.

"Don't be." Heather's gaze went a bit distant as she stared back to the house. "I think it's brave as hell of you to try to fix it. You two are good together. That's worth fighting for." I exhaled a shuddering breath. It felt like a literal weight had come off my shoulders, like I'd been wearing one of those lead smocks they put on you before an X-ray for months and I only just now had the chance to shed it. I hadn't realized until that moment how much I needed someone else—not a self-help book or an Internet board, someone I trusted, even looked up to—to validate this, to tell me it was okay to even *want* to forgive Blake. Heather gripped my right hand in both of hers, turning back to me with fierce determination in her eyes. "For the record, you can get through this. Trust me, I know from experience." Her lips twisted into a tight, sardonic smile.

I blinked, not quite able to process what she was saying. Did that mean Phil had actually cheated on her? I'd always assumed the flirting was meaningless, a personality quirk. She always took it in stride so well, and their marriage seemed so happy. Was that all just a show they put on when people came to visit? Or . . . was she right? Could you really move past it, so far past it, in fact, that you actually, fully *trusted* each other again?

She must have seen my shock on my face.

"You're surprised?"

"I just never would have guessed. The two of you seem so . . . solid."

"We are," she shrugged, eyes going distant again. "At least in the ways that really matter. Not that it always comes easy, it doesn't. We've had to fight for our marriage too. I'm still fighting for our marriage every single day."

"And . . . you think it's all worth it?" I whispered, hardly daring to hope, so desperately needing her to flash a light at the end of the tunnel, if only so I could guess at how long I'd be stuck in it.

"Absolutely." She bit into the word as if she was wrestling it to the ground, then closed her eyes for a moment, considering her next words. "I know right now it seems impossible, but it starts to hurt less eventually. And then one day you realize you've sort of . . . slid back into place when you weren't paying attention. And whatever you have to do to get back there . . ." She squinted, sighing. "It's okay, Becca. Whatever you have to go through is okay."

"I'm really, *really* hoping you're right about that. Because this is not my best look." I took another deep breath, swiping under my eyes one more time. "On that note, I think I need to wash my face."

"I'll walk you back?"

"That'd be nice."

We started picking our way back up the drive in comfortable silence.

"Are you enjoying this otherwise?" Heather said, gaze sliding over the grounds. "It seems like it might be a nice distraction, at least."

"I think so?" I laughed. "I think some of the generalized . . . *stuff* is making it hard to tell, if that makes sense."

"How do you mean?"

For just a moment I considered telling her my concerns—about Bethany, about the phone, and Manny and Drew and Gabby all acting so strange, and just that gut feeling that something was off—but I'd already just spewed so much crazy at her. Better not to put any more weight on that one.

"It's going to sound silly, but I needed a bathroom during lunch, and when I got back to the room, the door to the patio was open. Blake said he thought it might have been him, but I guess it just spooked me."

"I know you two are in a rough patch, but I don't think he'd make that up . . ." Heather's expression was a hair too gentle, lines around her eyes revealing the anxious undertow of *Just how far gone is Becca?* Good thing I hadn't said more.

"No, you're right. You definitely weren't wrong about the 'jumpy' thing." I rolled my eyes. "Or Blake's other explanation makes sense, too." She raised an eyebrow, urging me on. "He thinks the actors probably came into all our rooms to find the props for the bit with the armoire. I guess maybe . . . they went in through the patio so we wouldn't run into them in the halls? Since our room is on the first floor, I mean."

Heather stopped midstride, frowning hard at the ground, mouth hanging open in a slack little *o*.

"You think they went through our things? Did they *search* them?"

"I don't know. But they had stuff from everyone, it would make sense."

"Are they really allowed to do that?" Her entire face seemed to tighten with every huge flare of her nostrils. "What's in my room is none of their business."

"I honestly don't even know if that's what happened. Point is, I'm clearly a little more keyed up than your average player."

"I'd be keyed up too, if I thought someone had been through my things. I should talk to someone about this."

You could almost see the indignation rising through her thin frame, like mercury shooting up an old-fashioned thermometer. Heather was nothing if not a stickler for the rules.

"It probably wasn't even that, I think Blake just wanted me to know he was listening. You know, taking me seriously."

"Still, if that *were* the case . . . I just assumed people had given them the items, like with your earring—didn't Blake say he'd handed it off in advance?"

"That's right."

"Phil would never have let them touch that watch. It's a *Rolex*. He'd murder someone if anything happened to it. How didn't I realize . . ." Heather murmured, then turned to me, blinking rapidly. "Are you okay if I go on without you? I need to speak to someone about this."

"Go ahead, I'm fine." Frankly, now that the fever had passed, I was starting to feel a little embarrassed about having told her. I was the queen of the pseudo-overshare—the vulgar story or embarrassing moment that looked, at first glance, like opening up. But there's faux-coyly admitting to a dinner party of relative strangers that once you farted at a hilariously inopportune moment and the entire world seemed to stop to notice: *See, this is why Becca is so much fun, she's got no* filter. And then there's telling someone who you not only have to spend another twenty-four hours in *extremely* close quarters with, but who you'll continue seeing socially, that your marriage is midcollapse. Would she tell Phil? I wasn't sure if that would make it better or worse . . .

Heather squeezed my shoulder, leaning forward to look intently into my eyes.

"You really will get through this. You'd be shocked what you can get through in a marriage. But trying to save it, doing whatever you have to in order to make it to the other side . . . you should never regret that, Becca. Never."

"Thanks, Heather," I said, still absurdly grateful for every morsel of reassurance. "And thanks for letting me . . . you know, *explode* on you back there."

"Oh, honey, Isabelle and Olivia are now officially both teenagers. You having a little moment barely registers." She pulled away, and as she did, the tote snagged on me, sliding down her arm and onto the ground before she could stop it.

"Whoops, here, let me help." I bent to pick it up. The bag was shockingly heavy. I glanced inside, but it just looked like a bundle of workout clothes. "Wow, Heather. What have you got in here?"

She grabbed the bag from me, sliding it back onto her shoulder with a tight smile.

"Champagne." She rolled her eyes exaggeratedly. "I knew Phil would forget—we've been married a *very* long time—so I tucked some away in the trunk just in case. I don't want him to see it, but . . ." She shrugged, glancing up at the house. "I figure our anniversary deserves a *little* extra glamour."

"I applaud this decision." She smiled vaguely, eyes still on the house.

"I really should get going before all this starts up again. Sure you're okay?"

I nodded, and with one last squeeze of my shoulder, she hurried up the drive, nylon tote banging rhythmically against her hip with every stiff-backed step, intent in her quest to register her disapproval before the events resumed.

It was only when I was crossing the threshold to the house that it occurred to me: the earring.

My "stolen" item was the earring from the night before. *That* was why there hadn't been anything of mine in the armoire earlier. Every other couple had one item between them—Phil had probably guessed that taking something of Heather's as a "surprise" wouldn't go over well—and ours had been the earring.

My stomach sank. *That's no reason to freak out, Becca, Blake* told *you the door was probably him.* But I couldn't shake the uneasy feeling.

Wouldn't I have noticed it before? And if I hadn't . . . what else wasn't I noticing?

Phil, for one thing. I'd always thought their marriage was so bulletproof, but judging from what Heather said, he'd strayed at least once, maybe more. The flirting in the hallway floated into my mind again. But I still couldn't make it seem anything other than harmless. After all, a fling with a co-worker or a stranger on a business trip is a very different prospect than picking someone up *during* your anniversary weekend.

But not everyone here was a stranger to Bethany. Drew and Gabby knew her and they were hiding it, and Manny clearly hated her. It struck me again just how little I actually knew about all the people locked up in this hotel with me. I couldn't even tell when they were acting, whether their dropped hints and sidelong glances meant anything or whether they were all just part of the game we were playing.

Bethany's face flitted into my mind again, not as she'd looked behind the counter, cheerily printing key cards, but in the lounge, just after the discovery of the body, terror distorting her pretty features as she propped herself up on the bar.

"One of them—one of *you*—is a murderer!"

It was the whole point, the classic locked-room mystery. Blake had said as much again over lunch: No one has come or gone since the murder happened, ergo *one of us* must be responsible.

It was true for the game . . . but wasn't it true for Bethany, too? No one had been in or out since sometime Friday afternoon, all the staff stayed on the grounds during the weekends. Unless she'd managed to slip away without a car, without her phone, without a *trace,* someone here was involved.

I tried to force myself to be logical. She *might* have left. But what could be important enough to make her go so suddenly? An audition? She'd have taken her phone, if only for directions to the address. A family emergency? She'd at least *pack* for that, right? She could have taken a run and twisted her ankle . . . but who would do that after midnight on a dark woodland road?

Try as I might to mold an explanation into a shape that made some sense, I kept coming back to the one crouching at the back of my mind, skeletal and sharp: *Something must have happened to her. Something bad.*

And someone here was responsible for it.

EIGHTEEN

I couldn't face Blake. If I tried to explain all the imprecise, uneasy feelings swirling through me, he'd just shut down in that specifically Blake way where he kept nodding and mm-hmming in appropriately "concerned" tones while his eyes glazed over. We'd talked in therapy about how problems he couldn't fix made him feel helpless, useless, how knowing that people were in pain overloaded his circuits . . . which had led him to more than a few bad decisions, obviously. I wondered sometimes if Lara had seen that need in him, the almost visceral desire to make people happier, and had used it to draw him in. I wasn't quite curious enough to risk knowing the answer. But there was still half an hour until our next event, so instead of walking back into the main house, I veered off the drive, following a little footpath that skirted the eastern wing toward the gardens at the back.

Off to my right, thick woods pressed up around the edges of a charming stone cottage, probably some old gamekeeper's house. I wandered over to peer through the windows. Most of the furniture in the front room had been draped with heavy canvas, though the chair nearest the fireplace was uncovered. A wide, knotty slab of wood served as a mantelpiece, a single brass candlestick on the right-most edge its only adornment. I craned my neck around to see farther into the room, but all I could make out was an empty antique firewood rack on the far side of the hearth, its brass surface winking in the light from the window. I moved around the side of the building to another window. Through a gap in the curtains, I could make out a bare mattress next to a rustic dresser. It seemed clear that the place had been closed up for the season. I moved around to the front again, trying the door for good measure, but it was locked. *Not part of the game, then.* Though maybe they opened it up again over the holidays? An image of Blake and me huddling in front of a roaring fire with books and cocoa, just far enough away from the main building for it to feel like a private retreat, sprang to mind.

We'd be better by then, wouldn't we?

I drew back, swallowing against the lump in my throat, and hurried back onto the path. *Don't get ahead of yourself, Becca. Just focus on the present before you start building gingerbread fantasies of the future.*

I picked my way along the side of the house, trying to let all the nature soothe my frayed nerves. A dense blanket of grey cloud had rolled in since morning, so low to the ground that the trees climbing up the distant hillsides seemed to dissolve into it. It pressed down heavily, an impenetrable dome trapping everything beneath—including us—in eerie stillness. Despite all the open space in every direction, I was starting to feel vaguely claustrophobic.

The sound of a man and a woman speaking in low, intent voices drifted through the windows of the small library. *Maybe one of the "extra" clues the housekeeper kept talking about? They probably sat in there, replaying the scene, for the entire hour between rounds so we'd all have a chance to "uncover" it.* The distraction was beyond welcome, so I crept up under the windows until their voices became clear.

"Where do you want me to start?" the man said, voice flat with strain or exhaustion.

"The beginning." Some rustling sounds, then the woman coughed. *"You were sleeping with her? Did anyone else know?"* I thought I recognized the vaguely British accent as the housekeeper's.

"Just us. It had to be that way. She already had the old guy on the line. If he found out . . . she'd have lost everything. We both would have."

"You don't know that . . ."

"C'mon, Jen, I know you'd have fired her in a second."

"Manny—"

My whole body tensed at her suddenly clipped tone. Jen? Manny? I'd thought this was a set piece, but if they were using their real names . . .

Manny sighed heavily, voice softening a bit.

"Sorry, sorry. I know. It's just . . . you know how stressful this all is."

"Of course I do. But you have to compartmentalize, at least until the weekend's over. We both know what Drew and Gabby are capable of. Right now, I don't think they realize we know what they're planning. But you saw what they did to Barrington. If anything else goes wrong . . ."

Drew and Gabby? Did they *all* know each other? The swirl of thoughts was almost starting to make me dizzy.

"I said I know." I could feel the tension between them arcing out the window into the air. It crackled for a moment, then Manny sighed. *"Anyway."* He sucked in a deep breath, voice returning to the thin lilt from earlier in the conversation. *"He's here this weekend. Her guy. I got to thinking, if he knew about me and her . . ."*

For a moment the voices grew too low to hear. I wrapped my arms around myself, shivering as a colder wind blew through my thin dress.

"The gun's in the drawing room, make sure no one sees it. And find somewhere to put this, we'll figure out what to do with it when they're gone," Jen said.

Then the voices started to move out of range, hinges creaked genteelly . . . Drawing in a breath, I twisted around to peer through the windows just as the door to the library slammed shut behind a stiff, black-gowned figure.

They were clearly talking about Bethany. Manny seemed to be trying to convince Jen that someone else was behind the disappearance, this mysterious "other man." I couldn't tell if she was buying it, but regardless, she knew *something* had happened to Bethany, and she was clearly trying to help Manny cover it up. Which meant whatever Manny was supposed to get rid of . . .

I darted along the side of the house, trying to stay low, until I reached the side door near the guest rooms. I could just make out a swish of black tux tails at the opposite end of the hallway, turning left into the main lobby. *And no sign of Jen, thank god.* Heart thudding in my ears, I pulled open the door and padded down the hallway, trying my best to look nonchalant, which meant I was probably halfway to having a giant neon LOOK AT ME sign hovering overhead.

I stopped just before the carpet gave way to marble tile. I could hear Manny's wingtips clicking lightly against the surface, but the room distorted the sound, made it seem to come from everywhere. Was he about to catch me? Disappearing down the opposite hallway any second? I squeezed my eyes shut tight. I had to know what they were trying to hide. For Bethany . . . and for me.

Sucking in a deep breath, I started across the lobby, making for the main doors to the driveway. If he'd dashed up the stairs, I'd be able to spot him, otherwise . . . hopefully I could find him somewhere along the other wing.

But I was in luck. I was just passing the staircase when Manny popped up from behind the concierge desk, eyes a little wild as he turned toward me.

"Sorry, did I frighten you?" I forced out a laugh, then tried to remember the accent I'd been using the night before, a heaping mound of indiscriminate aww-shucks. "Mama always said I have cat feet. Used to scare the daylights out of her at least once a week."

Manny's face relaxed into an unreadable half-smile.

"It's no problem, Miss. I do tend to startle easily."

I slowed, hoping he'd leave the desk, but he stayed where he was.

"Is there anything I can help you with?"

"Just the time, if you don't mind. I wanted to take a stroll down the drive but I couldn't bear to be late."

He glanced down at the desk.

"Two forty-three, Miss."

"Then I'll just have to be quick!" With a lash-fluttering giggle, I continued to the main door, pushing it wide . . . and glanced back just in time to see him duck behind the desk again.

It had to be in there. Whatever *it* was. I stood outside, balling and unballing my fists, trying to ignore the tingling in my fingers and toes. Ten seconds . . . twenty . . . thirty . . . surely that had to be long enough. If it wasn't, hopefully he'd buy that I'd forgotten my sweater. I tugged the door open again and peered around it . . .

But the lobby was empty. I waited for footsteps, voices, anything to show that I wasn't alone, but the only sound was the faint echo of the door hinges ricocheting around the cavernous room.

I tiptoed to the desk, squatting behind it as soon as I could, and tugged open a drawer. Piles of blank plastic key cards. The next held toiletries—toothbrushes and razors, the things I always forgot to ask for at hotels. Below that a filing drawer, to the right of the stack a cupboard hiding a printer and office supplies.

Had I been wrong? Had he already stashed *it* somewhere else? I was about to give up, when I saw that the bottom file drawer stuck out a bit. I pressed it closed, and it rebounded. With one anxious glance around the room, I tugged it out as far as possible, snaking my hand over the tops of the folders, reaching behind the drawer for something, anything . . .

My hand rested on some sort of stiff fabric. I tugged it free, scraping my forearm in my hurry. Pressing the drawer closed with a toe, I sped out from behind the desk, crumpling the fabric beneath my armpit as I walked. My hands shook as I swiped the key at the door to our room once . . . twice . . . on the third time it finally opened and, with a whole-body liquefying sensation, I burst inside, pushing it closed behind me and flipping the hasp for good measure.

Once my heart rate descended from "hummingbird" to merely "call your doctor *now*," I shook out the bundle of fabric.

It was an apron, wrinkled by the time in the drawer (and my armpit), but clearly the same pinafore style Bethany had been wearing last night. And in the center . . .

A ragged hole radiating dried blood.

I tried to suck in air, but my lungs wouldn't comply, my chest heaving as I got more and more light-headed. I stumbled over to the chair near the vanity, the bloody apron talon-gripped in one hand. It was Bethany's costume. Covered in blood. And Jen had wanted to hide it. What had she said about the gun? And Drew and Gabby? A roaring sound filled my ears as I stared at the soiled fabric, the rusty splatter seeming to tentacle outward, threatening to wrap itself around me.

Suddenly a door creaked, and I barked out a scream. *They found you, they know you know, dear god what's going to* . . .

But it was just Blake, pushing through from the patio.

"Sorry, I didn't mean to scare you." He smiled vaguely as he crossed the room, but he didn't really seem to *see* me. One arm was supporting an open laptop, and his eyes were already back on the screen.

"Blake, I think maybe . . ."

"Hold that thought, I just need to focus on this email, then you'll have my undivided attention."

"No, Blake, listen. I just overheard a couple of the staff talking about hiding something, and it clearly had to do with Bethany going missing, so I followed them, and I found . . ."

I held the apron up in front of me, the words seeming to tangle around my tongue. Blake glanced up, then grinned.

"Damn, did you find one of those secret clues? I knew I shouldn't have let myself get bogged down in work stuff."

"It's not that. I think . . ." I glanced over my shoulder reflexively, to make sure no one was close, and nearly jumped out of my skin. The mirror over the vanity showed a too-pale face, wild dark curls, and the ghoulish black hollows my mascara had made of my eyes. Gulping, I turned back to Blake. "I think this is something else, Blake. Bethany going missing wasn't a coincidence, I—"

"Mmm? Sorry, I need to focus on this, Becks."

I blinked, his dismissal not fully registering. How could he not see how important this was? Too keyed up to even feel annoyed, I went into the bathroom and slammed the door behind me, leaning heavily on the sink and sucking in air until my body felt like it had settled back into place beneath my skin. Sighing, I turned on the tap, holding a hand under it to track the temperature.

Breathe . . . *in around the knot of anxiety that used to be your stomach, out through the gaps your logic is leaping over.*

Because that was still a possibility, right? I knew I wasn't thinking clearly—between the thick, woolly feeling just behind my eyes I always got the day after I cried, and the hangover, and the fact that I was a *little* on edge lately, there was a reasonable possibility I was blowing this out of proportion. Probably some part of the conversation *was* about the game; their voices had kept switching tone, though it was hard to pinpoint when, exactly, from beneath the library windows. So then, which parts mattered? The man, Drew and Gabby, the gun . . . it couldn't all be nothing, could it?

Still, any *single* bit of it could be. Drew and Gabby could just be tedious guests, and there was no way of knowing whether the apron, or the gun, or even most of the conversation was just a prop in the game.

Dammit, how could I figure out what was real and what was just for show?

I splashed some water on my face and glanced at the crumpled fabric. *She wasn't in costume when you saw her last, Becca.* Which didn't mean the apron *wasn't* evidence . . . but that would be the first thing Blake latched on to.

I tried to imagine explaining it to him, tried to imagine his responses so I could refute them . . . or possibly let them soothe me.

C'mon, Becks. It has to be part of the game.

But why were Manny and Jen so worried about Drew and Gabby? How did they all know one another? Most important, *where had Bethany gone?*

Anywhere. Some people are just flaky. And according to everyone who knew her, she had a history of not showing up to work. Doesn't sound like she had any friends on staff. Why would *she tell anyone if she was planning to leave?*

But her *phone.* And her *keys.*

Not everyone has their phone on them all the time. Plus, it hasn't even been twenty-four hours, she might come back for it by dinner. Besides . . . you once forgot your phone inside a washing machine.

Okay, but prenatal vitamins make *everyone* absentminded!

I gritted my teeth. Even in my head, Blake's implacable *logic* was frustrating. How dare he be so reasonable? Though maybe he'd see it my way if I just explained it clearly enough?

But then I thought about how much he hated loose ends, not to mention the thousand slivers of glass strewn on the ground between us, and I knew I wouldn't chance it. Even if he didn't actually tell me I was being paranoid, or that it was part of the game, I'd be waiting for him to say it, hunting for that first trace of tone to sink my teeth into and shake back and forth until the conversation was maimed and bloody on the floor between us. Even if he agreed with 98 percent of my wildest speculations, the chance that some word or phrase or look would raise my hackles, and we'd fight again, and I'd wind up feeling even fuzzier and jumpier and just more *miserable* than before, was . . . high. Very high, actually.

Sighing, I pushed open the bathroom door and slid the apron to the back corner of the closet. *He'd never look at it.*

"*Annnd* sent. What did you want to tell me?" Blake turned to me, eyes bright.

"Nothing. I thought I found a clue but it might just be a bar rag."

"The two are remarkably similar."

I forced myself to return his grin. Until I had something solid, I needed to deal with this on my own, for both our sakes.

We were just heading out to the next event when I decided to take Bethany's phone with me, telling myself it was in case she returned for it (but knowing I was itching for a free moment to try to unlock it again). As I slid it into my pocket, my fingers caught on something stiff.

I pulled out the thick black card Drew had left in the suite upstairs. On the front was the graphic of the noose. On the back, three words, in gory foiled red:

It was murder.

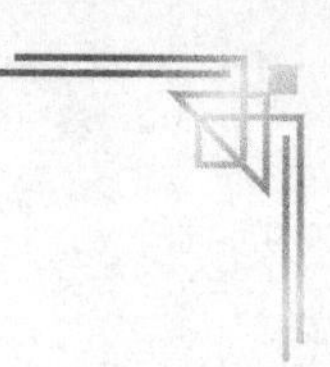

ROUND FOUR

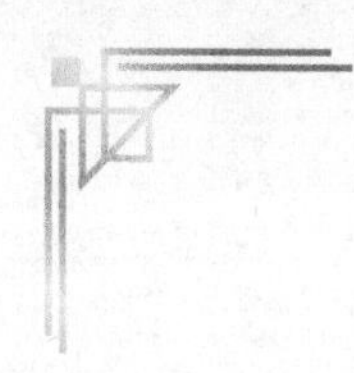

SEARCH PARTIES

A house like this was built to hold secrets. Miss Crooner's . . . and all your fellow guests'.

Each of you has been assigned a partner to help you in your search. Work together to find the clue that's been hidden in your section of the house or grounds. If you find it, you can decide whether to share this information with the rest of the group or keep it to yourselves. A murderer's in your midst, after all. You wouldn't want to be caught unawares . . . or caught out by the rest of the guests.

You've been assigned to search the attic.

Here's a hint to help you get started:

Ida's pipes have made her name,
Brought her fortune, stardom, fame!
She came up from a gritty scene,
And now she's New York's reigning queen.
But that jazz baby likes a strange mixture
Of low and high. You get the ***picture?***
Be careful, when you're on the makes
You might attract the gaze of rakes.
Or jealous fellows who couldn't stand
To lose you to another man . . .

Look high and low, you never know what you might turn up. And hoof it! You might not have as much time as you think . . .

When the gong sounds, turn the page . . .

NINETEEN

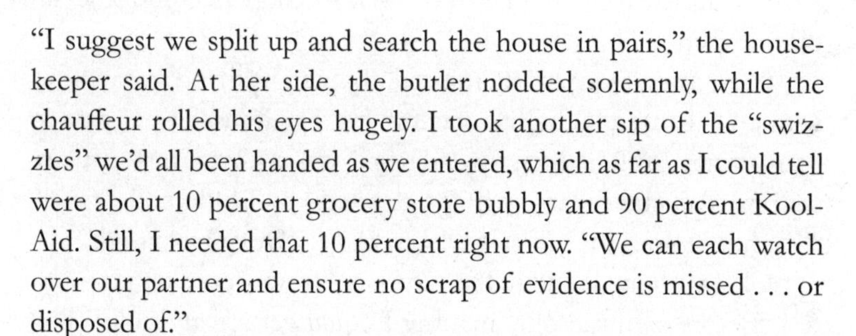

"I suggest we split up and search the house in pairs," the housekeeper said. At her side, the butler nodded solemnly, while the chauffeur rolled his eyes hugely. I took another sip of the "swizzles" we'd all been handed as we entered, which as far as I could tell were about 10 percent grocery store bubbly and 90 percent Kool-Aid. Still, I needed that 10 percent right now. "We can each watch over our partner and ensure no scrap of evidence is missed . . . or disposed of."

She narrowed her eyes, raking them over each of us in turn. As soon as she'd moved past me, I focused on her face even more intently. Was she sweating slightly? Surely if she'd actually had anything to do with whatever happened to Bethany, she wouldn't be able to hold it together like this. Unless the bad acting was all part of a *bigger* act. Or maybe Manny had fooled her about something crucial.

Dear lord, had I seriously convinced myself that the murder mystery weekend I was attending was the scene of *an actual murder*?

I could practically hear the cheesy thunder-peal soundtrack in my head.

Just drink your drink and try to look calm, Becca.

"Madam, if I might suggest we draw names? It would be the most *democratic* method." The butler twisted up his nose in vague disgust at the notion, but the housekeeper nodded.

"Excellent idea, Wynnham. We can use the candy dish. We'll have one pair search the cellars, another can cover the back garden, a third can search the ballroom—it is just below Miss Crooner's rooms, after all. The last pair can search the attic."

After some fussing with a notepad and an elaborate show of writing each of our names and dropping them into the frilled bowl Wynnham produced, she held it out to the chauffeur.

"Putters? Would you be so kind?"

"I don't know what you think they're gonna—"

"*Mister* Putters, might I remind you that your own name has been tarnished recently? You'd do well to cooperate until the authorities arrive."

"Yes, Miss Thrope," he minced, dipping his hand in the bowl with a final sneer. "The first victim . . ." The housekeeper gasped dramatically. "Oh, lighten up, lady, that was a joke. Anyway, we're starting with the cellars, yeah?" She gave a stiff little nod. "Swell. That honor goes to . . . Peter Oleum and . . . Dolly Diamond."

Gabby grinned at Phil. His return smile was more tepid.

"Before we head out, any way I could get a real drink?" Phil smirked at the butler. "I'd say put it on my tab, but that's your tab now, right?"

"What were you hoping for, sir?"

He rolled his eyes, patting his suit coat for a moment before retrieving a flask. He unscrewed it and proceeded to pour the contents over the ice left in the bottom of his swizzle cup.

"Don't worry, Wynnie, I come prepared. Fill this up again and we'll call it square." He grinned at the rest of us. "My daddy always said, you can take the man out of Texas, but you can't take the flask out of a Texas man's pocket."

I glanced at the liquid in his glass, tinted palest pink from the swizzle remnants. After the fuss he'd made over not wanting Heather to know how tipsy he'd gotten, why down straight liquor now? Everything I knew about them was starting to seem flimsier than I'd realized after Heather's conversation in the garden. Was his drinking another problem they'd managed to keep out of sight? Phil always maintained that specifically Wall Street veneer no matter what was going on around him, never dropping the confident smile that I was only now realizing papered over more than I'd ever guessed. The major firms must all include a personality-Teflon clause in the contracts.

The chauffeur kept plucking out names while the butler carefully filled Phil's flask. Reid and Maria in the ballroom. Scoops and Bugsy in the gardens. Which just left . . .

"Miss Lulu Larksong and Miss Debbie Taunte, looks like you two broads are a team." Jessica raised her eyebrows gleefully at me. I felt myself smiling automatically. It's *hard* not to smile back at really beautiful people. Plus, it was probably better not to be paired with the couple that might have had something to do with Bethany's disappearance, though I couldn't help but feel a little disappointed.

"If you'll all open your personal dossiers and turn the page labeled 'Search Parties.'" The housekeeper looked us all over. "Excellent. As soon as you're ready, Wynnham, Putters, and myself can lead each pair to your designated search area. With all of you covering the important sections of the house, Wynnham and I can secure Putters in his quarters and turn our eyes to the staff rooms. I'm starting to think our maid's absence might have more . . . *sinister* causes. Guest rooms, of course, are off limits even to ourselves." Heather gave a curt nod of approval, and I couldn't help but smile. She might have made a big show of wanting to be sure her privacy was protected, but I had a feeling that *specific* trip to the manager had been mainly for my benefit, a twist on the mother's instinct to buy ice cream when facing a problem you can't solve for a child, hoping against hope it would at least fix something adjacent.

"Please do not leave the room or area you've been assigned to until the gong sounds."

A few minutes later, Wynnham opened a slim door tucked in the juncture between the second floors of the west and central wings, revealing a long, narrow flight of stairs.

"You'll find the attic above, ladies. Good luck." With a furrowed look of concern and a final bow, he turned and strode off down the hall.

"After you?" Jessica gestured to the staircase and I nodded, hand tight on the worn wooden banister as I ascended the steep stairs.

They let out at the end of a long hall that stretched the entire length of the central wing. Overhead, the ceilings sloped steeply, following the pitch of the roof. The walls that ran along either side of the room were barely four feet high, occasional dormers along the right-hand side—where the front of the house would be—breaching the claustrophobically low surface every thirty feet or so. Weak puddles of light sloshed in around their edges, thinned on their way through the sieve of grey cloud that was hanging lower and lower over the mansion. The wall and ceiling running along the front side of the house had been papered with what must once have been a cheery floral print, but years of neglect had left it faded and water-splotched, the edges curling and withered where it hadn't fully torn away. The other half of the room had walls and ceilings of bare plaster, yellowed a bit by age, and more in places where water had seeped through the roof.

A long, rough strip of unvarnished wood near the center of the space ran the entire length of the attic floor, mirroring a central exposed beam that ran along the underside of the roof's crest. Every so often both were intersected by a half-wall stretching down to the back side of the house. On most of these, irregular sections of plaster had crumbled away from the beams beneath, giving the dark little nooks an eerie, gap-toothed look. Three gigantic chimneys, the bricks soft-edged with age, stood sentinel over the room, their surfaces slightly hazy beneath the shimmering veil of dust in the air.

In the first . . . pocket? It wasn't really a room, just the approximation of one, as though the attic had been deliberately divided to maximize dark corners. Anyway, off to the left of where we were standing was a spindly tower of rusting twin bed frames.

"Welp—that's even creepier than I expected." Jessica was standing just behind me, pointing to the teetering advertisement for tetanus with the edge of her dossier. "If our clue's in there, let's just pretend we found it and decided to keep it to ourselves, deal?"

"Deal," I said with a laugh, reaching over to flick on the ancient-looking light switch mounted just inside the door. A handful of sconces along the right-hand wall buzzed noisily to life, their yellow light revealing frosted glass shades streaked with grime, the ornate brass mounts below tarnished.

Jessica moved past me, glancing between the ceiling beam, the central unvarnished strip of flooring, and the left-hand walls.

"There must have been a wall here," she murmured, miming one through the air. "And doors. Look, you can see where it would have gone, the flooring is different. And these would have divided the servant bedrooms," she added, pointing at the remnants of the nearest half-sized wall. I blinked—once she pointed it out, the absence was obvious, but I wouldn't have noticed it myself. *Helpful reminder, Becca: Pay attention to the details if you think you're going to solve an actual crime.*

Together, we made our way past the first wall. The next pocket held a small table pushed up against the wall, a simple white vase filled with faded silk flowers cocooned in cobwebs the only item on top of it. Next to me, Jessica shivered elaborately, wrapping a hand around my arm and squeezing.

"*So* spooky. I love it."

We moved along to the next room, clearly a bathroom at some

point. A chipped enamel tub dominated one wall, a spindly cluster of pipes spidering up and over the edge. A plain pedestal sink stood opposite, a simple mirror tucked between its base and the wall behind. The floor was still tiled, a dizzying array of hexagons.

"Pretty luxurious for servants."

"What, were you expecting chamber pots?" I asked. "I looked online, apparently this place was a private home through the sixties."

"Honestly? The servants' bathroom needs hadn't really occurred to me. Do you think it still works?" She pointed at the old-fashioned toilet at the back, the water tank mounted high on the wall, a chain trickling down from one side.

"I'm just hoping there's nothing scary enough up here to make me find out." Jessica laughed softly, then drifted past me, peeking around the edge of the first chimney.

"Jackpot. I've found the steamer-trunks-and-artfully-decrepit-furniture section."

I picked my way over to her, decades of dust clouding around my feet with every step. The wall between this room and the next seemed to have been deliberately stripped down, leaving a row of bare two-by-fours as a very gappy fence between them. Both halves were filled with the kinds of things you only ever saw in antique stores: three wooden washstands, their glazed ceramic basins in various states of chipped; an old-fashioned telephone table, the red-and-gold brocade of the seat worn through at the center, revealing a nimbus of stuffing; an absolutely baffling piece that looked like a table without a top, its four curving legs held in place at both top and bottom with matching filigree rectangles, their delicate twists and twirls darkened with neglect. Books were piled with studied haphazardness on top of the furniture, and framed paintings and photographs were stacked several deep against the back wall. And of course there were the promised steamer trunks, conveniently propped open to reveal piles of suspiciously intact gowns, gloves, and stoles.

The rest of the attic felt legitimately abandoned, a remnant of the house's earlier life. This was clearly set design.

Jessica tugged the top off a hatbox at her feet and plucked out a suspiciously bright straw boater, moving over to place it on my head. She smiled and took a step back, hands on hips.

"You should take that."

I bent to catch myself in the mirror mounted above the nearest washstand. Actually . . . it was kinda cute, even if it was more Williamsburg than my usual style. I tilted it back a bit, studying the effect. Jessica caught my eye in the reflection.

"Don't pretend you don't know it looks good on you."

"Still, I think the staff will notice if I'm wearing one of their props."

"I didn't say you should *wear* it." She raised her eyebrows impishly. I smiled faintly and pulled the hat off, hanging it on the post of the mirror's frame.

"We'll see."

I slid between the two-by-fours, crossing to a walnut dresser, a faded porcelain shepherdess with a crack running up her coyly displayed petticoat—*how risqué*—reclining on the top. I tugged the top drawer back and forth until it jerked open. A stray pair of gloves was the only thing inside. I bent to tug open the next.

"Does this seem important?" When I turned, Jessica was wrapping one of those heads-still-on fur collars around her neck with a flourish. She flapped the long-gone little weasel's paw with two fingers.

"Not unless you think the secret killer was rabies." She laughed, tugging the fur loose and dropping it back into the trunk. "It's probably in one of those," I added, pointing at the stacks of frames leaning against the back wall. "'Picture' was the only word in the poem in bold."

"Good point. I guess I was so blinded by the lyricism that I glazed right over that."

"You noticed the floor thing, though," I said. "I should probably be more observant."

"That's just because Josh's work friends are always droning on about architectural details. They've ruined me."

I sensed Jessica moving up behind me. She leaned close, head just over my shoulder as she murmured "Finding anything good?"

"Not yet." I flashed a quick grin, then moved over to the first stack of frames, squatting down to flip slowly through them, making a show of turning each over to look for hidden documents or a too-obviously-torn corner of the backing. Jessica slipped back into the other half of the room for a moment before moving up next to me again, unfolding a faded, worn quilt on the floor in front of the wall. She sat on one half, patting the other invitingly. "Thanks," I said, settling down on the fabric, offering another tight smile before I turned back to my stack, feigning intense interest in a framed Currier and Ives print, as though the clue might be hidden between its snow and horses and women in muffs.

"It's okay, you know." I glanced over at Jessica. She was biting her lower lip, staring at the side of my face.

"What's okay?"

"If you're having second thoughts. About tonight, I mean. We won't be offended if you'd rather just stick to yourselves."

I flipped the frame, frowned at the backing. I'd thought I'd been convincingly friendly, *Who cares if my husband likes talking to the young, beautiful guest, certainly not me!* But apparently my acting was approximately on par with the housekeeper's.

"Why would you think that?" I set the picture aside, risking a quick glance at Jessica before grabbing the next from the stack, a faded photograph of an extremely solemn, plain little girl, in a stiff pinafore and even stiffer curls, cradling a doll.

"You just seem a little . . . 'standoffish' is too strong, but I can't think of a better word." I caught Jessica's shrug out of the corner of my eye. "Point is, we'd still really love to have you—both of you—but I get if you're having buyer's remorse."

A slick of oily guilt slid through me. I'd always hated making anyone else uncomfortable. Even when I was little, Mom had always called me "the peacemaker." Amy just called me a pushover. She'd been kind of evil as a teenager.

"It's not that, it's just . . ." I turned my gaze to the ceiling, unsure how to defuse this without going into a whole sob story again. I didn't regret telling Heather, precisely, but now that I'd vomited it all out and the pressure of it wasn't threatening to pop through my eyeballs anymore, it seemed a little melodramatic to air all that laundry to a relative stranger. Finally I shrugged. I didn't have to tell her the *whole* truth, just enough of it to make Jessica understand it wasn't her fault. "What can I say? I get jealous when Blake hits it off with beautiful women."

"Then forget Blake."

I sniffed.

"Seriously, I couldn't care less if he comes along. I'm much more interested in you." She smiled softly at me.

"You might be the first person to ever say that," I said, twisting my mouth to the side, half-hating myself for fishing so openly.

But it's how you feel. The voice inside was small, but unignorable. Maybe that was what was *really* hard for me to get past, more than the cheating, or even the lying: the nagging sense that, at the end of the day, I just wasn't that *interesting.* That the flaw wasn't in Blake, but in me. That underneath the big personality at parties and the self-deprecating jokes and the literal *costumes* I made such a big deal of planning months in advance, I was really just a slightly different pattern on the same basic look: middling marriage, just-interesting-enough job, biding time until you can move to the suburbs and have a baby and fully lean into a life of boring predictability, where you trade away novelty and passion for the twin comforts of knowing exactly what's waiting for you at the end of every day and a sharply increased "night pants to outfits where you actually try to look good" ratio. Worse . . . that Blake had finally woken up to it. That he'd finally glimpsed the real, desperately dull me.

Honestly, who wouldn't want an escape hatch out of *that*?

"I'm not sure how that's possible." Jessica leaned forward, placing her hand over mine and squeezing lightly. "Not that Blake's not great, but have you seen yourself? You're totally carrying the two of you."

"You're just trying to butter me up 'cause we're stuck in an attic together."

Jessica leaned farther forward, eyelids lowering, lips parting slightly . . .

"No. That's just a bonus."

And then, before I'd fully processed what was going on, she was leaning in to kiss me, her mouth soft and full against mine. I inhaled sharply, and some sort of feral instinct kicked in without my consciously approving it, and suddenly I was kissing her back, pressing forward, eager, shivers running down my spine as she trailed her hand up my arm to lightly cup the back of my neck.

And then the *What are you doing Becca what the actual fuck is happening right now* alarm finally sounded in my head and I pulled away sharply, trying to ignore the way it made my breath hitch to do it.

"I . . . that wasn't . . ." I blinked and bit my lip, scooting back along the blanket. Jessica's eyes widened as she took in the look on my face.

"Please tell me you wanted that to happen . . ."

I shook my head, words totally failing me.

"But . . . last night in the bar . . ."

I blinked again, trying to slot the pieces into place.

"Wait . . . you were *hitting* on me?"

"I thought you knew that."

"Why would I know that? I'm *married*." My voice was at least an octave too high. "Anyway, all you said was you wanted me to come up to your room for a *drink*."

"Well, yeah, because the bartender was right there. But I thought . . ." Jessica's entire face twisted into a grimace. "Oh my god, I'm sorry, I read that *so* wrong."

Embarrassment at what had just happened between us warred with a vague sense of superiority. Jessica and Josh *were* pretty attractive, after all. Especially Jessica. *And she hadn't even wanted Blake, she wanted* you.

"It's okay," I murmured, trying not to stare at her lips. Because of course now all I could think about was kissing her again. *C'mon, Becca, pull it together.* I swallowed, the heat in my face practically volcanic, and turned back to the stack of picture frames, just to have somewhere to look. "I get . . . friendly when I've had a couple drinks, I get how you might have thought . . ." I tried to focus on the image in front of me, an uninspired landscape filled with an assortment of stiff-looking animals, as though they'd been poorly taxidermied then returned to their natural habitats.

"Oh my god, please don't blame yourself. It was stupid to think . . . I mean what, just because I think you're hot, that means you're into me too? And Blake wasn't there with you, I shouldn't even have . . . *Christ,* talk about amateur hour."

We flipped through the frames in awkward silence for a few moments. Once all my pheromones had been tucked away again, the rest of my brain started working through it.

"So, Blake . . ." I finally ventured. Jessica cocked her head at me, but said nothing. "Were you clearer with him?"

She flushed in an alarmingly pretty way.

"I mean . . . yeah. In my defense, I thought you guys had already talked about it. More generally, that is." Her eyes slid to the side. "He seemed a little caught off guard, but then he said you two *had* talked about doing something like that. Just not recently?"

I knew the exact conversation he was thinking about, maybe three years back now, after a giddy, tipsy dinner party at Moira's, a college friend who'd just moved to the city after almost a decade on the West Coast. It was one of those clearly scraped-together affairs, a who's-who of the people Moira found on Facebook that she still knew reasonably well enough to invite. One of the women—she'd been Brittney in college, but since then had apparently decided that name hinted *far* too strongly at the suburban-white-girl background I knew for a fact we shared, and had therefore decided to start going by some random word I can't remember anymore, something like Grey, or Affectation. Anyway, between regular mentions of something she'd read in the *Paris Review* and offhand intelligentsia-dropping, *Of course ontologically the film is a complete muddle, but viewed as a metaphor for male insecurity in the face of* oh my god who talks like this in real life, Greyfectation had turned to her boyfriend and, with a smug little smile, noted:

"Of course neither of *us* believes in the construct of monogamy." He nodded solemnly, the motion loosing a lank strand of brown hair from behind his ear.

Moira was the first to respond.

"So, what . . . you fuck other people?"

Moira had been getting through her own dinner party via frequent refills of her wineglass. Greyfectation rolled her eyes indulgently.

"It's not off limits. But really, it's more a philosophical position than a sexual one. Leaving our relationship open just feels more *honest.*"

Blake and I had barely made it to the elevator before we were cracking up over Greyfectation's many, many choice tidbits. And we hadn't even hit the street before he turned to me, eyes sparkling with wine and desire, and asked:

"Have you ever wanted to try that?"

"Try what?" I raised an eyebrow, feeling daring and young and devastatingly unconventional in the way only one drink too many can make you feel.

"An open relationship."

"Not particularly. They've always seemed like a pit stop on the way to breaking up. Like . . . do you actually know anyone who has one that *works*?"

"Fair . . ." He'd turned away, slipped his hands into his coat pockets. "And honestly, I'm not sure I could handle the idea of you being with someone else. At least, not without me there."

For some reason, at the time, that had seemed really *touching*. "What, you'd want to watch?" I grinned, squeezed his arm playfully, trying to convey that it was still us against the world, that not even the idea of some other man could come between us.

"I mean, no. But I dunno. It might be kinda hot if it felt like . . . like it was *us* doing the thing together?"

"Less side piece, more swingers?"

"Exactly." He grinned again, back in the spirit of it.

"I could be into that."

He raised an eyebrow.

"No, really! I mean, we've talked about our crushes before. It's kinda like that, right? It wouldn't be some secret, it'd be . . . a safe way to introduce some variety. It'd be *honest*." When we stopped laughing he turned back to me.

"Seriously, though. Do you think that's something you'd like?"

"If it felt right, I'd be open to the possibility. As long as we did it together."

And somehow just talking about the idea of sleeping with other people had made *our* sex that night so incredibly hot that it never even occurred to me that it probably should have been a warning sign. But of what? How wide, exactly, is the gulf between tipsily flirting with the idea of bringing someone else into the bedroom, and leaving your wife at home alone while you and someone else build a secret world bounded by a wall she's never meant to peek over?

"I think I found it."

Jessica pulled a framed black-and-white photograph of obviously recent vintage out of her stack, tilting it between us. A flapper stood at the center, flanked by two men. The one on her right wore a tux and top hat and was grinning broadly at the camera, his arm around the woman. The man on her left—older, and a bit paunchy—

was staring behind her shoulder at the other man, face contorted with exaggerated fury.

"That's definitely the bartender in the center," I said. "And I think that guy was working in the gardens earlier," I added, gesturing to the middle-aged man.

Jessica shook the frame a bit to bring a white border covered in hand lettering at the bottom more into view.

"Oh good, they've labeled it for us. 'Peter Oleum, yours truly (Ida Crooner), and Reid A. Daily at Bugsy's New York place (the Jazz Baby).' Just in case the poem was too subtle."

I laughed harder than the quip deserved.

"I suppose it's good to know who everyone's meant to be," I said. "So what are we supposed to gather? Peter is Ida's jealous lover? We more or less knew that already, right?"

"I think repetition is a big part of these things. Who knows, maybe the point of the clue is supposed to be Reid. Confirming that he's her lover, I mean, not that he's jealous." Jessica flipped the frame over. A typed piece of paper had been laminated to the back.

> They always say a picture is worth a thousand words . . . and this one's telling you that your fellow guests might be more *intimate* with the murdered Miss Crooner than you realized.
>
> They're always sending **roses.** But as far as Miss Crooner is concerned, those fellas are all **wash(room)ed** up. You should be, too, if you want to proceed to the next round. Follow the clues you've found here and I'm sure you'll learn something **enlightening.**

"So . . . now we look in the weird servants' bathroom I guess? For roses?" I said.

"You really *are* good at this, you know that?" Jessica said, shaking her head appreciatively as she squinted at the words again. "I was about to start searching the picture for flowers and . . . I don't know, 'Ladies' Room' signs or something."

I felt a little surge of triumph blooming in my chest—or was that just lust? *Jesus,* why did Jessica have to be so confusingly attractive?

"I read a lot of mysteries, especially lately. And I watch all the shows," I said. "You start to pick up on the patterns."

"Well *you* do, at least."

I stood first, automatically extending my hand to help Jessica up, then jerking it halfway back as the kiss bobbed to the surface of my memory, then awkwardly putting it out again . . . all of which made things even *more* weird. With a rueful smile, she pushed herself up on her own and we made our way back to the bathroom. We pored over the porcelain and wood fixtures in silence for maybe a minute before I noticed that the brass sconces mounted on either side of the sink were shaped like roses where they met the wall.

"I think I found the roses," I said, pointing. "But . . . I don't know what to do with them."

Jessica moved up next to me, running her fingers over the brass, then stood up on tiptoe to see inside the frosted glass coupe-shaped shade. She shrugged, turning to me, lips slightly parted, revealing a tender, soft-colored strip at the inside where her lipstick had wiped away. I swallowed, trying to will myself not to move away . . . or closer . . .

"I thought maybe there'd be a note inside, but I don't see anything."

"Try turning it on?" I said. "The 'enlightening' bit, you know."

She turned the switch beneath the lamp nearer her. It crackled, then glowed dimly. I frowned, trying the sconce on my side of the sink. It made an electrical buzzing sound, but the light didn't come on.

"All right, I'm officially out of—"

Just then, a speaker in some unseen corner of the attic came to life with a crackling pop, and a low, round bell tone sounded.

"You have complcted the first portion of your search," a voice said through the speaker. "Please turn the page in your dossier."

Then the gong sounded again and the speaker fizzled off. I

flipped open my booklet, grateful to have somewhere to look, and turned to the next page.

HIDE AND SEEK

Lulu's going to try to give you the slip . . . will you let her? Follow her discreetly to learn what she's hiding, or use this opportunity to search the attic for a clue that certainly wouldn't **Currier** favor if she knew you had it.

Once you've found what you're looking for, please turn the page.

"I don't know what your thing says, but mine says to ditch you and . . . I think that might be a good idea?" Jessica grimaced at me across the sink. I couldn't quite trace the sinking feeling in my stomach to a source. "I can tell you whatever I learn, I don't want to screw with your weekend—I mean, any more than I have already. Not that I . . . sorry, this is just super awkward."

"No worries. I'm going to choose *not* to discreetly follow you, since they gave me options," I waved my booklet in the air for emphasis. "And no hard feelings. It was an honest mistake. Besides, how often do I get to make out with new people these days?"

She laughed in obvious relief.

"Great. Okay. I'll . . . see you later, then."

And with that, she hurried back down the length of the attic and out of sight, leaving me and the dusty remnants of the house's past alone.

With a sigh, I crossed back to the stack of frames, flipping through my discards until I found the Currier and Ives print. The brown cardboard backing had a thin line of writing at the bottom: "For Debbie Taunte's eyes only." I flipped open the catches holding it in place and pulled it out to reveal a glamorous black-and-white headshot—it *might* have been Bethany . . . but primped and curled and powdered into a convincing old-Hollywood "girl next door" type, hands folded under her chin, gaze tilted up to the sky, the better to take in distant angelic visions and show off her wide, false-lashed eyes. The border said "Ruth Spitz."

On the back, more handwriting:

> *This is the last of the old headshots, from now on Ruth Spitz of Dubuque is dead and gone and Lulu Larksong is taking her place. Isn't that name just divine? My agent came up with the most delicious backstory for me, all castles and European counts and the high life. I'll tell you all about it next time you come out to sunny California to visit. If you hoof it I might be able to get you an audition for a picture my agent thinks I'm good for. Wouldn't it be grand to be on set together?*
>
> *Keep it hush-hush, though. Apparently we're going all-in on this little deception. He thinks film fans will like a glamorous ex-countess better. So far, casting directors certainly do!*
>
> *See you soon, lots of love and all that. Let me practice my new signature here—someday hopefully it'll be in a lot of autograph books!*
>
> *—Lulu Larksong*

End of that round, then.

I turned the page in my little booklet.

BARGAINING

Join your fellow sleuths at 6:30 p.m. in the dining room for dinner. You can all reveal (or conceal) the things you learned then . . . but will it be enough to catch the killer?

I checked my phone: 5:15. Probably everyone was still searching, or sneaking away, or sneaking after someone sneaking away. And if the other groups had made it through as quickly as I had, and Blake was waiting in our room, I'd wind up telling him what happened, and I still needed to sort through how I felt about it, precisely.

I was annoyed—with everyone, except maybe Josh, he hadn't crossed any lines as far as I knew, at least not yet—but then I tried to think back to the night before, Jessica's sultry smiles, me letting them buy my drink and laughing with them at the bar. I *had* been flirting. Honestly, I always flirted a little with strangers, more when I was in a relationship. It felt safe—*Look, here's my significant other, you can't possibly take this the wrong way*—but with a tiny hint of danger, that little sprinkle of "but we *could* if we wanted" over the top.

I'd just never had anyone assume I meant it that . . . widely before. Was it really my fault for not realizing when I was being tag-team hit on? And really, what had Blake done wrong other than believe what he'd been told? Why wouldn't he, especially when believing gave him a clear path to sleeping with a beautiful stranger, which he'd already demonstrated was a favorite extracurricular?

Intellectually, I was exasperated to realize he must have thought *I'd* want that solution. How could he possibly think the fix for him fucking where he shouldn't was more fucking? But then since the big reveal, there'd been screaming matches, feral sex, a week when I watched the entire *series* of *Endeavour* while he slept on a college friend's couch, more screaming, a breakdown in the grocery store over a display of *kumquats* of all things, complete stonewalling in therapy, more feral sex, and me buying a pack of cigarettes and smoking them out the apartment window as I worked my way through a cheap bottle of wine, like an extra from a cut-rate community theater production of *Rent*. If I was going to be fair, I'd been slightly hard to predict lately. Even—especially—to myself.

Still, who said I owed him fair right now?

Even thinking about all this was starting to make my heart thump wildly against my sternum. Closing my eyes tight and sucking in one deep breath, I decided the emotional safety blanket of the game was the safest option.

I started toward the center of the attic. We'd come from the right, might as well search the area to the left. There could still be a clue up here, even if it was only "the secret of how to kill another few minutes without having to open the mental boxes you really, *really* don't want to open right now, Rebecca Wilson."

I took a few tentative steps past the edge of the next dividing wall. Without Jessica next to me, the eeriness of the attic had multiplied several times over. Somewhere to my right, the faint sound of nails skittering across wood. My heart jumped into my throat, the close, dust-thick air seeming to draw in tighter around me.

It's just a mouse, Becca. You don't care about mice. Or it could be a squirrel on the roof. You're not afraid of squirrels, for goodness' sake.

I kept walking.

The room just past the set piece was nearly bare, containing a bed frame topped by a thin, yellowed mattress pushed up against the dividing wall. Someone had papered this room in the same floral print that covered the long wall of the attic. Patches where the paper was brighter, the colors of the pattern more vivid, scarred the wall, the lingering spectral shadows of paintings, decorations, pictures of friends and family hung to give the narrow room the feel of home. Opposite the bed, a rusting metal clothes rack stood empty except for two simple wooden hangers. I moved over to it, running a finger along the edge of one hanger. It made a small scraping sound and I shivered, backing away from it, and the room, in a few quick steps.

The next room was full of junk. Not picturesque antique junk—this was all much more recent. A half dozen dining room chairs were stacked near the back wall, the veneer chipped away at various points on the legs, the seats and backs covered with a pastel-swoopy fabric that would have looked ultramodern on the set of *Miami Vice*. Deep plastic storage bins were stacked atop one another near me, strips of painter's tape across the front labeling them *Employment Records*

1985–2010, Taxes/financials (thru 2013), Purchase Orders 1982–~~Present~~ Aug. 2007, and other desperately exciting-sounding titles. A dented filing cabinet huddled in the back corner, bottom drawer stuck open at a drunken angle. At the center of the room, four giant cardboard boxes labeled XMAS DECORATIONS waited for their chance to molt the thick skin of dust built up over the last several months . . . or decades. All in all, it felt like the ultimate losing bid on one of those storage-space auction shows.

I moved over to the filing cabinet, tugging the bottom drawer all the way out and bending to peer inside; there was a single hanging file folder, seemingly empty, and a dead spider, shrouded in its own webs. The next drawer up had a few old guest registries, and the top drawer held a stack of carbon paper slips, tessellated with sections for name, room number, and all the things you were being charged for.

If there were any secret clues in this room, I did *not* have the patience—or quantities of allergy medication—necessary to find them. I moved to the next enclosure.

Holy serial killer.

The room had been repurposed, the walls mounted with pegboard, an array of rusting garden tools prickling out from the surface. There were spades, rakes, dented tin snow shovels, pruning shears with wickedly curved blades, seemingly custom-made for finger removal. Cracked lengths of garden hose dribbled over the tops of chipped ceramic planters. One whole wall was hung with various types of saws. I took a step toward them, running a finger over the teeth of a long, thin blade.

"Ouch." I stuck it in my mouth, sucking at what was probably already tetanus. *Brilliant maneuver, Becks.*

I took a step back, looking around the room more slowly. Everything in it was old, covered with rust, dust, or both. Probably it was the room of last resort for the groundskeeper if all his more functional tools crapped out at the same time. I was just turning to leave when I caught them out of the corner of my eye: faint tracks along the floor through the dust, not quite distinct enough to resolve into footprints, more like . . . someone had been shuffling around without fully lifting their feet. I followed the marks with my eyes all the way to the left-hand wall. All the spikes and blades and edges seemed to sharpen under my gaze.

Stepping straight back, hoping I was finding my own tracks, I moved out of the room, then tiptoed back to the set piece room, bending to peer at the floor.

No tracks that I could see. It wasn't spotless, obviously—dust seemed to be an atmospheric condition in the attic—but it had clearly been given a once-over before we'd been sent up, and all the furniture, trunks, dresses, and frames looked as though they'd recently been wiped down. This was clearly what we were *meant* to see.

I went back to the torture museum display, shining my phone flashlight on the ground. The tracks jumped out vividly, almost like one of those *Dateline* specials that make you never want to visit a hotel room again; they moved straight across the room to the left-hand wall, stopping about a foot away from a large metal-tined rake. A snow shovel was mounted to the left of it, the dented scoop nearly grazing the rake's outstretched skeletal fingertips. But between them and a bit lower, maybe four feet up from the floor, two pegs jutted out from adjoining slots in the wall, cradling . . . nothing.

I reached my hand out to the empty space, as though I could . . . what, sense the missing item's spirit, like some sort of garden tool medium?

I frowned at the wall for a few more seconds . . .

And then something *popped* behind me, and the room suddenly dimmed.

"Jesus *fuck*!"

Part of me registered that one of the ancient sconces must have given up the ghost, but the rest of me was a geyser of adrenaline. Slowing down just enough to snatch up the framed clues, I scurried down the length of the attic, not stopping for breath until I reached the bottom of the stairs where Wynnham had deposited us before.

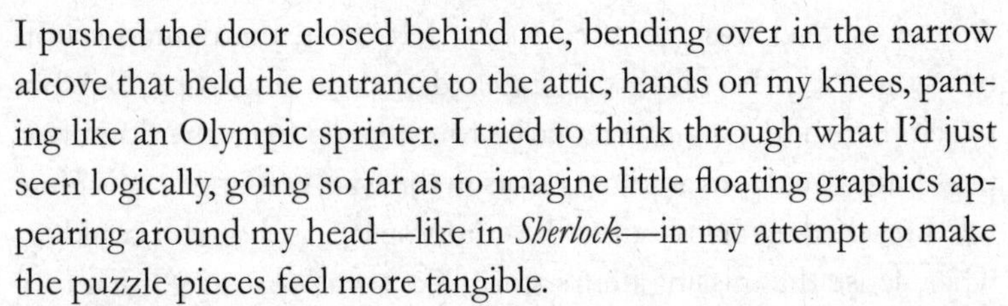

TWENTY

I pushed the door closed behind me, bending over in the narrow alcove that held the entrance to the attic, hands on my knees, panting like an Olympic sprinter. I tried to think through what I'd just seen logically, going so far as to imagine little floating graphics appearing around my head—like in *Sherlock*—in my attempt to make the puzzle pieces feel more tangible.

Someone had been in the attic recently in order to prepare it for Jessica's and my search, which would have required what? Cleaning supplies, surely—rags, a mop and bucket, glass cleaner. It was possible that someone had ducked into the tool room to grab something that would help them complete the task . . . but if that were the case, wouldn't that item be there now? It seemed clear that the room had been purpose-designed to store landscaping tools, likely ones that weren't even in use anymore. "Active duty" gardening equipment would be in one of the equipment sheds outside; cleaning equipment I'd seen in a closet near the guest rooms when I passed by a maid earlier—the real kind that the hotel presumably employed year-round. There were probably several such closets tucked around the main portion of the hotel; it would be too big a time-suck to send the cleaning staff up to the attic multiple times daily.

Unless there'd been a lot of inexplicable raking involved in prepping the set-piece room, the tools weren't involved. Which meant either some creepily antiquated landscaping tool was about to become important to the game, or this had nothing to do with the game at all. In which case . . . did it have something to do with wherever Bethany had disappeared to?

Which led to another question: What, specifically, was missing?

All the smaller, more vicious-looking tools had come to roost on the right-hand wall, but the footprints very clearly cut to the left, where large-handled tools were hanging.

So a rake, or spade, or . . . I don't know, *tiller*? What sorts of things did people with actual gardens need?

I startled at a sound from down the hallway and poked my head around the corner just in time to see the door to Manny and Bethany's room opening. Manny emerged, a dark look on his face, and I pressed myself back against the wall, praying I hadn't been spotted. I couldn't hear footsteps, but it could just be the hallway carpet muffling his steps. After a few moments I heard the soft click of the door closing.

"You have to keep that hidden." It was Manny, his voice strained and tight.

"Or what?" Another man, his voice lower and slightly sneering. I inched over to the edge of the doorframe, tilting my head in a desperate effort to make out the second speaker with my peripheral vision, but they were too far down the hallway—all I could see was the dark slick of Manny's hair disappearing into the collar of his tux.

"Or I could lose my job, for starters."

"I think that's the least of your worries." A sharp sniff. "I know things haven't been going to plan, but that's not my problem. If you want me to stay quiet about just what a shitshow you and Jen have made of this thing—"

"We all want that, I promise. But please, don't use—"

"Yeah, yeah. Just hand it over and I promise I'll keep my mouth shut about that and every other damned thing . . . at least for now."

I sucked a breath in through my nose, holding it in and pressing my back to the wall. I had to know who was threatening Manny, had to see whatever it was that Manny was giving him in exchange for his silence. One, two . . .

I leaned out around the frame for half a second, just long enough to see Manny passing something into the open, meaty hand . . .

. . . of Drew.

My eyes fluttered closed, vertigo overtaking me as I stood there, stock still, waiting for the two of them to make a move.

"What are you going to say?"

"You'll just have to wait and see, hmm?" Drew laughed cruelly. I could hear whatever he was holding slapping against the flat of his palm with a dull, heavy thud. "But I'm a man of my word. Your secret is safe . . . as long as you keep up your end of the bargain."

"Understood."

"Good. If we're clear . . . better *Scuttle* away before anyone turns up, hmm?"

A few more seconds of silence and then a loud creak of a door pulling open. Probably the exit door to the stairs at the other end of the hallway. I'd give it another ten seconds, just to make sure the coast was clear, and then I'd—

"How long have you been standing there?" Suddenly Drew was looming to my left, the shadow of his hat turning his eyes into dark pools. He was only just my height, but in the oversized suit, he seemed to tower over me. I startled so hard my shoulders banged into the wall behind me, setting the picture frames rattling.

"Oh, uh, not long. Sorry, you scared me." I tried to flash a weak smile. "I was searching the attic." I held out the pictures as proof.

"Really." He sneered, leaning ever so slightly closer. My breath seemed stuck somewhere around my sternum. "Find anything good?"

"Nothing we didn't know before." I dug the nails of my free hand into the butt of my palm, trying to steady my nerves. "What about you? Was that Man—um, Scuttles you were talking to just now?"

Drew's lips curled into a sinister smile.

"That's right."

"Did he have any clues? Because I'd love to—"

He planted a hand beside my shoulder, leaning closer, eyes going piggishly small as he glared at me.

"You were slinking around after us earlier—yeah, we noticed—and you're following me now. What's your game here, Becca? If that's even your real name . . ."

"I swear, I just came down from the attic and—"

"No, just listen. If you say anything, to *anyone,* about what you've seen and heard this weekend, there will be consequences. Not just for you, whoever you are, but for everyone in this hotel." He was so close I could smell his stale, slightly musty breath. "You don't want that, do you?"

I just shook my head.

"Good. Then stay out of it and I promise nothing bad will happen. At least not to you. After all, Gabby and I are professionals."

With a wide, wet grin he pushed away from the wall and lumbered off down the hall. It was only then that I registered the metal garden shears swinging jauntily from his fingertips with every step. The handles were patinaed by years of sweaty palms, the menacing metal smile of the curved blades smeared with brownish red. I leaned forward, but before I could get a better look, he pushed open the exit door and disappeared through it, leaving me alone to wonder what he was planning to do with them . . . and with me.

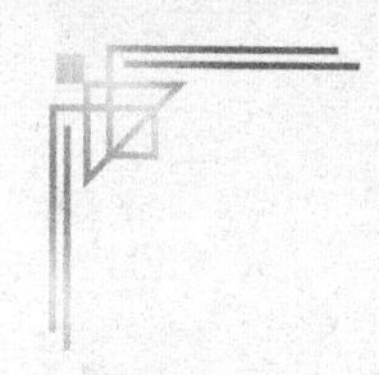

MR. BUGSY SLUGS

CONFIDE:

You were dropping in to chat with your old pal Ida when you saw her door open. Call it your mob-honed instincts, but you ducked out of sight before Miss Debbie Taunte could see you. There was something familiar about her face, and something Ida said to her just as the door was closing—"just like back in Chicago"—made you wonder what sort of history this dame was hiding. You decided right then and there to keep an eye on her.

HIDE:

Ida isn't the only member of the household you go way back with. Her maid, Terry, used to waitress for you in Chicago . . . that is, until you caught her stealing from the guests. You made it very clear how you deal with thieves . . . but the floozy skipped town before you had a chance to settle the score. Now that the two of you have so serendipitously met again, you're not going to lose your chance a second time. . . .

TWENTY-ONE

It took me several seconds to gather myself enough to make my way down the main staircase and across the great hall to the safety of our room, where I tugged my shoes off and nestled under the covers as though they could protect me against Drew . . . and Manny . . . and whatever had happened to Bethany.

The more I thought about it, the tighter my skin started to feel. *You have no proof it was anything bad. What if she just twisted her ankle on a walk in the woods? Or had a friend pick her up?*

Or what if someone—or several someones—had a reason to hurt her? And what if they realize you're on to them?

I swallowed hard against a wave of bile. What had I gotten myself into? If something had happened to Bethany—and it was getting harder and harder to believe my own feeble protests that *maybe it was something innocent, you never know*—then whoever was behind it was still in this house with me. How could I protect myself from them when I wasn't entirely sure who was involved or what they'd done?

Then it hit me, the one advantage I still had in all this:

The phone.

Heart in my throat, I tugged it out of my pocket, hiding its blue-white light beneath the covers. *Please dear god let her Uber history show a ride into town in the middle of the night.* I ran my thumb over the unlock screen, trying a random pattern. S shape?

Incorrect unlock pattern

Out of the corner of my eye, I caught movement. I glanced through the French doors to the gardens, heart catapulting into my throat. Whatever it was had already scurried away, probably some animal trying to find cover before the clouds, hanging lower and lower over the trees, delivered the squalling storm practically bursting through their pregnant bellies.

I tried a snaky pattern through all the dots.

Incorrect unlock pattern

I was about to start running through a more rigorous series of shapes, letters, numbers, when the door handle creaked.

I slid the phone back into my pocket as Blake walked in. There was no way I could explain any of this to him. If I could manage to be semicoherent, and if he somehow believed me that something really, truly wrong was going on here, he'd probably insist we call the police, and what would I tell them? *Hi, officer, I think something terrible happened to the woman I met last night. Why? Because I broke into her room, stole her cellphone, and overheard her roommate saying awful things on the phone—what more proof do you need?* The likelier option, of course, was that he wouldn't believe me, and then we'd be calling our therapist for an emergency intervention. Which might not be totally off base, but fuck if I wasn't sick of that half-pitying, half-fearful look Blake would give me when he thought I was spinning out over something.

He stopped just inside the door, grimaced, sucked air through his teeth, then carefully pushed it closed behind him.

"So, I uh . . . had to meet up with Jessica for the last part of the round . . ."

I almost laughed aloud. Right. *That.* But Blake looked so serious, I somehow managed to tamp it down.

"I'm guessing she told you what happened in the attic?" I raised one eyebrow, working hard to keep my voice level.

"Yeahhh . . ." He scrunched up his face in a look of pained sympathy. "Are you okay?"

"She kissed me, Blake; it wasn't like, an *attack* or anything." I almost added *I kissed her back,* but I could already taste the acid in the words.

"You know what I mean."

I scooted up the bed, patting the spot next to me, and he exhaled gratefully, taking a seat.

"For the record, she was super apologetic," he continued. "She clearly felt terrible about jumping to the wrong conclusion."

"With me too. Anyway, it's not her fault. Just . . . crossed wires." My cheeks went hot as the image of her leaning toward me along the bar, eyelids lowered, gaze fixed on mine, flashed into my mind again. And the rest of me went hotter as I imagined her lips against my own . . . "Honestly, I don't care about that. I just want to know why *you* thought I wanted to?"

He closed his eyes, shaking his head once.

"I didn't, not at first. You can ask her, I wasn't really buying it, I promise. But when you came back to the table you were so *sure* about it, and you seemed so happy . . ."

"That you assumed I wanted us to hook up with another couple?"

His eyes snapped open.

"Yes? No. I don't know. I mean, it surprised me obviously, but ever since . . ." He winced.

"Your affair." I'd expected the words to slice open a new section of me, but somehow naming it this way, casually, felt like the tiniest release of pressure. Maybe because half my mind was still on the phone in my pocket, the encounter with Drew, trying to dredge up a realistic explanation for where Bethany had gone . . .

"Right. Ever since *that,* I don't know what I'm supposed to do. I mean, I know apologizing isn't enough. But things feel so different now. I never know what you're going to do anymore, and . . ." He glanced at me nervously. "But I know it's supposed to take time, I get that. I guess I just thought you felt, like . . . empowered?"

"What?" I laughed, genuinely confused. "Why?"

"Being wanted." Blake's brow lowered a bit. "Like this was a way to take back control."

"Blake . . . you *do* know I could go out and sleep with someone else any time I wanted, right?"

He reeled back as though I'd slapped him.

"I'm sorry, I'm really not saying that to be mean," I squinted, genuinely confused by the shock lingering on his boyish features. Did he really not know how simple it was for younger, reasonably attractive women to get laid? Go to any bar, if it doesn't happen in the first hour, lower your standards half a point and it's practically guaranteed. "Sex is *easy*. This"—I gestured back and forth between us—"is what I'm having trouble with. The fact that you really think I'd just jump into bed with someone else—two someone elses—without talking to you about it . . ." I lowered my head, sighing.

"Fine. That's fair. But . . . Becca, I'm running out of ideas. It's not like you're telling me what *will* fix things."

I looked up at him, surprised by the edge in his voice.

"What's that supposed to mean?"

He sighed heavily, dropping his eyes to the floor.

"C'mon, Becca, you know how you get."

"How do I get?" Hello, jaw-headache, my old friend . . .

"Like *this*!" Blake whipped his head up to face me, and I was shocked to see the hurt in his eyes. "You get so *cold* when I'm not doing what you want. And sure, I know damn well when I've done something wrong, but not what's *right*. Or when you're going to talk to me in your normal voice again. You just freeze me out. You've *always* done that."

"How are you making this my fault?" I could feel my eyes narrowing to laser points, about to physically slice through him. "She kissed *me*. Because you believed that I'd just sign us up for, for *swinging* completely out of the blue."

"I'm not saying it's anyone's fault, Becca, I'm saying I can't read your mind." He ran both hands through his hair, eyes glistening as he stared at me. "I fucked up, okay? I fucked up huge, I still don't even know how it happened. But for *months* before that, any time I'd get home late, any time I wanted to go to bed at a different time than you, any time I didn't want to look at stupid houses in Scarborough with you on the laptop again you'd do . . . *this,* and it would be like suddenly you were a million miles away. You'd flinch if I tried to touch you. And I should have said something, and it doesn't let me off the hook, I know that, but god, Becca, sometimes you make it so *hard*."

Cold seeped out from my sternum, crackling along my ribs, through my guts, up to the base of my skull. I knew, deep down, that he was right.

It's what my mother had always done, what Amy had spent her entire teenage years shrieking about. The ultimate passive aggressive trump card: Of course I'm not mad, I'm fine. No, you're not, *clearly* you're not, but from that point forward, the wall is up—like, a *Game of Thrones* million-foot-tall ice fortress wall—and only backbreaking efforts to anticipate all future needs for some always indeterminate length of time can hope to thaw it.

But I couldn't exactly admit that now, with the ice wall rooting my feet to the oriental rug in real time. That was a several-more-solo-therapy-sessions issue.

"I really am trying, Blake."

He closed his eyes, exhaling heavily.

"I know. I'm not trying to say . . . Becca, I love you, okay? I want to do whatever I have to do to prove that to you. But I can't if you don't let me." He took another deep breath, shoulders lowering, bracing himself. "So, what do you want me to do to try to fix this?"

I looked at him, mind blank, body ice-welded to the bed—this was the entire problem with this weekend, the one mystery I actually needed to solve had no clues, no suspects, and no real answer—and then for some reason I blurted:

"Are you the killer?"

Blake's face was basically a mirror of the inside of my brain, which was just a giant, blaring *Where did that come from?*

"Maybe? I honestly hadn't . . . Sorry, did I miss something?"

"No. I don't know." I pinched my eyes shut. "Listen, I can't talk about this right now, okay? I'm not mad." Suddenly I just felt tired; we'd been trying to find an answer to this, a neat solution to the giant explosion of shit that had spattered every inch of our lives, but what if it wasn't even really the problem? What if the affair was just the symptom, a rotted limb we were frantically trying to hack off when the real issue was *gangrene*? I tried to grope around in my brain for something honest. Honest enough that it hurt to pick it up, hold it out to him. My breath caught in my throat as I whispered: "Do you think I'm boring?"

"What? Becca I'm not following this."

"Please just answer the question. And be honest, okay?"

"Becca . . . no. Of course I don't. Did someone tell you that you were?" His brow lowered further, jaw tightening angrily. Blake wasn't a violent guy, wasn't like half his college friends who tried to act ashamed of their teenage fistfights but brought them up just often enough that you could tell they felt ennobled by them, more authentically masculine. He was more than willing to state the truth: He'd never thrown a real punch. Something about how simply he put it, like it was no more or less important to his sense of self than the fact that he'd never really liked raisins, made me love him so much more. But now . . . he looked like he'd fight the person, whoever they were, that made me believe there was something wrong with me. My chest ached so much I thought it might burst.

Suddenly tears were streaming down my face.

"Becca? Did I do something?" He stood, hovering over me, my tears paralyzing him into inaction.

"Do you . . . promise?" I sniffed out between sobs.

"Of course." He sat again, tentatively putting an arm around my shuddering body. When he spoke his voice was rough. "Did *I* make you feel that way?"

I didn't—couldn't—respond. I could hear Blake swallowing heavily.

"Becca, you are the least boring person I've ever met. Every time we walk into a room, every single person's face lights up, and I get to look around and know that they only get to see a sliver of the person you are. Plus you're funny, and kind, and you do this thing with your tongue when you're cutting vegetables, where just the tip peeks out . . ." He swallowed again. "I didn't realize that . . ." Swallow. "I'm so sorry. What can I do?"

I shook my head back and forth, blinking until I could get my breathing under control.

"I think . . . something needs to change."

"About me?"

"About us."

"Did you have something specific in mind?"

"No. I just . . . I want us to stop pretending."

"Pretending what? I'm not pretending, Becca."

But I was. I'd been doing it all my life, smiling when I was uncomfortable, saying yes to things I didn't want, putting on a show—I would have called it a brave front—so no one would ever think anything about me, us, our lives, was less than.

And where had it gotten me? Even the one couple I was *certain* actually had it figured out were wading through the same crap that we were.

Bethany's face drifted into my mind, the jaw-set, determined,

Amy-like face when she'd refused to accept that this was all, that she couldn't will her own desires into existence. I'd thought it was heartbreakingly brave . . . but really, it just showed how scared she was. That jaw was her very flimsy armor against a truth she didn't want to let in.

And maybe my armor was that version of us I'd wanted everyone to believe in, that I'd willed myself to believe in . . . and it wasn't *real,* it was just a shimmer of rainbow on the surface of an oil slick, gone the second you turned your back. Why had I ever let myself believe that it was the most important thing about us? That it even had anything to do with us?

"Becca, I swear to you, you're all that I want."

He wrapped his arms around me, shaking with silent tears, and I let him hold on to me, let him believe that I believed him when I wasn't sure, anymore, if I even wanted that to be true.

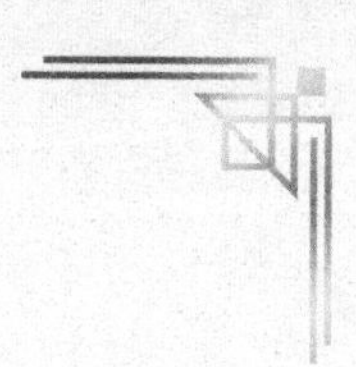

ROUND FIVE

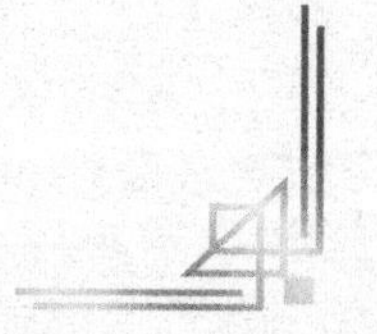

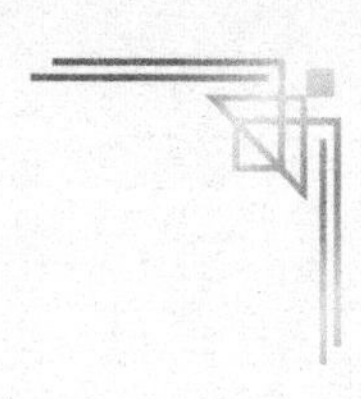

COMPARING NOTES

You've dug up secrets about each other (and yourself), one or more of which will point you to Ida's killer . . . if you know what to look for, at least.

Who has the most to hide? Who has the greatest motive to kill? Now is your chance to put your heads together and find out, before it's too late.

Share the clues you found and anything relevant you observed throughout today's rounds as you see fit, or keep them to yourself. Just remember, if you choose to share, or any of your fellow guests questions you directly, **you must tell the truth** about how and where you found the relevant item or information.

And before you clam up, remember, the most damning clue of all might be your silence . . .

TWENTY-TWO

"So Lulu isn't who she says she is. Interesting. Not that I'm surprised." Gabby rolled her elaborately—borderline clownishly—made-up eyes as she looked at the headshot I'd just offered up to the group. She flipped it over to glance at the note on the back again, then met my gaze. "I've never trusted actresses. Just liars for a living, if you ask me." She raised an eyebrow, mouth twisting into something like a challenge. Was that a hint that she knew something about Bethany? Jennifer was a full-time concierge, according to the bartender, so she'd have been the only actress around . . . unless she was referring to *me*.

I slipped my hand into my pocket, clasping the phone again, eyes darting around the table to each of the people assembled there, shuffling through piles of handkerchiefs and letters, headshots and compacts, their real motives constantly slipping into the shadows of the characters they were playing.

"Since you already spilled the beans"—Jessica pulled another headshot out of an envelope she'd tucked beneath her charger—"no point holding on to this anymore." She slid a picture of the same girl in my attic headshot—more glamorously made up but clearly recognizable, this time, as Bethany—into the center of the table. It must have been her clue from the earlier search of Ida's rooms. I glanced around to see if anyone would react to the sight of the missing girl, but if the picture brought anything up, I couldn't find it in their faces. "It basically says the same thing: I am not, in fact, a lost European princess."

"Well, if everyone else is sharin', I suppose we might as well, eh, Scoops?" Drew glanced across the table at Josh for approval, then bent down to grab something from under his chair. Sitting up, he slammed a brass candlestick in the center of the dining table with an impressive thud. "Whaddya think *that* is?" He raised an eyebrow, eyes darting around to take in all the other players' reactions.

"Something my grandmother would like," Phil said, sitting back in his chair and taking a sip from his never-empty glass of scotch.

"It's the *murder weapon,*" Drew said, obviously annoyed. "Someone tried to hide it in the bushes near the gazebo."

Then what were the gardening shears for? I physically bit down on my tongue to keep from saying it aloud. If the candlestick was part of the game . . . did that mean the shears were part of whatever happened to Bethany? An image of her costume, the entire front stained with gore, flashed into my mind again. *Maybe I'd been too quick to write that off . . .*

"You really think? But it's so small." Frowning, Heather reached across the table to lift the candlestick, weighing it in one hand and making an experimental half-swing through the air against her palm. "I don't know," she said, handing it to Jessica, seated to her left. "Could anyone actually *kill* someone with this?"

Jessica waved it through the air a couple times, then shrugged.

"I've never killed anyone, Maria, so I'd hardly know." She smiled pertly before setting it back on the table.

The housekeeper moved over to the table, frowning, and picked up the candlestick.

"You say you think *this* was the murder weapon?" she said, lifting it up. "I'm not sure that makes sense. There are no candlesticks like this in the lounge, I can assure you. Nor in any of the rooms that Miss Crooner has open at the moment, to my knowledge." She shook her head, setting it back down. "And I tend to agree with Mrs. Oleum. Something so slight could hardly have done the damage we saw."

Phil promptly leaned forward with a creak of his chair, reaching for the candlestick and weighing it one hand. He pushed up to standing, lifting an arm and swinging it through the air. Wind blew across the back of my neck and I tried to repress a shudder. Phil's height had never seemed so . . . intimidating.

"I think that could do the trick. In the right hands." He smirked, thumping it down in the center of the table, hard enough to rattle the plates, and sat back in his chair, swinging an ankle over his knee casually.

"There's also the fact that our clue specifically said . . ." Josh flipped back through his booklet. "Here, we were looking for *an object that somebody hastily hid, after cracking it over poor Ida's lid*." He sniffed. "Subtle, I know. Also, there's this." He twisted the candlestick around, tilting one edge up to the light and pointing at a brownish smear on the corner. "Pretty sure it's not meant to be brass polish."

"God, that's grisly," Jessica murmured, leaning across the table and turning the candlestick to get a closer look at the "blood." Unless it really *was* blood. Dammit, it was hard enough to know what was real when it was just my emotional shitshow getting in the way, how was I supposed to keep a disappearance *inside* a murder mystery straight?

"Where did you say you found that?" The housekeeper frowned at the candlestick. "If you ask me, that's simply old wax, maybe a bit of tarnish." She bent to peer at it, flicking at the speck with a nail. It crumbled, leaving a little pile of rusty dust on the tablecloth.

"Right next to the gazebo," Drew said. "Under some bushes."

"And there wasn't anything else in the area? Something a bit heftier perhaps?"

"I wondered about that too," Josh said, flipping open his book. "The poem said something about . . . there, *took a nasty turn after getting clocked with an urn.* But I figured maybe it was just to make the rhyme?"

"An urn. Now that *is* interesting," the housekeeper said, eyes widening as she looked at the other players around the table in turn. "I've seen several unique examples in Miss Crooner's collection, she usually likes to buy them in pairs. Some of them are quite weighty . . ."

"There weren't any urns around the garden, I'm certain. Scoops and I went over the place with a fine-toothed comb," Drew said, folding his arms across his broad chest. "If this isn't the murder weapon, fine, but then it's still missing."

"How unfortunate." Miss Thrope's lips pursed as she stared at the candlestick, as though she were trying to set it alight with the intensity of her gaze. "Scuttles," she finally said, turning to where Manny was standing against the wall, "would you mind helping me make our guests some more coffee? The pot is . . . out of my reach." She gave him a meaningful look and he scurried over to her. "We can also pick up those self-affixing papers you were asking for earlier, Mr. Slugs. They could be very useful in marking the locations of all of your clues on the map of the grounds."

"Be quick about it," he snarled, leaning back. "Some of us have better things to do than wait on dames that can't even remember to provide copies of a map for the houseguests."

The housekeeper smiled tightly and retreated, Manny just behind her. Just as he was leaving, he glanced back at Drew. *Did Drew nod to him, or did I just imagine it?*

"Finally," Drew muttered to Gabby. "I asked for Post-its how long ago? We need them to keep track of who's who in the picture clues, too. Since none of these people actually *look* like the players here." His lips pinching with obvious annoyance. He turned to his wife to murmur, not quite under his breath, "*I* expected *a laminated map and whiteboard markers to be able to track everyone's movements, at the very least, but I suppose that was aiming too high . . .*"

Josh pointed at the map.

"So if this is the gazebo, and we know where everyone's supposed to be staying . . . I'm guessing we're supposed to assume the murder weapon came from either Debbie's room"—he tapped on one corner of the map—"or Bugsy and Dolly's."

"But it doesn't even seem like that's supposed to be the murder weapon, right?" Everyone turned to stare at me. My heart fluttered a little. The more muddled everything got, the more my need to create *something* orderly, to find a single stupid answer, had grown, until suddenly it felt less like a dinner party, more like having to give a speech to the whole class in middle school. "I mean . . . the housekeeper as much as said so just now, right? Or . . . was I the only one that thought that?"

"I think you're right." Blake nodded, leaning forward, eyes fixed on the map. If his eagerness was just for my benefit, it was very convincing. "She was trying to point us toward something else. You said the poem made it sound like you were looking for an urn, right, Josh?"

"Yup. Right here, *urn*." He pointed at his book.

"And then she said all that about most of the urns being in pairs, right?" I could feel my excitement rising with the sense that we were finally actually on to something. I turned to Blake. "There must be a pair somewhere in the house with one missing!"

"Oh my god, yes! Probably in one of the rooms where everyone was just before the murder." Blake leaned forward to look at the map, pointing at each location in turn. "People had access to the library, the lounge, and the ballroom then. Maybe one of those rooms is missing an urn?"

"And the conservatory," Jessica said, our enthusiasm seeming to catch her. "I was taking tea in the conservatory when I saw

Scoops in the garden with the binoculars. But . . . what does that really tell us?" Her shoulders dropped heavily. "We all could have gone in and out of the rooms at any time, right?"

"All except Maria, she was supposed to be on a call until just before cocktails," I said. I *may have* been keeping extremely detailed notes since the afternoon session.

"That's right," Heather murmured, frowning as she squinted at the map, reading glasses presumably still tucked away in her purse.

"So . . . maybe this candlestick *was* the weapon?" Blake turned to me expectantly, certain I could solve it.

"Maybe . . ." I frowned, thinking. "Or maybe the urn came from somewhere only *one* of us had access to."

"Like one of our rooms?" Blake's eyes widened. "They all have weird decorations in them, don't they?" Blake glanced around the table as everyone nodded. "Are any of them urns?"

"We have urns in our room, right, babe?" Jessica turned to Josh. He nodded. "I can't remember how many, though."

"We all need to go back and check," I said, grinning as I turned to Blake. "Whoever's missing an urn . . . might be the murderer."

"Oh my god, *awesome*." Blake raised his hand and I slapped him five, a flare of warmth stirring in my chest. It had been so long since it had felt like this, like we were on a team, fully ourselves. Like we were just having *fun* together. I'd almost forgotten how enthusiastic he'd get about puzzling something out, whether it was a thorny problem at work or the final *Jeopardy!* answer. Like you'd done something so damned impressive he could hardly believe it. I wasn't quite sure how, but our conversation just before dinner seemed to have shifted something infinitesimally inside me, cracked open a release valve I'd thought had rusted shut.

"I'm confused. If there was supposed to be an urn, then how did you find this candlestick?" Gabby frowned in a way that made her eyes nearly disappear. "Did you look in the wrong place or something?"

"Absolutely not," Drew said, sniffing heavily. "The poem said

'Something like that you're looking to hide / would be far too likely to turn up inside. / But nobody'd think twice if you were to go / For an afternoon walk around the gazebo! / Vegetation near there's especially thick / You could stash something in it pretty damn quick.'"

"Wait, did you . . . memorize that?" Josh's forehead wrinkled up.

"I work in showbiz, bub. Learnin' lines is part of the gig."

"Not to burst anyone's bubble"—Heather turned to me with an apologetic smile—"it sounds like this is what they were supposed to find, don't you think?"

Drew sniffed loudly.

"Or else maybe one of the staff members just screwed up. They're already down a person—them getting sloppy makes the most sense." He shrugged a little too nonchalantly.

"I'm with Drew on this one," Phil muttered, taking a heavy swig of his drink. "Whole thing's been a goddammed circus if you ask me." Maybe this was why Heather didn't love him drinking too much. I'd never seen pissy-drunk Phil before, but then I'd never seen him drink scotch for an entire afternoon into the evening.

"Maybe that Scuttles guy broke the urn and tried to cover for it," Drew said, trying, and failing, to look innocent.

"But how can we know that?" Josh glanced around at each of us in turn.

"We couldn't. Which is why I say we just assume things went according to plan unless the staff tells us otherwise." Heather frowned reprovingly at her husband, who didn't seem to catch it. "We assume this is the right weapon . . . and that it probably can't tell us anything. At least not *yet,*" she added, smiling encouragingly at me.

I tried to return her smile, but I couldn't help but feel deflated. I'd really thought I was on to something there. Beneath the table, Blake reached over to squeeze my thigh, leaning closer to whisper in my ear. "I'm still keeping my eyes peeled for urns." Warmth surged through me, though not quite enough to eradicate my disappointment.

Everyone flipped through their booklets for a few moments in silence, apparently unsure where to turn next. Beneath the table, I slipped the phone out to try an N shape. If I wasn't going to get answers in the game, maybe I could here.

Incorrect unlock pattern

Jessica reached for a bread basket at the center of the table, plucking out a roll and pulling it apart slowly. Butter knife poised in the air, she looked around, eyes bright. *Guessing the silence felt extra awkward for her right then.* Still, I couldn't help but notice how flattering a little embarrassment was to her, how well the color in her cheeks served to define her cheekbones. "So let's assume we all could have gotten our hands on the weapon. I still say it comes down to motive."

"But we all have a motive, too," Blake said, smiling in a way that looked warm but that I recognized as merely polite. He might say the kiss hadn't bothered him, but I knew him better than that. "Opportunity is just as important."

"So what, you think murdering someone just comes down to 'right place, right time'?" Josh couldn't keep the smirk off his face. "I'd like to believe there's a *bit* more to it than that."

"We all would," Phil said, rocking forward heavily to pin Josh with an intense gaze. "But underneath all this"—he gestured at all of us, in our carefully chosen outfits, arm sweeping wide to take in the entire heavily curated room—"we're all just animals."

"I'm not sure I take your meaning, dear," Heather murmured as she gently took the glass from his hand before it spilled on her dress. Poor Heather, this weekend was supposed to be her big anniversary gift and instead she was spending it mothering a sloppy friend and a sloppier husband.

"People think murder is some bright red line only evil people cross. Really, anyone could do it. Get someone mad enough, threaten something dear to them . . ." He reached for the candlestick again, swinging it through the air in one short, sharp jab that made Heather startle back from him. "Lose control for just a second and suddenly . . . lights out." He discarded the candlestick with a sniff, and it juddered across the table until Gabby stopped it with a little yelp of surprise. "Anyone who tells themselves otherwise is a fool or a liar." Heather drew away, blinking at him, eyes wide with something close to fear. He held her gaze a moment longer, then levered up off the chair, crossing to the cocktail cart near the door to pour himself another couple inches of liquor, his hand remarkably steady. My throat ached for her as I saw the flush of embarrassment creeping up her neck.

No one seemed to know how to follow that.

I glanced back down at the phone, checking the battery life—19 percent—before clicking it dark again and sliding it back into my pocket. Was it just me, or did the air in the room feel closer since Phil's little pronouncement?

If he could make all of us feel this uncomfortable in a room full of people, couldn't he have scared Bethany alone in the middle of the night?

The thought felt traitorous, but I couldn't seem to shake it. So what if her room was shared—this house was cavernous, practically built for secret conversations well out of anyone's sight. Phil this deep in a bottle wasn't a person I recognized. And he was clearly a person Heather didn't like anyone else seeing . . .

The first drops of rain were tapping against the walls and windows of the dining room, a gust of wind driving a whole sheet against the glass in a staccato burst, just as the housekeeper reappeared in the doorway, a pack of Post-its in one hand.

"Mr. Slugs, you're in luck, I've found exactly the—"

Then her voice was drowned by a loud, staticky buzz, and everything went black.

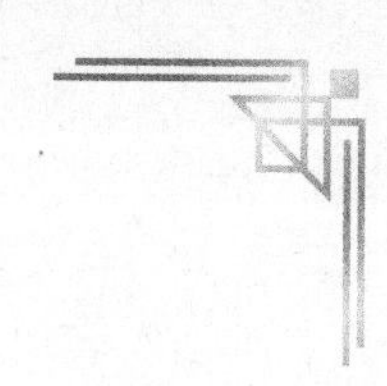

LIGHTS OUT

The only way to restore power to the mansion is to flip each of the eight breakers located around the house by hand. You've been assigned to find the breaker switch located in the

Large Library.
____

If you've forgotten the way, please use the map of the building below to help guide you.

Once you reach your designated room, look for the switch. It will be located behind a door, box, or panel bearing this symbol:

Once all eight switches have been flipped, the power can be restored. But don't be too hasty. You might find something else hidden in the dark that will help you solve the mystery.

And *be careful*. You never know what might be lurking in the shadows . . .

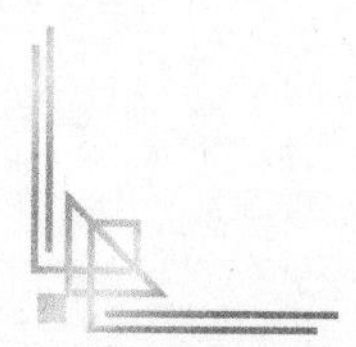

TWENTY-THREE

"Please, stay calm. I always keep a candle on my person. If I've said it once, I've said it a hundred times, you just can't *trust* electricity . . ."

A few seconds later, a match sizzled to life, illuminating the housekeeper's face in ghoulish gashes of shadow as she bent over the candle. I lifted a hand to my cheek. Was it already too late for preventive Botox?

"I think Wynnham keeps some lamps in the sideboard . . ." She crossed the room, the flame of the single candle swaying lazily back and forth as she moved. A distant bolt of lightning flashed, briefly illuminating the owlish expressions on everyone's faces. Several beats later a peal of thunder rolled over the distant hills. It was as if they'd made the storm to order. A chill shot through me. I was only just realizing that until now, my obsessing about Bethany's disappearancc had felt important, but distant. Huddling here in the dark, all these strangers' faces turned unrecognizable in the flickering candlelight, the house rising up around us in all its gothic horror, the threat felt very, very real. "Here they are."

The housekeeper set the candle on the sideboard, bending to unearth a wooden crate, which she carried over to the end of the table, setting it between Drew and Gabby with a thump. She reached in, fiddling around at the bottom until the box lit up, slivers of light slipping between the slats and out onto the polished wood. Inside were a dozen old-fashioned-looking hand lanterns.

"There should be enough for everyone here. If you'll pass them along the table."

One by one she "lit" and passed out the lanterns. They gave the room an almost claustrophobic intimacy, the table and guests bathed in their soft, forgiving yellow glow, the room around receding into ever deeper shadows. I glanced at Drew, lifting his lantern in one hand as though to test its weight. The light seemed to carve his face into a new shape, with a heavier, lower brow and the lantern jaw of a man used to picking a fight. He nodded, seemingly appeased, before lowering it back to the table. The memory of him casually twirling the cruel-looking gardening shears turned my stomach crawly.

"I hate to ask, but . . . would you all be willing to help me restore the power? The house is so large, I'm afraid there are several breakers we'll need to flip before the main breaker will work again. I'd ask my staff, but they've been . . . a bit on edge since the events of last night." The housekeeper raised a trembling hand to her mouth. Phil sniffed, taking a big swig of his drink. "If you turn the page in your dossiers, everything will be explained. I'll just be off to the guest quarters to handle the breakers there."

With that she blew out her candle, took one of the remaining lanterns, and strode out of the room, the doorway slowly going dark as the dry rustling of her skirts receded down the long hall. Lightning split the air outside, setting the hairs on the back of my neck on end. I glanced around the table. Everyone else seemed on edge, too, though it could just be a trick of the lights, the circles of protection they seemed to cast around each of us, and the inky shadows just beyond their borders. Blake laid a hand on my thigh and I startled so hard my chair scraped across the floor.

"Sorry," I said.

"Right there with you," Jessica muttered.

Everyone glanced over their booklets in silence. Heather frowned at her page for a second, turning it this way and that . . .

"Is anyone else supposed to go to the lower level?" she finally said.

"I'm in the kitchens," Blake said.

"Okay. I see those here." Heather squinted at the page a moment longer, then nodded. "If I get turned around, I'm yelling for you. Or, you know—in case of ghost attack."

"I'll make sure to keep an ear out," Blake said with a smile.

"Well? What are we waiting for?" Phil set his glass on the table with a hard crack. "Let's get this over with."

With that, he slid the booklet into his breast pocket, pushed back from the table, grabbed his lantern, and walked out, leaving Heather staring after him, mouth hanging open. Drew and Gabby followed close behind, but Drew stopped in the doorway, turning to catch my eye and shake his head once, sharply, in wordless warning. I swallowed hard against the lump in my throat, willing the inside of my nose and eyes to stop prickling.

"Chin up," Jessica said to me, smiling slyly. Maybe it was the dark, or maybe it was the cocktails with dinner, but she didn't seem to feel quite as constrained as she had a few hours before. "The only way out is through, right?"

TWENTY-FOUR

I turned right, raising my lantern in front of me as I made my way farther down the hall to the large library. It emitted a small circle of weak yellow light that slithered over the curves of the polished woods and pooled on the surfaces of the portraits, giving the bodies trapped in the oils an eerily lifelike glow. I glanced back over my shoulder as I tiptoed along past set after set of painted eyes, the thick carpet beneath my feet swallowing the sound of my steps.

Just don't look at the eyes and it won't seem like they're following you.

False.

Soon I reached the heavy wood door that led into the large library. I reached for the knob, my breath hitching as the door creaked open under the lightest touch of my hand. Raising the lantern higher, I stepped inside.

In the dark, all the sharp edges of the library—the carved lines of the shelves, the spines of the books bound in linen and leather, the tufted velvet chairs and couches tucked into the corners, spindly tables nestling against their protective bulk—all seemed to have smeared together, charcoal drawings of themselves that a careless hand had brushed over. The lantern brought just a few feet of shelving into focus, the light dissipating as it reached the upper atmosphere of the room. The narrow balcony that hugged the three interior walls was visible only as a suggestion of balustrades and deeper shadows beyond. Heavy velvet curtains had been pulled back from the floor-to-ceiling windows on the opposite side of the room, and the rain outside flitted past the glass like static.

I took a tentative step forward, the lantern light skittering across the gilded spines of the books. Another step, and something clattered.

"Jesus *god,*" I whispered, jumping back from an occasional table that seemed to have apparated out of the darkness of the room. I lowered the lantern until its polished surface took on a bit of color. Stepping carefully to the side, I continued past it.

Overhead, a door creaked open.

"Is someone here?"

Instinctively I crouched, tucking the lantern beneath the table, lungs bursting with the pressure of my held breath. The woman's voice sounded as though it was coming from the balcony, but when I glanced up, I couldn't see anyone. Leaving the lantern where it was, I crabbed back across the carpet toward the door, trying not to make even a whisper of sound. I wasn't sure if the game would change if I were caught, but better safe than sorry. Besides, with shadows undulating around the room, thunder cracking outside, and a draft creeping down the neck of my dress from somewhere unseen, it was hard to feel sure that any of this was just a game anymore.

"You're being paranoid, why would anyone be in the library *now*?"

The second voice was male, and unfamiliar. The woman's voice I thought I recognized . . .

"It doesn't hurt to take precautions," she said. A creak of wood overhead as they stepped inside. *It was Bethany.* But did that mean she had just . . . come back? I felt simultaneously elated and idiotic. *Had I really blown things that far out of proportion?*

Focus on the game, that still needs a solution.

"Listen, babe, this is our shot to hit it big. And he'll pay up, I'm certain of it. After all, he couldn't risk me ratting out his wife to the coppers."

"Are you sure that will work?"

"'Course it will. Ida told me, the guy's all talk. But his dough? That's *very* real. I tell him to cough it up if he doesn't want me to sing, and you and I'll be set for life."

"I told you I don't like that idea." Her voice had gone small, like a child scared to look under the bed.

"And I told *you* I'd handle it. Leave it to me. I'll meet up with him somewhere private—don't worry, I swear no one will see me—he'll hand over the money, and then as soon as you can get away, we'll meet up in New York."

"I'm scared, baby . . ."

"Of course you are. That's why you've got to trust a man to handle it. Now hurry up and talk to the old man before he starts getting big ideas about not paying up."

Then the floors creaked, and I realized the set piece was about to end. I jumped up.

"Bethany? Bethany, I know you're supposed to stay in character, but I really need to ask you—"

But the footsteps didn't even slow.

Fumbling for my lantern, I set out around the room, finally locating the spindly staircase up to the balcony. Three-quarters of the way around the narrow walkway I saw it—a small silver box in the middle of the carpet.

It was a tape player. The conversation had been a *recording.* Which meant it was just a part of the game.

"Dammit!" I picked the thing up and threw it at the nearest

shelf. It thudded against the spines of some ancient-looking almanacs and skittered out of sight.

Frustration surged through me. She'd never been here. Which meant I was no closer to an answer as to where she'd *gone*. And my brilliant game insights at dinner had all been proven pointless already. God, I just wanted to sort out *one thing* this weekend. Take your pick, just give me *one*.

After about a minute of deep breathing, I made my way back down the staircase, picking my way around the room again, lifting and lowering the lantern along the stacks of books, searching for anything that might resemble a lightning bolt. I almost shat myself when the recording started up again, garbled this time, presumably by my Hulk-out.

". . . were sleeping with her . . . anyone else . . . ?"

I could only make out every third or fourth word.

"Had to be that . . . had the old guy on the . . . found ouuu . . ."

Then there was a long, thin wheezing sound followed by a mechanical clacking.

Whoops.

I continued my search for the symbol, which in the end was typically unsubtle. Mounted between the shelves and the first window was a large plywood box that had been painted brown, a giant neon lightning bolt splitting its front. I pulled open the cover to reveal a porcelain mount with a small switch shaped like a miniature version of the handle on an electric chair. Beneath it, a small handwritten sign read FUSE: OFF. I flipped it up to FUSE: ON, then pushed my lantern closer to the box; I wasn't sure how we could have missed it the day before. A couple pokes and it slid down the wall slightly, revealing the sticky-tack holding it in place. I sighed, trying and failing to ignore the heavy blanket of disappointment settling over me. We'd probably *all* solve the case of "Who murdered Ida Crooner?" But if there was an answer to what had happened to Bethany, I was no closer to it.

I pulled the phone out again, tapping my thumbnail against the screen. Stairsteps from the top left to the bottom right?

Incorrect unlock pattern

Something was locked inside it, I was sure, something important. But unlike the game, there weren't any painfully obvious clues to help me crack the code.

I was about to try a new pattern when a flash of lightning split the sky. Barely a second later a thunderclap rang out.

Then another . . . and another . . . Then someone screamed, and I realized it wasn't thunder at all.

It was gunshots.

TWENTY-FIVE

Moments later, the lights came on and a speaker crackled to life.

"Everyone, hurry! Come to the great hall at once!"

Then the speaker crackled off.

Lantern still in hand, I strode out of the library, turning left down the hall, body still electric with anxiety, even with the lights back on. Behind me, a door slammed against the wall. I held back a shriek, but it was just Phil, looking haggard as he emerged from the ballroom . . . not to mention *soaked.*

"Phil . . . is everything okay?"

"Hmm?" He blinked, seeming only now to realize that he wasn't alone in the hallway. The closer he got, the greyer his skin looked. He swallowed hard, eyes narrowing with the effort of focusing. "I'm fine," he said. "Why wouldn't I be?"

"I mean . . . you're drenched, for one thing."

He frowned and lifted a hand to his hair, then pulled it away and stared in confusion at the water trickling over his palm. A small scrap of white fabric was crumpled between his fingers. Did he carry a handkerchief?

"They left the French doors open in the ballroom," he finally said. "The rain must have come in." He held an arm out in front of him, shooting a cuff experimentally, then looked back at me, eyes a bit glazed.

Either Phil's drinking had all caught up to him in about ten minutes flat, or something had happened in that ballroom that he wasn't sharing. I veered sideways subtly, trying to put more distance between us, the hallway becoming even more claustrophobic as we continued down it in silence.

In the great hall, Jessica was waiting next to Drew, who was wheezing, cheeks a bit red, forehead wrinkled in that vaguely anxious way. Had everyone been spooked by what they found? Or maybe it was simpler. You can pretend you outgrow it by adulthood, but who *isn't* a little afraid of the dark?

A few seconds later, Josh and Gabby emerged from the opposite wing, and after another minute, Blake and Heather made it up from the basement.

"Should we say what we found?" she finally said, then, taking a good look at her husband, "Phil . . . what in god's name happened to you?"

"The doors were open," he mumbled again. "I thought I saw someone . . ."

Frowning, she plucked the scrap of fabric from his limp fingers, holding it up to examine . . . a maid's cap? It looked exactly like the one Bethany had worn. And there hadn't been one with the mutilated costume I found. Anxiety skittered through me as Heather patted at Phil's collar with a napkin unearthed from her tiny clutch. Had he found that just now, or earlier? Then the housekeeper rushed in from the far corridor, panting in a way that threatened the integrity of the buttons on her bodice. She ran a hand over her hair, which did nothing to smooth the aureole of frizz escaping from the usually immaculate chignon securing her head to her neck.

"Is everyone safe?" she said, breathless. "I heard gunshots from this room . . . but no one was here, were they?"

Everyone shook their head. The housekeeper's neck swiveled above its solid platform of lace, then she cried out.

"There!" She pointed beneath one of the sideboards, hurrying over with a rustle of skirts, bending, scrabbling around beneath it with one hand. I couldn't help but notice the other slipping into her pocket. She unfolded and spun around, brandishing a small pistol. "I knew I'd heard gunshots! But . . ." Frowning, she lifted the gun to her ear, rattling it a bit, then flipped open the chamber. "No bullets left. I suppose that's a small mercy." With a dramatic shudder, she set the pistol on the table, shying away as though, bullets or no, it might fire itself suddenly.

"So you're saying . . ." Gabby narrowed her eyes at the housekeeper.

"Someone shot it off just now, but they must have abandoned it here before we made it back. Which means we don't know who fired this gun, and we don't know *why*." She squinted at each of us meaningfully. "I must ask . . . did anyone see any, well . . . *bodies*?"

Heather cleared her throat.

"I found the butler, but he was just drunk. I'm sorry, I can't remember his name at the moment. But when he popped up, it scared the bejeezus out of me. Ask Blake, I screamed my head off."

"Wynnham," Blake murmured. He'd always been so much better with names than me. It really helped at parties. I'd break the ice with the couple we didn't know, or the co-worker Blake wasn't sure he had anything in common with, and he kept track of who we were talking to, what they'd said. He jokingly called us the dream team, but we really were, in a way. "And she did," he added with a gentle smile. "Scream, that is."

"I *do* apologize for that, Mrs. Oleum. I assure you, our staff is of the highest caliber. It must be the shock of last night's events that led poor Wynnham into a bottle. Let me clarify my question: Have any of you found any . . . well, *corpses*?"

Everyone shook their heads slowly.

"Curiouser and curiouser," the housekeeper said, frowning. "I suppose that means the shots must not have been fired on this level of the house." She clapped her hands sharply. "I suggest we search the upstairs rooms. Perhaps the staff will know more about these gunshots."

Drew rolled his eyes hugely and Gabby leaned in to take his arm, whispering something in his ear, but he let the housekeeper rustle toward the stairs, pausing next to the gun with a stern frown until we all moved past her, then darting past us up the main staircase that led to the upstairs rooms.

We were about halfway up when the housekeeper screamed theatrically, running across the gallery to crouch in front of one of the occasional tables near the wall.

"Putters? Mr. Putters, can you hear me?"

She flipped the man over onto his back with a heavy thump, bending to press an ear to his chest, fingers to his throat . . .

"Oh, oh dear . . . I'm afraid . . ." She turned to us, her smallish eyes stretched as wide as they could go. "Mr. Putters is *dead*."

TWENTY-SIX

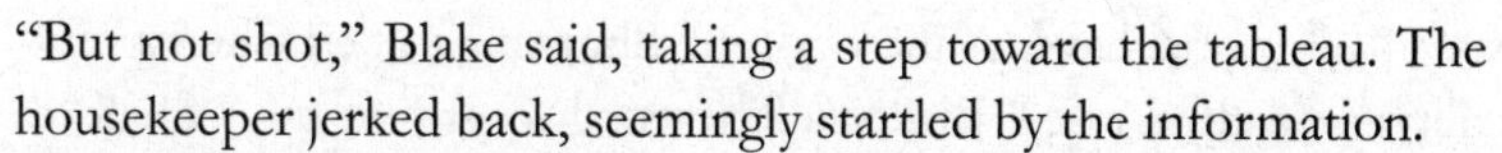

"But not shot," Blake said, taking a step toward the tableau. The housekeeper jerked back, seemingly startled by the information.

"My goodness, Mr. Daily . . . I believe you're right!" She pulled the lapels of the man's jacket open, running a hand lightly over his stomach, then turned his head to the side to be sure. The "body" wriggled his nose.

"Maybe somebody used this?" Blake tugged a length of rope out of his pocket, tossing it onto the ground next to the body. It had been twisted up into a noose. "I found it in the kitchens."

"Oh dear, this is too dreadful." The housekeeper started pacing the room, fist pressed to her mouth. "I simply can't stand this . . . my heart can't tolerate so many shocks . . ."

"Should we head downstairs to talk about what else we found?" I said, glancing around at the others, trying not to think too much about the disappointment still weighing down my limbs. We could still solve the game. That was *something.* "I heard something that made me think the staff were planning to blackmail the killer. I'm sure the rest of you had encounters as well?"

"By all means," the housekeeper said, lips pinched tight. "This night has been too much for my nerves. Of course, if you'd like to discuss the mystery over a cocktail in the lounge, that's your prerogative, but after all the shocks we've been through, I myself will be retiring. Just as soon as I find some of the footmen to help me remove the corpse."

With that, she strode down the steps, back ramrod-straight, several strands of dark brown hair slipping their pins to trickle down her back. I tried to tamp down my annoyance, the urge to scream after her *Forget the stupid game for five minutes and focus on the girl who's actually missing!* Hearing Bethany's voice on the tape had made me so sure she was okay . . . and realizing it wasn't really her left me feeling more twitchy than ever. I sighed. Yelling at the housekeeper wouldn't accomplish anything. She was just doing her best after getting dealt a crummy hand. *Weren't we all.*

"I, for one, have no intention of returning to bed when a murderer's on the loose," Blake said, turning to grin at me. "Shall we discuss what we've learned over cocktails in the lounge?"

"I'll never say no to giggle water," I chirped, and was rewarded with a glimpse of his dimple.

"Free drinks are about the only worthwhile part of this weekend," Phil muttered. Heather's face pinched up as she glanced over at him. "May as well take advantage."

The rest of the group followed us down the stairs.

"I suggest we take our drinks to the dining room," Drew said as he waited for the bartender to pour his lager. "We can give the clues another once-over. Now that we finally have some Post-its."

Before long we were all spread out around the dining room table again, bent over the clues.

"So, did *everyone* see something after the lights went out?" Blake asked, looking around.

"Not me," Drew said, face obscured by the giant fedora. "But I did find these."

He slapped the gardening shears down in the middle of the table with a loud, deadened *thump*. I sucked in a breath, eyes darting up to his. His lips were twisted in a sneer, practically daring me to say something.

"Those look grisly," Heather murmured, picking them up. "Do you have any idea where they came from?"

"They were wrapped in this." He tossed a scrap of fabric onto the table. It was covered in rusty stains, but the letters *P O* were still clearly visible in the corner. "Perfect match for the one that turned up in Ida's room, wouldn't you say, Peter?"

Wait . . . were the shears just part of the game? Or was he somehow trying to pass them *off* as part of the game?

"And?" Phil sniffed, picking up the handkerchief for a moment, then tossing it back to the center of the table with disdain. "The lady wasn't stabbed."

"*Ida* wasn't. But if you were trying to cover something up—"

"What? Not stabbing that other guy? Putters?"

"I think they seem pretty damning," Gabby piped in, after which no one else seemed to have anything more to add. I couldn't pull my eyes off them. Were they really just part of the game? But if they weren't . . . why show them to us all? *Maybe he wants to convince you—the one person who saw him holding them—that they were just for play . . .*

"If there was anything in the sitting room, I didn't find it," Jessica said with a graceful, feline shrug. She glanced up at me from under her eyelashes, held my gaze for a moment, then turned away. I tried to ignore the heat flooding my body.

"I didn't see anything, but I overheard a conversation," Josh said. "A man said his 'real employer' was at the house this weekend. So I guess one of the servants is supposed to be working for one of us?" He shrugged. "I think it was that footman guy."

“Red herring,” Drew said with a sniff. “Debbie’s thing probably is too. Things like that are always red herrings.”

“Since when are you such an expert?” Phil spat, sneering.

“Let’s just say this ain’t our first rodeo,” Drew said, throwing his arm around Gabby.

I frowned; I could swear Gabby had said something about never having come to these before. Though wouldn’t the ultimate red herring be Drew trying to push me off the Bethany scent by muddying the waters of the game?

Unless it had been Jessica who had said that about never doing one of these. The first night wasn’t entirely clear . . .

“Well, even if it’s a red herring, you might as well all know what I heard,” I offered when it seemed clear no one else planned to speak up. “I think it was the maid and the chauffeur talking, it sounded like they were blackmailing one of the men, and that one of the women probably did it.”

“The maid’s not here.” Phil leaned across the table, staring at me intently, the heat of his gaze seeming to burn straight through the fug of alcohol fumes. I jerked back reflexively. There was something almost feral about the look on his face, half a breath from teeth bared.

“I know that,” I said slowly, trying to keep the frown off my face. “Like I said, it was a recording. Anyway, I think it narrows the suspects down to the women.”

“Red. Herring,” Drew said, lip curled.

“What about you, Phil?” Blake took the opportunity to lean toward the older man, putting his body between the two of us so that I could retreat from the awkwardness. I could feel my body loosening, a swell of gratitude pushing into the newly available space in my chest. Blake could always tell when I was uncomfortable, noticing the tiniest changes in body language that said I was nervous, or ready to leave the party, or pissed about something, no matter how many times I told him I was fine. I reached for his leg under the table, squeezing it once, a silent *Thank you.* Blindly, he moved his hand over mine, and I was surprised to feel a familiar glow of comfort. The fact that Phil was someone we knew, someone he had to work with, only made me more grateful for the intervention.

"Did you see anything in the ballroom?" Blake continued.

"Nope. Nothing." Phil shrugged and took a swig of his scotch. His effort at nonchalance might have worked if he had been slightly more sober.

"You have to tell us if you did see something," Gabby said, arching an eyebrow. "It's in the rules."

"Believe it or not, I'm *also* literate," Phil said with a thin smile that was somehow more threatening than a frown. "My booklet said one of the staff would meet me to discuss an *arrangement,* but no one showed."

"Then . . . how'd you get so wet?" Jessica was frowning at him, nibbling lightly at her lower lip. Phil's eyes shot over to hers, and for just a moment, anger flashed on his face, then something else, a tightening around the edges of his eyes almost like . . . sorrow. He bent over his glass, swirling the cubes.

"Like I said, a set of doors was open. Got too close in the dark."

Something prickled at my spine. He'd been holding the maid's cap when he came back—no one else seemed to have noticed that—and something about the meeting had clearly shaken him up. I knew Phil, or at least I thought I did, but did I know him well enough to rule out that *animal* switch-flipping he'd demonstrated at dinner?

"Gabby . . . sorry, *Dolly,* did you see anything?" Josh said.

She frowned exaggeratedly.

"I thought maybe. But I think it was my imagination."

"What do you mean?" I pressed.

"Well, I thought I saw Miss Crooner. But either it was a ghost, or I just had the heebie-jeebies, y'know?"

Saw her ghost? Why would Dolly *specifically* see Ida's ghost? And if anyone here was "all talk," like the chauffeur had said in the library recording, it was Bugsy . . . though I was starting to think the man *playing* Bugsy was more dangerous. The ping-pong between anxiety over Bethany, wondering about who I was locked up in this hotel with, the lingering skin-crawl of the time in the dark, and then just the tangle of game clues, was starting to make my legs jitter.

"So . . . we don't really know anything new, then?" Josh said, looking around.

"No, that's not right," Blake said, turning to me. "Someone killed Putters while the lights were out, or at least they tried to, right? Maybe the killer needed to silence him?"

"Which might be useful information if we had any idea who the killer *is,*" Drew said, folding his arms across his chest and jutting his jaw out. "Frankly, this whole thing has been so muddled, I'm not sure it's possible to determine that."

"Oh, I don't know about that," Heather said. The tight look on her face, and the way her eyes darted over to Phil's, told me she had plenty of experience trying to defuse angry men. Clearly she'd been telling the truth out in the garden—their marriage might look perfect, but that didn't mean they *never* had problems. *Still, why was Phil so angry?* He didn't seem to care much about the game itself. Was he just a belligerent drunk? Or was there something else going on, something only Heather, with a lifetime of experience of the private Phil, could see? "We have the map of everyone's location just before the crime, and we know everyone's motives . . ."

"Which might be useful if the last two rounds of clues weren't a complete shitshow." Drew sniffed, brow lowering. The image of him leaning over me in the hallway brandishing the shears came to mind again. I repressed a shudder. "Let's assume that the housekeeper wasn't lying and the maid going AWOL hasn't changed much, which is a pretty big assumption. That doesn't excuse them screwing up the *clues.*"

"We can still work this out," Blake said, voice calm, a little quieter than usual, forcing Drew to focus on listening to him. It was a neat trick I knew he used on clients. "Jessica and Josh, or whatever their names are, they have urns in their room, right?"

"Yup," Jessica nodded eagerly. "But I checked, they're definitely a matched set."

"Right. Heather, Phil? Any urns?" She shook her head, eyes cutting to her husband again. "Becca and I don't have any either, just a couple of creepy dog statues. So: Drew, Gabby, do you guys have urns in your room?"

"Well . . ." Gabby twisted her mouth so far to one side it took her nose with it. "There's something that looks like a plant holder."

"Just one?"

"Yeah, but I'm not really sure—"

"Wait, wait, wait," Heather shook her head. "Are we *certain* the candlestick isn't the weapon? The housekeeper told us about the maid—why wouldn't she just clear that up, too?"

"My point exactly," Drew said, pointing at her with a grin of triumph. "We can't even tell what's supposed to be a frigging clue anymore."

I resisted the urge to point out that the shears were the least-clear clue yet. But I couldn't let Drew see me as a threat—or as *more* of one—until I could sort out what was really going on there.

"Okay, but we worked out that your room and Becca and Blake's room are closest to the drop point, right?" Josh bent over the map, picking out the points with a finger. "And we know Bugsy carries a gun. So even if we assume the candlestick's the weapon, it makes sense that—"

Drew pushed back from the table with a violent jerk.

"Keep playing with half a deck of cards if you want, I'm heading to bed." He tilted his frown onto Gabby. "Well, Dolly? You comin' or what?"

"'Course, Bugs. Whatever you say," she murmured, smiling apologetically at us as she rose to follow his stomping course out of the room. I stared after them, wondering just how much of it had been an act.

"Why don't we head to bed too, Phil." Heather took her husband's arm, then jerked her hand away, staring at her damp palm for a second before recovering herself. "You should get out of this suit anyway," she added in a murmur.

"I'm not done with my drink," he said, not even looking at her. "And anyway, I might want another."

"Phil, I really don't think—"

"Oh for chrissake, Heather, stop counting my drinks for *one* night."

"Fine," she said tightly, nostrils flaring. "*I'll* be in the room. Enjoy however many drinks you like."

With that, she strode away, shoulders pinching together behind her with restrained fury. Phil stared after her for a moment, brow low, then rolled his eyes.

"Probably oughta follow her if I want to get out of the doghouse sometime this year," he said, grimacing and trudging off after Heather.

"I still say it comes down to who had the weapon," Josh said, flipping through the pictures and maps slowly, occasionally stopping to take a closer look at something. "Which makes Drew, Gabby, or Debbie the likeliest option."

"You don't think that's a little simplistic?" Jessica grinned wickedly, igniting a thrill of something in the base of my stomach. *Stop it, genitals. Swinging was* her *plan, not yours.* "They give us the weapon and then we all just ask each other 'Hey, do you have something like this in your room?' We can't lie, remember?"

"Yeah, maybe you're right." He sat back, exhaling a happy sigh. "I just want it not to be me, you know?"

I chuckled appreciatively . . . and then we all seemed to realize at once that we were the only ones left in the room. Jessica cleared her throat, eyes widening meaningfully at Josh, darting to mine for half a second before finding his again.

"I think I'm turning into a pumpkin soon . . ." Jessica smiled a bit awkwardly. It pulled out the delicate swoop of her collarbone. "Ready to turn in, babe?"

An amused half-smile curled Josh's lips. "Sure, why not."

We lingered long enough for them to turn the corner at the end of the hallway, then made our way across the cavernous, empty lobby to our room.

"So," Blake said as he plopped onto the bed to carefully unlace a shoe. "Do you know who did it yet?"

"I have some ideas." My hand drifted to the phone in my pocket. "Actually . . . I'm a little keyed up still. I might go grab another drink at the bar."

"Do you want me to tag along? Two heads are better than one, right?" I felt another unexpected flood of warmth. He'd already shed both shoes, and he had that heavy-looking wrung-out-introvert posture he always got after a night out, when he'd insist *I had so much fun, I just haven't been sleeping all that well lately* so I wouldn't have to feel bad about being the reason that we'd lingered at the party or show or bar at least an hour longer than he'd have preferred.

Why had it never occurred to me that he only did that for me? He almost gleefully declined invitations with friends, postwork drinks with colleagues, a whole host of social events that he'd sparkle at so brightly his entire battery pack would've been drained before the end. But any time I wanted to go to a dinner party full of half-strangers, or throw a Halloween thing that wound up twice as crowded as we'd agreed to, or even just insisted we text a few friends to meet us at our local, he smiled, and agreed, and made sure to keep his face pleasant when we rehashed it at home, even as his slumping shoulders betrayed his exhaustion.

My thumb slid across the phone screen again. Should I tell him about Bethany? Invite him in? Would he play along or give me one of those wide-eyed, too-still *Oh god, this is* not *good* looks that had become unpleasantly frequent since I'd learned about the cheating (or, more specifically, since I'd started spinning out about it)? Wherever we were right now, whatever little glimmers of *us* had slipped into the weekend when I wasn't looking, it all still felt too ethereal to bear up under that.

"You stay here," I finally said. "It'll just be a nightcap."

"If you say so." The relief was palpable on his face. "Let me know if you change your mind."

I slipped out of the room before I could risk that possibility.

TWENTY-SEVEN

I glanced into the main hall before turning in the direction of the bar—was actually twisted around, foot raised to take me there—when it registered.

The gun was gone.

It should have been on the table at the foot of the main stairs, but there was nothing there.

The housekeeper could have grabbed it, put it away somewhere as she passed through . . .

But they made such a show of leaving everything out, telling us to keep looking at the clues, discuss things amongst ourselves. She'd turned leaving it there into a whole set piece.

I hurried down the dim west wing hallway back to the dining room. All the other clues we'd just been poring over were there: the pictures, the letters, the compact with DOLLY DIAMOND picked out in rhinestones, the IOU from Maria to Ida, even the opera glasses with S.C.M. "etched" on the frame in what was clearly Sharpie.

But no gun.

Frowning, I walked back along the hallway, thoughts tumbling through my brain on overdrive. It was just a prop, right? Nothing to worry about. Probably whoever'd shot the chauffeur picked it up when no one was around, so we couldn't guess who it belonged to.

Or it could be another of the real *disappearances.*

Except what good would a prop gun be, even if something *had* happened?

I made my way to the bar, expecting to find it empty, but the table in the back corner had a single occupant.

"Oh . . ." Jessica blinked at me.

"I thought you were going to bed."

"I was, but Josh was tired, and I didn't want to keep him up." She lifted a paperback in one hand.

Feeling suddenly aware of my body, I sat down at a table a few feet away. The idea of making small talk with the bartender sounded exhausting. And the idea of sitting near either of them and *not* talking was just . . . unfathomable. *Why is it so important that no one else ever feel uncomfortable?* I'd never really crystallized the thought before, but suddenly it seemed absurd how much time I spent ensuring that.

"I'll see you in the morning," Jessica said, taking the rest of her drink in one swig and tucking a slip of paper into the pages of her book. It was a Tana French that I hadn't read yet. *Those looks and good taste too.* She was just tucking her chair under the table when I surprised myself by blurting out:

"Can I ask you something?"

"Uh, sure. Go ahead."

"How does it work for you?" She stared at me for a moment, then her eyes widened. She moved closer to my table.

"You mean . . . our arrangement?" I nodded. "What do you want to know, exactly?"

I turned the question over in my head. What *did* I want to know? When I thought about Blake and Lara it twisted my insides so tight I almost couldn't breathe . . . but Josh and Jessica seemed so easy around each other. Like sex with someone else could slip in and out of their relationship without even leaving a smear on the carpet.

"How do you keep from getting jealous? Or hurt?" *Please let there be an answer to this.* Because there had been glimmers this weekend of what we were before, the Blake I'd married, maybe even the me *he'd* married, but as soon as I peered behind them at the giant hulking mass in the corner, they seemed to dissolve, sugar-spun fantasies in a heavy rain. And I was starting to realize now that as much as I loved him, as much as I knew he still loved me, the version of our lives we'd been living before this happened wasn't enough. *Neither of us was really happy.* The thought felt sacrilegious, and I was itching to paper over it immediately with smiles and a joke, but that wouldn't make it less true.

Jessica's lips curled as she assessed me.

"I guess the main thing is that it's always something we both agree to," she finally said. "Is there jealousy? Sure, sometimes. But we're honest with each other about what we want, and what we're comfortable with, which actually makes it kind of . . . exciting to share this other thing."

"Okay . . ." I frowned. That didn't really clarify anything.

"It can be something you do together, you know," she said with a little half-smile. "There's not just one way to do it." Then she heaved in a big breath and glanced over her shoulder toward the door. "Anyway, I should go. Enjoy your night." She held my gaze just a second too long, her large brown eyes half closed, almost languid, then swished out the door, leaving me watching her retreating form. A few seconds later the bartender appeared at my table.

"What can I get you? On the house, so don't hold back."

"Surprise me," I said, still too caught up in Jessica's response to process further, then added, "but nothing sugary. Like . . . professional drinker cocktails only, please."

"Music to my ears."

As soon as she left, I pulled out the phone, stroking it to life with a thumb. Just 12 percent charge left. If the secret of where Bethany had disappeared to was hiding inside, I didn't have much time left to find it. Through the window, I could hear the rain still falling, but the lights in the room had turned the panes into a wavery mirror. I leaned closer to the glass. If I shielded my eyes, I could just make out the flagstone path a few feet from the side of the house, glistening with wet.

The bartender came back and set a rocks glass on the table, the liquid inside a deep reddish-brown.

"In honor of the weekend's theme, a Blood and Sand," she said with a little flourish of her hands. I took a small sip.

"Oh, wow, that's so good."

"You know where to find me when you want another."

Okay, Becca: focus.

I started running through more random patterns while I sipped my drink, the part of my brain not tied up in inventing new ways to connect dots drifting back to what Jessica had just said. Spiral starting from the top left corner?

Incorrect unlock pattern

Could it possibly work that way? Bring people closer together instead of pull them apart? I started from the opposite corner.

Incorrect unlock pattern

Still . . . it made a weird kind of sense. The idea of Blake and Lara together put my lungs in a vise, but it wasn't really the sex that bothered me. That was just . . . *mechanical.* I remember once, about a year after Blake and I got together, Amy had called me up, livid that she had found porn on her husband's computer—not even weird porn, something generic like Tits Galore—and I'd been legitimately confused at why she was so jealous. It was just *fantasy.*

Like imagining a young Brad Pitt showing up on your doorstep with a crippling sexual desire only you could fulfill.

"That's different, Becca. That's pretend."

"What, and porn's real?"

That line of reasoning had not gone over well.

Maybe something simpler, like the letter *L*?

Incorrect unlock pattern

People had crushes. Hell, when we first started dating, Blake and I would tease each other about them. It had been weirdly hot. Like . . . extremely lazy role-play.

But could *I* really remove the betrayal from sex? Not intellectual Becca who says charmingly outré things over cocktails—actual, stuck-in-this-brain, saddled-with-my-history, still-reeling-from-this-thing Becca? Could that version of me get to a place where the idea that Blake would rather be with someone else—someone younger, unencumbered, wearing clothes with a real waistband—didn't just *hurt*?

I recalled Heather's earnest face as she'd stared at me, *You'd be amazed what you can get through in a marriage.* Could this be our way through?

Because if we were *both* involved . . . It's what Jessica had assumed we were planning in the first place. Imagining the possibilities almost felt like when I'd discovered masturbating, this *Eureka!* revelation of possible pleasure and *Why had no one told me about it before now?*

The number seven?

Incorrect unlock pattern

Seriously, though, why didn't anyone tell you this when you got married? *Any* of it? The fact that need never goes away; that being loved doesn't make you stop wanting to feel desired, *newly* desired; that knowing someone so well they feel like a part of you, a phantom limb you keep trying to reattach, still isn't enough to understand them, not really. It's not enough to fulfill them. Or you.

The more I sat with it, the more the idea started to cohere in my head: that the thing I needed to get over wasn't the cheating at all, it was the picture of marriage I'd always had, this idea that unless your relationship looked this way, and he acted that way, and you both never even *looked* away, you were failing. That if you took even one step off the path, you had to get back to that picture-perfect marriage immediately, *or else tragedy*. I'd let myself believe the picture version of Heather and Phil, possibly because it made it feel less futile to keep trying to force our marriage to look that way, but really, they had as many problems as anyone. So, what if the thing you actually needed to do was just . . . draw a new picture?

What about an *N*? No wait, I'd tried that already. A *Z,* then? . . .

A young woman in a sheer cotton babydoll dress smiled back at me from the phone screen. She was holding on to an old-fashioned lamppost with one hand, a triangle of city visible between it and her slim body. Her other arm was flung wide, long blond hair hanging down behind her in a sun-catching sheet. It was the kind of pose you'd find on a photo database if you searched "carefree."

I squinted at the picture.

"Holy fuck . . ."

It was Bethany. I'd unlocked her phone and the proof was right in front of me . . . and apparently she was the kind of girl who set her background as *herself*.

The text icon at the bottom of the screen was blaring *fifty-eight*. God, why was everyone younger than you so obnoxiously popular?

Stop whining, that's fifty-eight potential pieces of pay dirt.

I clicked into the texts, opening the first thread, from Manny. I had to scroll back through half a dozen new messages to find the last outgoing one.

SUNDAY

Bethany
(8:43 P.M.)
Is it okay for me to bring a couple boxes up with me? Can't stay at my apt
(8:44 P.M.)
And need a clean break

Manny
(9:02 P.M.)
sure you can put them in the attic
(9:10 P.M.)
Everything ok?

(9:15 P.M.)
Things just ended suddenly I'll be fine tho

TODAY

(9:26 A.M.)
Didn't hear you get up this morning where r u?
(11:01 A.M.)
Jen is pissed
(11:20 A.M.)
You can tell me it's not like I'll rat you out
(1:39 P.M.)
not showing up doesn't just hurt you Bethany
(2:17 P.M.)
fwiw I'm really offended you would do this when I worked so hard to get you the job

A bad breakup explained why Bethany had been so eager to get out of the city. Other than that . . . it felt like bog standard tense roommates. God, he hadn't even followed up on that heartbreaking "I'll be fine tho."

I clicked into the next set of messages.

TODAY

Jen

(12:05 P.M.)

Can you be here tomorrow for your final costume fitting?

Bethany

(12:32 P.M.)

Yes if I can leave by 4

(12:33 P.M.)

I have an audition in the city and I need to prepare

(12:46 P.M.)

It won't interfere with your commitment to the production, will it?

(12:46 P.M.)

You signed a contract

(12:46 P.M.)

Nope just for a commercial wld film midweek

There was a monthlong gap until the next message, which had come in this morning.

Jen

(9:48 A.M.)

Where are you? Cast meeting started at 9:30

(10:03 A.M.)

Have you left the grounds? You know that's not allowed on production weekends

(10:40 A.M.)

If I don't hear from you in the next 20 minutes consider your contract terminated. You've already had two warnings.

(11:11 A.M.)

I thought you were more professional than this. Don't expect to make it as an actor if you can't keep your commitments

Jen sounded humorless . . . but hardly murderous. Maybe all her whispering with Manny had just been gossip and scrambling to stitch together the rest of the weekend. I sighed, feeling bizarrely frustrated.

There was a thread with "Mom," one with a girl named Whimsy—literally, Whimsy—asking to borrow a straightening iron, and below that, a thread with "Sugar."

YESTERDAY

Bethany

(2:15 P.M.)

I don't know why you came but please don't make this harder than it has to be

Sugar
(2:22 P.M.)
You know I couldn't get out of it
(2:25 P.M.)
Can we meet later? Somewhere private?

Bethany
(2:39 P.M.)
There's nothing to talk about

Sugar
(2:45 P.M.)
Please

(6:01 P.M.)
Just saw maids cleaning 102, no one in it

(6:01 P.M.)
It can't happen while I'm working

(6:45 P.M.)
Of course. Name the time and I'll be there

But . . . that was the room they'd moved Blake and me into. A thread of cold wound from the pit of my stomach up and around my spine.

Bethany
(7:02 P.M.)
Midnight?

Sugar
(7:04 P.M.)
Counting the minutes

(9:05 P.M.)
Plans changed have to cancel

TODAY

(12:58 A.M.)
I need to see you
(12:59 A.M.)
Where can we meet that's private

(12:59 A.M.)
There's a groundskeeper's cottage on the edge of the gardens
(1:00 A.M.)
I checked earlier its open
(1:03 A.M.)
I can be there in 20
(1:04 A.M.)
But you have to promise to drop this afterward

(1:05 A.M.)
Promise.
(4:12 A.M.)
Did you change your mind? Waited a while but didn't see you
(7:35 A.M.)
Where were you last night?
(11:02 A.M.)
Am I the reason you left?
(12:26 P.M.)
Just let me know you're okay and I'll leave you alone
(12:26 P.M.)
If that's what you want.

(5:05 P.M.)

Why not at least hear me out? I
don't understand

I frowned at the phone. She'd meant to meet "Sugar" at midnight, apparently in our room . . . which was close to when Phil had arrived, loose from liquor and around the collar.

Manny had said something earlier about her "rich old guy." If that hadn't been part of the game . . . what if it wasn't just that Phil had crossed some line, what if he and Bethany were having a full-on affair? Hadn't he mentioned a studio he kept in New York for nights he was teaching?

Goosebumps broke out on my arms as I read through the messages again, trying to piece it all together.

She'd moved at the beginning of the week in a rush, come up here, asked Sugar to leave her alone when he pressed for a meeting . . . but after that encounter in the hall she must have figured it was easier to appease him. *She wasn't scared of something he'd said, she was scared I'd caught them.* Then either she put us into 102 on purpose or she canceled once the housekeeper told her to give it to us; Phil either missed the message or assumed she was just getting cold feet; he tried again, and Bethany agreed . . . but then just hadn't shown?

Or maybe she had.

And maybe he had too.

Oh my god that's where I'd seen it.

"How are you doing over here?"

"Aaahhh!"

I actually shrieked, which of course made the bartender shriek too and jump back, almost backflipping over one of the occasional tables that seemed to sprout up around this house organically. She put a hand on her chest, half-laughing. "Sorry to startle you."

"No, it's okay. I was just . . . focused," I said, waving the phone half-heartedly in the air. My heart felt like it had migrated to the space just behind my eyeballs.

"That's hilarious, Bethany has almost that exact same phone case." She pointed, and I flipped the phone over, absurdly relieved to realize it was glitter-shot pearlized pink, the kind of case you could find on a thousand end displays in a thousand big box stores.

But . . . they knew each other. Well enough to recognize each other's phone cases. And there was one more thing I needed to be sure of. So far, I only had overheard conversations, stabs in the dark. I needed an actual answer. Pasting on my most innocent smile, I flipped the phone back over and turned to the bartender.

"Oh? Who's Bethany?" I put a hand under my chin, tilting my head. *Just normal curiosity here!*

Very subtle, Becks. But the bartender seemed to buy it.

"One of the actresses. She plays the maid."

"Interesting . . ." I licked my lips, frowning slightly. "Can I ask you something?"

"Shoot."

"Do *you* believe she would just ditch the rest of you midweekend?"

The bartender's eyebrow crept up, but she didn't say anything.

"You don't have to tell me if you don't want to, I just got the sense that the housekeeper . . . what's her real name?"

"Jen."

"Right, Jen. She seemed pissed. I just wondered if they'd had a falling-out or something."

"Yeahhh . . ." The bartender rolled her eyes. "Bethany and Jen aren't exactly close. Bethany can be a little . . . flaky. Which I get, she's trying to make it as a real actress. If I were her and I got a last-minute audition in New York, I'd take it too."

"Oh, did she have an audition today?"

"If she did, she didn't tell me, I was just assuming." The bartender glanced at me, then shrugged. "I wouldn't put it past her to just bounce, she skipped a few rehearsals at the beginning. Like I said, she's *flaky*. But I guess I thought she needed the job." She sucked in a breath, putting on a bright face. "People do all kinds of weird things, right?"

"Totally." I laughed a little to cover the vertiginous feeling tumbling through me. "By the way, is it alright if I take this with me?" I lifted the remains of my cocktail. "I want to check the clues table now that I finally have a chance to hear myself think."

"Feel free. It's already been 'paid for,' right?"

"I guess I have Bethany to thank for that." I smiled and hurried out, making for the dining room once again.

It was right in the center of the pile, rising like a monolith.

The candlestick. We'd been so intent on figuring out whether it was the actual clue that I'd completely forgotten that I'd seen it before. Not in one of the rooms, not as part of the game. Through the windows of the empty, locked cottage at the edge of the grounds. The cottage Bethany had used—or tried to use—for her tryst with Phil.

I ducked out of the room and hurried to the lobby, where I heaved open the door that led out onto the drive.

A gust of wind blasted me in the face and I blinked away raindrops, craning my head to pick out the silhouette of the building against the dark forest.

I found it almost immediately. After all, it was hard to miss the thick clots of smoke belching from its stone chimney.

Either Bethany was there right now, playing house a few feet from all her things, her job, her *life,* just waiting for someone to knock on the door and find her . . .

. . . or someone had *already* found her. Someone who was looking less and less like the man I knew with every passing moment.

Either way, I planned to find out.

TWENTY-EIGHT

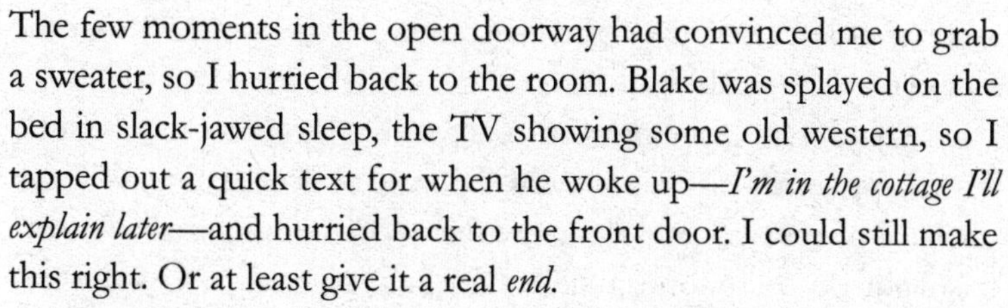

The few moments in the open doorway had convinced me to grab a sweater, so I hurried back to the room. Blake was splayed on the bed in slack-jawed sleep, the TV showing some old western, so I tapped out a quick text for when he woke up—*I'm in the cottage I'll explain later*—and hurried back to the front door. I could still make this right. Or at least give it a real *end.*

Impulsively, I opened the text chain on Bethany's phone again. The idea that Phil would do this so blithely, that he could smile at everyone and be this other person the moment you turned your back, made me so angry my fingers started curling into claws. He wasn't our charming friend with a perfect life, the good dad who showed up to every volleyball match, the picture of everything we could have someday; he was just another confirmed cheater, sowing hurt in every direction, sailing through life on a cloud of scotch fumes and a spokesman-ready smile. Fuck him, fuck all the Phils. It felt like he'd betrayed *me,* the idea of him I'd been holding in my head for so long, that I'd been holding us *up against* for so long. I wanted him to be terrified. Cornered. Feel what the women he used up and discarded probably felt.

Bethany

(9:50 P.M.)

Didn't mean to ghost you.

(9:50 P.M.)

Tho you can't really blame me.

The "read" icon showed up almost immediately. Stopping only to snatch a giant black umbrella from the stand near the front door, I hurried out into the night, huddling beneath its bat wings.

The rain had slowed to a steady drizzle, the sort that moves sideways as much as down, fuzzing every surface slightly, as though the world hadn't quite figured out the right strength lens to read the eye chart through. The lights along the front of the house barely managed to stretch halfway across the gravel drive, and the woods surrounding the estate seemed to have taken the opportunity to creep a little closer, the soft susurration of the rain covering the sound of their stealthy advance.

I shivered, wrapping an arm across my stomach for warmth. The damp, chilly air was already slipping its slender fingers down the back of my neck and along the furrow of my spine. Clicking the flashlight on my phone, I started picking my way across the wet gravel drive.

I immediately regretted not changing my shoes. How did I manage to specifically go back for a sweater and then still wear ballet flats out in this?

Oh right, alcohol.

Soon I'd made my way beyond the pale protective dome of light that huddled over the main house. The groundskeeper's cottage was only fifty yards away, but with the night starting to crowd in, it seemed farther. I glanced at the sky overhead. The clouds were woolly and low, pressing claustrophobically close to the tops of the trees. The rain started to bead on the sleeves of my sweater.

Finally, shivering slightly—if I pressed my toes down, little puddles of water sprang up between them from my insoles—I reached the front of the cottage. The edges of the living room window I'd peered through earlier seemed to glow, flickeringly, as though a will-o'-the-wisp had gotten trapped in the frame. My breath hitched in my throat as I made my way up to the door. Huddling beneath the narrow roof that jutted out over the entry, I tucked the umbrella away and reached for the knob, turned it . . . this time it opened . . .

"Hello? Phil, are you here?"

But no one answered. Sucking in a deep breath, rain prickling painfully at the backs of my legs, I stepped inside, pushing the door closed behind me with an ominous *click*.

It was almost over. The only thing left to do was drag the girl out through the bulkhead, into the forest, and then . . .

"Hello?"

The voice was faint and breathy, almost inaudible.

"Phil, are you here?"

Overhead, the floorboards creaked.

Someone was up there.

The bulkhead doors were still open, the impenetrable dark between them a perfect promise of escape.

But no, it was too late for that. For now, the only thing to do was slip out of sight . . . and wait.

TWENTY-NINE

The front room of the cottage was empty, lit only by the fire in the large stone hearth, burning low now, the flames undulating eerily in the draft from the door. I blinked, trying to force my eyes to adjust to the dim orange light.

Heavy canvas shrouds gave the furniture a bloated, organic feel, like gigantic fungi that had sprung up from the floor in the damp. All except for the loveseat just next to the fireplace; its covering was missing, and the dark brown leather beneath, stiff and shiny with age, had a bare, skinned look in the firelight.

It took me several seconds to notice that there were no logs in the fireplace.

Instead, the flames were steadily eating away at a large heap of thick canvas. The near corner had unfolded, spilling over the spindly metal grate and onto the hearth. I moved over, bending to pluck an edge up between my fingers. The fabric was stiff, the kind of material you'd use for a backpack.

It had to be the missing loveseat cover—it was the same beigey color as what covered all the rest of the furniture. *Speaking of* . . . I unfolded, turned to gaze along the mantel, and there, right where I knew it would be, the candlestick's mate. Before I could think twice, I picked it up to test its weight. *It's exactly the same.* A surge of triumph rose through me . . . and immediately plummeted back down.

The candlesticks were the same.

I'd been so elated that I'd noticed that detail—and also, *alcohol*—that I hadn't really thought about what it meant. What it practically *guaranteed.* Because why trade out the pretend weapon in your murder mystery game unless . . .

I heard a faint scraping, creaking noise, maybe a foot on an old floorboard, or a door opening somewhere out of sight.

"Bethany, are you here?" I whispered, hoping against hope, against all reason, that she might answer. "I'm here to help."

The stone walls sucked up the sound of my voice. I raised the candlestick, hardly daring to breathe. She might still be alive, somewhere deeper in this claustrophobic little building. What if she had been knocked unconscious, couldn't hear me? I couldn't *abandon* her.

Another creak.

Every muscle in me tensed, my neck telescoping to give my ears a better vantage point on the mysterious noise.

The sound hadn't come from the creepy hallway across from the entrance, it was coming from the far side of the kitchen. I narrowed my eyes, peering at the shadowy hulks of the counters, the shelves looming over them, until finally I could pick out the faint glimmer of a brass knob at the far side of the room.

There was a door there. And the sound was coming from somewhere behind it.

As I crept closer, I realized it was partway open. I trained my phone around the edge, revealing a narrow room lined with empty shelves, and at the far end, another door, this one coarser, and older-looking somehow.

It opened onto a rough wooden landing and an even rougher

wall, formed from a jumble of stones set in crumbling mortar. A set of old wooden stairs dribbled down to the right, set into the foundation wall but open on the other side, the gaps between each step vertigo-inducing. The sight of them tightened my throat nauseously.

"Bethany? Are you down there?" My voice was barely a whisper. I crept down a single step, then two, hand on the splintery wood of the railing, and crouched to look into the cellar.

The room . . . *opened up* wasn't right, really, the ceilings were so low they seemed to press down from above. More like it oozed out from the foot of the stairs, the packed-earth floor spreading off in all directions, the far walls disappearing beneath thick swaths of shadow. In one corner I could make out the heavy silhouette of some sort of workbench. Deeper patches of black against the walls hinted at chairs and boxes, the sort of detritus every basement seemed to collect, and at the far end of the room, a door gaped open, creaking slightly as a gust of wind barreled through it.

It was then that three things struck me in quick succession.

The first was that a light was on. It was faint, probably a single bulb suspended from the ceiling, but it was enough to carve out the basics of the room. Someone was definitely down here, and if it was Bethany, she didn't feel up to chatting.

The second was that this was not a TV show and I was not the lead detective. This was the real world, a world in which I was almost certain something terrible had happened to this young girl, and determining what, precisely, wasn't going to get me the end credits I'd been hoping for.

All of which pointed to: Get out of the murder house, *now*.

I turned, scrambling back up the stairs and through the narrow pantry, stumbling into the kitchen, wincing as the edge of a counter dug into my hip bone, fumbling my way around it toward the entrance. Even a few seconds in the dim light of the basement had blinded me, turning the ground floor into nothing but inky smears. I moved around the counter, hand on the top to guide me, aware of the too-slow, molasses feeling clinging to me, like when you try to run in nightmares.

"Dammit . . . where's the . . . ?"

Why couldn't I find the door handle? My fingers were just scraping on splinters, hooking onto rough wall planks, where did the wooden wall end and the wooden door begin?

Then the third thing struck me, hard on the back of the skull, and everything went black.

FINAL ROUND

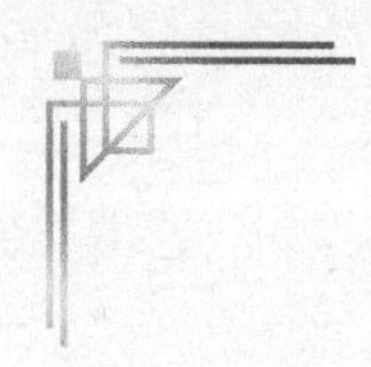

THE ACCUSATION

You've found all the clues, learned all your fellow guests' secrets, and weighed the evidence. There's only one thing left to do before the authorities arrive: decide who you'll accuse of the dark crimes committed here.

Is the murderer an obsessed fan, a jealous lover, a desperate rival, or a mysterious hanger-on from the past? Only you can decide.

Make your guess below. But remember, more than one person amongst you might be guilty . . . and there may be more foul deeds afoot than any of you realize . . .

Once everyone has written down their accusation, please turn the page . . .

THIRTY

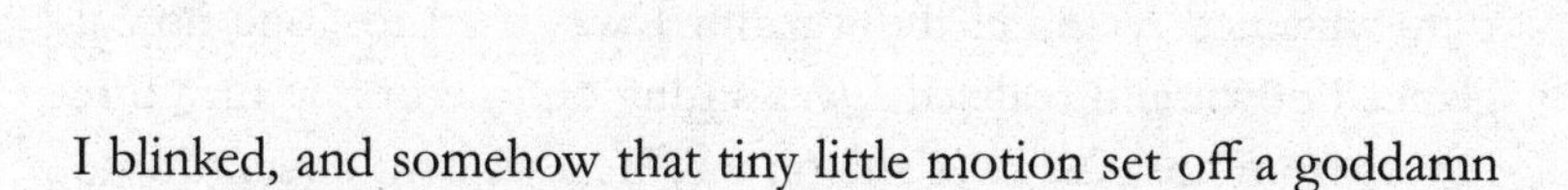

I blinked, and somehow that tiny little motion set off a goddamn tidal wave of pain through my head.

"Nnghhh . . ."

I tried to reach up to touch the pulsing mound of pain at the back of my skull . . . but my hand wouldn't move. Wincing, I opened my eyes a tiny slit, trying to sort out where I was.

I could see the underside of a set of stairs directly in front of me, their wooden planks splintered with age. Beneath them I could dimly make out a rough stone wall, and nestled between the two was . . .

"Jesus fucking Christ!"

I jerked back, hitting my head against the wall behind me, which set off another nauseating explosion of white in my head. Digging my heels into the packed earth, I tried to scoot away, but there was nowhere to go, and without my hands— I glanced down to find them bound at the wrists with a length of bright blue nylon rope, the ends tied off in a neat bow. What the actual—

"Calm *down,* Becca. My god." The gaps between the stairs started to go black as the speaker descended, their steps grinding into the ancient wood. "She can't hurt you. She's *dead.*"

The shadow slipped to the side, stepped around the edge of the stairs, and resolved into . . .

"Heather?" I frowned, trying to make sense of the familiar whip-thin middle-aged woman in front of me, her pale grey-and-pink yoga pants and matching zip-up athleisure top smeared with grime.

"I'm glad you're back. I was starting to worry I might have hit you a little *too* hard. Sometimes I don't know my own strength. Just ask my kickboxing instructor." She giggled, raising a hand to her mouth. "Though I'll have you know, I was very careful getting you down the stairs. So . . . you know, you're welcome." She dropped her hand to reveal the smile I knew so well, tight lips around carefully whitened teeth, all the warmth I was used to gone now. I glanced down and realized I was sitting on one of the furniture covers from upstairs. Eyes still on me, Heather bent down next to the body, lifting the dead girl's hand between two fingers. "See?" She let the arm flop back to the earth with a heavy thump. "Nothing to be afraid of."

"Heather . . . what's going on?"

"Oh, just the usual. Cleaning up my husband's messes. Though I guess Bethany over here is really more *my* mess this weekend." She giggled again, in a high, thin way that verged on manic. "What's mine is yours, right? Oh my god . . ."

"I don't understand . . ."

Her face snapped back to sharp attention.

"Of course you don't, Becca. You've been a mess since you got here. For god's sake, I swear there was a minute where you believed the bartender was *actually dead.*"

I frowned, blinking. Bizarrely, at least considering the circumstances, I felt stung. *I had to put a hell of a lot together to get here, Heather.*

"I'm sorry, that was . . . unkind. Especially knowing what you've been dealing with lately." Heather planted one hand on her hip, massaging either side of her forehead with the other, and sucked in a no-nonsense breath. "Forgive me, I've been a bit . . . occupied." She gestured at the body under the stairs.

"So he . . . killed her?" I said, the words seeming to stick on my parched tongue. Already I could sense that they were wrong, that I'd put together the puzzle pieces only to realize the thing was actually a Magic Eye.

"Oh god no. Phil would never have the balls to do something like *that*." She sniffed derisively, turning a disgusted sneer on the corpse. "He just *fucked* her."

"What, last night?" I frowned. "Or do you mean . . . after she . . ."

"Of course not." She turned back to me, eyebrows beetling. "Dear lord, Becca, I'd think you know us better than *that*." Her eyes drilled into me. I blinked, trying to piece it together . . .

"So then . . . *you* broke into our room?"

"Broke into your . . ." Heather's eyebrows knitted together. "Why would I break into your room? You told me it was the *staff*."

My stomach plummeted even lower. Blake had been right all along. *If I'd just listened to him* . . . Heather's gaze had grown so intense I could almost feel heat coming off it.

"Sorry," I swallowed hard, trying to push my thoughts past the throbbing wall of pain in my head. "I'm getting mixed up. I'm a little woozy."

"Aww, I know, sweetie," she cooed, her face twisted in genuine-looking concern. "Ryan had a concussion last year at the club tennis tournament, he was nauseous for weeks. But you understand, I had to act fast."

I blinked a few times, unable to reconcile the three Heathers: the one I thought I knew, the concerned parent in front of me, and the one who had apparently murdered this poor girl. Finally I nodded. It seemed to appease at least one of them; she turned back to the dead girl, shaking her head.

"The schmuck probably thought he was so *lucky,* that the *one* weekend his wife had her heart set on just happened to be his mistress's little dinner theater performance. Didn't even think to question why I was pushing so hard for us to come to this getaway for our anniversary. For god's sake, I put the reminders in his calendar and he still seemed to think his little dalliance was a secret." Her nose twisted up as she turned her eyes back on the girl's body. I tried to turn my head away, but I couldn't keep my eyes on Heather and off Bethany at the same time; limp snakes of blond hair slinked in at the edge of my vision no matter what I did. "Even if I hadn't known, what kind of man would think it was a good idea to risk us meeting? But that's Phil. Always trying to find efficiencies." She rolled her eyes. "I'm sure he just figured two birds, one stone."

What did they do at this point in the shows? *Keep them talking.*

"So you planned all this? God, that's like something out of a movie."

"Actually, no. I didn't plan *any* of this." Heather rolled her eyes again, spreading her hands wide in a "You caught me" gesture. "It's a bit hard to manufacture a chance encounter with some would-be actress flitting around the city, and I needed to make sure I'd have a chance to talk to her. Usually, realizing that I know, and that I'm not going anywhere, is more than enough to scare them off, though dipping into Phil's bank account can be a good fail-safe for the particularly *vicious* sluts. But this?" She winced. "This was a very unfortunate accident. I mean, honestly, Becca, what do you take me for?"

"I just thought . . . I mean, Drew and Josh found the candlestick, and . . . that's what you used, isn't it?"

"It was." Her eyes drifted to the girl again. "But that was just me doing what I always do. Cleaning up." She sniffed out a mirthless laugh. "You can find all these scripts online, you know. They even suggest what to serve for dinner, can you believe that?" She widened her eyes in exhausted incredulity. Heather was always lean, stretched, but right now she looked like an elastic about to break.

"The bits you can't be sure of aren't too hard to sort out if you just happen to grab someone else's 'dossier' after breakfast. Then easy-peasy, swap the candlestick in for the urn and wait for everyone to cover it in fingerprints." She glanced over at me with a rueful smile. "You're not the only one who reads a lot of mysteries, after all."

She gazed at the body for a few more seconds, then shook her head sharply, like a dog waking up.

"Before I forget, I'm going to have to get a bit intimate. I'm assuming you have the phone with you?"

"The phone?" Even I wasn't convinced by my play-dumb routine. Rolling her eyes, Heather started patting my pockets until she found what she was looking for, extracting Bethany's cellphone—and my own—and sliding them into the holsters of her yoga pants.

"Thanks for that. I assumed she'd have it on her last night. Once I realized she didn't, I sent a text to give Phil a little cover, but you saw. It was flimsy at *best*. Honestly, I'm not sure how I'd have found it if you hadn't turned up."

"Glad I could help," I murmured, stomach sinking further. Watching Heather tick through her boxes was almost as disorienting as the body under the stairs. How was she able to so thoroughly divorce herself from the reality of what she'd done? Yesterday, Bethany was smiling, making plans, worrying about her lines. She was a *human being*, but Heather was acting as though the biggest issue in the entire equation was wiping a few text messages. And if she could truly shut off the absolute horror of that so thoroughly . . . what did that mean for *me*, the wrench in her step-by-step-by-step plan?

Heather followed my gaze to the body, eyes going a bit unfocused as she stared at the vaguely girl-like heap. An image of Bethany from the night before, so triumphant when she'd managed to make the room key, flashed into my mind. I was suddenly aware of just how *young* she was.

"No time like the present, hmm? We should probably get to it."

"Get to . . . what, exactly?"

"Getting *rid* of her, Becca. For goodness' sake, try to keep up, we're in a time crunch here."

"You want me to . . ."

"I didn't *want* you here at all, not at this weekend, and *certainly* not now. You should be back in your room, trying to work things out with Blake, for goodness' sake, not trying to live out your own little mystery story." She folded her arms across her narrow chest. "But now you're here, so we have to make lemonade, hmm?" She quirked her head to one side like some maniacal bird. "Most of the hard work's done already. But if you help me carry her, we can finish much faster."

"Heather . . . please, you have to—"

"Was I not *clear,* Becca?" Her eyes narrowed, voice getting tighter and higher as she drilled into me with her stare. "You're the one who couldn't leave well enough alone—what happens in a marriage is nobody else's business, I would have thought your experience would at *least* have taught you that much. But now you're here. I can't exactly leave you alone here while I deal with her myself. So. You'll help."

"Right . . ." I swallowed hard. The room still felt swimmy from the bump on my head, but my heart was fluttering back to life, banging around my rib cage frantically as though it could somehow secure an escape for both of us. "What did you have in mind?"

"I can get her up through the bulkhead on my own—you just rest up. After that, it's your turn. Okay?" The tight little chirp in her voice was the same one she used to urge her kids to finish their homework, on Phil when she wanted help getting the meal on the table, on restaurant managers she was trying to get to comp our desserts. The dissonance of hearing it come out now was almost enough to bring up the drinks sloshing around in my stomach.

"Okay," I said, nodding slowly.

"Sit tight, then." She glanced at my wrists, giggling manically again. *She's legitimately starting to crack.* "I swear, that was totally unintentional."

Then she moved over to the body, which was splayed across a blue tarp, grabbed on to the end near the feet, and started tugging it after her across the basement, like the most grotesque Christmas sleigh you could imagine. I told myself not to watch—who the fuck needs *that* in their nightmares forever—but I couldn't seem to peel my eyes away from the scene, Heather tugging steadily as the girl on the tarp jostled and bounced over the rough floor, fingertips trailing in the dirt, head flopping crazily from side to side. Soon the shadows had swallowed them, and I exhaled, relieved.

I had to think through this. She knew us, *Phil* knew us . . . Surely that would count for something, especially if this was all just an accident. I just needed to snap her out of this. I tried to comb through all the mystery shows, the stories I'd steeped myself in over the last several months, searching for a way to convince her to rethink what I was becoming more and more certain was happening next. But for the life of me, I couldn't think of one that ended that way . . .

"Ready?"

I startled at her voice, directly overhead. Heather's cheeks were red from exertion, and a light film of water had smeared the streaks of dirt into a grimy tie-dye on her skin and clothes.

"Heather, listen, I know you didn't mean for this to happen. If we just head back to the main house—"

"Don't play dumb, Becca, you don't wear it well. You made your bed, now you're going to have to lie in it."

She crouched next to me, lifting the end of the rope around my hands, then stopped.

"Hold that thought, now where did I . . ." She patted around her spandex-clad body. "There." Unzipping the front pocket of her athletic jacket, she pulled out a dainty gun with pearlized inlays in the handle, then took up the rope again. "For insurance. You understand."

"But . . . that's the gun from the game, isn't it?"

"See? That's the smart girl we all love." She smiled and patted my cheek, never lowering the gun.

"I thought it was a prop."

"A five-in-one blank cartridge can turn any gun into a prop. I learned that in community theater." She smiled and flicked open the barrel, displaying the backs of six shiny bullets for me. "You know how much I love my afternoons at the range. They charge an arm and a leg if you buy your ammunition *there*." She flicked the barrel closed, pointing the gun at my chest again. "Lucky for me, thirty-eight specials are a very common handgun size, especially for female enthusiasts. So. Shall we?"

I nodded and she yanked the end of the rope with a hard jerk. She waited, training the gun on me as I tugged my hands apart, wincing as feeling prickled back through them. The rope slipped over my hands and onto the ground at my feet. I rubbed the insides of my wrists, never taking my eyes off her.

"What now?"

"Outside." She gestured toward the bulkhead door with the gun. "And for goodness' sake, don't try anything *stupid*."

We crossed the basement to a plain metal door that led to a short, narrow concrete staircase, the angled metal doors built into the rim flung wide open. The tarp was just to one side at the top. My throat tightened spastically as I glanced at it. The girl seemed to be floating in the small puddle of rainwater that had collected around her, and the area around her head looked distinctly . . . *swampier* than it had in the basement. I stared at the sharp, thin ledge of the bulkhead door that Heather must have banged her over the top of, then back at what remained of Bethany's head. Then I turned away, gagging, as a small chunk of something greyish bobbed past her cheek.

Probably just a piece of leaf. Definitely *not brain matter. Which you also definitely didn't just walk through on those stairs . . .*

"There's more slack by the feet," Heather said from behind and below me, pointing with the nose of the gun. I moved dutifully to the far end of the tarp, grateful to put a bit more distance between myself and the wreck of skull.

"Which way do you want me to go?"

"Through the woods over there," she gestured with the gun again. "I'll bring up the rear." Then she hurried up the last couple steps, eyes and gun trained on me as she bent to grab a large, handled flashlight tucked neatly alongside the bulkhead opening, lens down. She flicked it on, then aimed the watery beam of light at the trees. "Well? I don't have all night, Becca."

She fixed me with the same disapproving-mom stare I'd actually seen in action before, and I bent to grab the corners of the tarp, trying to ignore the wave of painful vertigo it brought on. With one last futile glance over my shoulder at the main house, its enormous bulk dotted by a few tiny patches of yellowish light, I started hauling my death sledge into the woods.

For a few minutes we trudged on in silence, the canopy of the trees slowing the rain. Every so often, Heather would shift the beam of light one way or another and bark out a simple order, "Left now," or "Go around the log," and I'd comply.

Soon my legs and shoulders were burning with exertion. But it seemed to have cleared some of the fog around my brain. The back of my head ached dully, but my thoughts were starting to cohere.

"I just don't get it, Heather," I said as I stopped, dropping the tarp briefly to pick up the base of a fallen sapling and move it off our path. "Why do all this if it was an accident?"

"Oh, come on, Becca. You confront your husband's tramp at her place of work and she ends up dead, you think anyone's going to buy that it's an accident?"

"But . . . it was, wasn't it?"

"Of *course* it was." Her voice sounded strained, near tears. "I told you, I only ever came here to talk to her, but she wouldn't listen, kept saying I had it all wrong, as if I hadn't been through this more times than I can count." She barked out a rough laugh. "I needed her to understand what she was risking. He was so much more enamored of her than I'd seen him in the past, you know? And it had been going on so much longer, I was starting to worry that he might actually . . ." She swallowed hard, pausing for a few long moments. "And I tried to explain all that, just ask her woman to woman to let him go, but she wouldn't even look at me, just kept shaking her head like some stupid fucking windup doll, and then she was running out the door, and I grabbed her arm but she wouldn't stop, and I saw the candlestick there and I just . . ." Even through the rain and the forest sounds, I could hear Heather's heavy gulp. "But it's not my fault. She was threatening my family. My kids deserve a mother *and* a father, I couldn't bear to have them ping-ponging back and forth between me and whatever tawdry penthouse Phil would wind up in, with a stepmom who looked like she stepped out of some porno."

Then it hit me in a sickening wave.

"But Heather . . . she'd already called things *off* with Phil."

"What?" Heather's voice was faint, lost-sounding.

"She told me last night that she was moving away from the city, and she texted Manny about bringing boxes here, plus she mentioned an ex . . ."

There was a long, pregnant pause, then an angry snort.

"Bullshit. That little bitch would never give up her meal ticket."

"Heather, I'm telling you, she had. Think about it—why would she be so cagey in their texts, tell him she didn't want him here? She was trying to avoid him because she'd ended things."

Heather went silent. I risked a glance over my shoulder. She was staring at her feet, eyes glazed, head shaking slowly back and forth.

"No . . . *no*. She wanted you to think that."

"Why would she care what I—"

"No, you know what? *Spare* me, Becca. Your husband has one fling and you think you understand how this works all of a sudden? This isn't my first rodeo, and *that* bitch"—her arm shook as she pointed furiously at the tarp—"knew *exactly* what she was doing. If she broke things off"—she shook her head rapidly, tongue darting over her lips—"it was just some tactic to wrap Phil around her even *tighter.*"

"Oh, Heather . . ." It slipped out before I could stop myself. Her eyes narrowed to feral slits. *Think, Becca* . . . But before I could come up with anything, she was pointing through the woods with the pistol.

"Move."

"Heather, please just—"

"*Move,* Becca."

I swallowed hard, mind whirring furiously. I had to make her believe there was another option. Make her remember it was me, her friend Becca, at the end of that gun.

"It must have been really hard for you," I said, glancing back at her as I bent to pick up my burden again. "And for Ryan. He's so bright." *Remember, Heather, I know them. And they know* me.

"It was, you know?" She had a slightly distant, sad smile on her face. "You'd think after all the flings Phil's had over the years, it would get easier, but it really never does."

I could hear her heavy sigh behind me.

"I considered trying to pin it on Phil—with all the messages between them, it wouldn't be hard." I glanced back and she raised an eyebrow at me meaningfully, then dropped it, shrugging. "But after everything he's done, can you believe that I still love him?"

"Yes," I murmured, stomach plunging even further south at the thought of Blake. *Did he realize I was gone yet? Would he wake up at all?* I was going to die here, alone with this homicidal soccer mom that had invaded Heather's body, and he would never even know why I'd left. A small part of me—buried beneath the aching muscles, throbbing head, and generalized disgust—felt sorry for Heather. I knew *exactly* what it felt like to be so deeply, eye-clawingly angry with someone and still need them in your life. Hate them so much it was hard to share the same air and yet still love them too much to let them go.

The rest of me just felt like it was falling through an unknowably long, vast void. *How could this have been inside her all this time?*

"Stop here," Heather said sharply, reaching forward to stretch the beam of the flashlight a bit farther. Just a few feet ahead of us, a long trench had been dug in the earth, an ancient shovel sticking up at one corner like a flagpole. A shiver went through me. Another few steps and I'd have fallen into it headfirst.

Though . . . that might be better than what was probably coming for me any minute. Bethany might have been an accident, but if Heather was going to all this trouble to cover her up, there was no way she'd leave me behind, no matter how much history we had.

I had to keep her talking. Slow her down until I could think of a plan, or even just get the feeling back in my arms and legs. A horror movie flashed into my mind, me stumbling through the woods, trying to run but my legs not responding, and Heather coming up from behind to finish what she'd started in the cottage . . .

"Forget what I said before," I said, dropping the body and turning to face her, rubbing at a shoulder with my thumb to loosen the muscles. It was a risky play, but I had to hope there was something still there, some part of her that recognized, if not how far gone she was, at least that I didn't deserve this. Bethany's face flashed before my eyes again, the way it had looked last night: confused, and scared, and determined. "I just want to understand what you were going through. You must need someone to talk to right now."

Heather's eyes narrowed.

"We both know it won't make a difference, so why not get it off your chest? What made this girl so different?"

She stared at me a moment longer, then her body relaxed infinitesimally. *At least it's a start.*

"It was just a feeling, you know? I mean . . . Phil has been stupid before, but never *that* stupid. Putting her up in his pied-à-terre? Ryan is going to start touring colleges any day now—what if we'd decided to pop down to the city to see NYU, or Columbia?" Her nostrils flared, lips tightening with indignation.

"But surely he would have moved on eventually, right?"

She chewed at her lower lip.

"His texts with her were more puppy-dog than I'd seen in ages. There was a chance . . ." She sucked in a deep breath, eyes seeming to go out of focus as she continued to stare at the girl's face. "All I actually wanted was for her to understand. I didn't spend all those years, *decades,* building our life just for some stupid midlife crisis to tear it all down. And I didn't want this, obviously, but once it was done . . . I realized it was better this way. *Cleaner.*"

"Cleaner?" I could hear the shock in my voice. *Dear lord, Becca, can you* never *keep your emotions to yourself?*

"If she just disappeared. Started . . . what's the word for it? *Ghosting* Phil. He'd get over her eventually, and in the meantime there wouldn't be all the *melodrama.*" Then she turned to me, giggling again. "Oh my god . . . *ghosting.* I just got it. See, I told you that you were a smart girl." She started laughing harder, bending at the waist with the force of it, until the laughter had turned into heaving wild sobs as she clutched her stomach.

Now. Now's the moment.

I took a step closer.

"Heather, listen . . . the stress of this is getting to you. If we just go back to the hotel, I'm sure they can—"

"No!" She whipped her pistol hand toward me. I leaped back just in time to avoid getting cracked across the jaw. "Don't you come near me! Just . . . *deal* with her."

She pointed at the body again.

"Heather, it's *me.* Blake's back at the hotel. You must know this can't end well . . ."

"This is going to end *however I fucking want it to*!" She was shrieking now, eyes bulging as she pointed the gun at me. Reflexively I put my hands up. "Did I want this? No. But am I sorry? Of *course* not!

She was trying to destroy my family. My entire *life*." She was leaning forward now, lips pulled back over her teeth. "You of all people should understand."

"Me?"

"Don't play all high and mighty with me." She sneered. "I know you've thought about it too."

"Thought about . . . what, *killing* the woman Blake slept with?" I could feel indignation ballooning in my chest. She widened her eyes, *Duh, Becca,* and something in me just . . . bubbled over. It was bad enough trying to sort things out with Blake, and Jessica, and what I even *wanted* anymore, but being lumped in with this wild-eyed escapee from Lululemon? "I didn't even *throw a vase,* Heather. Because I'm not a fucking *psycho*."

She reeled back. I had the briefest hope that rage had somehow gotten through to her where reason couldn't . . .

Then her eyes narrowed to slits, she pointed the gun straight at my forehead, and, in a low voice, so controlled it was terrifying, said:

"Get her in the hole. Now."

"Heather, I'm sorry, you have to understand . . ."

"This isn't a discussion, Becca."

"You don't need to do this. We can still—"

"Get her in the hole or I swear to god I will shoot you in the fucking head."

I gulped spastically. My whole body felt numb, even my lips. Somewhere, dimly, I wondered how I was aware of my lips being numb so quickly.

But I was out of time. Out of words. Arms and legs and heart feeling like bags of wet cement, I bent, tugging at the tarp again to inch the body closer to the hole.

"Good. Now flip her off it."

Too numb to even wince, I knelt in the muddy ground next to the grave to heave against Bethany's hip. I slid around for a few seconds, unable to get my grip, her body unwilling to budge, and then suddenly the momentum was enough and she slid sideways across the tarp and into the hole with a sickening splash of rain-water.

"Now you."

I turned to face her, but mud and leaves were sliming my legs, and I fell to my hands in the muck. I looked up at her, heart beating so loud that the sound of it was starting to drown out the soft static of the rain.

"Please. I'll stay here. I won't run . . ."

"In the hole, Becca."

"Heather, it doesn't have to be this way."

"*You're* the one who's made me do this, Becca. You." Her arm lowered as she spat at me, face tight with fury. "You had to come poking into other people's lives, where you're not welcome, not *wanted.* And you know what? This is what you get."

A movement over her shoulder caught my eye. Was I imagining it?

"Get. In. The. Hole." She gestured with the gun again, lips pursed.

It was still dim, distant, but there was definitely a light in the trees from back the way we had come.

Keep her focus on you, Becca. You just need a few more seconds.

"I'm getting in, okay?" I started scooting backward, eyes on her face, willing her to hold my gaze. The light was closer now, just beyond the perimeter of the small clearing Heather had dug the grave in, but Heather wouldn't see it if she just kept her eyes on me. "I just don't want to . . . to *step* on her, you know?"

"I doubt she'll mind."

"Right," I glanced over my shoulder at the hole, then back to Heather. "But before you . . . *do* this, I have to know . . ."

"Yes?" She tilted her chin down expectantly. Her gun hand hadn't wavered.

"Who was the murderer?"

"Who was the— What are you *talking* about?" Her eyebrows crinkled. Over her shoulder, the light turned off abruptly. Somehow

I managed not to look at the place where it had been, the glimmer of hope still burned into my retinas.

"In the game. You said you looked it up after all . . . this. Which, hats off, I never would've thought of that. I just need to know if I'm right. Bugsy seems like too obvious a choice, but the stuff about Lulu had me wondering . . ."

"You're honestly using your last moments on earth trying to solve a *stupid mystery game*?"

Her hand dropped for just a second, but it was all I needed. With a guttural grunt I sprang for her knees, wrapping my arms around them before she could retrain the pistol on me, taking her to the ground with me in a tangled mass of limbs and dirt and leaves.

"What the *hell*?" She shrieked, struggling to sit up as I rolled away from her. "You tore my pants!" I started crawling across the forest floor, limbs slipping out from under me . . . I could almost *feel* the gun finding its way back to my head, and then . . .

"Aaahhh!"

I turned back just in time to see the rusty shovel head connect with her wrist with a sickening crunch, sending the pistol skittering off into the dark. And before I could even process the sight of Heather clawing her way up to face her attacker, lips bared in a rabid snarl, eyes wild, feral . . .

. . . Blake swung the shovel again, straight at her face, and she crumpled to the ground in a ragged heap, a marionette with her strings cut.

He stood over her for a second, chest heaving as he drew in a few ragged breaths, then turned to me, eyes wide, the shovel thudding to earth as he slid across the wet ground, dropping to his knees by my side.

"Are you okay?" He reached a hand up to my shoulder, tentative, as though he might break me.

"I think so?" I stared at Heather's body for a few more seconds, still not quite processing what had happened, then turned back to him, frowning. "How did you find me?"

"I woke up to that text—why would you ever go to that place in the middle of the night, Becks? It was fucking *horrifying*. Like even before the basement." He shuddered.

"I don't know," I murmured. My need for answers . . . somewhere between the bulkhead doors and the graveside it had disappeared, melted by the rain.

"You weren't there, and I thought it was too late, but when I came up through the bulkhead I saw a light in the forest, and I thought: *What would they do on Becca's shows?* And when I looked down there was this *path,* almost. So I followed it until I heard someone yelling. And then . . . I'm just glad I got here before . . ." He glanced over at Heather, and his shoulders started to hitch up and down, breath going more ragged. "Becca, if she'd . . . if I hadn't . . ."

Then he dissolved into body-shaking, heaving sobs, and I wrapped my arms around him, and the two of us sat there, holding on to each other until the storm passed.

THIRTY-ONE

"Is it okay if we go get some breakfast? I think I need something real in my stomach . . ."

I was still wrapped in an afghan from the groundskeeper's cottage, my sweater beneath it damp in places, body stiff from holding it tight around my chest. Though that might be the sleeplessness. Or maybe one of those weird concussion side effects? Basically, I felt creaky and ancient and crusted in filth and if they were going to keep asking me the same questions *I needed coffee yesterday.*

Blake had wound up using his tie to bind Heather's wrists, but she was just waking up by the time the police arrived. It turned out we were only a quarter of a mile or so into the woods, well within cellphone range, and by the time the sky started turning pearly with approaching dawn, the scene was safely swathed in rolls of neon caution tape, Heather had been cuffed and carted off to the police station, and Blake and I had been escorted to a pair of benches just behind the cottage in order to be questioned half a dozen times by half a dozen different officers about "the incidents."

"That's fine. We'll be by the main house shortly to question the other guests. They've told the hotel manager already, but make sure none of you leave the premises before the chief has explicitly cleared you to go, okay?"

I nodded at the officer standing over me, his freckled face chipmunky with youth, spine achingly straight as he turned to stare in the general direction of the "secondary crime scene." *Felt pretty primary to me.*

Already the track that Blake had followed between the trees was hard to make out, the relentless onslaught of the night's rain erasing the furrows the tarp had carved through the muck of the forest floor. The officers had swept out the chimney, but the furniture cover had burned down to cinders, along with, presumably, the outfit Heather had been wearing when she went to meet Bethany, posing as her husband. A slender strip of metal, still painted lavender under the grime, and a zipper, the teeth still clinging tightly together, emerged from the soot, the Ghosts of Lululemon Tops Past.

Honestly, it was pretty impressive as a plan, especially considering she'd basically been winging it after the fact. Anything weird that happened around the mansion could be chalked up to the game, anyone acting strange was just in character. Unless, like me, you came into the thing with your skin five sizes too small. Heather might be psychotic, but give her this—the woman really was a hell of a planner.

God, was that the only thing about the Heather I thought I knew that was actually real? Had she ever even stopped to consider what she'd done, what she'd taken away from some other mother, sibling, friend? Or had it really just been as simple in Heather's mind as a mess to clean up? I pulled the afghan tighter around me against the chill of the thought. Somehow it had never occurred to me, in the hundreds—maybe thousands—of hours I'd spent bingeing stories just like this, that every whodunit really involved a double murder: of the victim, but also of some intangible but deeply vital part of the killer's own humanity.

Blake stood and held a hand out to help me up, and together we made our way back to the main house, the bright fall sunshine gilding the edges of the leaves in a way that felt like an attempted cover-up. As we passed the edge of the cottage, I saw Phil through the windows, ashen as he spoke to an officer inside. Seeming to feel my gaze, he looked up, eyes meeting mine for a moment. I could see his throat working, mouth opening as though he wanted to say something, then he dropped his head, whole body slumping. It was the first time I'd ever seen the tall, confident man look truly small—weak, even. I gripped Blake's hand tighter as I turned away. Looking at Phil too long felt dangerous, almost contagious.

The great hall was empty, the concierge desk abandoned. Through an open door behind it, I could hear a man crying. I glanced over, vaguely curious.

"She's really dead?" It took me a moment to recognize the slim man in the fitted button-down and jeans as Manny. He turned his tear-stained face up to the housekeeper, who was standing over him with a hand on his shoulder.

"I'm sorry, Manny, but yes. Bethany is gone."

He hiccupped a few times, then buried his face in his palms.

"I thought she was just . . . being flaky again . . ."

Blake and I picked our way down the hallway to the dining room. There was something comforting about the breakfast buffet on the sideboard. The world can tilt on its axis, people can die, you can nearly get brained by a Victorian-era shovel, but the rubbery eggs of free hotel breakfasts will keep marching on, lumpy standard-bearers of mediocrity.

"Finally."

Drew folded his arms across his belly—straining hard against a pinstriped vest—with a huff.

"Don't be that way, the round doesn't start for another five minutes," Gabby murmured, turning to flash an apologetic smile at Blake and me. "Anyway, Heather and Phil still aren't here either."

"Pretty sure they're not gonna make it," Blake said flatly.

"*Perfect.* As if this weekend hasn't been enough of a disaster already." Drew rolled his eyes, chin jutting out with annoyance. "Did they really think a few cop cars would salvage it? Especially when they're so painfully anachronistic?"

"You have no fucking *clue* what you're talking about," Blake said. Drew pulled back, eyebrows beetling. He looked so ridiculous, a cartoon of shock, that it was hard to imagine that just yesterday I'd thought he might have something to do with all this. Before he could interject, Blake continued. "This isn't part of some ridiculous game, Drew, so just . . . slow your roll, okay?"

Drew's mouth hung open for another moment, then he nodded. I wrapped a hand around Blake's arm, just above the elbow, leaning in to whisper to him.

"Let's just get some food?"

He nodded.

We filled our plates with heaps of god knows what and sat down across from Jessica and Josh, ignoring Drew's muttered *"If they think I don't know they were part of this from the beginning, then . . ."*

"Are you . . . okay?" Jessica leaned across the table, eyes wide. "No offense, but you both look *terrible.*"

"I'd say something about being rude, but she's not wrong," Josh said with a tentative half-smile.

"It's . . . been a really long night," I finally said.

"Is that a leaf in your hair?" Jessica reached across the table to gently pluck it free.

"I hope so," I muttered, the image of Bethany on the tarp, rainwater sloshing from the inside of her head to the outside, flashed into my mind for probably the twentieth time that morning. *Goodbye, oatmeal.*

The housekeeper hurried into the dining room, exhaling heavy relief when she saw us all gathered there. She was wearing the same stiff black dress she'd had on all weekend, but her hair was loose around her shoulders in a way that turned all her imposing stiffness sort of . . . Amish-girls-gone-wild.

"Thank god you're all still here. The police have asked you to stay on the premises until they have a chance to question you."

"Don't you mean the *inspector*?" Gabby smiled pertly at the housekeeper, who stared blankly back.

"These are real police," she said, then turned and hurried out without another word.

"Wait, I'm sorry . . . *what* is happening right now?" Gabby said, the smile still lingering around her mouth.

By the time Blake and I managed to fill everyone in on the barest outline of the details—and none of the elements that felt most important, the fact that we'd sat across a dinner table with these people and talked about their kids, had drunk beers in loungers in their backyard while they smiled and laughed and sparkled for their friends, had performed our small supporting roles in the yearslong run of the play that was *Heather and Phil's Marriage*—Gabby's and Drew's mouths were actually hanging open.

"So you're saying there was an *actual* murder here this weekend?" She turned to Drew for confirmation.

"Yes," I said, unable to muster any inflection whatsoever.

"And *you* figured it out?"

Jesus, why did everyone have so much shade for my detective skills?

"I realized something serious was going on," I finally said. "The rest I sort of pieced together from Heather."

"Oh my god, that is . . . *so* cool," Drew murmured, eyes lighting up. "We should put that in the review, babe. It kinda redeems the whole thing when you think about it."

"Review?" Jessica's eyes darted over to them. At some point during the story, her hand had crept across the table to cover mine. It was more comforting than I wanted to admit.

"Shoot . . . sorry," Drew grimaced at Gabby. She shrugged.

"I suppose it doesn't matter now. It's not like we're going to get to finish the game, so it won't be an *official* review anyway."

"Really? But if they have an extra copy of Heather's and Phil's booklets, maybe we could—"

"Drew."

"Right, right. Yeah, that makes sense."

"Review of what?" Josh pressed. "The hotel? Or . . ."

"It seems silly to even talk about it now, considering what you all went through, but it turns out . . . we're 'It Was Murder.'" Gabby flashed a rueful "You caught us!" grin.

"Wait . . . *that's* why you left this?" I stuffed my hand into my pocket, and there, crumpled and softened with damp, was the little black card from the room search.

"I thought you took that because you knew us. Or actually . . ." Drew jutted out his chin and heaved out a breath that tickled the hairs escaping from his fedora. "I assumed you were a plant. I mean, I told you as much yesterday in the hallway."

I blinked, remembering the shears, the looming bulk of him. Clearly we'd been having two *very* different conversations.

"I'm sorry, so this is about a website, or . . . ?" Blake finally said.

"Really? None of you have heard of us?" Drew's eyebrows furrowed in disbelief as everyone shook their heads. "Wow. Okay, umm . . . we're kinda the biggest murder mystery weekend review site in the whole Northeast?"

"Well, there *is* 'A Weekend Most Foul,'" Gabby said with a beleaguered sigh.

"We both know that's just Gretchen's cosplay site now," Drew said, voice dripping with disdain. Gabby's eyes rolled to the side in tacit agreement.

"Anyway, we're basically a resource for fans hoping to find the best murder mystery weekends near them. We help with costuming ideas, hosting your own parties, developing a backstory for your character. All the basics, really. Honestly, we were going to three-star this event, even with that neat secret-passage trick. It's *pretty* unprofessional not to have a backup plan in place in case one of the actors can't perform, plus the clue mix-ups . . ." Gabby stopped short, eyes widening meaningfully. "Though I guess that wasn't really their fault. And if the actress actually *died* . . . ?" She turned to Drew, the question on her face. After a moment of beetle-browed consideration, he shrugged.

"I guess we just write this one off as research."

"Sorry . . . what sort of *plant* was I?" I frowned at Drew.

He grimaced awkwardly.

"Sometimes the staff puts a shill in with the guests, to keep things on track. Once we saw Bethany was working this weekend—erm, before she . . . you know—we thought they must be pretty aware of the 'tricks of the trade,' so to speak."

"You knew Bethany from other murder mystery weekends?"

"Of course. Where else would we have met?" He blinked, clearly baffled by the idea that paths could cross outside his subculture. "Anyway, you reacted so strongly to the body, and then you were tailing me and Gabby after lunch, I just figured . . ." He raised a finger, eyes lighting up. "But if you ever *wanted* to do something like that, I know a guy who might hire you. I mean, we know our stuff, and you were *really* good. Anyone else would totally buy you."

"Thanks," I said, taking the paper, "but I might be a little tapped out on these for the moment."

"Right." His eyebrows tented and he grimaced again. "Right, of course. That was stupid. Anyway, if we're really not going to finish the round"—Drew looked around, clearly hoping to be corrected, then continued—"I think I might head up to the room to pack. Can you tell the police that's where we are if they ask?"

"Sure," Jessica said, flashing me an almost imperceptible eyebrow raise.

"But wait," I said as he stood. "If you were reviewing it . . . why did you *want* us to stop playing last night?"

"Oh, that," he laughed. "I couldn't get any of you to bite on

Phil stabbing the maid with the shears. And I figured I was the one that 'shot at' the chauffeur. I mean, you saw the gun."

"What?" Josh frowned.

"It was right there on the handle!" Drew's eyes wrinkled in disbelief. "B.S. Bugsy Slugs. My gun, my shot."

"Couldn't one of us have swiped it from you?" Jessica said.

"Trust me, it's never that complicated." With that, he crossed to the door. Gabby stopped to wave awkwardly at us, then followed him down the hallway.

"Okay, I know we're all wondering: How bad do we think things need to get for a dreaded two-star?" Josh raised his eyebrows meaningfully.

I was recapping the night's events for Josh and Jessica for the third time when the housekeeper appeared in the doorway again. She'd changed into a flowy cardigan and leggings. Without the period garb, she had transformed from the prim matron to something like your chatty colleague who's really into crafting.

"I just wanted to see how you all were doing. Is there anything I can get you? Also, please know that I've already spoken to the management team and they agree that considering the circumstances, it'd only be fair for us to offer you all a complimentary weekend stay in the future. You can use it for one of our theme weekends or just a getaway."

"Thank you," I said automatically. "That's so generous." Sometimes my default, avoid-the-conflict-at-all-costs Midwesternness annoyed me, but it wasn't necessarily the worst secret power.

"It's the least we can do," she said with the practiced half-smile of a lifelong service professional. "If you need anything, I'll be at the front desk. And I know things were a little . . . *hectic* this weekend. I hope you won't be too hard on us if you do post a review. I assure you, we usually put on a much cleaner performance."

"Of course," Blake said, and she nodded, a look of desperate gratitude on her face, turning on her heel—*not just for the part, then*—to hurry off down the hall.

"So . . ." Josh said after she left. "You guys want to coordinate our next freebie weekend in what is now *absolutely* a haunted hotel?"

I automatically reached for Blake's hand. He was wearing his polite mask, the one that got him through every party, the one that seemed to magically blunt any issue I wanted to bring up, the one that was impossible to read even after knowing him as long as I had. I glanced at Jessica. She was looking at me, face composed.

After what we'd just been through, I should be grateful. That my husband loved me, that he knew me well enough to find me in the middle of the woods in the rain, that the worst hadn't happened, even just that we weren't Heather and Phil.

God, I'd spent so much time thinking we needed to be more like Heather and Phil. But couldn't we become them someday?

I'd always thought the worst that could happen to us was what happened to my parents. Us ending. But I was realizing there were so many other ways it could go wrong, much darker ways, things that could twist and mutate love into something violent and horrible, turn us into versions of ourselves that were so used to mounting the show of our marriage for other people that eventually we forgot to take off our costumes when we got home, to look beneath them for the people we really were, the things we really wanted, the uncomfortable but necessary fights I'd always thought meant failure. If the version of marriage I'd spent so long idealizing, the Heather and Phil marriage, was wrong—or at least could *go* so wrong—it had to mean there were other and different ways to be *right*.

I'd spent all this time trying to "fix" us, but really, I'd just been trying to slot us back into the same places we'd been in before, the smile-for-company, bite-back-your-resentments version of our lives that suddenly felt so deeply hollow. After everything that had happened, I wanted to start over—*really* start over, on a new path together . . . or else I had to be willing to head off on my own. If Blake wouldn't, or couldn't, come along with me, I could get through that.

I could get through whatever I had to. Last night had made it starkly clear: There is *always* more to a relationship than you see from the outside, and losing yourself, especially in some empty, meaningless performance of what you think you ought to want, was much, *much* worse than losing someone else.

I sucked in a breath, releasing my hand from Blake's. This was my choice to make, I didn't need his permission or his approval. But . . . I also didn't need to run from one wrong version of us into another. We needed some sort of resolution, but we didn't need to decide on what it would look like *right now.*

"I could be into that," I said slowly, closing my eyes briefly to get my bearings. All the Heathers I'd known, and thought I'd known, and seen unmasked in just the last few hours, flashed through my mind in rapid succession. Each of them had felt real, at least in the moment. Each of them had felt *true.* "But we should probably get to know each other a little better first."

We were halfway home when Blake turned to me.

"I meant to ask . . . who were you going to put down?"

"Sorry . . . what do you mean?"

"As the murderer. Who did you think it was?"

I laughed.

"Really? *That's* what you want to know?"

"I mean, I also want to know what Bethany saw in Phil, but I doubt he's taking calls at the moment." Blake's dimple popped out as he grinned at me, and a surge of utterly familiar tenderness suffused my chest. It almost surprised me with how strong it was; I hadn't thought it had disappeared, exactly, but the affair and its aftermath had hidden it from view for so long I'd forgotten the shape of it, the giant groundswell of *us* that underpinned everything. And some part of me felt sure that whatever path I set us on, whatever we reshaped this marriage into, we'd find a way to be in it together. But *fuck* we would be having a lot more painful conversations along the way about what we both wanted and needed.

I stared out the window, letting the brilliant golds and reds go blurry. Finally, eyes still on the side of the road, I murmured:

"It had to be Dolly."

"Really? How do you figure?"

"I'm assuming their room had the urn . . ."

"Right. The urn."

"Beyond that it's just down to motive. Everyone else's secrets were about hidden identities, or money, or reputation. Hers were about love." I shrugged. "Why else would anyone go that far?"

Blake reached across the console to lay his hand on my leg.

"Are we . . . okay?" When I looked at him, his face was more vulnerable than I'd seen it in years, almost childlike. I could hurt him if I wanted to. Gut him the way he'd gutted me. His defenses were finally fully down. A small part of me still wanted to.

But more of me wanted to find a more honest way to be with him, especially now that he finally seemed to see the real damage he'd done, now that he was trying not to pretend anymore, either. Whatever it meant, however much it might hurt along the way, dropping the act we'd been keeping up with each other was the only way forward.

"No," I finally said. Then slid my hand into his. "Not yet. But I think we can be. We just have to be . . . open to new possibilities."

ACKNOWLEDGMENTS

I wrote the first draft of this book in the early days of the pandemic, trapped in my tiny L.A. apartment, feeling desperate (as we all did) for a mental escape, since physically, I wasn't going *anywhere.* Without the help and support of so many people, *All Dressed Up* never would have broken free from those beginnings and made it out into the world.

An incredibly heartfelt thank-you to my fabulous agent, Taylor Haggerty, who has believed in this story—and in me—from the beginning. You're always able to cut straight to the heart of any thorny issues I'm getting stuck on; I'm so very lucky to be able to rely on your wisdom and guidance on problems big and small.

I can't say enough good things about Anne Speyer and the entire team at Bantam. Anne, I'm in awe of your editorial brilliance and so grateful for the time and care you've shown this story. I've said it before and I'll say it again here: I won the editor lottery.

A big thanks to my critique partners Lana Harper, Adriana Mather, and Chelsea Sedoti. You're the readers I trust most, not to mention my de facto support group. I'm so lucky to have you in my corner.

Thank you to all the friends who have supported me through the difficult times and who have made celebrating the good things so much more meaningful. You know who you are, and I love you deeply.

To my mother, Pam, and to my sisters, who are there for me no matter what. Mom, you always said "family is forever," and I'm old enough now to admit you were right (about this and so many other things). Claire and Janie, you are and always will be my best friends.

And, finally, to Danny. You believe in me more completely than just about anyone I know (including myself), and you pick me back up whenever things don't go according to one of my many, many plans. Only slightly less important, you make the coffee every morning. Thank you for everything you do for me every single day. I love you.

Jilly Gagnon's humor writing, personal essays, and op-eds have appeared in *Newsweek, Elle, Vanity Fair, Boston, McSweeney's Internet Tendency, The Toast,* and *The Hairpin,* among others. Her young adult novel, *#famous,* was published in 2017. She lives in Salem, Massachusetts, with her spouse and—fittingly—two black cats.

jillygagnon.com
Facebook.com/JillyGagnonWriter
Twitter: @jillygagnon
Instagram: @jillygagnon

ABOUT THE TYPE

This book was set in Garamond, a typeface originally designed by the Parisian type cutter Claude Garamond (c. 1500–61). This version of Garamond was modeled on a 1592 specimen sheet from the Egenolff-Berner foundry, which was produced from types assumed to have been brought to Frankfurt by the punch cutter Jacques Sabon (c. 1535–80).

Claude Garamond's distinguished romans and italics first appeared in *Opera Ciceronis* in 1543–44. The Garamond types are clear, open, and elegant.